*A mi madre Cirenia que nos dio la luz
en Xalapa, y a mi hijo Agustín que
descubrió el Barrio Cósmico a los 7 años
en Los Ángeles...*

MUSIC STORIES FROM THE COSMIC BARRIO
©2020 by Betto Arcos

Editorial design: Insensato Studio / Carlos Villajuárez
Cover art and illustrations: Alec Dempster
Style editor: María José Giménez
Index: Marco A. Villa Juárez
Images: Various authors

1st edition, December 2020
All rights reserved

ISBN: 978-607-9178-33-8

Printed and made in Mexico by Fogra Editorial

MUSIC STORIES
FROM THE
COSMIC
BARRIO
BETTO ARCOS

FOREWORD

Betto Arcos has taken me around the world. To places I've always dreamed of visiting, like Brazil and North Africa. And places I never imagined, like Colombia's Caribbean coast. He's introduced me to artists whose work I didn't know: Nella from Venezuela, Carlos do Carmo from Portugal, Gabriela Ortiz from Mexico and Rajery from Madagascar. Betto's taught me about Cuban bolero, Colombian vallenato, Mexican son huasteco. As jazz musicians say, he's got big ears. He is, of course, informed by his Latin American heritage. But his interests go far beyond its many cultures, histories and musical styles. He helped create a public radio show on KPFK in Los Angeles called "Global Village" in 1997 and co-hosted it — with a brief break — until 2015. As the name implies, the goal was to show the connections between cultures, musics and the people who create them — to highlight the things that unite us.

And that's what he does in the stories you're about to read, drawn from his feature reporting for NPR and other public radio outlets. Music is informed by the lives of the people who make it. The great Cuban guitarist and composer Leo Brouwer was an orphan. He told Betto this in his 2017 NPR profile: "To be useful is something incredible. Humans, when they teach, when they show, when they give, they're doing one of the most beautiful things in life. Perhaps because of my roots in solitude, of being an orphan, it forces me to these reflections."

Classically-trained singer Silvia Perez Cruz draws from a different childhood experience: "The song has to have a story that I believe in, and I can make it my own. I think I have that influence from my mother. My mother is a good storyteller, and she's always believed that songs are stories."

And Lebanese musician Ibrahim Maalouf got something invaluable from his father: a four-valve trumpet that allows him to play quarter tones: "This trumpet that he invented is pure genius. He invented the only Arabic instrument in which you blow that allows you to play all modes, all scales, in all the tonalities. He invented a new way to play the trumpet."

Through Betto's writing and interviews, I've gotten to know these people and their music, if only vicariously. Betto travels and reports; as his NPR editor, I sit in the office, wait and listen. We've collaborated on nearly 40 stories over the course of a decade and I've learned something new in every one. And going back through the NPR archives, I found I remember each one. That's a testament to Betto's storytelling.

Now you can get to know some of these musicians, too, in this collection. So read, enjoy, learn and, above all, go out and find the music and listen. Because that's what brings us together.

Tom Cole
Senior Editor, NPR Arts and Culture Desk and host
of "G-Strings" on WPFW in Washington, D.C.

ACKNOWLEDGMENTS

I started writing stories for radio, right before I graduated from the University of Colorado in May 1993. But my radio career goes back to 1987, when a Brazilian friend introduced me to the host of a program called "Latin Jam" on public radio station KGNU in Boulder, Colorado. The program was hosted by Javier Garcés, a Colombian who had been doing the show for a few years and wanted to pass the baton to another Latino. I didn't have any radio experience and I was undocumented. The only thing I had going for me was a passion for music. I did the training, took over the show and changed the name to "Tierra Mestiza." I also invited a friend and singer-songwriter Ellen Klaver to co-host the show with me and the rest is history.

From May of 1993 to the Spring of 1996, I wrote and produced stories for Latino USA and Radio Bilingüe's "Edición Semanaria," most of them about news and culture, with a few music pieces in between. Then, when I moved to Los Angeles in 1995 and created KPFK's "Global Village" two years later, I found a bigger and more diverse music scene with many stories to tell. From 1997 to 2002, and from 2005-2015, Global Village became the outlet for many local, national and international stories about music. I got a chance to interview musicians from Africa, Europe, the Middle East, Asia, Latin America and Los Angeles. The list is long but here are a few of the artists I interviewed during those years: Hossein Alizadeh, Omar Faruk Tekbilek, Lila Downs, Waldemar Bastos, Chucho Valdés, Astrid Hadad, Chango Spasiuk, Ronu Majumdar, Baaba Maal, Manu Chao, Paddy Moloney, Flaco Jiménez, Hamza El Din, Gonzalo Rubalcaba, Rachid Taha, Radio Tarifa, Ry Cooder, Compay Segundo, Ibrahim Ferrer, Charlie Haden, Bill Frisell, Jordi Savall, Carlos Varela, Eugenia León, Cimarrón, Susana Baca, Vicente Amigo, Seun Kuti, Santiago Auserón, Kronos Quartet's David Harrington, Boubacar Traoré, and many more.

In December 2008, I decided to revive my storytelling career and pitched a story about the Iranian rock band called Kiosk to Marco Werman, host of "The World" and he accepted it. That story is included here along with more than 50 music pieces I wrote for the program from 2009 to 2016. Then, in August of 2010, with the encouragement of my friend and colleague Mandalit del Barco, I pitched a story about the French band Caravan Palace to Tom Cole, senior editor of the arts and culture desk at NPR and he accepted it. Ten years and 40 stories later, I'm still pitching and writing music pieces for NPR. The most recent was a profile of one my heroes, Silvio Rodríguez. Finally, in 2016, I started doing stories for KPCC's programs "The Frame" and "Take Two." The last piece I wrote for KPCC aired last April, on Candelas Guitar Shop in East LA — a different version of the story aired on NPR in June, included here.

I've always believed that I'm the sum of my family and friends, without them I would never be able to achieve anything. First and foremost, thank you Josephine for supporting this project and all the work I've done in music since I moved to LA in 1995 – your encouragement and advice have been essential all these years and without your love, none of this would have been possible. My friends and colleagues Rubén Martínez, Raúl Silva, Jaime Andrés Monsalve who are always there when I need them for advice and support. Thank you David Barsamian for helping me to find a radio voice and María Martin who was my first editor at Latino USA. Big thanks to my NPR editor Tom Cole for his kind words and more than 10 years teaching me how to tell stories. Thank you to the staff at "The World", especially Marco Werman, April Peavey and Jennifer Goren for giving me the platform to tell these stories." Thank you Oscar Garza and Megan Larson for the opportunity to contribute to KPCC; Roger Short, Felix Carey and Michael Rossi at BBC Radio 3. Last but not least, a big thank you to my style editor, María José Giménez, who has helped this book shine from beginning to end; Alec Dempster for his fantastic cover art; Betty Van Cauwelaert and Carlos Villajuárez from Fogra Editorial for their exceptional work.

WELCOME TO THE COSMIC BARRIO

I was 6 years old when I listened to a radio program called "La legión infantil de madrugadores" (the children's legion of early risers). My mother turned on the radio every morning to get her kids in the mood for school. The program was a world onto itself, two hosts — how could I forget their names, Griselda Hernández Portilla and Martín Casillas — taught us about nutrition, health, civics and everything kids need to learn during the grade-school years. But to a kid like me, the best part was the music of Francisco Gabilondo Soler, better known as Cri-Cri, "el grillo cantor" (the singing cricket). I loved listening to his songs because each one of them told a story I identified with: "Gato de Barrio," "El Comal y la Olla," "El Ropavejero," "La Patita." Cri-Cri's songs were complex masterpieces filled with subtle social commentary, and each song featured a different style of music. All those songs, the lyrics and the music, are deeply embedded in my consciousness, along with the songs I heard in the evening, when my father tuned the dial to his favorite radio stations, XEW in Mexico City and XEQ in Monterrey. Every weeknight he listened to "Trios Famosos," an hourlong program of boleros featuring some of the major trios that popularized the genre from the 1940s on: Los Panchos, Los Tres Reyes, Los Montejo, Los Fantasmas, Los Tres Caballeros, Los Dandys, and so on. But he was especially fond of a program called "La Hora de Agustín Lara" and, occasionally, he'd grab a guitar and sing them in the carpentry shop — a space filled with a strong smell of cedar, mahogany, walnut and pine — where I also worked with my older brothers Luis and Quinto.

In my early teens, my older sister Esther — who worked as nanny for an upper-class family in Mexico City — would visit during the Christmas holidays and she'd bring home vinyl records of the latest pop stars: Roberto Carlos, Juan Gabriel, Rocío Dúrcal, The Carpenters, The Jackson Five. In the shop, during the afternoon, we tuned the dial to a handful of local stations offering a diverse variety of music: The Beatles, Santana, La Revolución de Emiliano Zapata, Los Corraleros de Majagual, Los Socios del Ritmo, Los Ángeles Negros, Sandro, Leonardo Favio and my brother Quinto's all-time favorite Rigo Tovar. That was my life in Xalapa, Veracruz, until 1977. At age 15, I was invited to live with the Donald family in Palo Alto, California. I attended 8th grade and learned to read and write in English. A completely different world suddenly opened up to my ears. The following year, when I returned to Xalapa, I had a new sense of who I was and what I could do. I joined a church choir led by my brother Quinto, and I learned how to play the guitar and sing in two languages. As I approached college, I began to collect the albums of Silvio Rodríguez and Pablo Milanés from Cuba; Inti-illimani and Quilapayún from Chile; and Joan Manuel Serrat from Spain. Then, in 1985, I decided to return to the U.S. to work and I landed in Boulder, Colorado. When I crossed the Matamoros-Brownsville border, without papers, I had Bruce Springsteen's "Born to Run" playing on my Walkman.

All the stories contained in this book are in some way part of my personal story. When I talked to Mateo Kingman in Quito, Ecuador, and he told me about getting lost in the Amazon jungle, I couldn't help but identify with him — I've been lost too, in a different kind of jungle. Mexican classical composer Arturo Márquez described how he fell in love with danzón, and when I listen to his music I'm transported to the port city of Veracruz, where I lived temporarily and would see well-dressed elderly couples and children dance every Saturday night. The week I spent in Fes, Morocco, in June 2010, attending the World Sacred Music Festival, helped me understand the Arab roots of Mexico's cultural heritage. After seven intense days in Rio de Janeiro, interviewing musicians and going to see live shows, in September 2013, I began to understand the importance of samba in Brazil: samba, like almost any music, is a mirror of society, a daily valve that helps people vent their happiness and their sadness, their disillusions and their dreams. One evening in Cartagena, my dear friend and colleague Jaime Andrés Monsalve said that, for Colombians, "music is a balm to help heal the wounds of so much pain."

As I look back at my career as a music and culture journalist working in public radio, in English, I must say I've taken a great responsibility, especially with regard to Latin American music. It's not only about translating a language or a style of music, but explaining who we are, the complexity of our history and diverse cultures, the hopes and dreams yet to be fulfilled by the future generations. Every story I've written about music and identity, music and immigration, music and education, music and community-building, has to do with who I am as a person. Music has the power to transform lives. I know it transformed me.

TABLE OF CONTENTS

IDENTITY

Carlos Vives 19

Colombian Music 21

Pasatono Orquesta 25

Taiko in Los Angeles 27

Lupita Infante 29

Dhafer Youssef 31

Diego El Cigala 33

El Personal 35

Gustavo Galindo 37

Caravan Palace 39

Los Cenzontles 41

Magos Herrera 43

Noel Petro 45

Making Movies 47

Celso Piña 51

Elisapie Isaac 53

Simon Lynge 55

Alec Dempster 57

Armenian Music in the USA 59

Buika (Part 1) 61

Buika (Part 2) 63

Lara Bello 65

Antonio Zambujo 67

Toña La Negra 69

Linda Ronstadt 71

El Compa Negro 75

Jungle Fire 77

Renaud Garcia-Fons 79

La Cuneta Son Machín (Part 1) 81

La Cuneta Son Machín (Part 2) 83

Carlos Núñez 85

María Márquez 87

Los Gaiteros de San Jacinto 89

Flamenco, after Paco de Lucía 91

POWER

Gabriela Ortíz 95

Women Mariachis in Los Angeles 97

Violeta Parra 99

Ana Tijoux 101

Silvia Pérez Cruz 103

María Volonté 105

Flor de Toloache 107

Francisca Valenzuela 109

Carla Morrison 111

Y La Bamba 113

Las Hermanas García 115

LEARNING

Areni Agbabian 119

CalArts Salsa Band 121

Cameron Graves 125

Vahagni (Part 1) 127

Vahagni (Part 2) 129

Chicago's Mariachi Herencia de Mexico 131

Oaxacan Brass Bands in Los Angeles 133

Estrella Arias and Primero Sueño 135

César Castro 137

Son Mayor 139

Leon "Ndugu" Chancler 141

Rosalía 143

Polka Madre 145

YOLA: Youth Orchestra of Los Angeles 147

BRAZIL

Bibí Ferreira 153

Joyce Cândido 155

Leandro Fregonesi and Samba 157

Luiz Gonzaga: A Lenda 159

Guinga 161

Hermeto Pascoal 163

Hamilton de Holanda 165

Vinicius Cantuaria and Bill Frisell 167

CUBA AND THE DIASPORA

Rock in Cuba 171

Carlos Varela 173

The Endless Tour of Silvio Rodríguez 175

Cien Sones Cubanos 177

Leo Brouwer 179

Harold López-Nussa 181

Omara Portuondo 183

Daymé Arocena (Part 1) 185

Daymé Arocena (Part 2) 187

Cimafunk 189

Jazz Plaza Festival in Havana 193

Cuban Musicians in Los Angeles 195

Alfredo Rodríguez 197

Note: All the stories contained in the book were previously broadcast on NPR, "The World" from PRX, KPCC, BBC Radio 3 and Latino USA. Broadcast dates are included at the top right of each story. Some of the interview excerpts in the book have been condensed and lightly edited as needed for clarity.

Rumbankete 199
Dayramir González 201
San Miguel 203
Silvio Rodríguez 205

ADVERSITY

Nella 209
Malawi Mouse Boys 211
Colombian Music and Peace 213
León Gieco and Mundo Alas 215
The Lost Cuban Trios of Casa Marina 217
Mateo Kingman 219
Chéjere 221
Canzoniere Grecanico Salentino 223
Los Angeles Master Chorale 225

SOCIAL UNREST AND VIOLENCE

Emel Mathlouthi 229
Arturo Márquez 231
Abjeez 233
Anouar Brahem 235
Los Aguas Aguas 237
Artists' Reaction to Violence in Mexico 239
Edgar Quintero 241
"Únicamente la Verdad" 243
Jordi Savall and Hesperion XXI 245

IMMIGRATION

SB 1070 and Music 249
Arturo O'Farrill and Fandango at The Wall 251
Ibrahim Maalouf and Oxmo Puccino 255
Lila Downs 257
John Daversa and American Dreamers 259
Gaby Moreno 263
La Santa Cecilia 265
El Conjunto Nueva Ola 267
Jon Balke and Siwan 269

COMMUNITY BUILDING

Quetzal in Veracruz 273
Yo-Yo Ma in Mexico City 275
Las Posadas 277
Jorge Drexler (Part 1) 279

Jorge Drexler (Part 2) 281
The World Stage 283
Boleros de Noche 285

INSTRUMENTS

Cristina Pato 289
Ibrahim Maalouf 291
Guillermo Contreras 293
Partch Ensemble 295
Rodrigo y Gabriela 297
Los Angeles Balalaika Orchestra 299
Rubén Luengas 301
Candelas Guitar Shop 303

PRODUCERS

Gabe Roth 307
Sebastian Krys 309
Gustavo Santaolalla 311
Eduardo Llerenas 313
Joe Castro 315

PLACE AND NATION

Jordi Savall and El Nuevo Mundo 319
Samba and Brazil 321
Vallenato and Colombia 323
Carlos Do Carmo and Portugal 327
Astrid Hadad and Mexico 329
Kiosk and Iran 331
Daniel "Tatita" Márquez and Uruguay 333
3MA and Africa 335
World Festival of Sacred Music 337
Son Jarocho in Los Angeles 339
Guarania and Paraguay 341
Chamamé and El Litoral 343
Champeta in Cartagena, Colombia 345
Festival de la Mejorana, Panama 347
Carranga and Boyacá 349
Galician Music and El Camino de Santiago 351
La Chiva Rumbera in Cartagena, Colombia 355
Candombe and Montevideo 357
La Trova Suriana 359

Index 363
Permission credits 377
Betto Arcos 379

IDENTITY

CARLOS VIVES

Vallenato is a traditional music from Colombia — it's country-and-roots music and, these days, it's enjoying a revival and a much wider recognition thanks largely to the efforts of a young and talented Colombian named Carlos Vives. A former soap opera star turned singer, Vives has successfully managed to take the polyrhythmic sounds of vallenato from the streets of his native Colombia to major concert venues worldwide.

The roots of Vallenato are as diverse as Colombia's multi-ethnic population, a combination of Indian, African and Spanish heritage. Vallenato's beat is driven by polyrhythmic drumming, as well as the infectious sound of the accordion. One of the most noticeable ways in which Carlos Vives approaches vallenato is the constant use of a Colombian instrument called "gaita," an Indigenous flute that evokes a recognizable mountain sound. Vives says the use of Indigenous instruments in vallenato is something that was being lost but is a fundamental element of traditional vallenato which his band has reclaimed:

> "We're not making something new. We're making something that has been there. America is a continent where a lot of things got mixed and that's our music, and it's not only ours, it's everybody's. Because here in Colombia, many things happened culturally and that's who we are — a mixture of all these things."

In his new album, "La tierra del olvido" (The Land of Oblivion), Vives pays tribute to the old guard of vallenato composers, updating classic songs with new arrangements, without taking away the essence of the style, as in the song "La cachucha bacana" by composer Alejo Durán.

The transition of Carlos Vives from a soap opera star to a modern-day vallenato singer came after he portrayed a famous vallenato composer on a Colombian soap opera. The soundtrack from that series became so popular that he decided to pursue a musical career. Because of his movie star good looks, Vives enjoys a great following particularly among young women. But Vives says that making music is still the most important thing, he says music has the power to teach people about their world and their roots: "This music comes out of very natural sounds of life, humans, nature, and the animals. It's humble music from peasants, it has to do with the countryside and everything that's natural. We try not to lose those roots." And in this way, says Vives, his recording of "La tierra del olvido" has some things in common with the quintessential Colombian novel by Gabriel García Márquez: "'La tierra del olvido' es como 'Cien años de soledad,' es un lugar pero no es una pequeña aldea solamente." "'La tierra del olvido' is like 'One Hundred Years of Solitude' — it's a place, but not just a small village. It's a large region that has to do with a state of mind but also with people, and the feelings of these humble people. 'La Tierra del Olvido' is everything here in the third world."

Carlos Vives | Photo by Andrés Oyuela

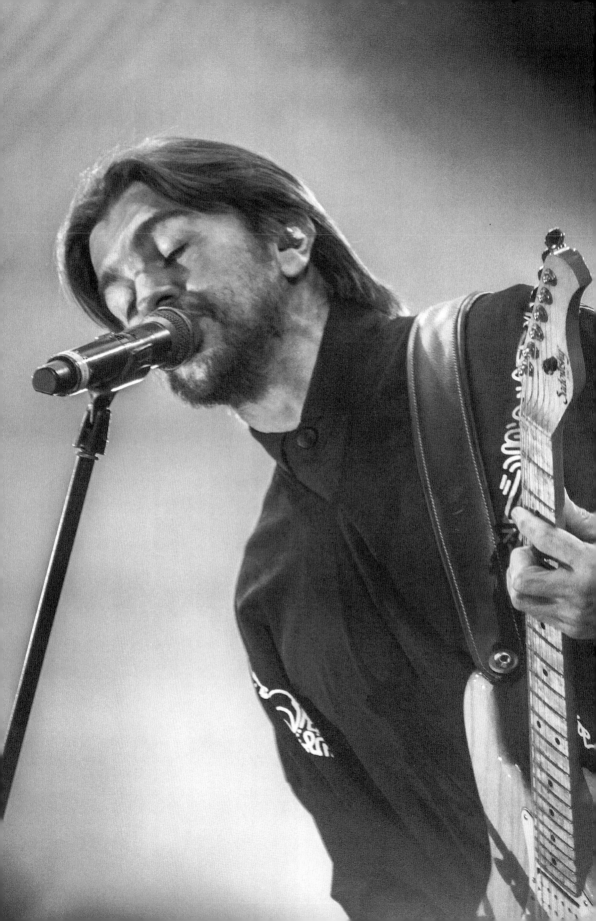

COLOMBIAN MUSIC

From Carlos Vives to Shakira, from Juanes to J Balvin, Colombian artists have been making a significant impact on the international music scene for decades. To find out more about Colombia's footprint in pop music, I traveled to Colombia's capital, Bogotá, to talk with some of the movers and shakers.

At the Art&co Recording Studios in Bogotá, producer and composer David Trujillo aka "García" talks about his forthcoming pop album, anchored in Colombian traditional music. He'll record up to 35 songs, and then he'll choose a third of them for the album. The first song he's recorded is based on the rhythm called Bambuco. Trujillo says, today's Colombian music global explosion has a precedent in previous decades: "For many years, we've had Colombian artists that have been at the forefront, who clearly understood that our music could be mixed with other styles and made in a more universal way."

The Colombian artist who helped pave the way is Carlos Vives. In 1995, after the global success of the album "Clásicos de la Provincia," Vives released "La Tierra del Olvido" — this album marked the birth of a "new Colombian music" with its fusion of traditional music with pop rhythms. Chucky García, programmer of Bogotá's biggest music festival "Rock al Parque" says Vives paved the way: "Carlos Vives is the one that takes the commercial leap, with the backing of a major Colombian label, Sonolux, and that's how at that

specific time, in some way, Vives becomes the father of new Colombian music."

García says the international explosion of the new Colombian music can be explained by looking at several factors. The hip-hop band Chocquibtown is a good example of a group who started underground and is now an international success. They migrated from the Pacific coast of Colombia to Bogotá and established their musical project:

> "When I met them, the band was selling their demo. They played in bars and wherever they could play. So the Colombian artist who's succeeding today has already experienced an underground journey. When people see them today, it's already packaged, but it's the result of all that work they did for years."

If anyone knows the Colombian music market and its success worldwide, it's Diana Rodriguez, founder and chief executive of Criteria Entertainment, a management agency based in Los Angeles. Rodriguez currently manages the Colombian rock band Diamante Eléctrico. She's been working in the music industry for almost 30 years and has seen the ups and downs of Colombian pop music:

> "Colombia is very particular in the sense that it has a lot of talent. And it sounds like a mouthful because I'm Colombian. But I think its biggest problem was that the ceiling or the industry ceiling for the

Juanes performing at Bogotá's "Rock al Parque" festival | Photo by María Paunks

Colombian talent was very low. It didn't meet the needs of the talent to export. So within the last years, what you've seen, with a lot of Spotify and the Internet and everything else, artists being able to travel outside of Colombia."

Rodriguez says Colombia's own music market can help explain the success of its international artists:

"We don't yet have that market where the audience is used to discovering artists. Our artists get discovered outside and then come back, and that's the truth. It's a market that's still growing and learning to discover its own artists, but it's a market that has been delivering nonstop hits for international audiences from a while back."

Until July, Colombia's pop rocker Juanes had never performed at the country's biggest festival, "Rock al Parque." Festival programmer Chucky Garcia says at first he was criticized for booking Juanes, a mainstream pop act, at an alternative rock festival. But after the concert, public opinion changed: "He's an artist whose significant international experience has a lot of things to offer, and he's a model and a reference. And people who did not want him to be in the Festival later admitted: 'I don't like Juanes, but that's how you do a show in a rock festival.'"

Criteria's Diana Rodríguez says there's a particular quality about Colombian music that makes global the new local: "Even if J Balvin is pop worldwide, his Colombian sound is very noticeable. Same for Monsieur Periné, same for Bomba Estéreo. There's always this footprint they leave in the sound that is very unique to them. I think it's the identity. We've never really lost the Colombian identity as much pop as we go … but I think the roots are there. Our new talent has managed to kind of intertwine with other sounds without losing its identity, so we've been able to grow and travel a lot and become part of that global movement but without losing our local sound."

Back at the Art&co Studio in Bogotá, producer David Trujillo says a country like Colombia, with such a rich musical culture, will continue to have a big part in the global pop sound. He also has a prediction:

"Music is so homogeneous today — everything sounds the same, you can't tell if it's Puerto Rican, Colombian or Argentine, everybody sings the same. There will be a need and a demand for new rhythms and new ways to mix music. We're starting to see it in other countries. If you listen to Rosalía, it's the result of mixing pop with flamenco."

Trujillo says the future Colombian pop music will be shaped by artists and producers who combine traditional rhythms and modern sounds with innovative mixing techniques. And maybe that will be the next wave of Latin pop music.

Colombia's hip-hop band Chocquibtown | Photo courtesy of @chocquibtown @davidmicolta

PASATONO ORQUESTA

Pasatono Orquesta is led by a couple who do double duty as ethnomusicologists and performers. The band plays traditional music from the Mixtec region of Oaxaca. They research and document the music and sometimes they record and perform it. Rubén Luengas plays a 10-string instrument called "bajo quinto." Patricia García plays violin. Their second album is called "La Tiricia: Music and Stories to Cure Sadness."

A few years ago, while doing research in the Mixtec region, Luengas and García discovered groups that play their own version of early American swing music on the banjo. Mixtec migrant workers brought the instrument to the region in the 1920s. But Luengas says that their most exciting find was the enduring popularity of the music known as "Yaa Sii": "This Indigenous music is an amalgam of traditional and modern styles known in the Mixtec language as 'Joyful Music.'" The Mixtec are one of the largest Indigenous groups in the state of Oaxaca. And Yaa Sii is the most popular Indigenous music in the Mixtec region. Luengas and García found that the music is played by solo musicians, small groups, and orchestras.

Patricia García says the Mixtec language plays an important role in understanding the Yaa Sii musical style and its meaning in everyday life: "The only ones who call this music and identify it as 'Yaa Sii' are the Mixtec speakers. The speakers of the Mixtec language have the knowledge of this music, not the Mixtec people in general." Luengas says Mixtec people have a special belief about music: "the best joyful music is the one that makes you cry. There's a sadness, an implicit melancholy in this music, but it must be enjoyed and danced, when there's a birth or and offering, when there's a wake or a party. It's music that's present in everyday life, and it's very Mixtec."

García says this music is a window into the Mixtec worldview. And to appreciate this view, you have to understand the function of music in daily life: "It's not only about understanding a musical genre or a specific instrument. We have to look into the history of the group of instruments, the purpose of the musical events, and every aspect that has to do with the world of Mixtec music."

More than 10 years ago, when they started doing research in the Mixtec region, Luengas and García were concerned that traditional music was in danger of dying off. Today, they have a different opinion: "We believe it would be very hard for this strong musical culture to disappear. Pasatono Orquesta is now part of this music scene and they're also part of the preservation and continuity of the music of the Mixtec Region of Oaxaca."

Pasatono Orquesta | Photo by Estanislao Ortiz

TAIKO IN LOS ANGELES

It starts with a loud, guttural scream, a sort of call by a leader to the rest of the drummers. The others respond and the drumming gradually builds, gathering sonic energy, until an aural explosion envelops everything. This is taiko, a Japanese tradition that goes back more than 500 years. But in the last six decades or so, it's been brought to the main stage by way of Los Angeles and a universal immigrant story. Halle Fukawa started playing at age seven. She's now 15 and said she just can't stop. "It's just something that's so powerful, and I think a lot of the times, especially in [a] society that women aren't really encouraged as much to be powerful. Taiko, hitting the drums, showing energy, showing emotion, it's something that is so addictive." Fukawa is part of a youth group, Kitsune Taiko, who along with Bombu Taiko and Taiko Project are rehearsing in the basement of the Higashi Honganji Buddhist Temple in Little Tokyo. It's a group of more than 40 drummers, ages 10 to mid-50s, rehearsing the opening piece of the show they'll be performing at the Ford Theatre in Hollywood.

Taiko drumming is dynamic, visceral, physical and, of course, loud. At one recent rehearsal, women make up the majority of the performers — about two-thirds. Women's participation in taiko goes back 50 years, when it began taking root in LA. Bryan Yamami, executive director of Taiko Project said the original taiko drums came to the city as part of the Buddhist tradition — but it wasn't practiced much. A temple had one taiko drum to be used once a year during the Obon festival. Yamami explained:

"They would play it at this festival to remember one's ancestors and to dance in this idea of joy. But back in the late '60s, early '70s, some members of the Senshin Buddhist Temple, they pulled out this drum, they just kind of looked at each other and said, 'hey, we should play this more than once a year.' They just started banging on it and a few hours later, they're sweaty, their hands were bleeding, and they said, 'let's do this more often.'"

Johnny Mori, one of the founding members of the Kinnara Taiko group, explains how taiko planted roots in LA's Japanese American community: "Because of our parents' sacrifice, during the war and after the war," he said, "we were given the opportunity that allowed us to create our own culture and to understand and study Japanese culture, but it also gave us a situation so that we could develop our own Japanese American culture or American culture." During the groups' rehearsal at the Little Tokyo temple, Lisa Shimamoto takes the lead, with an opening call to more than 40 Taiko drummers. Shimamoto, 57, lives in Monterey Park and started drumming in 2002: "My nieces were playing Taiko in Monterey Park so I was taking them to their events. Almost every weekend I have to take them to practice or I had to drive them to a gig. I'd bring them home and they'd say, 'oh auntie, you should try it one day,' so that's what I did."

Anyone can play taiko — age or background doesn't matter. "I'm not Japanese myself," says drummer Jen Baik, who's Korean American and has been with Taiko Project since 2004. "I found taiko through my love of music [and] I've really come to love the traditions and the culture behind it and how it's changing in the U.S. as well." Masato Baba, the artistic director of Taiko Project, says he wants to continue teaching the style the same way he learned it from his parents:

"I definitely think that preserving the culture and the music of taiko is important, and so, as much as I can, I try to teach that way to our students, and hold on to those traditions as much as possible. For here in Los Angeles, it seems to me it's a little bit more wide-open right now. There's no certain restrictions, there's no one person here saying you need to do this way or that way."

Fifteen-year-old Halle Fukawa, of the youth group Kitsune Taiko, said there's something special about the community she's been a part of for seven years: "The thing that sets us apart from everybody else is our synergy and how well we work together, and how much energy is on that stage. I really hope that people coming to watch for the first time will walk away and just say like, 'Wow, that was amazing, I felt like I was up there with them.'"

The seed that was planted 50 years ago, by both Kinnara Taiko in Southern California and Taiko Dojo in the Bay area, has spread across North America. Today, there are more than 200 taiko groups in the U.S. and Canada.

Taiko Project | Photo by Kim Nakashima

LUPITA INFANTE

Singer Lupita Infante is heir to a Mexican music dynasty. Her grandfather, Pedro Infante, was Mexico's most beloved actor and singer. The 31-year-old, LA-born singer is starting to carve her own path, but it hasn't been an easy road.

It's a Saturday night at the Ford Theater in Hollywood. A packed house is here to see two of LA's top female mariachi groups — Reyna de Los Angeles and Las Colibrí. Tonight, the special guest is singer Lupita Infante. In the second half of the program, Infante comes out in a black mariachi outfit. After belting out a couple of classic rancheras, she starts crooning "Cien años," a song made famous by her grandfather, Pedro Infante. Backstage, Infante tells me the mariachi outfit she's wearing tonight was a gift from her father, singer and actor Pedro Infante Jr. "I forget that my dad got me this. This is my first suit ever."

Last week, I met Infante at her label's offices in Burbank. She told me about growing up in Downey, the complicated relationship with her father, who lived in Mexico City and visited only sporadically. From an early age, her mother began to shape her artistic path. "Basically, in every class you can think of: dance class, modeling class, at a very young age, like 3 years old. There's pictures of me in the cutest little outfits. I did Hawaiian dancing, I did piano classes, I did guitar classes."

In her freshman year of high school, Infante took a jazz choir class and later played drums in a Ska band she formed. After graduating from high school, she attended community college. Around this time, her father decided to move to LA. Then, in 2009, "My dad, he passed away tragically. He took his own life, after many years of struggling with addiction."

Ten years ago, after her father's passing, Infante decided to focus on a career as a singer and continue her grandfather's legacy. In the 1940s and 1950s, Pedro Infante was Mexico's most popular singer and actor. He died in 1957 at the age of 39 in a plane crash. But his music remains popular to this day. "I started learning all of the standards, the canciones that everybody asks for, like 'Cien años' and 'Amorcito corazón.' And from then on, I started kind of building on that and I kept going to classes." At first, Infante says it was a big struggle to satisfy audiences. "People expected the granddaughter of Pedro Infante to sound like this incredible singing angel and I think I was refining my craft and my style. I still am, but I've come a long way."

In 2015, she transferred to UCLA's Department of Ethnomusicology. She says her two years there were difficult. "I was commuting from Downey to UCLA, so it was like an hour and half each way, and I was trying to keep my part-time job teaching, and I was also recording independently, working on this album that I would sell at my shows." After graduating from UCLA in 2017, Infante auditioned for the reality show "La Voz — Mexico" and got in. Infante says the manager of one of the TV program's coaches saw her perform during the semifinals: "And right away he sent me a message on Instagram. He's like, 'hey, I want to talk to you about possibly working together' and since, there has been so many wonderful things that have come out it."

Infante got a publishing and record label deal with Peer Music — the same company that operates her grandfather's publishing catalog. Early this month, she was signed to the Creative Artists Agency. Her debut album comes out September 27. The album's title is "La Serenata." Infante says the songs are meant as a repertoire for a serenade: "For someone that you're so in love with and you want to serenade them, or somebody that you're kind of mad and then you want to go tell them off in a serenade. I kind of like that idea of a female figure taking a serenata to a man, or it could be a female figure to a woman."

"Her point of view comes across so clearly, particularly in 'La Serenata' there is that feminist side to her that I know that she has that brings a different, youthful, bicultural perspective that we have not had a tremendous amount of in the genre," says Ivonne Drazan, Vice President of the Latin Division at Peer Music. Drazan says having a pedigree will only get you so far: "And I've said this to Lupita: I know that your last name will open the door for you, but only you can walk through that door. Your talent will take you through that door. If you have a last name that's very famous but you can't back it up with anything, it really means nothing."

Infante says her grandfather created an image of Mexican identity. Her father, with the burden of that famous name, struggled to find his own identity. Lupita Infante says, as a woman, born and raised in the U.S., she is forging a completely new identity. "I'm a 100% Mexican, but I'm also a 100% de los Estados Unidos. And that's a whole other identity and I feel that that's what's really going to shape my music. It's this whole story of where I come from and at the same time this new perspective of where the Infante dynasty is going."

Lupita Infante | Photo by Greg Watermann

DHAFER YOUSSEF

Dhafer Youssef grew up in the small Tunisian town of Teboulba. When he was a boy, he was a "muezzin," calling Muslims to prayer from the local mosque. As a teenager, he saved up money to buy his first 'oud' and taught himself to play. Then, one day he saw Tunisian oud master Anouar Brahem on television: "I saw him in Tunisia, playing alone, solo oud. It was like a shock for me, to see an oud player not with a band. I mean, it was opening big doors for me, to believe that everything is possible with the oud."

When Dhafer Youssef turned 19 he moved to Vienna and his career took off. Today, he's recorded six solo albums and collaborated on many different projects. His latest is an album called "Abu Nawas Rhapsody," inspired by the Persian-Arabic poet Abu Nawas. Nawas was known for his tributes to dissipation including the joys of drinking wine. Dhafer Youssef says, even though Abu Nawas lived in the eight and ninth century, his poetry seems to address present-day issues of censorship, intolerance and religious fundamentalism:

"Today, the whole world, especially in the Arab-Islamic world, people are confusing a lot of things, confusing the sacred with the profane and the profane with the sacred. They're stressed about the moral of religion. And I'm sick of that, I'm out of that. I'm Dhafer Youssef, I'm a human being, I know how to love."

"I think that's the role of any good art. It should be provocative," says Hussein Rashid a professor of religion at Hofstra University. "It should make the listener, the viewer think. It should say, 'I'm throwing this out there. What is happening that has caused me to create this?'"

Dhafer Youssef says that's what he's hoping to achieve with his new record: "Abu Nawas Rhapsody is a CD today for me like the explanation, I drink wine because I love it. I don't drink bad wine and it's healthy. I'm not talking directly about wine. I'm talking about the philosophy of life." Ultimately, Dhafer Youssef says "Abu Nawas Rhapsody is a statement about personal freedom, to say what you want to say."

Dhafer Youssef | Photo by Flavien Prioreau

DIEGO EL CIGALA

Diego El Cigala's new album "Cigala & Tango" is an unusual convergence of two different genres: tango and flamenco. But when you listen to this classic tango by one of today's top flamenco singers, the spirit is one and the same. Flamenco's ability to absorb other styles may be one reason it's growing in popularity. Cigala says flamenco used to be something you played for a group of friends. You'd only hear it in small clubs and a handful of festivals in Spain: "But today, flamenco is universal, and it's at the same level of other great music, and has the ability to transmit feelings beyond language. But you need to have the chops to transmit the feeling, just as you do with Jazz, Latin jazz or Afro-Cuban music, that's what flamenco can do."

Currently playing with Cigala is guitarist Diego del Morao from Jerez de la Frontera, one of the cradles of flamenco in Andalucía. As flamenco continues to adapt and reinvent itself in the 21st century, musicians like Diego del Morao strive to keep the traditional styles alive: "Musicians in Jerez are very conscious of their roots. But young musicians of my generation, also try to create something new, because that's the secret of this music and its evolution."

Del Morao says he's very proud that they still hold onto tradition in Jerez. That's why musicians from this region of Andalucía have a special sound, an aged aroma, which today is almost on the verge of extinction. As long as flamenco musicians keep learning the traditional forms, says Del Morao, the music will hold onto its roots.

Diego El Cigala, in concert at the Los Angeles International Flamenco Festival | Photo by Sari Makki-Phillips & Los Angeles International Flamenco Festival

EL PERSONAL

The Mexican city of Guadalajara is known as the birthplace of mariachi. But it's also the city where an unusual band called El Personal flourished in the late 1980s and early 1990s.

The story of El Personal takes place in Guadalajara, the quintessential Mexican city where Mexican identity was forged centuries ago. "La tapatía" is considered the city's unofficial anthem. The song talks about food and famous sites in Guadalajara. It's about a man who falls in love with a drag queen, as they stroll the local streets. It's a little unusual to hear popular Mexican tunes featuring gay characters. But El Personal's lead singer and songwriter Julio Haro and the band's original drummer Pedro Fernandez were openly gay. Both died of AIDS in the early '90s. "Many of the songs were about not exactly homosexuality, but about morality, about the behavior of the people in Guadalajara who is very hypocritical," says Alfredo Sánchez, one of the band's remaining founding members.

Guadalajara is a city of contrasts, says journalist Rubén Martínez, who has written about El Personal. He says their songs capture this tension:

"It is a city that is known for its machismo, through the figure of the charro, the Mexican male with the spangled outfit, the rodeo mariachi-type figure, on the one hand. On the other hand, it's known for its gay underground, and Julio Haro comes out, right from the fault line between those two extremes and he gives voice to that contradiction with sarcasm, with biting irony, and he erupts onto the pop music scene and gives voice to that very contradiction."

In the song "No te hagas" (Don't Fake It), Julio Haro poked fun at people who were afraid to admit their sexual orientation. Diego Escobar is a young music promoter in Guadalajara. He says many "tapatíos," as the people of Guadalajara are called, live a kind of double life: "Many people complain about tapatíos being sort of 'two-faced.' They frown upon some things and then have a few tequilas at night and then go about doing the same things they were frowning upon in the morning in mass."

You can hear those contradictions in the more introspective lyrics of El Personal. In the song called "No me hallo" (I Can't Find Myself), Julio Haro addressed his concern about not "fitting in" in a traditional society, a feeling that resonates with many Mexicans today. El Personal disbanded some years ago, but their songs of are still embraced by their home city. At a recent tribute concert to El Personal in Guadalajara, Café Tacvba's lead singer Rubén Albarrán performed the band's songs. He was accompanied by the surviving three original members, a few guest musicians, and a house full of tapatíos. El Personal's Alfredo Sánchez says he's been surprised how popular the band still is, especially among young people.

"They still are touched by the songs; they still understand what they say. I think the songs are very relevant now in these days, in the 21st century." Alfredo Sánchez says there's talk about doing more reunion concerts with the original surviving members and continue celebrating El Personal's legacy.

El Personal | Photo by Flor Acosta

GUSTAVO GALINDO

A few years ago, Gustavo Galindo made a demo of five songs as a gift to his family but somehow the demo tape landed in the hands of the star-making team at Surco Studios. The team produces Latin rock artists such as Mexico's Café Tacvba and Colombia's Juanes. Galindo says he was stunned to hear from the producers: "The only person that I wanted to work with was Gustavo Santaolalla, Anibal and Adrián. But that was like a wish that I sent out to the universe and they were the only people that called back, so it was meant to be."

"The first thing for me that caught my attention was the songwriting. That's the soul of Gustavo Galindo as an artist," says Adrián Sosa, who, along with Gustavo Santaolalla and Anibal Kerpel, produced Galindo's album: "He's an artist that you can put just with a guitar or with a 60-people orchestra. There's something that will always be there which is the songwriting he has. I think that's his main potential. He's an artist of songs."

The album shows two sides of Galindo's songwriting: one is focused on social commentary, as in the song "Canción pa'l norte," about a young Mexican woman who goes to the U.S. in search of a better life. The other side is more personal, as it reflects on the duality of being both Mexican and American. Galindo says it was difficult growing up not knowing where he belonged: "Because I was never Mexican enough for Mexicans and I was never American enough for the Americans, the kids I grew up with. They'd ask, 'are you Mexican? Are you American?' When I was younger I tried to go to the extreme. I was hanging with my Cholo friends down in the barrio in Sacramento." Galindo says music has helped him define who he is. In the song "Chasing Lightin" he sings in Spanish and English, creating one identity, all his own.

Producer Adrián Sosa says in all his years at Surco Studios he's never come upon someone like Gustavo Galindo before: "We receive, I would say, a hundred demos every month. And this was one of those stories that you can read in magazines. This was a kid that sent a demo, and I actually listened to it." Two years later, Gustavo Galindo's debut album is out. It's called "Entre la ciudad y el mar," and his producers say he has everything going for him, he's talented, he has a unique voice, and he knows how to write songs.

Gustavo Galindo | Photo courtesy of the artist

CARAVAN PALACE

Imagine sashaying into a nightclub, looking to get down to some thumping electro, only to hear swing music from the 1930s. That's just what you'd hear if you happen into a club where the band Caravan Palace is playing. And if you hang for just a moment, you'll be dancing. The group had one of the top records in France last year.

Caravan Palace formed when the band was recruited to compose the soundtrack for a silent porn movie. Even with an anonymous beginning, last year the group sold over 150,000 copies of its first CD and reached No. 11 on the French album chart. At the heart of the group's popularity is a confluence of Gypsy jazz, American swing from the '30s and a high-energy electronic beat. Guitarist Arnaud Vial points out that back in the '30s and '40s, people danced to swing music, so combining swing and today's dance makes perfect sense. "We come back with this old stuff, with modern electronic beats and so people just think, 'Oh, I'm swinging, I'm swinging,'" he says. "Just they needed more, more bass!"

From the beginning the musicians were well aware that they would face all kinds of criticism from traditionalists — especially the Roma (also known as Gypsies), who depend on the continued interest in their music to make a living. Violinist and Caravan Palace co-founder Hugo Payen says he was worried about their reaction. "We were very afraid of the reaction of Gypsies, and really understood that we weren't here to do the same job as them," he says. "We were inspired by their music, by their culture, so they listen to our music for what it is: dance music — dance music inspired by their own culture."

Caravan Palace's three founding members, violinist Payen, guitarist Vial and bassist Charles Delaporte

started out as jazz musicians, playing standards in a swing band. But this group of 20-somethings all had side projects with electronica bands. Payen says they found a way to respect tradition and still have fun. "We didn't have the talent to do virtuoso music, very technical music, virtuoso exactly, so we asked ourselves to know what we found interesting in that style and, in my opinion, it was entertainment," he says. "We try to do that job, to entertain the people, and we found that it was a strong characteristic of our music."

The band's concert in Los Angeles drew an audience of nearly 4,000 dancers. The show's promoter, Leigh Ann Hahn, director of programming at Grand Performances, compares Caravan Palace to another Paris-based band that mixes tango with electronic beats:

> "Same way the Gotan Project did it. It's that same sort of hybridity that really works, where they're being respectful of the tradition but bringing it into the modern-day sensibility. It's timeless music, it has an immediacy, it's classic, it's got great energy and you don't have to understand anything that's being sung. All you have to do is dance."

For its second album, Caravan Palace plans to stay true to the spirit of swing. Vial says the record will be more focused on the sound of the '40s, with an emphasis on brass instruments. "Now we like a lot of big-band stuff, Count Basie, Duke Ellington, all this stuff," he says. "I think we're thinking about it for the second album, to make something maybe different, more you know, trumpets, trombones, stuff like this."

That will be the band's next challenge: finding the bridge between the sound of the big-band era and the ever-changing electronic music landscape.

Caravan Palace | Photo by Florent Drillon, courtesy of the artist

LOS CENZONTLES

The group Los Cenzontles have the ability to absorb a Mexican musical style and make it their own. Their new record, "Songs of Wood and Steel," takes that idea one step further. The opening track is called "Mi único camino," a classic ranchera by Tejano legends Conjunto Bernal, rearranged with a blues flavor. This is not your grandpa's Mexican music: it's Mexican music with an American sensibility.

This approach to music-making has been an integral part of Los Cenzontles from the beginning, says Eugene Rodríguez, director of the band and the arts center of the same name based in San Pablo, California:

> "When you think about the origins of our group, the word Los Cenzontles, the mockingbird, the bird of 400 voices, we've been through many different styles of music and more than just imitating these styles, which isn't what our intent is, it's really to incorporate all these styles and to create something that's our own voice."

Rodríguez says that's the main reason he wanted to record an album with David Hidalgo:

> "He has this profound soul, it reminds me of my grandma's Indian soul, and he's able to infuse it with this incredible music fluidity, and cross boundaries and borders, which really all Mexican Americans deal with. We come from these distinct worlds that really don't interact with each other very much, the Mexican and the American. So this record is really the realization of that."

The record features a guest appearance by Linda Ronstadt in a duet with David Hidalgo singing the popular Mexican song called "El Chubasco." For musician Hugo Arroyo, this song had a special meaning as part of his childhood's soundtrack, growing up in California:

> "It's basically a memory of traveling with my family, I remember we used to take long trips, there was eight of us, we would all hop in my dad's van. I remember almost every single one of those trips, my dad had a tape, I don't remember who the performer was, it was actually an eight-track tape, which made it kinda cool."

Los Cenzontles also reached a magical moment of creativity while recording this album. They were outside taking a break from the studio and found themselves looking at the full moon. Eugene Rodríguez says that's where the words for the song "Howling Moon" came from, and that moment encapsulated the whole recording experience with David Hidalgo:

> "Even though we're in this converted liquor store in a pretty rough neighborhood in urban California, there was no ceiling. We were free to be ourselves — we were free to be who we wanted to be. So often, Mexicans, Mexican Americans we're confined into this box as an identity. You can only play this, you can only sing that, you can only do this, you can only be that. And I feel like this project, the experience of recording this record, was really about liberating ourselves from those constraints."

Rodríguez says this record is also a statement about the place of Latinos in American culture. He hopes that the people who listen to the album will identify with the same feelings in expressing their culture, without being boxed in or constrained by society.

Los Cenzontles | Photo by Craig Sherod, courtesy of the artist

MAGOS HERRERA

Imagine you're a singer and a major record label gives you an opportunity to do an album of songs to celebrate your country's bicentennial. For Mexican singer Magos Herrera it was a dream project. Herrera decided to record songs by composers who emerged in the heyday of Mexican cinema, in the 1930s and 1940s. One of those composers was Agustín Lara. Herrera says she was drawn to Lara's embrace of African roots in Mexico: "You can see he had a very strong view and acknowledgment of Blackness in Mexico and how we were influenced by Africa in our culture. That is something that is not very obvious, right. We don't hear that much from Mexico. We can hear that very strong in Brazilian music, in Peruvian music, in Venezuelan music — but in Mexico it's not that obvious."

One of Lara's popular songs, "Noche criolla," is a tribute to the port city of Veracruz, on the Gulf of Mexico. Another Mexican composer that Herrera connected with was Álvaro Carrillo. She remembers listening to her father singing Carrillo's songs in the living room. But she says she didn't really know all that much about him: "When I started researching about repertoire of this era, Álvaro Carrillo was one of the great beautiful surprises. He had this African background, and the way he wrote his lyrics were so poetic and so, so beautiful."

Magos Herrera moved to New York three years ago. The experience of living away from home has allowed her to see Mexico from a different vantage point. Herrera says this album is an effort to point out the richness of Mexican music: "And I really try to do that, to rescue this 'Africanness' that we have in our culture. That we could really dig into that."

Magos Herrera | Photo by Adrien Tillman

NOEL PETRO

Noel Petro is a larger-than-life character, considered something of a Colombian Chuck Berry for his innovation on the electric guitar. Since the 1950s, Petro has had hit after hit. Among his most famous tunes are: "Cabeza de hacha," "Azucena," "El ñato," "El burro mocho" and "Loco rock." He's from Cereté, a small town in the province of Córdoba, Colombia.

In the early 1960s, inspired by Mexico's Trio Los Panchos, Petro created the electric "requinto," a lead guitar with a very tropical flavor. His songs are filled with humor and slapstick, including his own self-deprecating song "El burro mocho" (The Blunt or Broken Donkey).

In addition to being such a funny, unusual character, there's another thing that blows you away: He's also a bullfighter. Petro has even played a number of gigs where he does a bullfight and a music performance at the same venue. Once he was badly wounded by the bull and still went on stage, bleeding, singing his funny tunes. He likes to tell the story when he played

a double bill with Los Panchos in the Colombian city of Medellín: he was so excited to play a show with his long-time heroes, only to find out that Los Panchos were just as thrilled to meet him.

A promoter in Bogotá once said to him: "Play and do the bullfight, people want to see you do both." But Petro says he prefers to do them separately and that it's very uncomfortable to do both. It's not always in the artist's hands. And sometimes, the president of the bullring will decide which comes first, the music or the bullfight. A bullfighter friend once told Petro, "I would not sing in the bullring, not knowing what kind of bulls you're going to fight. They could be good or they could be ready to put up a fight." And Petro knows all about angry bulls. "I've been gored and I played with a crack in my head and three loose ribs, and the 'donkey' sings as if nothing happened — and after the show to the hospital!" he says. "It's incredible. That's happened to me, it's very serious." He pauses and says with a smile, "I'm used to it."

Noel Petro | Photo by Betto Arcos

MAKING MOVIES

It's a late Wednesday afternoon at the Moroccan Lounge, a small club a few blocks from Little Tokyo, downtown Los Angeles. The band Making Movies is doing its sound check, and rehearsing one of the tunes it will play with trumpeter and singer Asdru Sierra, of the LA band Ozomatli. After the sound check, I sat down to talk with the band members backstage.

Making Movies started 10 years ago in Kansas City, says guitarist and lead singer Enrique Chi: "I met Juan Carlos and Andres' mother who has a ballet folklórico, and she came up to me, 'cause I was playing some acoustic music at that time, and she's like, 'you should meet my sons, they're musicians and they're very talented.'"

"She started the group 40 years ago, in the West Side of Kansas City, where a lot of the Mexican immigrants went to," says percussionist and keyboard player Juan Carlos Chaurand. "That's where they first got, because there's a lot of work there for meat packaging and the railroads, and so they built a community in that area."

Chaurand's younger brother Andrés plays drums in the band. Juan Carlos says their mother's folklórico troupe was their anchor: "We just grew up loving it and being around it all the time and so, that's definitely helped us maintain our culture and our raíces as Mexicanos, even though we grew up in Kansas City, in the middle of the United States." Enrique Chi says the concept behind ballet folklórico — using the art form as a way for immigrant children to retain their identity — helped them create a foundation for the band. "Her

work, became a bit of the blueprint for Making Movies' mission, even though it's a completely different vehicle, but to accomplish the same thing. So we started playing rock-and-roll music, but using folkloric rhythm from Latin America as the foundation."

A few years ago, the quartet traveled together to Panama to explore the traditional music scene. That's where the Chi family is from. Enrique's younger brother, bassist Diego Chi, says the Chaurand brothers noticed the similarities between Panama's traditional "mejorana" and son jarocho from Veracruz, Mexico: "So that showed us even then, the lesson of how interconnected we all are, that even though you would think that these cultures are so different, that there was already a thread that was connecting them, even if that thread was just a rhythmic pulse."

"Ameri'kana" is the band's third album. Diego Chi says the concept behind it began to take shape when they learned that fellow Panamanian Rubén Blades was interested in collaborating with them: "Which came as a great surprise a couple years ago at the Latin Grammys. He had apparently listened to our music at some point. He liked it and he mentioned us on the red carpet. And the next day he went on social media and said 'I would love to collaborate with Making Movies.'"

In Panama, the Chi brothers grew up listening to Rubén Blades at home. As they began their music career, Blades' political and socially conscious songs were a template they wanted to follow:

Making Movies | Photo by Luis Cantillo

"For him to call us out was not only an honor but we basically cried and screamed and ordered a round of shots right away. That began a conversation that resulted in "No te calles," and that song speaks to Latinoamérica, but it speaks to anyone and it invites people to raise their voices against corruptionand injustice."

After they recorded the song, Blades asked if they wanted to put the song on an album, says Diego Chi.

"And well, we thought: well Maestro, if that's OK with you, we would love to make an album based on this idea. And he agreed and so we set down this path to kind of make an album that faced a lot of the issues that our society seems to be facing right now — things that we need to speak out about right now."

The album's songs address social and political issues by telling stories. To that end, Blades also proved helpful to the band. He advised them to think of the album as a book, says guitarist and lead singer Enrique Chi: "And every song is a chapter and picture what the chapters need to say, and then that's how you can select the songs and that's why there is a thread." They were almost done with the record, then, according to Enrique Chi, his brother Diego came up with a final touch:

"He had the idea of thinking of the album as a radio station in the future, as if it was something that we'd gone to utopian future, we had resolved all these social issues and now we're just listening to an oldies station. A station that was reminding us of the things that we had to overcome."

Making Movies also invited a few musicians from Los Angeles to help them tell some personal stories. Los Lobos saxophonist Steven Berlin co-produced the album. His band-mate, David Hidalgo, played accordion and sang on a classic corrido by Los Tigres del Norte, "De paisano a paisano." For the song "Tormenta" (Storm), they invited Las Cafeteras. Ozomatli's Asdru Sierra joined them for the song "Pedacito de Papel" (Little Piece of Paper). The song tells the story of an immigrant family's struggle trying to get a visa in the U.S.:

"So that really hit me. I'm obviously second-, third-generation Latino and I remember, right here in LA, my parents trying to do the paperwork, the money, the lawyer fees and everything, just to get another visa, to get the green card, to get citizenship. It's a long an arduous thing — it's a journey and it's painful."

But there was one more surprise from Rubén Blades. He gave the band a demo of a song he wrote in 1987 with Lou Reed, during the sessions for his album "Nothing but the Truth." The song, "Delilah," never made it to the album. The band was ecstatic:

"OMG, What?! So we made an arrangement, we played it for him in New York, and he decided to sing a duet with me on the tune. And it's one of my favorite songs on the record because it swings a little different than our music normally would, but the lyrics sound as fresh today as they did 30 years ago, and we're just incredibly honored to be the band that get to show the world this Lou Reed and Rubén Blades song from 30 years ago."

Rubén Blades invited them to play with him this November in Mexico City. This will be their first performance in Mexico, and their first gig with one of their heroes.

Making Movies | Photo courtesy of the band

CELSO PIÑA

Celso Piña likes to reminisce about the days when he was learning to play the accordion in his barrio in Monterrey, Mexico. He plays the first tune he recorded and says, to learn this seemingly simple cumbia he spent months playing the accordion, in the late 1970s. Today, he's celebrating a 30-year career with a new album called "Sin fecha de caducidad." Piña invited a wide range of singers to join him on vocals, including singer Natalia Lafourcade.

Celso Piña began a quiet music revolution in Monterrey, a region known as the cradle of Mexican accordion music. But Piña wanted to share his love of Colombian vallenato and cumbia with people. He recorded more than a dozen albums of Colombian-flavored music. Then, in the late 1990s, his record label told him to drop the Colombian sound and try something more commercial. Piña refused: "Si vieras lo que batallé para imponer este género musical aquí en mi tierra." Piña told the label manager he struggled for many years to establish Colombian music in Mexico, and he would not change it simply to satisfy a market. For four years, he did not record a song. Then, a Monterrey producer suggested he try an album of duets and he invited artists from a wide range of music styles.

With the release of his album called "Barrio Bravo," Piña reestablished his career, not just in Mexico but all over Latin America. "Porque a la gente le gusta. Yo me siento a gusto trabajando con diferentes músicos" — people appreciate the music, working with different artists. Better yet, he doesn't have to satisfy a record label and he can invite whomever he wants, from Mexico's rock legend Alex Lora to France's Sergent García.

When asked about the music scene in his native Monterrey, Celso Piña does not mince words: "A nosotros nos ha perjudicado mucho." He says, the increase in violence has hurt the music scene. Instead of playing for three or four thousand people, now it's hard to get a venue with two or three hundred folks. People are afraid to stay out till 3 in the morning." On a more positive note, Celso Piña says he wanted to close this album with a duet with his father, Isaac Piña. After all, it was his father's unwavering support, 30 years ago, that got him where he is today.

Celso Piña | Photo by Betto Arcos

ELISAPIE ISAAC

Elisapie Isaac grew up in Salluit. It's a small isolated Inuit village in Nunavik, the northernmost region of Quebec. When she was 14, she got her first job: "Which nobody wanted in the village. Everybody took, you know, cashier at the co-op, stuff like that, working at the school, and the only thing that nobody applied to is the TV and radio station and I was like, are you guys crazy?"

She began working as a radio and TV host. Elisapie says it was a turning point for her. "I realized that I may be shy, but in front of the camera, I think I sort of transformed into another person, maybe the artist that I wanted to become, slowly going towards music." Today, Elisapie lives in Montreal, where she has recorded two albums.

For her latest album, "There will be Stars," Elisapie asked Quebecois folk singer, filmmaker and activist Richard Desjardins to write a song for her. The song, "Moi, Elsie," tells the story of a white man who works in a northern village and then leaves. And it's told from the perspective of young Inuit women: "So I thought it would be nice to sing a song from these girls to this man who's taking the plane at the end of the month, and to tell all their dreams and their hopes and despair also."

Elisapie also writes her own songs, in English and her native language, Inuktitut. She says back in the 1980s, many Inuit feared the loss of their native language. Not in her village though:

"Where I'm from, it's still very, very strong. Because we're so isolated probably. But we're still very Inuit-speaking. Young people, they become trilingual at one point. We're still very, very strong with our language. So it really depends where you're from. I think we're so proud of that — I think it's our identity."

Elisapie Isaac is also an award-winning documentary filmmaker. But she's put that work on hold for now to focus on music.

Elisapie Isaac | Photo by Jonathan Brisson, courtesy of the artist

SIMON LYNGE

"The future" is singer-songwriter Simon Lynge's debut album. Lynge has Inuit roots and grew up in a little village on the southern tip of Greenland:

> "It was very simple, I helped out with the sheep a lot when I was a kid, there was lots of shepherds, so I helped out the neighboring shepherds starting when I was about 5 years old. There were no stores there, no electricity, no running water. Beautiful place. Four generations of my family were born there and grew up there."

In his late teens, Lynge moved with his parents to the Danish capital, Copenhagen, where he began to pursue a music career. He says music runs deep in the family. His grandfather is a musician, his father plays the accordion. So Lynge picked up the guitar and began writing soulful, deeply melodic songs. "We've had problems in my country with alcoholism," Lynge says. He wrote "The Promised Land" in English and Inuit, after meeting a guy who was from a town near his village in Greenland. Lynge says the man's story is part of a bigger, difficult reality:

> "So a lot of young people from Greenland go to Denmark to get an education, but it's a very different country, it's a very different culture and often, we from Greenland, people get lost in Denmark, 'cause they don't feel like they know how to live in that kind of society and often people turn to the bottle — and this man had done that. But when I started talking to him, he was so intelligent, he was so lucid and told such great stories of where he came from."

Simon Lynge now lives in Washington State. He mostly writes and sings in English, but he says he continues to be inspired by his Greenlandic heritage.

Simon Lynge in Greenland | Photo courtesy of the artist

ALEC DEMPSTER

Alec Dempster is not a typical "son jarocho" musician. He was born in Mexico City to a French mother and British father. The family moved to Toronto when he was 5: "And I grew up playing music, studying classical guitar, but really being close to all kinds of other music that was around me. My dad plays baroque music, he also plays Zambas Argentinas. And then I started going back to Mexico much later — I was about 18 or 19."

Dempster says it was during one of these trips that he discovered son jarocho, the southern Veracruz style. He went to the town of Santiago Tuxtla, one of the cradles of this music:

> "With the intention of getting there in time for the annual son jarocho festival and the celebration of their patron saint — it's all kinds of festivities are happening alongside the son. I got to see son jarocho music in its context and the fandango and musicians just all over town playing music that had come from all over, from rural communities, from other cities. That's how I got in touch with son jarocho music."

In 1998, Dempster settled in the capital city of Xalapa, Veracruz, and got immersed in the local son jarocho community. But not as a musician. Dempster created a series of linocuts and wood prints inspired by son jarocho songs. Later on, he produced six field recordings and learned how to play the music. Three years ago, he and his wife Kali Niño left Mexico for Toronto. They formed a group called Café con Pan, the only son jarocho group in Toronto, as far as they know. Their debut album is titled "Nuevos Caminos a Santiago."

The album includes collaborations with musicians from Veracruz, Los Angeles and Toronto. One of them, Araz Salek, plays the "tar," a traditional Iranian stringed instrument. He'd never played son jarocho before: "And we invited him into the studio, without really knowing what he was going to do. He was very nervous. He wasn't even sure if he would let us use the recording unless he was happy with it. But by the end of the day he was." Dempster says they wanted to take chances with their debut recording. So he did something he'd never done before. He wrote some verses in French for the popular son jarocho tune "Los Pollos" (The Chickens):

> "I don't think we could have done more to shock people, perhaps. It's a language, it's my mother tongue. My mother is French. I hadn't sung in French before. I don't sing in English I only sing in Spanish. I wasn't really a singer until I started son jarocho. I thought it would be interesting to try singing in French because I think it's a musical language and it's a language that is close to my heart."

Alec Dempster is still a professional visual artist. He's had solo exhibitions in the U.S., Canada, France, Spain and Mexico. He recently published a book of 60 linocut prints inspired by son jarocho tunes. It's called "Lotería Jarocha," a play on a popular Mexican board game.

Alec Dempster | Photo by Teresa Irene Barrera

ARMENIAN MUSIC IN THE USA

It's 90 degrees and very humid on a Friday afternoon at the National Mall in Washington. At the 52nd Smithsonian Folklife Festival, singer Samuel Galstian and his group perform a set of Armenian folk songs, in a jazz setting. Galstian is an Armenian American singer based in Boston. He says jazz has been a popular style in Armenia since the early 1950s. His new album features traditional Armenian songs from the 1940s to the 1970s: "So these are very well-known songs in Armenia. So the Armenian music element is in there, even if I sing as a jazz, as contemporary jazz, it's still there, the flavor of Armenian words and music." Vardan Ovsepian is an Armenian American pianist based in Los Angeles. He says it may be surprising, but Armenian and American music have a lot in common:

> "Armenians grew up with lots of different odd meters and syncopations which coincides with jazz a lot. Also the improvisational element too. As you heard, some of the Armenian traditional music is not all rigid and written. There's lots of improvisation, so that aspect also is very similar to jazz."

Also performing at the Smithsonian Folklife Festival is Zulal, a vocal trio of women who sing Armenian folk songs, a cappella. Singers Teni Apelian, Yeraz Markarian and Anaïs Tekerian are the three members of Zulal. Tekerian says when they met in New York City, 15 years ago, they discovered all three had a cappella backgrounds:

> "Teni had a background in a cappella jazz and Yeraz in more pop rock, and for me it was more Slavic, college a cappella, and decided to put together a group, since we were all, at least half, if not fully Armenian, put together a group and concentrate on Armenian music. And so definitely the arrangements that we create are very much informed by our backgrounds in a cappella, which is an American form."

Singer Teni Apelian says a cappella singing does not exist in Armenian folk music. She says harmony was introduced to Armenia by Komitas, the renowned musician, composer and ethnomusicologist, at the turn of the 20th century: "The harmony that we bring is very much Western influence, although there's a bit of Balkan influence coming from Anaïs' background, so it's a mix. But I think our presentation has that in mind: to move this music into an arena that it can be, sort of 'digested' by a wider audience."

The concept of interpreting Armenian folk songs with an American music style, has also inspired a pop trio in Los Angeles. At a restaurant in Little Armenia near Hollywood, guitarist Mher Ajamian says his group "Armenian Public Radio" interpret traditional songs with an American flavor: "In a style that is more congruent with the country that we grew up in, the U.S. A lot of Americana, blues and folk, American folk influence in our music." Ajamian, who is 37 years old, says one of the reasons they decided to interpret traditional songs stems from the trio's efforts to get more Armenians to listen to their own folk music: "None of our friends and our contemporary, really actively listen to traditional Armenian folk music, so we wanted to kind of make it more accessible to them."

From Boston to New York to Los Angeles, the common denominator among Armenian American musicians is traditional music, says Anaïs Tekerian of the vocal trio Zulal:

> "The thing that ties us together is Armenian folk itself. Really, you can't be an Armenian who doesn't know at least a dozen of the songs that just everyone knows. And so we all have that in common so it's very easy for us to pull on that and to create our own version of Armenian folk jazz, Armenian folk a cappella, or whatever. I think that's what connects us, that basic canon that we all have."

Above: Armenian Public Radio in concert | Photo by Shant Gharibian / *Below:* Armenian-American vocal trio Zulal in concert at the Smithsonian Folklife Fest | Photo by Betto Arcos

BUIKA (PART I)

"El Último Trago" is Spanish singer Buika's collaboration with Cuban pianist Chucho Valdés. The record is a tribute to one of Buika's earliest influences, the great singer of Mexican rancheras Chavela Vargas.

Buika remembers the first time she heard Mexican rancheras growing up on the Spanish island of Mallorca: "My dad left when I was 9 years old, and my mom used to listen a lot to Chavela, and you know, to just take care about his sadness." It was only as a teenager that Buika really understood the meaning of those Mexican songs she heard growing up: "I remember that I understand my first ranchera, and it was when my first boyfriend left me." Buika says since that time, she's felt an affinity with Chavela Vargas because she heard the sound of solitude in Chavela's voice. As she started singing and writing her own songs, Buika realized that Mexican rancheras dealt with sadness and pain in a very direct way, like the song "Un Mundo Raro," by one of the most respected composers of rancheras, José Alfredo Jiménez: "To sing José Alfredo songs or, you know, all those amazing composers from this record, to sing these songs, it hurts. You know, it hurts — and it hurts because it makes you open some doors from your past, from your memories."

Buika's album includes seven rancheras, four of them by José Alfredo Jiménez and three other classics, such as "Cruz de Olvido." When she finished the album, Buika sent it to Chavela. After she listened to the album, Chavela sent her approval in the form of a poem. In it, she called Buika "passion": "She has told me something that makes me feel like really special someone. You know what? I think that we have to learn words and sing to please the others."

Buika will be pleasing many people this coming weekend in Mexico City, where she will perform songs from her new album. She's especially excited because Chavela called to tell her she will be attending the concert.

Buika | Photo by Natalia Aguilera, courtesy of the artist

BUIKA (PART 2)

Spanish singer Buika is at a new stage in her career. She just published her second book of poetry and she's currently producing her first film, based on a tale from that book. She also has a new album, "La Noche Más Larga" (The Longest Night) — and it's the first one she's produced herself. The title could be a metaphor for the many years it took her to be able to produce her own record. As Buika says, "I just got out from the longest night of my life." Buika's previous records were all sung in Spanish and focused on popular songs made famous by other singers. On the new album, she does take up the classic Jacques Brel chanson "Ne Me Quitte Pas" in French, and chooses a handful of popular Latin American ballads. She also interprets a couple of jazz songs: Abbey Lincoln's "Throw it Away," sung as an Afro-Cuban ballad, and Billie Holiday's "Don't Explain," sung in the flamenco idiom. "In a world where one is constantly struggling to balance art with commerce, you see that there's someone who's uncompromising," says songwriter and record producer Desmond Child, who has been working in the music industry for more than 40 years, both in the pop and Latin music scenes. "She doesn't care whether she sells one record or millions of records," Child says. "It doesn't matter to her. All she can do is be herself."

Concha Buika was born in Palma de Mallorca, Spain, to parents from Equatorial Guinea — the only black family in a neighborhood of Roma (or Gypsies, as they're sometimes called). She became an international star in the Pedro Almodóvar film "The Skin I Live In," and she's traveled the world, performing in more than 20 countries. But she says she's never felt at home anywhere. "Because I don't have no identity, to build myself I need information from different countries," she says. "My mission is to go around the world discovering. I'm just discovering myself."

But a couple of years ago, Buika decided to leave her home base in Spain and settle in Miami. "I have a son," Buika says. "My son is 13 years old. I want him to live the reality of a place that is made by all the nationalities of the world." Her own songs speak to her personal story. On the track "Los Solos" she sings in Spanish: "The night helped me to see something I want to tell you / That in your company, I feel free / I feel in peace."

Desmond Child says the lyrics don't need translating. Hearing Buika's voice is enough to know what she's singing about. "There were a few moments in my life that changed the course of everything — the first time I heard Laura Nyro's music and her raw emotion," Child says. "When I heard Buika, I had that same feeling."

Buika says it's taken her a while to get to where she is now, but she's not regretting anything.

"It was beautiful; I saw everything," Buika says. "Because in the night there's a really powerful light shining and you can see a lot of things in the night. But I just wake up. I'm happy that I'm here."

Buika | Photo by Alvaro Villarubia, courtesy of the artist

LARA BELLO

Lara Bello grew up surrounded by flamenco music and dance. Granada is one of the cradles of this emblematic Spanish tradition. As a teenager, Bello studied voice and violin at a conservatory. But before that, she learned how to sing and dance flamenco: "I started as a musician, then I was a dancer. I love very much to connect the sounds with the movements of the body. So I also trained in flamenco and contemporary dance and Arabic dance because also the Arabic culture there is very strong."

Lara Bello's new album is called "Primero Amarillo, Después Malva" (First Yellow, Then Purple). She says the title refers to the changing colors of springtime in Granada: "The beginning of the springtime, the flowers are yellow, and with the time, that flowers they died and in their place appear the purple ones. So that's why I dedicated that title to the cycles of life." Bello says she used to see these colors on the road from her house to her flamenco teacher's studio. Bello's flamenco dance teacher was an American woman named nicknamed "La Presy." She moved from San Antonio, Texas, to Granada some 30 years ago to learn flamenco:

"And that means that she came into a very, very strong community, very closed. It's not easy, even for people that we are from Granada, which is a city that we all know a little bit about flamenco, even people that they don't play or they are not musicians or dancers, they know about flamenco. And it's difficult for us, so imagine for somebody that is from the other side of the ocean."

"La Presy" became a well-respected figure in the flamenco world. She died in 2011. But Lara Bello says she continues to be an important influence in her career. In fact, she dedicated her album to "La Presy": "So for all of us, all the students, she gave us a lot of power and also she taught us that your house, home is where the heart is. It's not a question about where were you born, or where you belong or where is the city that is written in your passport. It's where your heart is."

Lara Bello moved to New York two and a half years ago. And she found a new home in the diverse community of musicians from Latin America:

"When I was living in Spain I didn't know anything about Peruvian rhythms. I started to work with them. I met great musicians and also great composers like Samuel Torres. And with these already two years living in the city I wanted to put these strong roots into my music. So that's how this CD has a little bit of rhythms from Latin America, and colors from Latin America but from New York, also."

Lara Bello | Photo courtesy of the artist

ANTONIO ZAMBUJO

Antonio Zambujo is a guy in a world dominated by women. He sings "fado," the style of music often called Portugal's blues. And for decades, its mournful songs have been popularized by female singers. But Antonio Zambujo is starting to carve his own territory with a different approach to fado. Zambujo is not your typical fado singer. His style is closer to Brazil's Joao Gilberto and American Chet Baker than Amalia Rodrigues. "You associate a fado singer to a guy that sings with a very strong feeling, sometimes screaming a lot, yelling," he says. That's the traditional way of singing Fados. Zambujo deliberately chose a different path. "I don't know how to explain it. It's the way I feel it, the way I like to sing the poems, the way I like to say the lyrics."

Zambujo grew up far from the Lisbon neighborhoods where fado was born, in Southern Portugal, listening to polyphonic male choirs. Zambujo says the exposure to this ancient musical tradition at local taverns and social events was a huge influence. But his music director, Ricardo Cruz, says the singer has a firm grasp of fado. "The fado is always there. The way that the song is seen and the words are sung, it's the way of fado; to respect the words, to respect the story." From its early days in the Lisbon and Coimbra neighborhoods, fado is rooted in the musical dialogue between the singer and the player of the Portuguese guitar, an instrument with 12 strings and a body similar to a mandolin's.

Bernardo Couto is Zambujo's accompanist. He says the Portuguese guitar plays a very specific role. "Having a counter-melody to the melody that the fado singer is making, the guitar player gives a boost to the fado singer, and the fado singer gives a boost to the guitar player. So we try to pull the thing up together." Couto says he doesn't play a traditional style with Zambujo.

"If we were talking about another kind of singer or another kind of musical project, maybe, like other singers that are in Portugal that are more connected with the way you usually do fado. But here, things are a little bit more different. The musical approach and the musical influences are a little bit more wider, and so things aren't so simple."

Fado musicians and singers can be criticized for not respecting the tradition. But music director Ricardo Cruz likens fado to jazz or skiing. "Fado is an improvised music or should be an improvised music. It's that the musicians are improvising always, like, you're skiing and you have some banners that you have to respect, but you have always to create each concert.

When Antonio Zambujo released his first album 12 years ago, he says it was difficult getting gigs. But now he's performing in the same places as the female singers. Surrounded by his fellow musicians, Zambujo says there might be a reason he's been able to get away with it. "Maybe it's because I'm a little bit too feminine. That's the only reason." Whatever the reason, Antonio Zambujo is out to change the way fado is perceived at home and abroad.

Antonio Zambujo & Rancho de Cantadores de Aldeia Nova de São Bento | Photo by Betto Arcos

TOÑA LA NEGRA

Antonia del Carmen Peregrino Álvarez was born into a family of musicians in the port city of Veracruz, on the Gulf Coast of Mexico. She started singing at social events, music competitions and carnivals at an early age. The name "Toña la Negra" came later. In 1932, when she was 20, she moved with her husband and child to Mexico City. It wasn't long before she was discovered by the star-maker of the day, radio station XEW.

"She began singing at a place called 'El Retiro,' that was like the 'hip place' to be for bolero in Mexico City," says writer Rafael Figueroa, who just published a book on Toña La Negra. "It was close by the Plaza de Toros, the bullfight ring, and everybody who was anybody was there. The owner of XEW, he saw her and asked her to be part of the lineup of XEW."

Soon after, Toña La Negra met one of Mexico's biggest songwriters, Agustín Lara, and her career took off. Legend has it that Lara was the one who named her Toña La Negra. He wrote songs especially for her, such as "Lamento Jarocho." Rafael Figueroa says Lara found his muse in Toña La Negra and she became the vehicle for his musical exploration of the black contribution to Mexican culture: "And he acknowledged that, not only by naming Toña La Negra, but also by composing a lot of music based on the black Caribbean influence on culture in Veracruz. He began like a whole book of compositions devoted to the blackness of Veracruz and, of course, Mexico."

From the early 1930s to the mid-1950s, Toña La Negra focused on performing, making records and radio shows. But she also appeared in more than 20 films, as a performer and as an actor. Figueroa says people in Veracruz couldn't be more proud: "Well of course for us in Veracruz, Toña La Negra is THE singer of the 20th century — that's it, without discussion. The miracle is that she never really did any promotion of herself, she didn't give interviews or anything. It was just the power of her voice, that was it." And Rafael Figueroa says her voice retains that power. One hundred years after her birth, people are still listening to Toña La Negra.

Toña La Negra with Agustín Lara in a still from the film "Mujeres en mi vida" (1950) directed by Fernando A. Rivero | Photo courtesy of Filmoteca de la UNAM

LINDA RONSTADT

"Live in Hollywood," a concert recording by singer Linda Ronstadt was released a few months ago. The popular singer is also the subject of a new documentary coming out in September. Ronstadt was recently in Los Angeles at an event celebrating her life. I sat down with Linda Ronstadt at her hotel room, the day after she was honored at La Plaza de Cultura y Artes, an arts center in downtown LA.

Throughout her career, Ronstadt has received all kinds of major awards and recognitions. But she says the celebration that took place at La Plaza was special. "I don't usually like things like that, but with Mexicans it's fun. It's a different feeling, I feel like I'm at home." Ronstadt's celebration was indeed close to home. Her uncle, José Ronstadt shared a family story from the stage. In the late 1990s, in the middle of a concert in Tucson, the great Mexican ranchera singer Lola Beltrán stopped the show and asked a question: "Is Mr. Ronstadt here?" Gilbert Ronstadt, Linda's dad. She asked Gilbert come up to the front of the stage, she had a beautiful zarape, 'un rebozo blanco de seda.' She took it off and she says:

'Mr. Ronstadt, on behalf of every Mexicano, I want you to give this to your daughter Linda. It's because of Linda that the music of mariachi will never die.'"

Mexican music and culture have been a part of Ronstadt since she can remember. She was 8 years old, when she first heard Beltrán, who made a strong impression on her: "My dad would make a business trip to Mexico every year and he'd always come back with a bunch or records. He'd bring back Trio Los Panchos, Los Calaveras, Trio Tariácuri, Amalia Mendoza, Miguel Aceves Mejía and Lola Beltrán, primarily. I just fell in love with her music." In 1987, and again in 1991, Ronstadt released albums that paid homage to that music.

"When I wanted to become a professional singer I wanted to learn those songs. And in those days, you couldn't look up on the internet and find it. I had a scratchy record from my dad and I couldn't find the lyrics. And I don't speak Spanish, I didn't have a way to write them down from the records, so I just learned the melodies."

Linda Ronstadt | Photo by Piero F. Giunti, courtesy of La Plaza de Cultura y Artes

The influence of Mexican music in her pop songs first appeared in Roy Orbison's "Blue Bayou," a song she recorded in 1977. Ronstadt says she was trying to channel the deep emotion of the Mexican singer she adored: "It just made me think of a Mexican song, especially that big chorus. And I had a hard time finding a resonance in American pop music because the rhythm culture is really black church, the time that we were doing it, late 1960s and early 1970s." "Blue Bayou" and 11 other songs are part of the album "Live in Hollywood," recorded before a small audience in 1980. Ronstadt remembers vividly the night of the fabled concert. "It was a television studio and it was a small audience and it was hotter than hell — it was just too hot to work. I remember just sweating and trying to sing."

Ronstadt reminisced about the exciting time when she arrived in Los Angeles from Tucson. The Troubadour Club was at the heart of the music scene in the mid-1960s. She says anybody who played well hung out at the club, and it became like a big close-knit family. "And Joni Mitchell and Carole King and Elton John and James Taylor, everybody, Neil Young, Crosby, Stills and Nash, they all played The Troubadour. So you got to hear them over several nights." I read recently in an article that you were there when Elton John made his debut at The Troubadour:

"I was. He came in and did a guest set. It was crowded that night, so we were all standing up in the balcony. I remember hearing him on stage, it was just like an explosion. But I saw Joni Mitchell there for two weeks. She played two weeks, I went and saw every single show, two shows a night, three shows on the weekends. I went a saw every show she did. It was amazing."

These days, Ronstadt rarely goes out to concerts. She retired in 2011 and was diagnosed with Parkinson's in 2012: "But going into a big place is physically impossible for me. I go to the opera when I can get a chance, the opera and the ballet." I asked Ronstadt if she's seen any young singers recently. When I mentioned La Marisoul, lead vocalist of La Santa Cecilia, who performed at La Plaza, Ronstadt was excited to talk about her: "I love her. I've loved her already. I've been stalking her on Youtube. She's so honest, she's got a great voice and she's dead serious about the music and it just shows."

When I asked her about "The Sound of my Voice," an upcoming documentary about Ronstadt's career, at first she appeared reluctant to comment: "I saw a rough cut. I didn't have anything to do with it. It's a weird feeling being examined that closely. It was weird to watch it, like watching your whole life flash before your eyes."

Linda Ronstadt surrounded by United Farm Workers leader Dolores Huerta, producer Dan Guerrero, director Luis Valdez and Mariachi Angeles de Pepe Martínez Jr. at La Plaza de Cultura y Artes in Los Angeles | Photo by Piero F. Giunti

EL COMPA NEGRO

This a story "Straight Outta Compton" about a 19-year-old African American singer of Mexican regional music. Rhyan Lowery grew up listening to Mexican regional music in Compton, styles such as corridos, banda and cumbia. So it's no surprise he loves some of its signature sounds: "The accordion — it's amazing what they can do with the accordion, and what sounds you can get from it, and also banda. I love the tuba, and the charchetta, it's awesome! So I guess that's what draws me to it." Lowery didn't just love the music. "I love Mexican women. And Mexican women, they go to the 'Bailes,' and they dance banda and cumbias and 'norteñas' and 'pues la música es la llave del corazón,' music is the key to the heart. So if I'm gonna win the heart of a Latina, I have to do my homework." But he says his African American friends didn't understand his love of all things Mexican:

"What are you doing? You're supposed to be singing rap and hip-hop. Why are you hanging out with the Mexicans, those are the enemies. I'm like, 'no, they're not enemies, they're my friends.' And because of that, in high school, my first 9th grade and 10th grade year, I had like no Black friends. No one wanted to hang out with me, because they were embarrassed that I would sing and hang out and speak Spanish."

A couple years ago, a friend from high school started calling him "El Compa Negro." Even though Lowery was learning Spanish, he didn't know what it meant. So he asked his friend. He said, "oh, no te preocupes, it means like 'My Black friend,' you know." And right then, everyone started calling me "hey El Compa Negro," and I mean, it stuck with me.

"I was like, wait a minute this guy is actually on tune — he's in key, he's singing pretty good and I was like,

no, this guy is good," says Antonio Lopez, El Compa Negro's manager. He's the one who discovered Lowery singing on Youtube, when Lowery was just 16. That was three years ago. Last May, El Compa Negro appeared in the LA-based TV show "Tengo Talento Mucho Talento." He came in third. In the song "Negro Claro" (Black, Of Course), written by Lopez, El Compa Negro lays out his unusual position as a singer of Mexican regional music.

The lyrics say:

I'm Black, of course, African American
Heart and soul of a Mexican…
Sinaloa and Jalisco are supporting me
I sing with Banda or Norteño
My band "Los Mas Poderosos" are on my side
Black and of course, I insist, here's my hand
Black and of course, I respect all the Mexicans.

Lopez says while some of El Compa Negro's old friends don't get him, he also faces discrimination in the Mexican community in the U.S. He says people complain about Donald Trump's attack on Mexicans, but some Mexicans are doing the same thing to El Compa Negro.

"There's a lot of doors, here locally and outside the state that have not been able to be open for the same, just because he is Black. And that's a problem, that's a very serious problem. Why? Because, here we are complaining that someone is stereotyping us, yet they're stereotyping my singer. They're saying, well you guys can't play here."

But El Compa Negro says he's not discouraged. "Look what I've started, I've made something like Obama, he's the first African American president. Well, I'm the first African American in the "Regional Música Mexicana."

El Compa Negro performing at a Mexican music festival in Santa Anita Park, California | Photo by Betto Arcos

JUNGLE FIRE

The band Jungle Fire draws influences from a wide array of music icons: James Brown to Fela Kuti, Irakere to War. In their second album, called "Jambú," they establish an original sound the band calls "Tropi-Funk." On a recent evening at the group's studio and rehearsal space, on Pico Boulevard near Vermont, the 10-piece band forms a circle and starts its monthly ritual. Various members explain the band's sound and purpose: "It's been described as a 10-piece Tropi-Funk juggernaut from the City of Angels ... I think Jungle Fire is just kind of a melt-your-face, audio-slap-to-the-face party band ... It's a party, it's love, it's forget about everything else and just let yourself loose and bring it all together."

Jungle Fire came together as a jam between friends six years ago. Bass player Joey Reina says a friend called him and said he needed a band for a music festival he was organizing: "And ever since then, it just started to gain popularity and people liked it and became more serious. We got the core members of the band, kind of figured it out, and it became what it is today." Jungle Fire plays a wide range of related music styles. They can lay down a groove of deep funk. They can re-invent Latin America's most popular dance music — in a tune called "Cumbia de Sal" — and tip their hat to a major figure of West African music in the tune "LA Kossa" — a reference to Manu Dibango's "Soul Makossa."

Steve Haney is one of three percussionists — the foundation of the Jungle Fire sound. He says the band recreates Colombian funk sounds from the 1970s: "We gravitated towards that because that's how we heard the sound of the group going. And we wanted to bring some flavors of LA, Southern California, obviously War — that's a big part of what we listened to, as a lot of us were born in the '70s." Guitarist Patrick Bailey says Jungle Fire is a musical reflection of the LA metropolitan area:

"C'mon, it's 2017! It's such an amazing cauldron of so many cultures — it just gets more and more diverse and I think this band is definitely, definitely a product of that. We don't sit down and think about what sound we're going to do. We're gonna do afrobeat, we're gonna combine this Colombian rhythm. The beautiful thing about this band is it just kind of happens."

Percussionist Alberto López says the group's debut album was like a first date for the band — a musical explosion of friendship among the members: "But then we had a couple years of playing together and touring together between the first and the second record, and I think that shows. The second record showcases experiences that we could have not have imagined when we first got together." Haney says anytime the band plays a show, they want to make sure people have a good time: "Letting them forget at that moment, forget about all this BS that's happening, because there's so much evil that seems to be opening up everyday." And if the fans like the music, and take it home and share it with their friends and family, Jungle Fire is doing their part for a better world.

Jungle Fire | Photo courtesy of the band

RENAUD GARCIA-FONS

Renaud Garcia-Fons is known among jazz fans as an ear-popping virtuoso of the acoustic bass. The sounds he conjures from his five-string instrument have won him admirers around the world. But for his latest project, the Spanish-French musician says he wanted to concentrate on composition — specifically the sounds of the Mediterranean — while searching for a bridge between the music of the East and the West.

Garcia-Fons says the initial thinking behind his new album, "Mediterranées," was not to compose music for a band, but to make a concept album inspired by music across the Mediterranean and the search for a common identity. That process took him back to his childhood. "When I was in family, I was of course listening to Spanish music," he says. "But when I grew up in Paris, I had a chance to listen to many different music from north of Africa, which is Mediterranean. After that, I had really a passion for all music coming from Middle East, from Turkey, Lebanon, Egypt." Garcia-Fons says all of these different styles of music share common elements, and that he wanted to find the connections. "We have some bridges, but also, of course, each tradition is unique," he says. "The sense of this music was also to try to establish some bridges between."

Garcia-Fons' exploration begins in Andalucía, in the south of Spain, with a piece called "Aljamiado" — its title a reference to the Spanish language from the time when the region was ruled by the Moors. "For me, it's a good illustration of the union between Occident and Orient," Garcia-Fons says. His music moves from West to East, from Spain to the South of France, Italy and Greece, to the northern tip of the Mediterranean: "So all the first pieces are more on the 'occidental way,' and then the big change starts in the piece called 'Bosphore.' Because the trip arrives finally on the Bosphorus, so we reach the border with the Orient and start more Oriental influences."

Unlike some of Garcia-Fons' previous recordings, the new album is not centered on his five-string acoustic bass, but rather on composition. Nevertheless, Yatrika Shah-Rais — music director at the Skirball Cultural Center in Los Angeles, where Garcia-Fons performed recently with his quartet — says Garcia-Fons is a virtuoso:

"This is a world-class musician that deserves to be truly acknowledged for what he does. He's unique in every sense of the word. He's unique in his approach to compositions, to his music. He's unique in his technique. He's unique in the way that he has revolutionized the bass, and simply he has a fantastic band."

Garcia-Fons says he's always been intrigued with the notion that the roots of Western music come from the East. And he says that thread is present, not just in Western Europe, but also in the Americas:

"This is a fascinating point for me. And this is what I also really appreciate in all American music, from South to North, is that we can feel this influence from the Mediterranean area. I think maybe the common relative is baroque music. I heard that many baroque musicians find some codex, for example, in Mexico, so I think this was one of the bridges for the music to come here and to meet other cultures, other people."

Renaud Garcia-Fons | Photo by Patrick Hinely, Work/Play®

LA CUNETA SON MACHÍN (PART 1)

In the early 1980s, when the Sandinistas took power in Nicaragua, "Son Tus Perjúmenes Mujer" is one song you'd hear on the radio. The band was Carlos Mejía Godoy y Los de Palacagüina. Carlos and his brother Luis Enrique Mejía Godoy were the leading voices of the Nueva Canción movement in Nicaragua during the Sandinista revolution.

And these days, what's popular in Nicaragua is the song "Mondongo." That's a song by La Cuneta Son Machín, also known as La Cuneta. Three of the members are children of the Mejía Godoy clan. They started playing in 2009 on the sidewalk, in front of lead singer Carlos Guillén's house ("cuneta" means "sidewalk"). The band's new album, "Mondongo," is named after a beef tripe stew, a popular dish for hangovers. Carlos Guillén says the title is a metaphor: "of all the ingredients that we use in our music, because our music is kind of mix, a mixture between a lot of rhythms, rhythms from the United States, another rhythm of Cuba, rhythm of our country, of our traditional popular music in Nicaragua."

Guillén says La Cuneta's songs may not be as overtly political as their parents' music, but the spirit is there: "As a child I remember listening always the music of Carlos y Luis Enrique Mejía Godoy and other kind of music related to this movement. So there's a big influence, not only as a musician but as ideological thinking about the social movements and the social revolutions in all Latin America."

Last year, when La Cuneta were getting ready to record a new album, they asked their father Carlos Mejía Godoy for advice: "They asked Carlos what they should do. They wanted to expand their sound and he told them to go talk to Gregorio. And they called me and they came to San Francisco and we began working." Greg Landau is a music producer in the San Francisco Bay Area. Back in the '80s he lived in Nicaragua and played music with an uncle of La Cuneta: "What they liked is that I understood their roots, where they were coming from, and I was able to create a vision for where they wanted to go — and I think that was important, to try to take the project of the '80s into this era."

Luis Mejía, La Cuneta's Marimba player, says members of the band often ask their parents to weigh in on their songs: "We have the same influence that our parents had, in always talking about what happens in Nicaragua. All our music it's always talking about our culture and way of living. It's nice listening from them, that what we do is like the new way of doing what they have done in the '70s and the '80s. So that's also like a green light to us, like 'aprobado,' like they approve." This is the first time that a band based in Nicaragua has been nominated for a Grammy. They'll find out whether they'll be taking one home next month.

La Cuneta Son Machín | Photo courtesy of the band

LA CUNETA SON MACHÍN (PART 2)

The Nicaraguan band La Cuneta was nominated for a Grammy last year. For the Central American country with a population half the size of LA County, this was a big deal. That nomination and all the media attention reinforced the band members' approach of digging into their country's roots and culture for a new album. While in LA for a performance at the Nicaragua Festival in Huntington Park, three band members gathered for coffee at La Adelita Bakery, a popular hang-out in the heart of LA's Central American community. The Nicaraguan musicians looked right at home as they talked about the band's roots. It was eight years ago, on the streets of Managua, during the city's patron saint celebration, when La Cuneta was born.

These musicians knew each other, but they were part of other bands. So they decided to create a new group. Drummer Fabio Buitrago says the band started out playing traditional Nicaraguan music: "But then we decided to mix it up a little bit in the process to include other rhythms and more — let's say — contemporary tendencies on the music. So we included rock, funk, ska and new sounds." Buitrago says mixing traditional music with contemporary sounds helps young Nicaraguans appreciate the richness of their own culture. And that's one of the band's goals, to keep Nicaraguan culture alive, Buitrago says:

> "Young people do not know about the traditions. Young people are losing the knowledge of where the traditions come from. So what we want to do with this project is just to gather all the music, the tradition, the culture of Nicaragua, give it a fresh update, a fresh sound and new rhythm, and then put it back into the people."

One example of La Cuneta's reinvention of popular music is one of Nicaragua's most famous cumbias. Singer Carlos Guillén says they transformed the song with some rock elements and a hip-hop flavor: "The songs feels a little bit more modern and the sound of course it has synthesizers, electric guitars and things like that. So it is a like a new version of a very folk song called "La Cumbia Chinandegana." Greg Landau, who has produced albums by top Latin acts including Quetzal, Maldita Vecindad, Susana Baca and Jerry González, was behind the mixing board for the Grammy-nominated song: "'Mondongo' was more rock and had a lot of electronic elements, tropical rhythms, this was more to explore the Nicaraguan cumbia and to explore new ways to create Nicaraguan rock, celebrating the tradition of Carlos Mejía Godoy, who's also on the record."

Mejía Godoy is one of Nicaragua's most respected musical icons. He and his brother, Luis Enrique, provided the soundtrack during the Sandinista Revolution in the late 1970s and early 1980s. Marimba player Carlos Luis Mejía says his father, Carlos, and uncle, Luis Enrique, dedicated their entire lives working for Nicaragua, its music and culture: "Since we were little, they have always tell us about the importance about doing this job and tell us the importance of working with dignity, as brothers, with honesty of what we do."

Landau, who also produced the band's new album, "Cañambuco," says La Cuneta's Grammy nomination acknowledged the Mejía Godoy family and the band's fresh approach, compared to the other albums in the Latin rock, urban and alternative category: "They kind of push the boundaries of rock en español, including a lot of Indigenous and Nicaraguan folk elements — something that had gotten a little bit lost in that category and was what made Latin rock something unique." A Grammy nomination can also send a message to the naysayers. Nobody in Nicaragua, or in Latin America for that matter, thought it was possible for a little-known band from Managua to get that far.

La Cuneta Son Machín | Photo by Betto Arcos

CARLOS NÚÑEZ

When he was 8 years old, Carlos Núñez started playing the bagpipes. The "gaita," as the bagpipe is known in Galicia, opened a whole world of music around him. "For me, the magical thing about the bagpipes, it was to discover that other countries, like Scotland, like Ireland, like the Bretons in France, all the Celtic countries, we play the same music but we speak different languages," Núñez says. "But the music makes us only one nation. I think Celtic music is a sort of Atlantic nation and we are part of the same family. I think this is what I really love it when I was a child." Núñez says during the dictatorship of Generalissimo Franco, Galician music was forbidden — Celtic musicians could only play underground. After Franco died in the mid-1970s, there was an explosion of Galician music. Núñez says he's the direct result of this energy that had built up over decades.

In the late 1980s, when he was still a boy, he met the masters of traditional Celtic music, The Chieftains. Núñez says:

> "And I had the opportunity of start to play with The Chieftains when I was 13 years old. And with 18 years old I was playing with The Chieftains and then they invite me to come to America. My first concert in America it was with The Chieftains in this tribute to The Who. Roger Daltrey, we played with Alice Cooper, with Sinéad O'Connor. Wow!"

Núñez launched his solo career, built on a long list of collaborations. He's played with artists as varied as Laurie Anderson, Ry Cooder, Compay Segundo, Ryuichi Sakamoto and Jordi Savall. But Núñez says it was The Chieftains who had the biggest impact on his life. "They always said to me, 'Carlos, don't think about your little country — think international, think that the world is all connected and all the traditions are really the same, are really connected.' This is the idea The Chieftains gave me."

For his first album, "Brotherhood of Stars," Núñez invited musicians from all over the world. And at the suggestion of The Chieftains, he also invited musicians from Andalucia's flamenco world, to collaborate with musicians from the north of Spain. He says during the Franco dictatorship, Galician and flamenco musicians never played or recorded music together. "Never, ever. Because of the flamenco, it was the enemy for the music in the north," he says. "Think that for 50 years of dictatorship with Franco the flamenco was the official music of Spain. The only possible music of Spain, the official Spain. And well, for us, the democracy was a liberation."

Today, Núñez says he's on a musical mission. He wants to explore the links between the music of Galicia, and by extension, the music of Spain, to the diverse musical cultures of Latin America and beyond:

> "I think Latin America is like a cathedral with many traditions at the same time. So absolutely, I want to connect, to make all these connections, in the same way so many people as The Chieftains, Los Lobos, Linda Ronstadt, all those people. They gave me the opportunity of playing with them one day, and to learn."

Carlos Núñez just released a double CD called "Discover." And this week, he starts his first major tour of the U.S.

Carlos Núñez and his teacher, luthier Antón Corral at his shop in Tui, Galicia | Photo by Betto Arcos

MARÍA MÁRQUEZ

María Márquez started singing in Venezuela when she was 19 years old. It was the early 1970s, and the renowned German-Venezuelan musician Vytas Brenner, invited Márquez to form a duo with him called Vytas y María Fernanda. The duo lasted only two years, but the music became very popular and well-known in Venezuela. Márquez says Vytas Brenner went on to become an influential musician. "A very important figure because he was the first one to mix or fuse folklore with rock, in those days, and electronic music," Márquez says. "So he obviously, if you listen to the arrangements and so on, I do have a lot of influence from Vytas, really. He was a major, major influence on me."

In the late 1970s, Márquez moved to Boston to study at the Berklee College of Music. It was there that she heard about the San Francisco Bay Area music scene and some of the figures she wanted to learn from. Since her move there, Márquez has recorded three distinctive albums, every one of them with a unique and soulful Venezuelan flavor. For her new record, "Tonada," Márquez invited the renowned master of the Venezuelan "cuatro" — Hernán Gamboa. She says

her intention was to record only two songs, with him playing the traditional four-string instrument:

> "And we were in the studio and he said, let's do this one, let's do that one. So a lot of them were improvised, spontaneously done in the studio. And it was just out of his generosity that I ended up with all these tunes, so I decided to include them here and there as miniatures to showcase the cuatro."

Márquez says this album represents her career coming full circle. Part of the sound goes back to her early days as a singer in Venezuela with Vytas Brenner. But she says the new record is also peppered with an American flavor. "My roots of course are in Venezuela — that's where I grew up, where I was born," Márquez says. "But I've lived here half of my life in the United States, so really I cannot deny the influence and what impact it has had on me." Márquez says it took her more than four years to complete this album. She's now working on a special concert in San Francisco that will highlight the confluence of Venezuelan and American music that infuse her beloved songs.

María Márquez | Photo by Hugh Lovell

LOS GAITEROS DE SAN JACINTO

Los Gaiteros de San Jacinto take their name from the "gaita," an Indigenous flute made from a hollowed cactus stem, about a yard long, from Colombia's Caribbean coast. Los Gaiteros have been playing Colombian cumbia since the late 1930s. Gabriel Torregrosa is one of the younger members of the group. He's in his late 30s and he's the musical director of the band: "This is the group, the music genre and our Indigenous instruments from which every form of Colombian cumbia originates. Our music is tri-ethnic. There's the Indigenous influence of the gaita and the maracas, the African polyrhythms on the drums, and the Spanish lyrics."

Cumbia is one of Latin America's most popular dance forms. The cumbia beat is played in every country. But the instruments that play it can vary, from accordion to keyboards, electric guitar or acoustic bass. But no matter the trends, Los Gaiteros continue to play with the original Indigenous instruments. Torregrosa says for Los Gaiteros cumbia is the foundation of everything they do: "Although the music remains popular in small towns and cities around Colombia, radio stations don't play it much." Still, he hopes that by teaching young musicians their traditions, Los Gaiteros de San Jacinto will keep the fire of this music going for years to come.

Los Gaiteros de San Jacinto | Photo courtesy of the artist

FLAMENCO,
AFTER PACO DE LUCÍA

Paco de Lucía died more than three years ago, leaving behind an immense impact on flamenco music. He expanded what once was a very strict, traditional form by adding jazz and world music influences, and by collaborating with musicians outside of the genre. Members of his last touring band, led by guitarist-producer Javier Limón, are currently on the road as the Flamenco Legends, revisiting the late guitarist's music while paying tribute to his legacy.

The tour is fittingly called The Paco de Lucía Project, and Limón says the loss of their namesake will be felt for a long time. "We lost a leader that was even bigger than flamenco itself," he says. "Paco de Lucía was like Astor Piazzolla or like Carlos Gardel for the tango. Paco de Lucía was like Antonio Carlos Jobim for bossa nova, or like Miles Davis for jazz. And I think we're going to need decades to have a musician or a guitarist that big."

The flamenco guitar was primarily an instrument to accompany singers. Then came the great guitarists of the genre: Ramón Montoya, his nephew Carlos Montoya, Sabicas and Niño de Ricardo. Fellow guitarist José Fernández Torres, better known as Tomatito, says that de Lucía learned from all of them. "But he went beyond them," Torres says. "He changed the music, he changed the way of playing, he changed flamenco harmony. He did everything." Limón says that besides being the "best flamenco guitarist ever," de Lucía was also a consummate composer and musician. "He was a great producer," he says. "He was the producer of

Camarón de la Isla's albums and many others. So he created, as a producer, a new sound with this band."

Now that the band is on tour, people might ask, "Why present programs with de Lucía's band without the leader?" Which, Limón says, is a fair question. "All these artists, all these young members of the band, are very good leaders and are very good soloists," he says. "So now we have the opportunity of get deeper in every one of them. So even without Paco, the sound is there, the sound of the band is there. That has a very important value."

Nevertheless, another flamenco guitarist, Raúl Rodríguez, says that what's missing in today's flamenco scene is a guiding creative figure. "For many decades, flamenco has been thought of as music that's already made, already finished," Rodríguez says. "So now, it's not so much that we miss Paco de Lucía — it's that we urgently need to have creative minds within our music so we don't repeat the old scheme, or else it's going to fall asleep."

Though the void left by de Lucía will take a long time to fill, Limón believes that the future looks bright, as long as artists learn the roots of flamenco and embrace the open ears de Lucía brought to the music. "We need to really get deep in the knowledge of rhythm, harmony, sound, melody," Limón says. "And quality, basically. It's about quality." He adds that there's still plenty of room to make flamenco a bigger musical language. And it's more important than ever to keep playing it for as many audiences as possible.

Members of The Paco de Lucía Project | Photo by Luis Malibrán

POWER

GABRIELA ORTÍZ

Gabriela Ortíz's "Yanga" had its world premiere late last month at the Walt Disney Concert Hall in Los Angeles. Ortíz is one of Mexico's most sought-after classical composers and her work has been performed by musicians all over the world, from soprano Dawn Upshaw to the Royal Liverpool Philharmonic to Kronos Quartet. "Yanga," her most recent commission, came from the LA Philharmonic's music and artistic director, Gustavo Dudamel, who asked Gabriela Ortíz earlier this year to write a piece for orchestra and choir, with the choral parts sung in Spanish. "Gabriela is one of the most talented composers in the world," Dudamel says. "Not only in Mexico, not only in our continent — in the world. She has an ability to bring colors, to bring rhythm [and] harmonies that connect with you. That is something beautiful, something unique."

Ortíz's work, "Yanga," is named for a 16th-century liberator of slaves in Veracruz. As the story goes, Yanga was a prince from what is now the country of Gabon, in West Africa. "He came in the 16th century to Mexico as a slave and he managed to escape. And then with other slaves [who] also escaped from the Spanish crown, they start organizing a revolt," Ortíz says. "And finally, he was able to negotiate with the Spanish crown and founded the first free town in [North] America."

Gabriela Ortíz grew up in Mexico City. Her father was an architect and her mother was a psychoanalyst, but they were also founding members of Mexico's leading folk music ensemble Los Folkloristas. "During my childhood, I had the opportunity to meet people like Víctor Jara, the Chilean singer that came to Mexico. He stayed in my house," Ortíz says. "I met Mercedes Sosa. And so I was exposed to all this music, not only from Mexico, but from Latin America." Ortíz remembers visiting a small town in the Gulf state of Veracruz with her parents when she was 6 years old: "They were doing some research about music from Veracruz, so I remember that we rented a boat through the Papaloapan River, and my parents used to play folk music along with the people from Tlacotalpan," she says. That family experience was the foundation for a piece she composed in 1995 called "Río de las Mariposas (River of Butterflies).

Ortíz's music doesn't only draw from the sounds of Mexico. One day, when she was a teenager, her piano teacher introduced her to "Mikrokosmos," a series of pieces by Hungarian composer Béla Bartók. "For me, it was a window open to the 20th century music. That definitely changed my mind in a completely new way," Ortíz says. "And then I decided: I want to be a composer." Ortíz went on to study at the Conservatorio Nacional de Música (National Conservatory of Music) in Mexico City and got her advanced degrees in London. She brings both influences to bear in a work commissioned by Kronos Quartet. "Altar de Muertos," a piece about the Mexican tradition Day of the Dead, uses Aztec percussion instruments called "huesos de fraile" ("friar bones," also known as "ayoyotes") that the musicians attach to their ankles. "Every time they see an accent on the score, they have to step," Ortíz says. "It's a very energetic movement, very rhythmic, and it has a lot of influence from the 'Danza de Concheros,' one of the oldest dances that we know [from] when the Spanish came." That period is also the setting for her latest work and it, too, uses percussion. LA Phil's Gustavo Dudamel thinks Gabriela Ortíz's compositions need to be heard: "This piece deserves to be played many times because it sends a beautiful message. It shows our culture, our blood, our rhythm as one America and that beautiful connection and that beautiful message of 'libertad,' of freedom."

But getting her music into the concert hall hasn't always been easy, says the composer. "It's even more difficult if you're a woman and if you're Latin American," Ortíz says. "Because normally, in the concert music world, people look to Europe. They don't look to Latin America. They don't know that, in Mexico, we have a very important scene of composers doing lots of things." Gabriela Ortíz says one of the things she wants to do in her music is create a connection between tradition and the modern world, between different kinds of music and different cultures. Yanga's cross-cultural roots with a debut for an American audience just might accomplish that mission.

Gabriela Ortíz | Photo courtesy of the artist

WOMEN MARIACHIS in LOS ANGELES

It's a late Friday night at the Dorothy Chandler Pavilion in downtown Los Angeles. The all-female Mariachi Las Colibrí are playing in front of a couple hundred people at an event called "Quinceañera Reimagined," part of an ongoing late-night series at the Music Center called "Sleepless." In her own way, Las Colibrí's director, violinist Susie García, has also reimagined the traditional mariachi sound and look:

> "Because not any women mariachi had really taken the step to be really without trumpets to present themselves, and then to take a different take on what they are wearing. So we no longer wear the 'charro' suits, but as Las Colibrí, we've taken this '40s and '50s type of look of Mexican cinema and we made it our own and we're very colorful, like the colibrí [hummingbird]."

In Los Angeles, there are several female mariachi groups, all with individual styles. There's two-time Grammy winner Mariachi Divas de Cindy Shea, who play not only the standards, but also American pop tunes. And there's Mariachi Lindas Mexicanas whose aesthetic is quintessentially Mexican, with a strong trumpet sound. Mary Alfaro is a guitarist and singer, an educator and a museum curator who worked on a mariachi exhibit at La Plaza de Cultura y Artes downtown: "There's like a wide breadth of various styles and I guess goals of each group. You have the hardcore mariachi traditionalists. You have groups that appeal to a wider audience with that kind of pop aesthetic, you have groups that present themselves more in the 'traje de charro.'" Alfaro says in a region as big as the LA area, an all-female mariachi has to be different from the rest to be able to compete: "In LA, there are so many mariachis, there is demand for live music, in any genre of music, you're going to want to innovate, you're going to want to stand out and a lot of these groups are finding ways to do so."

The first all-female mariachi group to really make a name for itself was Mariachi Reyna de Los Angeles, founded in 1994 by José Hernández, director of Mariachi Sol de Mexico. At the "Cielito Lindo" Restaurant in South El Monte, home to Mariachi Reyna, the group is playing a set of classic tunes to a full house during a Sunday brunch. Reyna is considered the first all-female mariachi in the U.S., says violinist and singer Laura Peña: "And we were able to start something that wasn't seen before in such a male-dominated genre, do it with passion as well, show that we can also love our music, love what we do and do it in a very traditional and respectful way." Peña says, in the beginning, it was a challenge to work in a music scene filled with all kinds of macho behavior, but 25 years later: "I think we've proven ourselves. I think nowadays you won't see it as often anymore. I think definitely you'll have the token man that says 'ha, they're good, but they're not going to sound like the guys.'"

Julie Murillo is the leader of Mariachi Reyna de Los Angeles. When her band formed more than 20 years ago, she says men were the only role models for female mariachi musicians. Reyna broke the ground for women:

> "Until Reyna came along, that's when you kind like, OK, there's a different way. Reyna has its own sound, its own mariachi sound. You hear a difference there. If the guys could sound this way, then this is the girls' sound for mariachi. Yes, there have been other groups that have come out, looking up to Reyna, and they each have their own unique sound, but I don't think everybody has kept it traditional as well as Reyna has."

There are a few key factors why there are so many women into mariachi music in the region: LA is the second largest Mexican city after Mexico City, with a population that's almost 50% Latino. In addition, Mary Alfaro says the U.S. has a fairly strong public music education in schools: "That, along with other nonprofit ensembles, university groups, that have been around for decades now, those settings help cultivate a large population of women being able to participate in the tradition." And mariachi music is no different than any other popular music, says Alfaro: "Women, just like men, we enjoy performing music. We enjoy teaching kids this tradition, we enjoy being role models, helping people have a great time at their daughter's quinceañera, at a baptism, comforting a family during a funeral. We enjoy all the facets of mariachi music."

Mariachi Las Colibrí leader Susie García says there's no question Reyna de Los Angeles paved the way for women in mariachi. But ultimately, García says it's a natural cycle, like everything else in society: "There are more women lawyers, then we see them and we want to be them. More women senators, we want to be them."

Mariachi Reyna de Los Angeles, performing at Cielito Lindo Restaurant in South El Monte, California | Photo by Betto Arcos

VIOLETA PARRA

In a scene from the film "Violeta Went to Heaven," the Chilean singer Violeta Parra (played by Francisca Gavilán) walks through the countryside with her son Angel in search of a woman whose songs she wants to learn and record. Her son asks her, "What if we can't find this lady? Isn't she old?" Parra responds, "Of course we'll find her. But if she's not there, it will be very sad that no one will remember her."

Remembering people and their music was Violeta Parra's mission. She brought the sounds of the Chilean countryside to the city and, in so doing, inspired people elsewhere to do a similar kind of thing. Emily Pinkerton is a singer, songwriter and ethnomusicologist who teaches Latin American music at the University of Pittsburgh. Pinkerton says Parra's work was a revelation to a lot of people in Chile: "Through the traditional songs she sang, through the songs she composed inspired in that music, she also brought rural musicians and their lives and experiences and practices to the radio — so just really bringing the reality of Chilean rural culture to urban centers."

Parra grew up in rural Southern Chile. She learned how to sing and play guitar when she was 10 and soon joined her relatives, who had a traveling show. In the early 1950s, she began to research, document and record Chilean folk songs. Many of those songs inspired her to write her own compositions. Parra's son Angel picked up her research, and his own memoir provides the basis for "Violeta Went to Heaven." Director Andrés Wood says his admiration for Violeta Parra inspired him to make the movie, but that in some ways her personality proved too big to capture. "Actually getting to her work," Wood says, "and trying to actually put all this energy, all her knowledge, all her life, all her character in one movie was a very big task that we wanted to try to do — and we failed because we decided not to put everything."

Parra had a complex life. She was a sophisticated songwriter and performer who toured Europe in the mid-1950s. She was also a visual artist whose work in paintings, embroidery and sculpture was exhibited at the Louvre in Paris. But Parra had an emotionally complicated personality, with sudden bouts of depression. She committed suicide at the age of 49. Actress Francisca Gavilán, who is Chilean herself, says playing Parra in "Violeta Went to Heaven" was a huge responsibility: "The first time I met Andrés Wood, and he told me that I was going to be Violeta, it felt like carrying a heavy backpack on my shoulders. I think it was one of the most difficult, most painful, most beautiful jobs I'd ever done."

Pinkerton says Violeta Parra's efforts to popularize traditional music still reverberate with folk musicians across the continent. "She fused this specific sound and all these different traditions to her desires and aspirations for a better future for Chile and for Latin America," Pinkerton says. As difficult as it was to capture Parra's life on film, Wood says there's one thing that comes across loud and clear. "Violeta Parra is very transparent through her work," he says. "So you can know a lot about her, almost everything about her, just reading her, or just watching her paintings." Or, perhaps most of all, just listening to her songs.

Paloma Ausente | Linoleum print by Alec Dempster

ANA TIJOUX

Ana Tijoux is not your typical hip-hop MC. She was born in France, the daughter of a French mother and a Chilean father who fled during Pinochet's military dictatorship. Her mother worked in the immigrant suburbs of Paris as a youth social worker. Ana Tijoux grew up listening to music that was popular in those neighborhoods, Rai and African music by artists like Faudel and Khaled. But she also gravitated toward Latin American musicians like Victor Jara, Violeta Parra and Chico Buarque. Tijoux's listening to such a wide range of music helped her define her own style. The album's title song "1977" is Tijoux's autobiographical tribute to both hip-hop and punk rock — the year both exploded onto the scene and the year she was born.

Tijoux says she arrived at hip-hop almost by default. She admits she was not exactly an "A" student in high school, and poetry was the most exciting class:

"I remember at the time I fell in love with Dada and with the surrealismo in the poetry. So at the time,

I didn't know what I was going to make after. When I began to rhyme, for me it was so perfect because it was the perfect mixture between poetry and music. I always say, for me to rhyme it's like yes, sing poetry."

Tijoux speaks French and Spanish but she prefers to write in her father's language. Still, the album includes one song in French called "Oulala," about friendship: "It's a song about a friend of mine, we were growing up together in France, her parents were from the Congo. She was like me, she was born in France, her parents from the Congo. I came back to Chile and a year after me she come back to Congo. So it doesn't matter how faraway we are — we got a connection."

Tijoux moved to Chile in 2005 and now makes her home in Santiago. In fact, she was there when the earthquake struck in February: "I'm very proud to live in South America. We got so much beauty in our land even if there's so many problems, we got to be there and we got to change it."

Ana Tijoux | Photo by Pilar Castro, courtesy of the artist

SILVIA PÉREZ CRUZ

For Spanish singer Silvia Pérez Cruz, stories are everything: "Style is not what matters to me, but the result. The song has to have a story that I believe in and I can make my own. I think I have that influence from my mother. My mother is a good storyteller, and she's always believed that songs are stories." Pérez Cruz's own story is pretty remarkable. The 31-year-old is a classically trained singer from Catalonia. She studied piano and classical saxophone and has a degree in vocal jazz. While still at the Catalonia College of Music in Barcelona, Pérez Cruz co-founded a flamenco group called Las Migas with three other women. She says that none of them were the best players or singers, but that that helped them take a different approach to flamenco. "I think that's the best thing we did," she says. "It was a sound that really did not exist in Spain, based on our limitations, which was to make a more accessible type of flamenco." Before long, Pérez Cruz was the buzz of the Spanish music scene.

Javier Colina, a jazz bassist, invited her to record an album with his trio. Colina sent her a CD of classic Cuban songs with a note telling her to listen to the lyrics. "Of course, he liked the melody and the harmony," Pérez Cruz says, "but he selected them because of the text and the stories they told." She says he told her, "Don't study the songs. Listen to them at home. Let them keep you company until they stay with you." Again, it was the stories in the songs that were at the heart of the recording they made. Finally, just two years ago, it was time for Pérez Cruz to record her own solo album. She asked guitarist and producer Raul Fernández Miró, who's worked with artists ranging from Sonic Youth's Lee Ranaldo to Spanish rapper La Mala Rodríguez, to help her. "She has like a complete vision of music," he says. "She's not thinking just about vocals, about the voice. She's thinking about everything." The recording they made, "11 de Novembre," earned Album of the Year

nominations in Spain and France. That same year, one of her own compositions, "No Te Puedo Encontrar," won a Goya — the Spanish equivalent of an Oscar — for Best Original Song.

Silvia Pérez Cruz sings in four Iberian languages, as well as French, German and English. She uses them all on her new album, "Granada." She sings an iconic Catalan folk song called "El Cant Dells Ocells," made famous by cellist Pablo Casals; a lied from the mid-1800s by Robert Schumann, and the Edith Piaf classic "Hymne a l'Amour." Once again, Fernandez Miró was her collaborator. For "Granada," he says they chose songs with stories they liked, but they had to figure out how to unite such a wide range of material:

"I think that if you don't know that they come from different styles, and they have different languages, I think you can imagine the record or you can see the record as a whole thing. Which is something that we were looking for — not to be impressed by playing so many different styles, just to play them as the way that we want to play."

One of them is "Gallo Rojo, Gallo Negro," a popular song from the Spanish Civil War. The words read, in part: *The black rooster was big / but the red one was brave … The red rooster is brave / but the black one is treacherous.* Pérez Cruz learned the song when she was part of a concert to honor the remaining members of the International Brigades, who went to Spain to fight against dictator Francisco Franco. "At the concert, these men were singing the song in their own language with tears in their eyes," she says. "This song made a big impression on me. They stood up with their arms raised, and I thought, 'These people have lived through so much. It's good that I can sing and help them remember.'" It's just one example of the way Silvia Pérez Cruz comes to understand the stories she sings.

Silvia Pérez Cruz | Photo by Alex Rademakers

MARÍA VOLONTÉ

María Volonté grew up in a small town just outside of Buenos Aires. She was one of six sisters. Their father filled the house with music and art. Volonté recalls those years in "Ituzaingó," a song she titled after her hometown: "I started as a singer-songwriter playing in the streets and plazas of Buenos Aires in the 1980s when Buenos Aires was a big explosion of democracy, relief and reencounter with democracy after long years of dictatorship." Then in the 1990s, Volonté fell in love with the classic tangos of the 1920s, 1930s and 1940s. She recorded a number of tango albums and toured the world. She won a Gardel prize, Argentina's top music award, and was nominated for a Latin Grammy.

But with all her success as a tango singer Volonté felt there was something missing. She went back to the singer-songwriter side of her career. In her latest album, aptly titled "Nueve Vidas," Volonté brings together the many influences that have shaped her; that includes some renowned singers who inspired her to hone her own voice:

> "Strong women, all these characters, coming from (Edith) Piaf, Amalia Rodrigues from Portugal, Chabuca Granda from Perú, Violeta Parra from Chile. I was strongly inspired both ways, through the vision of women, different visions about the world. I think all that not only pushed me to this need of reinventing this new version of the songs. But also, all of it is in my songwriting for sure."

Currently on tour in the U.S., Volonté is heading in a new direction. This time, she's exploring the confluence of two musical traditions: "Blues and tango were born in sin on the margins of society from people who had lost a lot. I think tango and blues have a lot in common and our songs are completely infused, both perfumes put together."

Maria Volonté | Photo by Kevin Carrel Footer

FLOR DE TOLOACHE

It's midday at the LATV Studios in West LA, and Flor de Toloache is warming up for a performance on the show "Acoustic Sessions." After their performance, I sat down with the three leading members for an interview. Violinist and singer Mireya Ramos grew up in Puerto Rico — her mother is from the Dominican Republic; her father was a mariachi musician from Michoacán, Mexico. Ramos says one day she felt a calling: "I had the desire to collaborate with other women. I was one of the only female musicians playing mariachi in New York City during that time — this is about seven years before 2008. And I wanted to do my own arrangements as well, and my own compositions." In 2008, Ramos called Cuban American singer and guitarist Shae Fiol and together they decided to form the group Flor de Toloache. In the beginning, they played all the regular mariachi gigs — quinceañeras, weddings, birthdays, funerals. And they were also buskers, playing in Manhattan's subway stations — Times Square, Union Square and Grand Central Station. Singer Shae Fiol says the subway gigs helped to audition potential new members: "We also knew who was committed by the players who would come out to the subway with us and then we got to try out a lot of new stuff. It was basically like rehearsal, a paid rehearsal with an audience, but that wasn't technically a show."

There was one thing they had clear from the get go: their goal as a group was to do a fusion of mariachi and other music styles, says violinist Mireya Ramos:

"It wouldn't be genuine to us to do traditional mariachi because none of the girls actually come from a mariachi tradition, other than me, and I wasn't raised in Mexico. My approach to the mariachi was from far away, from Puerto Rico, so even for me, it wasn't that genuine to do just traditional Mexican mariachi, so the goal was always to do new arrangements and to kind of experiment with the genre."

When they decided to record their first album, Fiol says they needed songs:

"And we had some of our own songs written already, from our own projects, and we're like, 'let's bring these in and do them, Flor de Toloache-style.' And so 'Let down' was one of the first ones, and it definitely had R&B vocals already, but what we needed to do was adapt it, using the guitarrón, the vihuela and the trumpet — put all these different mariachi technical styles into the song."

In their new album titled "Indestructible," Flor de Toloache collaborated in a song with pop singer Miguel, who happens to be Ramos's cousin:

"It was an amazing experience to be in the studio with him. And also, it was so emotional because his grandmother and my grandmother used to sing together in Michoacán, Mexico. They used to have a duet called 'El Dueto Heredia,' and Heredia is their last name. And they had just passed away, not too long ago before the session. So it was a really emotional session — it felt like they were there with us. They made this whole thing happen for us, so it was really pretty."

For the song "Quisiera," Shae Fiol says their producer Rafa Sardina, offered to talk to invite pop singer John Legend.

"He's like, 'let me see, I'll talk to him. We'll see if he can sing in Spanish.' But we wrote it in English first just in case. And he was into it, so we're like, OK, we shot for the stars. We shoot for the stars and think 'who would we want to sing on this album? John Legend of course!' Still, Cuban American singer-guitarist Shae Fiol says there's a certain responsibility that comes with being part of a mariachi group, playing Mexican music: "Not being Mexican, there's a lot of pressure. You gotta show up and really know your stuff. And not only that, respect the tradition and the culture, not being Mexican, because people are looking at you, because you're not, so they want to be like: 'and? what are you doing? and why?' I think it's obvious, if you know anything about mariachi, and how rooted it is in Mexican culture."

Flor de Toloache won a Latin Grammy for Best Mariachi Album in 2017 for their previous album called "Las Caras Lindas." Despite all the recognition, violinist Mireya Ramos says they're still criticized for not following the traditional mariachi aesthetic:

"They still come to us and say, 'oh that doesn't look good, you should wear a skirt. Oh those shoes don't look good' — like we should wear botines, or specific moños, even our hair back, it should be back, and not curly and out, it's wrong. It's like there are these mariachi laws that we shouldn't cross and I don't know who put them there!"

I asked the members of Flor de Toloache to tell me the story behind the band's name. They said "flor de Toloache" is a desert flower. It's also called "Devil's Trumpet" and its seed is protected by spikes — a flower you don't want to mess with. Flor de Toloache lives up to its name.

Flor de Toloache, from left to right: Mireya Ramos, Shae Fiol and Julie Acosta | Photo by Betto Arcos

FRANCISCA VALENZUELA

Francisca Valenzuela was born in San Francisco to Chilean parents. When she was 12, her parents decided to move the family back to Chile. By then, Valenzuela was already playing piano and guitar and writing her first songs. When Valenzuela was only 13, she published her first book of poetry with an introduction by renowned author Isabel Allende. It was only a matter of time before Valenzuela would bring the two crafts together. She wrote the song "Los Peces" as a teen and later recorded in 2006:

> "I worry about my lyrics when I write a song because I love the music to be fun and to have its voice and its life, but at the same time if you can extract the lyrics and look at them on their own. Hopefully they have some sense, hopefully they look fun, hopefully they have some story or some sort of charm. Whether it's a fun song or a sad song or a diary, more of a confessional song or a more intellectual song."

Some years ago, Valenzuela was invited to take part in a musical tribute to Salvador Allende of Chile — Latin America's first democratically elected socialist leader who was later ousted in a military coup. She wrote the song "Salvador" as a social critique on the lack of political leadership in Latin America: "More than speaking of Salvador Allende as a political figure, and being a left wing or a right wing, or whatever, it speaks more about this, poetic ideal of changing the status quo of our world, of our unjust, kind of psychopathic societies."

But that's just one aspect of Valenzuela's music. Her songs sometimes veer towards the silly: "To not be serious, to be fun, to be playful, to be young, to be authentic and goofy and not always be in this persona that you have to be grave and you have to be serious and you have to be somber all the time." Valenzuela continues to challenge herself with new ways of writing songs and telling stories: "These fantasies of becoming other characters and singing as them, whether it's a "Buen Soldado" in a bar, or whether it's a revolutionary like in "Salvador" or whether it's a man going to a work interview in "Entrevista.""

Valenzuela's new album is called "Buen Soldado": *I always get what I want, I'm a good soldier, and I will always be.* She says she chose this title as a metaphor for the struggles she had to go through to make an independent album. She said it took courage and will, but she got it done her way.

Francisca Valenzuela | Photo by Rocio Mascayano

CARLA MORRISON

Carla Morrison grew up listening to Patsy Cline records in the small border town of Tecate, Baja California, a place known for its beer and its bread. "I actually was born right next to the most famous factory of good bread over there," Morrison says. "And it's nice, it's a nice place, but right now I can't be there because I have too much demand on singing and traveling, going throughout the country and sometimes the world to show my music."

Morrison moved to Mexico City six months ago and she's been selling out concerts across the country. She says she has been overwhelmed by her success and her fans' response to her songs: "When I talk about love and when I talk about not being loved and when I talk about my own issues in life and all that, I feel like I'm really honest. And I try to be as clear as I can and I speak the language of the people." She says she is not trying to be a really well-spoken person and intelligent person who only speaks all these great words, but more like the people in the street: "I'm from a little town, I'm from a pueblo," she says. Morrison says she has been able to tap into an emotional aspect of Mexican music that's not as common now as it was decades ago. She refers to songwriters like José Alfredo Jiménez who poured their hearts out in rancheras with lyrics addressing all kinds of intimate feelings.

"Morrison's ability to connect with Mexico's young audience has to do with her personal approach to making music," says Enrique Blanc, a music critic based in Guadalajara. Blanc says Morrison symbolizes the opposite of all the other pop stars, built by television emporiums or multi-national labels: "She's real. Carla Morrison has an indie attitude that makes her songs so convincing." Morrison got involved in the student movement called "Yo Soy 132," participating in a massive rally in Mexico City two weeks ago. The movement was started by university students protesting against the resurgence of the PRI, the former ruling party, and the mainstream media's support of the PRI presidential candidate. The students view the PRI as the embodiment of old-style Mexican corruption. Morrison says, as a musician she has to support her fans and make sure that just as they are free to decide on their feelings about life love and about a certain person, they should be free to decide who is going to lead their country: "They can't make us have this leader that we don't want."

This week, Morrison will send out a new song to her fans. It's an anthem written by a friend, who produced her first album — pop singer Natalia Lafourcade. The song, "Un Derecho de Nacimiento" (A Birth Right) is meant to encourage Mexican youth to make their voices heard and their votes count in Sunday's presidential election.

Carla Morrison | Photo by Lana Mack

Y LA BAMBA

It's a Saturday night at the El Rey Theater in LA's Miracle Mile district. Luz Elena Mendoza and her band Y La Bamba are playing a song from their new album "Mujeres" to a full house. The band's music is a solid blend of indie rock, electronica, Latin rhythms and ambient effects. If you weren't familiar with the group, you might not be able to tell that Mendoza is the frontwoman. She stands off to one side of the stage and shares many of the vocals with the keyboardist. But Mendoza does stand out. She's tall and angular, and her multi-colored hair is a modified bowl cut that is long in the back. And when she cuts loose, her voice is at times ethereal, a bit dreamy, yet deeply soulful.

Mendoza's parents migrated from Mexico's state of Michoacán to Redwood City, in the Bay Area. After Mendoza was born, her parents moved the family to Medford, in southern Oregon. She began writing songs in English and Spanish and at age 25 she moved to Portland. Mendoza says writing songs in both languages has been a natural experience — like a plant, growing: "I don't know, there's no way I can forget my culture — it's just there, I contemplate with it constantly. So it's very beautiful to see how I've just kind of evolved and continued evolving, and when you heal, and you move through things, you grow, and you evolve."

Mendoza says everything that she heard growing up — from the Cumbias of Rigo Tovar to the rancheras of Chavela Vargas — plus the music scene in Portland, has helped her to become who she is today:

"I just write music. I don't ever think about like a sound or a genre or whatever. I just kind of do it, whatever happens. I definitely have to connect with the heart — if the heart is not behind the expression, I can feel it intuitively, I'm not interested in it. And there are some really good people in Portland that we all share the heart of music, so I am influenced by that a hundred percent."

Ryan Oxford is the band's lead guitarist; he's been with Y La Bamba for two years. The new album was recorded in his studio in Portland. Oxford says he was impressed with Mendoza's talent from the first time they met: "Yeah, I think she just has a limitless imagination, just has so many ideas all the time in her head, it's incredible."

When asked if the songs on "Mujeres" were inspired by the recent empowerment of women and the #MeToo movement, Mendoza says the subject is nothing new to her: "I feel like it's just intuitive. I've always felt this way. I've always felt this confusion about why feeling this thing, the female has inherited feeling less than. It's really hard, and then you get used to it. Especially, just growing up seeing how some women were getting treated and it's just normalized." Mendoza says there's something special about being able to express your feelings through music:

"And then through sound there's a word, 'una letra,' there's like a message. And for me it's always been like a catharsis and I feel very grateful and privileged that I get to share that with people on this platform. And I'm basically just talking about how I'm coming to terms with my boundaries, with like patriarchy and misogyny and wanting to protect my mom and all of us, all women."

Y La Bamba also includes bass player Grace Bugbee and drummer Miguel Jimenez Cruz. Julia Andrea Mendiolea is the band's keyboard player and also sings background vocals. She listened to Y La Bamba for many years, before recently joining the band. She says she identifies with the songs on the new album:

"It really touches a lot of personal things about growing up Mexican American and kind of all the different things that can even mean. It's titled 'Mujeres' so, a lot of things about being a woman I think a lot of people that don't have that specific experience understand. And I just love the way that the music is super personal, like playing it, it's really, it felt really easy to learn all the songs because I felt personally, emotionally invested."

Luz Elena Mendoza has a clear understanding of her role as an artist. For her, playing and touring with her musician friends comes with a responsibility: "It's like a form of activism. And I really hope that while I'm here, and doing what I'm doing it, and sharing it in this way, I can continue to make a difference. And I hope that I can continue to cultivate family and protect my family during these hard times."

As for the band's odd name, Mendoza recalls when she started uploading music on a long-forgotten social network, more than 10 years ago: "I came up with that name because I had a cat named Bamba and I got her when I was living in Ashland, a month before I moved to Portland, Oregon. And when I started to put my songs on MySpace, I needed a band name. What can my band be called? But I was like "Y La Bamba," I didn't want to put my name before it." The band's name became the symbol of moving to the big city, to start her career at age 25 — Luz Elena Mendoza and her cat Y La Bamba.

Luz Elena Mendoza | Photo courtesy of the artist

LAS HERMANAS GARCÍA

As the sun sets on the Pacific Coast town of Ometepec, Mexico, musicians and fans gather on a rooftop to enjoy boleros. The crowd of about 70 people listens attentively to Las Hermanas García perform "Que Sepan Todos." Most of the audience is made up of teenagers — and the García sisters take note. Celia García is 16; Laura is 17.

Bolero, the romantic Latin music style, was born in Cuba and migrated around the world. It took root in Mexico and became extremely popular in the 1950s. Now, with acts like Las Hermanas García, it's enjoying a revival. Laura notes part of the excitement to perform is because they are "helping to spread the bolero." Celia says boleros are part of their DNA. "It's a genre that we heard since we were in my mother's womb," Celia says. "This region has always been known to be very romantic. My father used to sing serenades to my mother and now we listen to this music." Mariano García, Celia and Laura's father, is also their arranger and lead guitarist. He says his daughters started singing together before they were 10. "I coached them a little bit with their voices, but really they're natural singers," Mariano explains. "Early on, I saw them singing in two-part harmonies. I don't know how they did it. Celia took the first voice and Laura second and suddenly they were making music."

The bolero planted roots in Mexico's Pacific Coast, known as the Costa Chica, in the mid-1950s, when a prolific composer from the region named Álvaro Carrillo began to score hits in Mexico City and beyond. His most famous tune, "Sabor a mí," has been recorded by dozens of singers worldwide, including Doris Day, Frank Sinatra and Eydie Gormé. The legacy of Carrillo and other composers of his generation is still felt today across the country. Mexico City has a boleros-only radio station and national pop stars have made boleros a regular part of their repertoires.

Ramón Estrada, the host of a radio program in Ometepec, says boleros are so popular in the Costa Chica, that you can go to any party and hear a bolero group. "For more than 50 years, those boleros from that period have been transmitted from one generation to the next. And with this new revival, this tradition will continue for a long time," Estrada says. Boleros have become such a big part of people's lives, they take them wherever they go:

> "They're listening to Radio Ometepec and to the García sisters in the U.S. They call us from New York, Los Angeles, Texas and Miami. There are a lot of people there who are from all these towns along the Coast. Just imagine how they feel being so far away from the Costa Chica and listening to songs from here."

The García sisters are in the process of rehearsing songs they plan to record for their second album. This time, they want to sing boleros from other coasts of Latin America. And their music is spreading even further. Celia and Laura recently performed at La Clave Festival in London in front of thousands of people. "We're doing what we like to do," Celia says. "And I think that when you're doing what you really like to do, you don't feel pressure, you just do it."

From left, Mariano García with his daughters, Las Hermanas García, surrounded by friends on the Costa Chica of Guerrero state, Mexico | Photo by Betto Arcos

LEARNING

ARENI AGBABIAN

Armenian American pianist and vocalist Areni Agbabian's debut album on the renowned ECM record label is out this week. I visited her home studio to learn about her music. Agbabian sits in front of the Mason & Hamlin piano she inherited from her aunt, Lucina Agbabian, who was also her music teacher and mentor. Areni says her aunt taught her everything she knows about music: "All the fundamentals that I have in musicianship, musicality, performance, vocal technique. I studied with other teachers too after her, but she gave me my foundation."

Areni Agbabian lives in an area called Sherwood Forest, in the San Fernando Valley. When we spoke on a recent afternoon, she recalled her aunt's advice at a time when she was at a crossroads, considering a career as an academic: "She told me actually, a few weeks before she died, she said: 'you know, you can learn and you can learn and you can learn. But then what? Go and sing! She said, go into the world and sing. Forget about being an academic." Agbabian took her aunt's advice — and much of what she learned from her is present in the new album, titled "Bloom." She composed most of the pieces on her aunt's piano: "I have played on this piano since I was a kid, coming to her house for voice and music lessons. We would have children's music lessons at her house and this piano was there all the time. And then, when she passed away, I inherited it."

Every Sunday morning, for the past three years, Agbabian has sung at a ritual called the "Offices of the Armenian Church." It takes place weekly, at St. Peter Armenian Apostolic Church in Van Nuys. Agbabian says she wants to learn as much as possible about this ritual, before the last torch-bearers pass on: "The monastic tradition in the Armenian church died, sadly due to the Genocide in 1915. All of the monasteries were destroyed. So there isn't really a monastic life left in the Armenian church like there is in the Coptic or Greek churches. So there's just a few people singing these songs, these hymns." On Easter Sunday, she and a group of singers performed a series of Armenian hymns called "Sharagan," written by various composers throughout the early and medieval church history.

"The master, he's about 88 years old and they're from Istanbul.. So it's from the Constantinopolitan tradition of Armenian Chant. I discovered him after having gone to Paris to study with a master singer who is also from Istanbul. So within that lineage I was searching for other singers and I heard that this church in Van Nuys has people who sing from that tradition."

At her home studio, Agbabian offers to play a song from the new album. The song is called "Mother." Agbabian wrote it when she was still living at her aunt's house, after she had passed away. The inspiration behind the song came during a Sunday liturgy: "Chanting in the church, I had an experience on the day of, they call it 'Khaghogh Orhnek,' it's the Assumption of the Virgin Mary. And we were chanting and all of a sudden I had this really — I can't explain —experience where I felt changed during the chanting and this is related to that experience." The album also has a recurrent melody linked to the title, "Bloom." This is called "Petal One."

Agbabian has a special gift for melody. She says the more rhythmic elements in the album come from her collaboration with percussionist Nicolas Stocker: "I wanted to use the piano also as a purely a percussive-sounding instrument, so I incorporated different ways of piano preparations to create different sounds that I wanted." Agbabian's album is a diverse collection of melodic songs, rhythmic music and a couple of traditional Armenian songs — including one called "Anganim Arachi Ko." This was one of the first sacred hymns her aunt taught her. She liked it so much she wrote a new arrangement and called it "Anganim Revisited." Agbabian says traditional Armenian music was more present in her work five years ago: "At this point, I feel more inclined to writing my own music and then singing Armenian traditional music on its own, in its original form."

In addition to her aunt, Agbabian also honors her mother, Alidz Agbabian, a professional storyteller. One of the stories she heard from her is an Armenian legend called "The Water Bride": "I just really like this short legend because of the different ideas in it, like grace, and forgiveness and transformation. Those are things that I've experienced a lot in my life and really grateful that I can continue to live my life and just try to always become a better person." Areni Agbabian said her aunt Lucy would be really proud of her. She would be happy that she finished this album, and that it was out in the world.

Areni Agbabian | Photo by Mher Vahakn / ECM Records

CALARTS SALSA BAND

The California Institute of the Arts — more commonly known as CalArts — opened its doors in 1970 and soon established itself as one of the leading private art schools in the nation. It became known for its animation and visual art departments, but from the beginning it also developed an expansive music department with an interest in sounds from around the globe. This weekend, CalArts holds its annual World Music and Arts Festival. Among the groups performing at the festival for the first time is the CalArts Salsa Band.

Every Wednesday afternoon, the band gathers for a rehearsal, in the same classroom where the members began learning about Latin music last September. The band was formed only seven months ago, but the young musicians sound like they've been playing together for years.

The band was created 27 years ago, when Aaron Serfaty, a renowned percussionist from Venezuela, attended CalArts to finish his degree in music. "So we put together a very small group," says pianist David Roitstein, chair of the jazz program at CalArts and director of the salsa band. "It was only about six or eight people, and we played a set of Afro-Cuban music at a noon concert and everybody got so excited that they all said, I want to do that with you."

That small group grew into a regular ensemble and, for the first few years, Roitstein accepted any student who wanted to join. But having a band of more than 20 members was no easy task. Roitstein says he downsized the group to 12:

"Three or four singers, four horns, three percussion, bass and piano. And that's the instrumentation that

CalArts Salsa Band, performing at the World Music Festival 2018 | Photo courtesy of CalArts

we arrange for. I start over every single year with new music. We learn a couple of easy descargas by ear, but then I spend a lot of one-on-one time, helping them arrange songs for our book. And by this time in the year we have probably 25 or 30 songs."

Roitstein says every band member contributes with at least two arrangements and that's how they learn to get into the heartbeat of the music.

The Latin music program at CalArts appears to be expanding. Every Tuesday, a group of 15 students get together in a large classroom for the Brazilian Drumming Ensemble. Today, they're rehearsing the "bloco" Afro style of Carnaval drumming from Salvador, Bahia. Percussionist Alex Shaw co-directs the drum ensemble. He's a second year MFA student in the World Percussion program and producer of the World Music and Dance Festival. He says this year's event includes the addition of a second Latin percussion stage: "There are more Latino students on campus than we've ever had before, and so I think the fact that these ensembles are present and growing is a reflection of who's on campus these days."

At the salsa band's rehearsal, 25-year-old Tiffany Lantello takes the lead, singing a classic cumbia from Colombia. Lantello is pursuing an MFA in performance and composition — and she also plays the sitar. After a year at Cal Arts, Lantello says she decided to join the salsa band to improve her musicality:

"My mom is from El Salvador and every time we were at family parties they would be playing the music. So it wasn't like I was actively seeking out that kind of music, but it was sort of around through my childhood. And so when I started singing with [the band] it was just so much fun and I'm so glad that I'm doing it."

In a small rehearsal room, 24-year-old pianist Pablo Leñero plays an original classical improvisation. Leñero, who is from Mexico, is getting an MFA in composition, piano performance and conducting. He's also a singer with the salsa band. He says he wanted to play piano in the group so he asked director David Roitstein: "'Let me play, por favor,' and he was like, 'Pablo, the thing is, I am the bandleader and if I'm not the pianist, the band doesn't run.' And he said, 'Well, can you sing?' I said, 'Sure. I'll try it!'" Leñero says, as a classical pianist, the experience he's getting with the salsa band is more than he could have imagined:

"Performing and having people dance to your music is mind-blowing and it has made me reassess what I want to do. Because sometimes I don't necessarily get the same satisfaction about performing piano. I like making people happy and I like when people enjoy when we're singing, when we're dancing or rolling Rs in very high pitches."

Renowned Latin percussionist Joey De León co-teaches the band with Roitstein. De León says a year later, the results are clear: "It's funny where you start and where they finish. The seed is sprouted and now you see this unwavering sense of relief [from the students]: OK, man, I broke through this passage and now I'm feeling comfortable. And you instill confidence [in them]." That confidence has given students the tools they need to take the next steps, after they graduate. Roitstein says many students who've played in the CalArts Salsa Band are now successful professional musicians: "Two or three years after they finish school, I might go to a club and see them with a band and they're burning it up." That's what the CalArts Salsa Band can do — besides getting people to dance.

CalArts Salsa Band during rehearsal | Photo by Betto Arcos

CAMERON GRAVES

Pianist Cameron Graves grew up in Van Nuys. As a teen, he began to play jazz with the likes of Kamasi Washington and Thundercat. Today, Graves leads his own band and tours the world. I caught up with Graves at the Asunción Jazz Festival in Paraguay. On a mid-Saturday afternoon, Cameron Graves and his band are doing their sound check at the Teatro Municipal, Asunción's oldest venue, which dates back to the mid-1800s. When he's done, Graves and I run into Víctor Morel, artistic director of the Festival, the person responsible for booking the 37-year-old pianist.

Morel tells Graves that the last time he saw him play was in Chicago, with the Stanley Clarke Band. Graves says everything he's doing today, he owes to Clarke — the acclaimed bass player: "Touring, business, flights, all that stuff man — we learned it all from Stanley, man! He's a great mentor." Graves said he began working with the jazz fusion pioneer in 2014: "It was almost like going to Stanley Clarke School of music. That's what Stanley Clarke's band is like. When you're in his band it's just a learning experience, it's an educational experience — it's almost like going to college. That's the real college, man, it's Stanley Clarke's band. Because, first of all he's going to take you everywhere."

Cameron Graves attended Hamilton High School in West LA. Like many students of his generation, he grew up listening to hip-hop: "It was kind of in the gang era, where there was like gang members and stuff, so we had to deal with a lot of that, and music was our way to kind of like get out of, not being in gangs, you know what I mean. It was the '90s, man, the '90s."

Then he met a teacher named Reggie Andrews at Locke High School in Watts. Andrews started a program called "Multi-School Jazz Band," bringing together students from various LA high schools:

> "That was my first teaching of jazz, where we were just playing a lot of tunes, performing different places and that's how I was able to meet all the great musicians I still play with — Kamasi Washington, Thundercat, Steven Brunner, Ronald Brunner, Ryan Porter, a trombone player that plays with Kamasi, Miles Moseley, Tony Austin, Terrace Martin who works a lot with Kendrick Lamar and Herbie Hancock."

That group of musicians became Graves' high school "hangout buddies." They used to perform at Leimert Park and at a club in Hollywood called Piano Bar. "For about seven, eight years, we really honed our tunes and our sound with the 10 guys, the 10-piece band. And then finally, Kamasi got a deal, he did his record and he took the band on the road." After a few years of playing, touring and recording with both Kamasi Washington and The Stanley Clarke Band, Graves was ready for his solo debut. Last year, he released "Planetary Prince" — inspired by The Urantia Book. The philosophical book about spirituality has been popular among musicians.

"I wanted to bring it to the public, somehow. But I do instrumental music. I don't have a lot of lyrics. I'm not a rapper, I'm not a singer so I did that through using the titles of the book, and I illustrated those titles with music. So that's the titles you see on the first record."

Graves and his band — electric guitar, electric bass and drums — delivered a strident set at the Teatro Municipal. Most of the music was a preview of his second album. Graves says it feels good to be a leader of a band with a completely new sound and he has a name for the type of music he's making: "Yeah, 'thrash jazz,' absolutely, it's like a new thing and we're coming with it." Victor Morel, artistic director of ASUJAZZ says, one of the goals of the festival is to show its audience that jazz can be found in every music genre. Last year, when Morel saw Graves play with Stanley Clarke, he knew he had to book him: "He blew my mind. Graves was the keyboard player — he was doing the solos. And if you saw him, you'd say 'who is this guy who looks like a rocker,' doing incredible solos and improvising. His project mixes classical music, jazz, hip-hop, soul music, and thrash metal."

Cameron Graves says he couldn't be happier that the music he and his buddies started playing in high school and developed together over the last decade, is now gaining steam around the world: "The whole new sound is like 'progressive advanced music.' I mean, that's basically what we're trying to do, is just carry on the legacy of Stanley Clarke and Chick Corea, and John McLaughlin and all these guys. And that's the purpose me and Kamasi and all of us are trying to bring."

Cameron Graves | Photo by Anna Webber, courtesy of Mack Avenue Records

VAHAGNI (PART I)

This is the story of a flamenco musician in Los Angeles whose family left Armenia in September of 1991, just a few weeks before the collapse of the Soviet Union. Flamenco guitarist Vahagni was 6 years old when he and his family landed at LAX. He thought they were going to arrive at Disneyland:

> "And I remember when we got to LAX I was kind of disappointed 'cause I thought we were literally going to land into Disneyland, or something like that. After a while, I think my first impressions was just constantly having to adapt because I didn't speak the language. I didn't know anything about America, I was 6. It was the transitional period that I remember a lot."

They arrived at the home of relatives — Los Angeles is home to the largest Armenian community in the U.S. Vahagni's father was a guitar soloist for the National Philharmonic Orchestra of Armenia, and in the early 1980s, he heard flamenco for the first time. "So my father saw a recording of Paco de Lucía, and it just blew his mind because it was the first time he'd seen something like that and someone play guitar that way, so he was fascinated and just started doing all the research he can to find out more about this and it became like an obsession." Vahagni says his father taught himself how to play flamenco. He treasured albums and one day he gifted one of his favorite flamenco records to his girlfriend:

> "When he met my mom, she happened to really like the music. So I guess maybe he had too much wine to drink or something, he gifted it to her as a present,

and then I think the next morning he woke up and said 'Jesus, what did I do.' And so it was kind of forced to marry her to get the disc back. That's the anecdote in the family — that's how they got together."

Vahagni began playing the guitar at the age of 9. His father didn't allow him to play anything else until he learned the classical repertoire. At home, he listened to three types of music: classical, Armenian and flamenco: "That was the soundtrack of my growing up. I was already so exposed to it, it was something very normal for me. It wasn't like a decision I made: oh, I want to learn more about flamenco and I want to play flamenco. It was just, that was part of life from a very young age — it was that music." Following in the footsteps of his father, he learned everything he could about flamenco. Then, in 2004, at the age of 18, Vahagni moved to Andalucía to learn from the source: "When you're studying any sort of music, that is rooted in its culture, it's very important that you spend some time within that culture, that's the only way you're really going to understand the depth of the music. So I went there. I was very blessed — I got to study with some amazing guitarists. Besides that, just living there, just being there and going out and having a beer in Andalucía, you learn a lot from that as well."

Last year, Vahagni got a chance to work with the Spanish singer Buika. While on tour, he played some Armenian melodies for Buika and asked her to record the Armenian folk song "Hov Arek Sarer Jan." The song is included in his new album titled "Imagined Frequencies."

Vahagni with his father in Yerevan, Armenia | Photo courtesy of the artist

VAHAGNI (PART 2)

At his studio, on the second floor of his Burbank home, flamenco guitarist Vahagn Turgutyan practices a "falseta," a guitar riff or hook essential to flamenco. Turgutyan, who performs as Vahagni, was born in Armenia in 1985. His family moved to Los Angeles when he was 6 years old: "I actually think I became the musician, the guitarist I am, in this room. My father and mother bought this house in like 2000, somewhere around there. And this was my room growing up, and it was just covered with Paco de Lucía posters and my corner with my metronome and all my guitar stuff."

Vahagni used to spend all day practicing, trying to understand flamenco. But he didn't have a formal instructor. His father, a classical guitarist who played with the Armenian National Symphony, was his only teacher. Vahagni says his father didn't have the proper knowledge of flamenco: he discovered Spanish guitarist Paco de Lucía on a TV program in Armenia, when it was still part of the Soviet Union. And he began to teach himself: "But flamenco is just such a deeper culture. It's not that easy, you don't just watch and learn, you have to participate. To do that, you have to be around Flamencos."

When he turned 18, having learned more than the basic knowledge of flamenco's "palos," or guitar styles, Vahagni decided to immerse himself in the culture. He moved to Andalucía, in Southern Spain, the cradle of flamenco. He wanted to learn more than just the technical aspect of flamenco. He was very interested in its rhythmic quality, and how to play behind a singer:

"And that's what I actually learned more of when I went to Spain. It wasn't so much about, hey learn this little lick or this little falseta; it was more about how to actually project the right sound, the right emotion, and treat each 'palo' the right way. It's like a chef, learning how to cook certain meals the right way and treat the ingredients the right way. And you can only do that in a kitchen surrounded by other chefs."

Vahagni and his group perform occasionally at The Stage club in Burbank. At a recent show there, I met flamenco dancer Manuel Gutiérrez. He's originally from Córdoba, Spain, and has been performing with Vahagni for five years. He says Vahagni's musicality is different: "He also brings his own personality inside, in his own music and the music is super rich, and full of lot influences, jazz — I mean Armenian for sure, Armenian music." Vahagni says every project he's been involved with has some aspect of his Armenian heritage: "Because I'm Armenian, because it's my culture, and I listen to that music and I grew up with that music, the folk music. It's something that naturally comes out when you're creating." Vahagni plays the first part of a melody: "But when you play it, like in a more flamenco tradition, with the low ends and the rhythms, it really translates. So I try to mess around with finding the right melodies, the right pieces, to kind of convert them into something that can sound flamenco."

Recently, Vahagni has been working on a completely new approach to flamenco. At a studio in Venice, Vahagni and his music partner, singer Ryan Merchant, are working on a mix of their latest single. Early last year, Merchant and Vahagni created a project called "Paco Versailles." Vahagni says after brainstorming back and forth, trying to find a name for their new musical concept, they settled on two meaningful words: Paco, from Paco de Lucía, Vahagni's biggest influence:

"And Versailles being Daft Punk, and Air, and Phoenix and all these bands that Ryan is extremely influenced by, who come from the Parisian suburb of Versailles. So we kind of put that together, 'Paco Versailles,' which is also how the music sounds: it's flamenco-influenced, yet it also has this kind of EDM-dance-French-electronica vibe to it."

Singer Ryan Merchant says, this is not your typical EDM project: "The key, or one of the keys to having something that can break through is having a sonic identity and having a point of view." In addition to Vahagni on flamenco guitar and Merchant on vocals, the live show includes a bass player, a drummer, an electric guitarist and a flamenco dancer: "Bringing something to life and exceeding people's expectations and just blowing them away with a live performance is what's exciting ultimately — it's the best way to get the word out there. There's nothing like a live performance."

Vahagni says the flamenco guitar has always had a cult-like following. But he's always wanted to help bring it into the mainstream: "My thing is, 'if I can get some 13-year-old kid to be excited about playing flamenco guitar that would be really awesome. And the only way you can do that is to present it to them with the language they can understand." As pop music has the capacity to reach a bigger audience, Paco Versailles may well reach a younger crowd too.

Vahagni | Photo by Martin Yernazyan

CHICAGO'S MARIACHI HERENCIA DE MEXICO

It's a Friday evening at La Fonda de Los Camperos, near MacArthur Park, LA's most revered venue for mariachi music and home to the Grammy-winning ensemble Los Camperos. But the stars of tonight's show are from Chicago. Sixteen teenagers, eight boys and eight girls. They're called Mariachi Herencia de Mexico. Melanie Juarez, 13, plays guitar and is one of the lead singers. She's thrilled to be playing tonight at La Fonda. "It's just really a big honor to be here, knowing that those mariachi Camperos actually perform here and they're here and me having to be here it's something amazing." Marco Villela is 14. He plays the trumpet and sings: "I am quite very honored to be here because I'm a very huge admirer of the Camperos and it's just unexplainable how amazing this is."

The man behind Mariachi Herencia is Cesar Maldonado, an investment banker who grew up in Brighton Park, a Mexican immigrant barrio in Chicago. Maldonado is passionate about mariachi music and was determined to give back to his community:

> "I think in this time, where people continue to question the contributions of our community in this country, I wanted to do something different, something relevant to our community, to our kids, at the same time recognizing the importance of saving mariachi music for future generations and teaching young kids, young students about the music of Mexico."

Maldonado started out as a promoter, scouting out mariachi groups from LA to and booking them in Chicago's performing venues. In 2012, he took LA's Mariachi Los Camperos to Chicago's Mexican community. He remembers a day, during that trip, when he was having breakfast with the legendary leader of Los Camperos, the late Nati Cano: "Nati told me at that breakfast meeting, he said, 'Cesar, if anyone is going to push mariachi to the next level, it's you. The way you're going to do it is with the kids.'"

In 2013, Maldonado helped to integrate mariachi education into the general curriculum of Chicago's public schools. Many were schools that had no arts programs: "So all of a sudden we hired mariachi teachers, credentialed mariachi teachers, we put them and we start a program, we have a curriculum going and these kids without this program would have never touched a violin, a vihuela, a guitarrón, etc." A couple years into the school program the effort began to bear fruit: "There was a lot of natural talent that we awoke, and we decided to hold an audition for an all-city program which is Mariachi Herencia de Mexico. And then, a year and some months later, here we are performing at La Fonda de Los Camperos."

Harpist Checo Alonso is a 20-year member of Los Camperos and a special guest in Mariachi Herencia's debut album. Alonso says LA is a microcosm of mariachi culture:

> "For many years, Los Angeles, outside of Mexico City and Guadalajara, has been the mecca of mariachi music, not only for American-born musicians but also many immigrants that come either permanently or temporarily to come work in Los Angeles. It is a large, living, breathing phenomenon where you have a constant mixture of different generations performing, learning either from their parents or their parents' parents, learning in schools, conferences, studying with some of the most revered mariachi musicians. And, of course, some of those originated and still exist in Los Angeles, including Mariachi Los Camperos, Mariachi Sol de Mexico."

When Chicago's Cesar Maldonado decided to record Mariachi Herencia's first album, he knew he had to bring his group to Los Angeles. Trumpet player José Hernández is founder and director of Mariachi Sol de Mexico and Reyna de Los Angeles. He produced Mariachi Herencia's debut album. Hernandez sees it as part of an ongoing cycle — elders passing on the tradition to the young. He says the older musicians who first came to LA from Mexico right after World War Two laid down the groundwork for the mariachi scene of today. Musicians like his father:

> "He was playing in places, like, it was called 'Jeanette's Place,' I think it was on Figueroa, and also 'El Granada,' one of the first places that had mariachis. For the mariachis in LA to have influence on other mariachis in the United States really doesn't surprise me. I feel personally that the best mariachis in the world are in LA."

Many of the kids in Mariachi Herencia de Mexico come from rough neighborhoods. José Hernández says music is a powerful tool to get kids out of trouble:

> "Music saves lives. Mariachi music gives it even an extra, something more special, because not all of them come from families that have a lot of money, so for them to have the opportunity to belong in a group like this, that gets to travel, that gets to play with the best mariachis in the world — it's something that I know that they appreciate."

This week, Mariachi Herencia will be traveling to the International Mariachi Festival in Guadalajara, for what they expect to be their biggest show yet.

Mariachi Herencia de Mexico, performing at La Fonda in Los Angeles | Photo by Betto Arcos

OAXACAN BRASS BANDS
IN LOS ANGELES

Los Angeles is home to the largest number of immigrants from the Mexican state of Oaxaca. The LA Oaxacan community has a rich musical culture, supported in part by a tradition of schools that promote music education through brass bands. Two years ago, Esteban Zúñiga had to stop teaching music in his garage. His neighbors kept calling the police and he was repeatedly fined. He went to court, and the judge dismissed the fines. But to stay out of trouble, he decided to save money from his landscaping job to soundproof the garage: "It's a lot, it's a lot of investment. Why? Because it's community work. It's for our culture. I prefer my community or the descendants learning their culture, instead of being in the streets or getting hypnotized by the technology that we have," he said.

Tonight, in that soundproof garage, complete with air conditioning and a bathroom, Zúñiga teaches a group of 15 students, ranging in ages 8 to 16. Saúl Martinez is one of Zúñiga's students. He's 8 years old and plays soprano saxophone. Norma Policarpo is Saúl's mother. She's been bringing her son to Zúñiga's music school for the past 10 months. She says Saul puts a lot of effort into it, learns more every day and is persistent. She has seen his progress, that's why she keeps bringing him — that, and the fact that her son is learning Oaxacan customs, and keeping its traditions alive. Esteban Zúñiga and other teachers like him are replicating a tradition from Oaxaca called "Escoleta": a music school based in a village. "Each village has one. The most important thing is, once they have an Escoleta, it's music for everybody in their hometown, basically free, so they can keep passing the musical tradition," said Zúñiga.

That musical tradition is focused on the brass band, usually made up of 20 to 35 instruments — trumpets, trombones, sousaphones, along with clarinets, saxophones, and two drums. Here in Los Angeles, there are more than a dozen Oaxacan brass bands, and each has its own Escoleta. Zúñiga is preparing his students for a new brass band he's forming. They've been practicing for six months. Once he's worked with them for about a year, he says they'll be ready to play in public.

Two miles from Zúñiga's garage, a storefront on Pico Boulevard is Maqueos Music Academy, home to a 30-piece brass band and a large dance troupe. They're rehearsing for a traditional music and dance festival called Guelaguetza. Estanislao Maqueos was director of his hometown's municipal brass band. He moved to LA in 2000. After a few years working odd jobs and gaining the respect of the local Oaxacan community, he established his music school. Since then, he's helped form several brass bands. "It's difficult for the children because they were born here and it's another culture," Maqueos says. "We're imposing our children to play our music and it's hard, but after so much persistence, they do learn to love our Oaxacan music, they dance to it, and they make it their own." Maqueos says the goal is to help their children find their identity: "Even though they were born in this country, their roots are in Oaxaca, the roots of their parents are there, and part of their identity is this music." Oaxacan brass bands play at all kinds of private and public events — from religious processions to dance festivals.

Tonight, at the home of Maqueos Music Academy, there's a party celebrating a baptism. Nineteen-year-old Yulisa Maqueos is directing the band. She plays clarinet and is the daughter of Maestro Maqueos. She says her father has built an impressive body of work: "As immigrants, we come here with nothing and we work hard, and seeing how someone from the pueblo can actually succeed in any other way that a citizen could do it. I think it just gives me a feeling of hope that everything is possible." There are people who call Maqueos Music Academy "the hotbed" of brass bands in Los Angeles. In 17 years, Maqueos has taught music to more than 500 students. Still, he says he has bigger dreams: "I want to have a big band with strings — a complete symphonic orchestra."

Above: Esteba Zúñiga and his students / Below: Yulisa Maqueos directs the Maqueos Music Academy Band | Photos by Betto Arcos

ESTRELLA ARIAS
AND PRIMERO SUEÑO

For the last 28 years, music students at CalArts have been recording at the renowned Capitol Studio B. This afternoon, outside the studio, five young band members are feeling pretty emotional. After all, recording at this legendary studio, doesn't happen every day. The group is called "Primero Sueño." The band takes its name from the most important work written by Mexico's renowned 17th-century poet Sor Juana Inés de la Cruz. It was founded at CalArts by bassist-singer Estrella Arias last September, at the suggestion of band-mate and singer Elsa Lund: "When I first listened to the song Estrella wrote over the summer, I thought it was so beautiful and I thought it sounded like the sound of a group I would also like to write for."

Arias's instrument is called "Leona," a small, four-string bass played in the traditional folk style of Veracruz known as son jarocho: "I was mostly playing jazz a lot, last year. Then over the summer I started writing songs, with the instruments that I play all my life. One way or another I identify with this music because it's the earliest memory of music that I've had."

Arias moved from San Miguel de Allende to Los Angeles in 2015 to attend CalArts and enrolled in the Jazz Program. When Arias and Lund put together the core members of Primero Sueño, they decided to invite other female musicians. Mandolinist Vera Webber heard them perform and was immediately attracted to their unique sound, created by classical and traditional instruments: "This group is such a great opportunity just to experiment and hear what these instruments sound like with each other and that's one of the greatest things about this group." Violinist Rachel Iba says the band creates exciting new sounds by exploring the intersections of music traditions from different cultures: "There's a huge world music environment, it's a big part of CalArts. So we all come to the group with different experience, both of music from our own cultures and things we've studied at CalArts."

Primero Sueño is now in Studio B, recording the main track for the song "Canto." Arias says the rhythms of "Canto" are based on son jarocho and the lyrics have a message of empowerment: "Canto" is about using music as a way to cleanse your emotional sorrows, your emotional pains, whatever you are holding onto. Let the singing wash away your sorrows." David Roitstein, director of the Jazz Program at CalArts says there are a few reasons why "Primero Sueño" was selected to record this year at Capitol: "When you hear the music, you'll understand. It just sounds great, it's beautiful songwriting, wonderful arranging. They're all really strong individually, but it's a real, it's a real band."

Rosy Sackstein, a professor of flute and piano at CalArts and a big supporter of the band, couldn't hold her thoughts: "I have ideas for this group, so I can't talk about that right now but I definitely see a lot in their future." For now, Primero Sueño's first dream is over. But no one in their circle of friends doubts that the band will continue on the same path of success.

Estrella Arias (center) and Primero Sueño | Photo courtesy of the artist

CÉSAR CASTRO

If you've ever heard "La Bamba," then you've heard son jarocho. The Mexican folk music style has been popular in the LA area for many decades. In the late 1950s, Ritchie Valens helped to bring a spotlight to it. And in the '70s and '80s, Los Lobos continued to popularize the sound.

César Castro is a contemporary son jarocho musician who lives in LA but comes from the place where the music was born — Veracruz. Castro is a 21st-century renaissance man of son jarocho in Los Angeles. Since he arrived from Veracruz 12 years ago, he's become a bandleader, an instrument maker, a teacher, and a few other things. But at the center of Castro's work is the music he plays.

While he plays "La Bamba," Castro demonstrates the genre's two main instruments: requinto or "guitarra de son" — a small four-string lead guitar — and jarana, also a small, eight-string guitar-like instrument. Castro says this music opened a whole new world to him when he first heard it:

> "When I was 13, I had no music background. What I heard was happiness, harmony. But I couldn't put that in words. I just felt good to walk in that little space, watching people about my age, doing something and I was like, wait, what's that, curiosity. And finally, when I was able to throw a chord in the jarana, it was amazing."

Something similar happened to East LA guitarist Chuy Sandoval when he first heard this music, eight years ago: "When I heard son jarocho, and most importantly what hit me first was the lyrics, the verses. When I heard what these people were singing about. They were saying words and phrases that I had heard my mom use at home. I had an emotional response to it. And not only that but it's so much fun to play!"

Sandoval is one of the four members of Cambalache, a son jarocho band led by César Castro. Their new album is called "Constelación de Sonidos — Constellation of Sounds," a collection of son jarocho tunes. But they're played on something more familiar to Los Angeles— electric guitars. Sandoval says every song in the album

is a traditional son jarocho: "But we're playing them with sounds that are 'us' — when I say 'us' I mean the Chicanos that are in the band, the sounds that the Chicanos grew up with. So, there's going to be a lot of electric guitar, a lot of rock-and-roll influence, oldies influence in there, but throwing it in there with sones jarochos."

Rafael Figueroa is a researcher from Veracruz who writes about the music and culture of son jarocho. He says it's easy to see why it's become so popular in the LA area. Figueroa says son jarocho is an alternative to Mariachi and it's an easily accessible style of traditional Mexican music:

> "You can adapt it to your own needs, you can play with it, you can add some things, you can add people. It's flexible enough to accommodate almost any taste, you can play it slow, you can play it fast, you can participate even if you're not really an accomplished musician, you can participate in son jarocho somehow."

A big part of participating in son jarocho is the celebration of music and dance called fandango. This is a gathering where musicians play their instruments and sing, while dancers take turns on a wood platform called Tarima. Castro says the fandango is an engaging ritual:

> "So it's easy to start participating and you can do it with percussion which can be an easy in — let's say that way with a simple pattern and you're already participating. And then when you feel that, when you feel welcome to a new community then you want to be part of it right, you want to come back. Music makes you feel good then you want to keep practicing it."

César Castro's band Cambalache will be doing a special concert on June 3 at the Aratani Theater in Little Tokyo. It will be his opportunity to honor some of the musicians from Veracruz that have helped him along the way — and a chance for many local musicians to honor a teacher who continues to spread the word about son jarocho to anyone who will listen.

César Castro at his shop playing a "guitarra de son" | Photo by Betto Arcos

SON MAYOR

If you dance salsa in Los Angeles, chances are you've danced to the music of Son Mayor. The salsa orchestra has been playing in Southland clubs for almost 30 years. I visited a couple of those clubs to learn more about a true "Band of Brothers."

It's a late Monday night at El Floridita in Hollywood, as Orquesta Son Mayor takes the stage. The club is packed and couples hit the dance floor the minute the band starts playing. Son Mayor was founded by percussionist Eddie Ortíz in Long Beach, in the late 1980s. Ortíz says he got into music when he was 12 years old, in his hometown of Jalpa, in the state of Zacatecas, Mexico: "I heard of a guy that had the Santana records. I didn't have them, so I decided to make him my friend, just so I could listen to those albums. And listening to that sound of Santana is what changed my life." In 1976, Eddie and his brothers, Julian and Mario, moved to Long Beach from Mexico. Alfredo Ortíz and two other brothers were already in Southern California. Within a few years, Eddie started playing a few local salsa groups and then, in 1989, he started his own band with all his six brothers. Three brothers left the band years ago to pursue other careers, but four of the Ortíz brothers continue to play.

Alfred Ortíz plays the congas — something he picked up in High School: "I consider myself somebody that's been lucky that had someone that taught me, that brought me into this, and I really enjoy playing music, but I only play with Son Mayor. This is our band." He couldn't afford to buy his own, so he borrowed a neighbor's conga to practice: "He didn't use it. But I knew that he had it and I would go beg him: 'hey man, let me borrow that drum, please.' And sometimes he would lend it to me and other times he would torture me, but I do remember that I wanted to play that badly." Brother George plays timbales. He says he was 12 when his older brother Julian bought him a flute but: "I couldn't stand it. You start blowing into the flute and you get dizzy, right, so I couldn't handle that! Then I started messing around with drums."

Son Mayor may be the hardest working salsa band in the LA area, but only one of the four brothers makes a living from music. Eddie has been an inspector for 23 years with LA County's Agriculture Commission. Julian has worked in the City of South Gate police department for 30 years. And George is a registered nurse at Centinela Hospital's ER in Inglewood. Alfredo Ortíz plays in seven other Latin music bands: "I'm barely scraping by sometimes, but at the same time I know what it's like to work a day job, and to have to play here at night, go home at two in the morning, get up at five or six in the morning. Can't do that." For more than two decades, Son Mayor has played three to four gigs, every week, across the LA area. I caught them at Steven's Steakhouse, in the City of Commerce. The band of 10 musicians could barely fit on the stage — 15 feet wide by 10 feet deep— but the music was as good as it gets. Trombonist Erik Jorgensen has been playing with the band the longest, 28 years. He's played with many other salsa bands but he says there's something special about Son Mayor: "They're absolutely one of the best, and the brothers are like no others. When you hear them, when you play with them, when you dance to them, when you feel their music — you can tell they're very amazing, they have a great sound. It's a good feel — it's a good-sounding band."

In the last three decades since the band's founding, salsa clubs have come and gone, but Son Mayor remains, says timbales player George Ortíz: "So it's a tough thing but you have to have a lot of patience but most importantly, no BS with promoters or musicians. I think that's why musicians like to play with the band, because we treat them well, they treat us well — we respect them, more than anything." Son Mayor lead singer Norell Thompson has been with the band eight years. She also sings with other bands but says Son Mayor has been a training ground for a lot of salsa musicians in the LA area, including herself: "There's a whole bunch of cats waiting to have their opportunity to even just be considered. It is an institution in LA. It's, bar none, the best band in LA when it comes to salsa, and that's because of the brothers. There's no other reason. That is it."

Son Mayor founder Eddie Ortíz is hoping his 9-year-old son will eventually take over the band. He just has to get him into the music, like he did with his brothers.

Son Mayor, brothers Julián, Alfredo, George and Eddie Ortíz at El Floridita in Los Angeles | Photo by Betto Arcos

LEON "NDUGU" CHANCLER

The world-renowned drummer Leon Ndugu died tragically of prostate cancer at the age of 65. Chancler was a Grammy winner whose work with a long list of major music figures earned him respect in the music industry. Chancler was also a professor at USC's Thornton School of Music. I spent a few hours on the USC campus to find out how Chancler's replacement was selected.

Ndugu Chancler was a living legend. He played and recorded with some of the top musicians in jazz, R&B, and pop music, including Donna Summer, Frank Sinatra, Miles Davis and Carlos Santana. But he's perhaps best known for his work on Michael Jackson's "Thriller." Chancler was one of the founders of USC's Popular Music Program. He wrote the drum curriculum for the department and was a very popular figure among the students. Patrice Rushen, Chair of the Popular Music Program at USC, says Chancler cultivated more than the usual teacher-student relationship. He was a beloved figure: "A mentor, a friend, a brother and, for some of the kids, a father figure. So when he tragically passed away, he left a big, big hole in the hearts of all of the students and certainly in trying to determine what to do so that their education could continue — but also the legacy that Ndugu had left with the style of teaching and the success that we had been enjoying with so many students getting out and working. We really had big shoes to fill."

Rushen made a list of drummers she knew who had a relationship with Chancler and started calling them, asking them to help finish his semester. The first seven drummers said yes. She called them The Magnificent Seven": "Because after they all said yes, I was like wow! This already is magnificent!" Rushen says bringing all those renowned drummers to USC was a life-changing experience for many of the students:

> "It helped them appreciate how great a teacher they had in Ndugu, and it helped them appreciate what good teaching and good mentorship really can look like. These were names that they had heard on records, these are names that had crossed Ndugu's lips or mine or other people's. It would have been a lifetime to meet any one of them, let alone sitting across from them having lessons each week, for seven weeks, from some of the greatest drummers around."

It's Wednesday morning at Will Kennedy's teaching studio at USC's Music Complex. This was Ndugu Chancler's studio. Kennedy says his spirit is in the room. The walls still have photos of Chancler with the artists he recorded and played with: "One of the most notable ones is a trio shot with brother Michael Jackson and Quincy Jones. That was the day of the session that he recorded "Billie Jean." That's an awesome photo." Kennedy is sitting in front of a small drum kit, going over techniques with Cameron Lee, a 19-year-old student from Sacramento. Lee is in his second year, majoring in Popular Music with an emphasis in drum performance. He's one of the students who had a say in the decision to hire Kennedy, after Chancler passed away. He says Rushen had a meeting with all the students, from pop music and jazz, who had taken lessons with the seven drummers and asked them: "Point-blank, pretty much: 'who is your favorite, who did you guys like the most?' And that was when we all kinda looked at each other and had that moment of like 'oh my gosh, we're deciding who we want to come in here next year, this is amazing.'"

Will Kennedy has performed with Herbie Hancock, Bobby McFerrin, and Esperanza Spalding, among others. He's also conducted drum workshops around the world and produced educational videos. Since 1988, he's been the drummer for the Grammy-winning jazz band Yellowjackets: "I wasn't viewing it as an audition. I didn't know that I was applying for the job unknowingly." Kennedy says he knew Chancler's position needed to be filled. It didn't occur to him that he was a contender until he got a call from Patrice Rushen: "Next thing I knew, I was asked to come back! I guess people like me! So it was a very challenging offer for me because my home is Houston, Texas." Rushen says teaching had not been on Kennedy's radar, up to that point. But he told her: "'I got a certain feeling about the students, and about the faculty and about the program and about the type of curriculum and education that's going on there, and it's really pretty cool. I want to look at this.' So he looked at it and here we are."

Cameron Lee says that, ultimately, Kennedy's teaching style won them over:

> "Will's approach to the drums is so musical and so much different than so many other drummers that we maybe studied with or listened to. I feel that I can speak for most of us: it's changed how we're listening to music, and our approach to playing the parts within the music, because it's really just not playing the parts, It's so much interacting with those that are on stage, and making sure that your awareness of melody and the bass parts and the guitar parts, no matter what it is — it really just helps to make you a well-rounded musician. So I think we've really just grown as musicians in this past semester and a half, more than anything."

And that's something Ndugu Chancler would approve.

Leon "Ndugu" Chancler | Photo by Noé Montes

ROSALÍA

Spanish singer Rosalía has taken the world by storm. In the past year, her career has skyrocketed — she has recorded with Pharrell Williams and appears in Almodóvar's latest film. On the eve of her new album release, I met Rosalía in Madrid, Spain. Perhaps it's fitting that I met Rosalía in a 16th century palace. These days, Rosalía is the equivalent of Spanish royalty. It's midafternoon in Madrid. Rosalía has been doing press interviews all day in a lavish salon and appears a bit frazzled. But she perks up when I tell her I just returned from walking 150 miles on the Camino de Santiago — a sacred pilgrimage in Northern Spain. She says she walked the Camino five years ago and would like to repeat the experience — if she ever has free time again.

Rosalía is from a small town in Catalonia. She's 25 years old and grew up listening to the music her parents played at home — The Beatles, Queen, Supertramp. Then, when she was 13, flamenco entered her consciousness: "I heard it in the street, with my friends. They were older than me, they had the cars with the doors open, hearing the music super loud in the street. They used to hear flamenco, they used to hear Camarón." Camarón de la Isla is considered the top flamenco figure of the 20th century: "And Camarón, it was like something that changed my life completely. It was like, before and after Camarón, you know. I fell in love with this music and the way he used his voice."

Rosalía doesn't come from a musical family. She didn't know anything about flamenco when she began studying it: "And this music is so difficult, it's so difficult. I'm telling you, like the rhythms, it's so, so difficult to understand. At the beginning you have to get very focused and study a lot to understand this type of music." Rosalía says Camarón has been a major influence in her career: "And was so inspiring for my generation and he was very open-minded, he always took risks doing his records." Rosalía is also taking risks on her own records. Many in the traditional flamenco community criticized her first album called "Los Angeles." Among other things, she was accused by a Roma activist of cultural appropriation: "I guess that when you do something with risk, that risk makes you connect with a lot of people and not connect with a lot of people too, right?" José Manuel Gómez is a music critic based in Madrid. Gómez says

Rosalía has engaged a new generation that has never heard flamenco before with an essential element every artist should have: "The good flamenco artists will tell you the important thing is to communicate, to transmit. And Rosalía communicates. It's true, there are songs that communicate and others simply don't, but that happens with every other artist I listen to."

Rosalía's new album is a departure from the previous one. If the first album was minimalist — guitar and voice — this one has many layers of production and influences, from electronic music to R&B. It's flamenco for the 21st century, inspired by an anonymous novel from the Middle Ages called "Flamenca." Rosalía says there are some traditional flamenco melodies, but there are many pieces she composed specifically for it. It's also a concept album: "And every song is a chapter. There's a whole story in the record which is 'El Mal Querer,' this 'Bad Loving,' this story about a dark love." Rosalía recently recorded two songs with singer and producer Pharrell Williams. The songs will appear in a future album of his. She says it was a privilege to work with him in the studio, where she came to appreciate something special about him:

> "Wow! He loves flamenco too! He likes that, he was interested in that. He was like telling me that he believed in me, that he loved this culture, these flamenco melodies, that he was excited about that. And that was a surprise for me. That made me feel very happy and comfortable to make music with him."

Spanish director Pedro Almodóvar invited Rosalía to do a scene in his film "Dolor y Gloria": "Yeah, it was like a beautiful experience. It was my first scene in a movie, and the first scene with Almodóvar — it's kind of mind-blowing because he's my favorite artist in the world probably."

Rosalía can only guess what the late legend Camarón de la Isla would say if he heard her music today. She certainly knows what she would say to him if she had the chance: "Because of him I'm here. He changed my life when I was 13. And he's been the most inspiring icon and musician from my country for me and he's been so important he was the door that I opened to discover all this music and I love him."

Rosalía at the Palacio de Santoña in Madrid | Photo by Betto Arcos

POLKA MADRE

Ten years ago, at a spontaneous jam session at the Mexico City home of accordionist Marina de Ita, the band Polka Madre was born — by accident. De Ita remembers:

> "We were not professional musicians. We were not studying as the others that came from the conservatories, we just wanted to jam and play, so we started the band together. And then we met Enrique, the clarinet player, in Coyoacán. He was busking. He used to play more jazz and bossa nova, but the sound — he sounded like this klezmer clarinet player so we invited him."

No one was even intending to start a band at the beginning, de Ita says, but Polka Madre ended up launching an unlikely Balkan music scene in Mexico. She says it makes sense because Balkan music has a lot in common with Mexican traditional music. At least how it sounds. "I don't know the history, actually," de Ita admits. "I haven't been, like, researching. But if you hear the polkas, norteño, sometimes it sounds the same as the Balkan music. Because you can hear some polka and they say it's from Mexico, but a German friend came and he said, oh, this is from Munich."

Bruno Bartra, aka DJ Sultán Balkanero, is leader of another Balkan band called La Internacional Sonora Balkanera. He says the Balkan scene in Mexico really took off when Goran Bregovic, one of the most renowned artists in the genre, came to play at a massive festival in Mexico City: "Ten thousand persons showed up and it was madness," Bartra recalls. "He also played alongside an orchestra from Oaxaca, so, since then, there was a symbol of this link between the Balkans and Mexico City." Bartra says many of the musicians who joined the Balkan scene in Mexico came from other counter-cultural communities like "the ska movement, which was pretty linked to the Zapatista ideology, or the World music movement, which was much linked to a multicultural idea."

Today, there are dozens of Balkan-influenced bands in Mexico City and across the country. For the past three years, there has even been an annual Balkan music festival in Mexico City featuring bands from Mexico, the U.S. and even eastern Europe. So far, there's only one place Mexico's Balkan bands don't seem to have reached: the Balkans.

Polka Madre | Photo by Raúl Pérez-Mejía, courtesy of the band

YOLA: YOUTH ORCHESTRA OF LOS ANGELES

The LA Philharmonic's Youth Orchestra of Los Angeles, better known as YOLA, is on tour in Mexico City all this week, culminating in a free, open rehearsal with Gustavo Dudamel at the renowned Palacio de Bellas Artes. It's the first time YOLA has traveled there to perform. As the group got ready for this trip, I went to talk to the musicians and hear them play.

It's a late afternoon at the Shatto Recreation Center near Koreatown. All 96 members of the aptly called YOLA CDMX Tour Orchestra are here for a rehearsal, before a free community concert. The first piece they're going over is "Danse Bacchanale" by French composer Camille Saint-Saëns. Right before the rehearsal, I talked to 15-year-old musician Judith García. She's from South LA and plays the trumpet. She says she's torn between this piece and the next one by Tchaikovsky called "March Slav": "I feel like my favorite piece of music would be between 'Bacchanale' and 'March Slav,' because it's so intense and it just gives me chills whenever we play it."

YOLA was launched 12 years ago by the LA Phil and various community partners. Initially, it was a program for 80 students, but now it serves 1,300 young musicians across the city in four sites. The program is LA's version of El Sistema, Venezuela's country-wide, free, classical music program. "YOLA provides children ages 6 to 18, from under-resourced neighborhoods, with free intensive music instruction, up to 18 hours a week, free instruments, academic support and leadership training," says Elsje Kibler-Vermass, the LA Phil's vice-president of

learning. But to the kids, YOLA is about more than just music. Sixteen-year-old Sergio Páez plays violin. He lives in East LA and has been in YOLA since he was 10:

> "YOLA has quite literally changed my life. I honestly can't imagine life without YOLA and I think that's pretty relatable for a lot of the students here in the program. YOLA is kind of summed up in one word, like a family. I don't think there's many other orchestra programs throughout the country that feel really as much as a family as this one does."

Fourteen-year-old Rebeca Márquez lives in West Adams. She plays trombone and has been in YOLA since age seven. She says YOLA has helped her become a bit more disciplined:

> "I remember when I was younger, I did not want to do anything at all wherever my parents told me — I just didn't care. But then, music really helped me try to, it helped me find something that I wanted to do, something that I wanted to pursue, and now I'm just trying to focus in on it. And it's taught me that, in order to get an end result that I would like, I need to put in the time and effort to do it."

Rebeca's father, Oscar Márquez, is appreciative of the program: "I think it's an amazing opportunity that we've been given. Something that we couldn't buy, and something that we definitely couldn't cost financially. How do you express the gratitude that you have for such an opportunity where my daughter is now entertaining

YOLA performs at the Music Center Plaza prior to the CDMX Tour, November 9, 2019 | Photo by Paul Cressey

the idea of pursuing music as a career. Something that I would not have been able to probably expose her to, to this level. And at such a high caliber. And the fact that she's pursued it with such passion. She's found her passion and often it takes a lifetime to find that."

Gustavo Dudamel is the LA Phil's music and artistic director. He says, though YOLA members may not all want to become professional musicians, it's important to offer children art as part of their education, as an essential part of their lives:

"For me, as a son of El Sistema, it was the most important thing. Because it was a way for me to bring the reason of why I am a musician: to give these children the possibility of seeing that everything is possible. It's joy, it's access to beauty, it's interaction with other, creating harmony, creating beautiful music, to share with other people — that changes completely the community."

Last Saturday, at The Music Center's Día de la Familia, hundreds of families came to the YOLA CDMX Orchestra send-off concert. Miriam Sunderman has four kids in YOLA — two of them play percussion, one plays violin, and the other bassoon. They've been part of the program for seven years. Three of them are in Mexico City this week. Sunderman's family in Guadalajara will be making the trip to see them at two of the performance venues: "Yes! Palacio de Bellas Artes and Auditorio Nacional. Whenever I tell my family members or friends that they're gonna be playing there, they're like, Woooow! Do you know who plays there?! Only the

big musicians get to play there, like, we're talking about Andrea Bocelli."

The LA Phil's vice-president of learning, Elsje Kibler-Vermass knows how meaningful the trip to Mexico City is:

"I can tell from our families how important it is for their families to see their family members, their cousins, their nieces and nephews come to Mexico. There's such a strong culture here within our own city, which also is so alive within our programs. So being able to build that bridge between the two countries and also between the two cities, between LA and Mexico City on this tour is really — it's beautiful."

One of the pieces the kids will play this week is the emblematic "Huapango" by Mexico's Jose Pablo Moncayo, so they rehearsed it a lot before leaving. After listening to YOLA's impressive "Huapango" rendition, I talked to David Rejano, principal trombonist with the LA Phil. He teaches YOLA students one-on-one lessons, and he regularly coaches the brass section of the orchestra. Rejano has been with the LA Phil just three years, but he says in that short time he's seen the orchestra grow in leaps and bounds: "And the change that I have experienced is huge. The level of maturity they're acquiring and the level of their playing, their commitment, everything is getting bigger and bigger and it's super exciting for me to be a little tiny part of it." Rejano says YOLA and what it stands for — providing an opportunity to have a brighter future for our kids — should mean everything for Los Angeles.

YOLA performs at the Music Center Plaza prior to the CDMX Tour, November 9, 2019 | Photo by Paul Cressey

BRAZIL

BIBÍ FERREIRA

At 91 years old, actress and singer Bibí Ferreira is still performing to packed houses in her native Brazil and beyond. Her fans range from superstar soccer player Pelé to Liza Minnelli. Many consider her the single most important theater actor in Brazil. Bibí, as Brazilians fondly call her, has been performing on stage and television for most of her life. Her father, Procópio Ferreira, was Brazil's most respected stage actor when he invited his teenage daughter to join his company.

"When I was still 17, I opened with my father at the Teatro Serrador here in Rio de Janeiro, on February the 28th of 1941," Ferreira says. "And I opened with a classical play by Carlo Goldoni, Italian — La Locandiera. It was a great success because it was interesting to see the great Procópio presenting his daughter." Three years later, she started her own theater company in Rio. She performed and directed all over Brazil and before long, her career had eclipsed that of her father. In 1962, she was contacted by the American producers of "My Fair Lady." They wanted to stage the musical in Brazil, and they needed someone who could act and sing: "I made a test. Funny, making a test after years and years of working as a professional. But I made a test for the Americans," says Ferreira. She got the part and "My Fair Lady" broke records in Brazil, playing in theaters for two and a half years. After this success, she took the lead in "Hello Dolly," and a few years later, "Man of La Mancha." These musicals ushered in the era of large theater productions in Brazil, with Ferreira at the forefront.

In 1970, she directed a musical about beloved composers Dolores Duran and Antonio Maria. One of the leads was singer Maria Bethânia, who says Ferreira cast a huge shadow on the Brazilian stage: "Bibí has been very important for Brazil. Everything that she does has helped Brazil with its identity," Bethânia says. "She's a master of theater, of the stage — of the arena, as she likes to call it." Bethânia says working under Ferreira's direction had a major impact on her own career: "Bibí taught me about the stage, and about respect, dedication, and how risk teaches you about life."

In the mid-1970s, Ferreira performed the lead in the musical "Gota D'Agua." It was written by her husband, Paulo Pontes, and featured songs by the renowned singer-songwriter Chico Buarque. It was inspired by the classic Greek tragedy of Medea. "Gota D'Agua" is set in a favela — a slum — in Rio. It's a tragic portrait of people living in poverty, and Ferreira says she took a risk bringing it to the stage. "Some said, 'That's going to be a terrible flop.' Imagine this tragedy, killing the kids and all that," she says. But once again, it was a success — and Ferreira followed with another challenge. Her agent had gone to New York and brought back a play about French singer Edith Piaf. But Ferreira felt most of Piaf's songs were too tragic and didn't think Brazilians would come out to see the show.

One day, a friend of hers, a Piaf fan, sat her down to listen to the renowned vocalist. Ferreira remembers the exchange: "She said, 'Well, Piaf is not only a singer of drama, my dear. You are wrong.' And what she put first — 'Milord' — is very happy." In May of 1983, Ferreira premiered the play "Piaf: Uma Estrela da Canção" (Piaf: A Star of Song) in Rio. She toured Brazil and took the show to Europe. Two years later, the French government awarded her the Commendation of Arts and Letters. This year, to commemorate the 50th anniversary of Edith Piaf's death and the 30 years she's been performing the show, Ferreira started a new tour. Bethânia says she's not surprised that Brazilians have enjoyed this show for so long: "Bibí singing Piaf is spectacular and we understand it and applaud it. What Bibí does is great," Bethânia says.

After Ferreira's performance at the Casa Grande theatre in Rio, Carlos Carneiro, a fan who'd taken a four-hour flight from Fortaleza in northern Brazil just to see the singer, couldn't contain himself. "I had the opportunity to see her in Fortaleza, 15 years ago," Carneiro says. "She was already singing Edith Piaf, and today she was spectacular, marvelous, really great, incomparable!"

Ferreira is returning to New York to perform Piaf at Town Hall, but even at the age of 91, she's ready for a new challenge: "I'm playing Sinatra! At the end of this show, I say, 'Now I'm going to give you a trailer: Next year's show.' So I sing two songs of Sinatra. They adore it, they sing it with me, it's beautiful. So I believe Sinatra is going to be an even greater success than Piaf has been in my career." At the rate she's going, she's got plenty of time to develop her next act.

Bibí Ferreira| Photo by Wilian Aguiar

JOYCE CÂNDIDO

Joyce Cândido was just 14 when her career in music got started:

> "I'm from a very small town, so I was the only one, the only teenager who was able to play and sing — so I got a lot of jobs, I got a lot of gigs, weddings and little parties and after that I start teaching piano lessons. When I went to college, I start singing bars, like Brazilian music with my band, so I guess when I was 18 years old, I decide to be a singer."

Cândido recorded her first album when she was 25. But she figured that to really succeed she'd have to leave her hometown. So she decided to move to New York. She attended classes at a Broadway dance school and took voice lessons. And she sang in small clubs. After a few years she went back and settled in Rio de Janeiro, where she met one of the top Samba producers. She had decided to focus her new record on Samba and called it "O Bom e Velho Samba Novo" (Good Old New Samba). Cândido says she first got into Samba when she was in college. She'd go to the local radio station and ask the DJ to help her find the old samba singers in the vinyl collection. She says a friend gave her a cassette of classics by the Godmother of samba, Beth Carvalho: "And I started listening to that music. It was only Beth Carvalho songs and then I felt WOW! And she was singing Cartola, Nelson Cavaquinho, only very very special composers." Then the friend told her that his band was looking for a singer: "And I felt so happy, so lucky to be invited to sing this kind of music. I really liked that — that's what I want to sing."

Joyce Cândido says many young Brazilians consider Samba "old-fashioned music." But when she performs in the Rio clubs, she's noticed that Samba is starting to gain some ground, even with the younger crowd. She says people approach her:

> "'I'm so happy to see a very young singer like you singing this kind of music that I really love.' My dad used to like this music, my grandfather. So this is good. I know I look 18 — I'm 30 years old but I feel like people think I'm very very young to sing this kind of music because it's not very common to see young singers."

One of the older songs she chose for her new album is "Deixe a Menina." It's a samba composed by Chico Buarque, one of Brazil's most revered songwriters. One day, her producer took her to meet Buarque: "He listened to my music, my voice and everything. He said, 'wow, I really like that. And what's the next step?' I said, 'Well, I need a label and manager and everything.' And he introduced me to people from the label and also some managers. So he just said, 'oh she's a great singer, just listen to her, you're gonna like it.'" Cândido says the samba capital has been good to her. She's gotten to meet some of Brazil's major music figures and even perform with a few of them. And in a country with so many talented musicians and so much competition it doesn't hurt that Joyce Cândido is so good at what she does.

Joyce Cândido and her group at samba club in Rio de Janeiro | Photo by Betto Arcos

LEANDRO FREGONESI AND SAMBA

When I was in Rio de Janeiro a few weeks ago, I sang and danced to samba in the clubs, I heard it on the radio and I ate a "Feijoada," Brazil's national dish, while listening to a live samba group.

But I wanted more insight into the world of samba. So I asked young samba composer and singer Leandro Fregonesi to take me to some clubs and educate me. I asked what drew him into samba: "It's very complete, in terms of rhythm, melody, harmony," he said. "Here in Brazil, samba, it's the most representative way to express our emotions, when we are happy, when we are not happy." And as we hopped from club to club, I realized this music lets you express lots of different emotions. Fregonesi says that's partly because there are so many different kinds of sambas:

> "We have samba de enredo, which is from the samba schools. We have samba de partido alto, [where] sometimes the singers, they improvise on the song, on the theme. We have samba-canção, which is a slower way to do the samba. We have samba-jazz. We have many types of samba. This classification 'samba' brings together many possibilities."

Samba's roots are in Africa, and drumming is a key element. So are the lyrics. Samba composers write about love and heartache, separation and reconciliation, tragedy and triumph. Sambas can be about food, soccer, even politics. For instance, "Vai Passar," by the great Chico Buarque, is about the arrival of democracy in the early 1980s. Fregonesi says a good samba composer is a storyteller who's sharp and insightful: "This is very important in Brazil. The more witty the composer, [the] more respected he is by others. It's a kind of measure. The wittier, the better." "Samba Mestiço," co-written by Fregonesi and recorded by the Godmother of samba Beth Carvalho, shows that kind of wit. It talks about the origins of the music and how samba became an anthem of freedom.

On my last night in Rio, my friend Nilson Raman surprised me with a special gift. He got tickets to a samba song competition at one of the oldest institutions of Brazilian Carnival, the Mangueira Escola de Samba near the famous Maracanã Stadium. There were hundreds of people dancing and singing like there was no tomorrow. I was in samba heaven. Never in my life had I even imagined I'd get a chance to see this kind of spectacle, the biggest party I've ever attended.

So the next time you hear samba, you'll know why it's such a rich and vibrant music tradition. It's a way of life!

Leandro Fregonesi, samba singer and composer | Photo by Betto Arcos

LUIZ GONZAGA: A LENDA

One evening when I was hanging out with samba singer and composer Leandro Fregonesi, he asked me to name some of my favorite Brazilian artists. I rattled off a few names, but when I came to Luiz Gonzaga, he stopped me and said, "If you like Luiz Gonzaga, then you have to go see this amazing musical about his life." So on the last afternoon I was in Rio, Fregonesi's mother took me to the working class neighborhood called Ramos to see the musical "Gonzagão A Lenda." Within a few minutes, I was transported to the northeast of Brazil, one of the most musically rich areas of the country. There, in the dry, poor region of Sertão is the birthplace of Luiz Gonzaga, the "King of Baião."

Gonzaga was a master accordionist and storyteller whose popularity spans decades. His songs have been covered by musicians from Gilberto Gil to David Byrne. Brazilians consider Gonzaga a mythical figure, says the musical's producer Andrea Alves: "My parents are from the northeast, I grew up listening to Luiz Gonzaga. Any person that's from the northeast considers Gonzaga their greatest icon of their culture, he sings about their pains, about the drought of the sertão, and talks about the northeastern culture like no one else." Alves says "Gonzagão A Lenda" is not only a portrait of the Brazilian northeast but of the entire country: "Wherever we take this show, we see how people get emotional about it, because we all have a little bit of the northeast. You might have been born in Rio or in São Paulo, but everyone has relatives who come from the northeast and have that common history."

"Asa Branca" is the anthem of the Brazilian northeast. It's a sweet, melancholic song about the plight of poor people, who must leave their home, in search of a better life. But still yearn to go back. That late afternoon in Rio, halfway through the musical about Luiz Gonzaga, I was moved to tears. Perhaps it was Gonzaga's story or the touching performances of his songs of love and despair. Marcelo Mimoso portrays Gonzaga in his 30s. He says Gonzaga's music is universal: "Fifty years from now, they're going to be teaching 'Asa Branca' in schools," Mimoso says. "It's music that will never die." Brazilians have a word that best describes how I felt after I got back to the U.S.: "saudade." It's a feeling of longing for something you love that's no longer with you.

True, I miss Rio, but the week I spent in this amazing city renewed my appreciation, not just for the music of Brazil, but for its rich and diverse culture. It opened my ears to new sounds and new ways to see a country that's distant yet so familiar.

The cast of "Gonzagão A Lenda" (Gonzaga the legend) | Photo by Betto Arcos

GUINGA

Guitarist and composer Guinga is a popular songwriter in Brazil: his songs have been recorded by the likes of superstar Elis Regina, and he's a favorite of musicians around the world like Michel Legrand and Sergio Mendes. But Guinga is less well-known in the U.S. — he rarely comes here to perform, and considering his successful five-decade career, he's an unusually modest musician. "I met so many virtuoso players in Brazil and had the opportunity to interact with so many virtuoso guitarists, including one called Hélio Delmiro," he says. "Everything that I tried to do in life is to play like him. And since I could never achieve it, I ended up playing like Guinga. It was better for me."

Guinga's full name is Carlos Althier de Souza Lemos Escobar. He got the name "Guinga" after his aunt took to calling him "Gringo" as a toddler, because he had pale skin. The youngster pronounced it "Guinga," and the nickname stuck. He grew up in a working-class suburb of Rio de Janeiro and his uncle taught him how to play the guitar when he was 11. At home, he heard Italian bel canto, Brazilian and American music on his parents' Victrola. "I listened to everything I could," Guinga says. "I knew who Leonard Bernstein was. I knew 'Somewhere' when I was 11 years old; I didn't know how to play it, but when I listened to 'Somewhere,' I cried. American music is inside of me as much as Brazilian music." Guinga combined both styles of music when he started composing as a teenager. Then, in the 1970s, when he was in his 20s, Guinga accompanied some of Brazil's biggest Samba stars and wrote the music for a hit by Elis Regina. Guinga started studying classical guitar when he was 26 and got really good, says John Paul Trotter, a Los Angeles-based classical guitarist. He first heard about Guinga's music 10 years ago, when he traveled to Rio. "I started taking guitar lessons with a teacher down there," Trotter explains, "and one of the first things he did was he put a Guinga piece in front of me and said, 'This is what you really need to look at, and

there's a lot of meat on this. So learn this well, come back to me next week and we go from there.'"

In addition to mastering his instrument and composing popular songs, Guinga also got a college degree — in dentistry. He says he did it for his dad, and because he knew he couldn't make a living as a musician. "I did not want to struggle financially. I didn't want to live the misery I lived as an adolescent and the first part of my adult life," Guinga says. "I did quite well as a dentist. At age 27, I earned $8,000 a month. In Brazil, that's a lot of money." Reflecting on the hardships his parents experienced when he was growing up, Guinga couldn't help but get emotional. "Everything that I tried to be in life was to try to redeem what my father and mother could not be. That's why I think I make music," he says. So, at the age of 56, Guinga stepped out of the dentist's office and into his music studio full time. Sergio Mendes met Guinga in the early 1980s in Rio when Mendes was recording a new album. He included two of Guinga's co-compositions on it and invited the guitarist to record with him: "I sent the album to Henry Mancini, one of the greatest melodists and writers of the century, and he heard the Guinga song and he said, 'Who's that? Who wrote that?'" Mendes recalls. "I said, 'Oh, a friend of mine.' He told me, 'We don't write music like that anymore in the United States.'"

Guinga says that, in the end, his instrument is not only the guitar, but also the songs it sings. That's something he learned from the great Brazilian songwriters. "I saw the way in which the synchronicity of the hand of those composers — their thoughts over the guitar is impressive," he says. "They are the creators, the true creators. Someone like João Gilberto: with that minimalist guitar, he transformed the world." Guinga may not be transforming the world with his guitar, but he definitely makes it a better place to live.

Guinga performing at the Blue Whale jazz club in Los Angeles | Photo by Betto Arcos

HERMETO PASCOAL

Brazil's Hermeto Pascoal is a legend among musicians and fans for his ability to conjure beautiful sounds out of just about anything — from tea kettles to PVC pipes to traditional woodwinds. Earlier this May, the New England Conservatory awarded Pascoal an honorary Doctorate of Music degree and in July, the 81-year-old released "No Mundo Dos Sons," the first album from him and his group in 15 years.

Pascoal can come up with a melody at the drop of a hat. He says he's written 9,000 compositions and most, if not all, were created on the spot. "It's because I'm 100% intuitive," he says. "I don't premeditate anything. I feel it. When something happens, I don't say, 'Now I'm going to do that.' No. If I want to write the music, I start creating. Every piece of my music, even the one I write on a piece of paper, I consider an improvisation." Pianist Jovino Santos Neto is a professor of music at Seattle's Cornish College of the Arts and agrees with the impromptu nature of Pascoal's work. Santos Neto was also a member of Pascoal's band for 15 years and is now the archivist of his work:

> "Hermeto is music. He is the current. He's like a source or a spring that's just gushing that water, and that water is music. … There's a saying, I think it's a John Cage thing that said, 'Music is playing all the time. Music continues, we just kind of dip into it once in a while.' Well, Hermeto is fully immersed in it. So because of that, whenever you are close to him, you just see [that] the music is just coming out."

Pascoal was born in a small farming town in the northeastern Brazilian state of Alagoas. He dropped out of school in the fourth grade — there was no such thing as special education back then for a child with the vision problems that come with albinism. His father taught him to play the accordion and in the early 1960s, Pascoal moved to Rio de Janeiro. By then, he'd picked up piano and flute and began recording with some of the new generation of Brazilian musicians, including Quarteto Novo. Quarteto Novo's percussionist was Airto Moreira who went on to play with Chick Corea and Miles Davis. Moreira recommended Pascoal to Davis and, together, the trumpeter recorded with the Brazilian on the album "Live-Evil." Santos Neto says one of Pascoal's compositions for Miles, "Little Church," was inspired by the Brazilian's childhood memory of hearing his mother and her friends singing novenas to the Virgin Mary. "He would hear these voices wafting through the walls of the church," Santos Neto says. "He was scared to go inside, so he'd sit outside and listen as his mother was singing. So he wrote this gorgeous melody."

Pascoal recalls an interview Davis gave in which the trumpeter was asked how he'd like to return from the afterlife. "'I would like to be a musician like that 'crazy albino,'" he says, recalling Davis' response to the question. "He used to call me 'crazy Brazilian albino.' And to make music like that of Hermeto Pascoal, the 'crazy albino.' I was very happy when I heard that." That's typical of Pascoal's personality, says Santos Neto. In the more than 40 years Santos Neto has known the older musician, Pascoal has never changed. "He never aged and he's at the same time — a very complex personality," Santos Neto says. "He's both the wise old man, because of the white hair, but he's also the prankster, the 16-year-old who's really crazy to play a prank on somebody and to laugh and to make jokes."

Pascoal doesn't make jokes about his honorary Doctor of Music degree from the New England Conservatory. He says it's one of the greatest recognitions of his life. But this acknowledgement reinforces something he's believed for a long time. "Hermeto doesn't make Brazilian music, he makes music in Brazil," Pascoal says. "Therefore, Hermeto is a Brazilian citizen only on a piece of paper. But in my music, I'm universal." And, as the title of his new album says, Pascoal will always be "No Mundo Dos Sons" — in the world of sounds.

Hermeto Pascoal | Photo by Pedro Dimitrow

HAMILTON DE HOLANDA

Alfredo Viana was one of the superstars of the Brazilian musical style known as choro. The flautist and saxophonist, better known by the nickname Pixinguinha, pushed the boundaries of choro by incorporating jazz and ragtime into his compositions. Hamilton de Holanda explores that connection on the new album "Mundo de Pixinguinha." De Holanda recorded with Cuban pianist Chucho Valdés, French accordionist Richard Galliano, and American trumpeter Wynton Marsalis. "As I've traveled around the world in the past 10 years, I became friends with a few musicians and I recorded with a few of them," de Holanda says. "I thought it would be an opportunity for the music of Pixinguinha to be played by jazz musicians who know about improvisation, and who know how to interpret music that's not theirs."

De Holanda plays an instrument called "bandolim." It evolved from the mandolin, brought to Brazil by Portuguese colonizers, and its acknowledged master was a man named Jacob do Bandolim. De Holanda says do Bandolim's genius lay in his ability to blend music brought by the Portuguese with that brought by enslaved Africans to create a perfect balance. "He created a Brazilian way, with a lot of emotion," he says. "You hear in his music a little bit of the fado nostalgia, but also the joy of Brazilian music, and African music too — and with such care in the refinement of a sound and the arrangements." But de Holanda wanted to take the music further — and he does, says Sergio Mielniczenko. He's the producer and host of "The Brazilian Hour," a radio program distributed across the U.S. and around the world. Mielniczenko says of de Holanda:

"He's a musician with an incredible technique and a deep interpretation to the soul of Brazilian music. If you look at his repertoire, he plays everything from Jacob do Bandolim to Egberto Gismonti to Hermeto Pascoal — and more recently he has been pairing with very outstanding musicians as well. But that's what is interesting about Hamilton: You cannot see him as a choro composer, only. Obviously he plays choro, but he's beyond."

De Holanda plays a special kind of bandolim. Normally, the instrument has eight strings, just like the mandolin. De Holanda had one built with 10 strings. "I wanted to create a polyphony in my instrument, and be able to play the melody, the accompaniment and the rhythm, all at the same time," he says. "Just as you see in a piano soloist or a guitar soloist, I wanted to express some polyphonic ideas in the bandolim — the same way a piano works in a jazz trio." De Holanda's ideas about what the bandolim can do led him to collaborate with a pianist, Italian Stefano Bollani, for another recent recording, "O Que Será." "The bandolim has certain musical 'off-keys.' The piano is always perfectly in tune. Perhaps the defect of the bandolim," de Holanda says, "is that when it's paired with a piano, magic is born, which is something I cannot explain."

De Holanda says though he started out playing choro, he's emphatic about where he's taking the music. "What I'm doing today is not exactly choro, it's not only samba, and it's not just jazz. It's all of the above, the confluence of all of it," he says. "Out of all that is the music of Hamilton de Holanda." It's safe to say Pixinguinha would approve.

Hamilton de Holanda | Photo by Marcos Portinari

VINICIUS CANTUARIA AND BILL FRISELL

American guitarist Bill Frisell and Brazilian songwriter Vinicius Cantuaria have a new record out called "Lágrimas Mexicanas." Vinicius Cantuaria says the title of the album "Lágrimas Mexicanas" was inspired by his memories as a child in Brazil, watching movies from the Golden Age of Mexico's cinema. In the mid-1990s, Cantuaria moved from Rio de Janeiro to Brooklyn and he was struck by the rich mix of Latin American immigrants from all over: "And then I talked to Bill. Bill, I have this idea to do 'Lágrimas Mexicanas' and Bill loved the idea." Bill is the guitar great Bill Frisell. They've played together on each other's records for more 15 years. Frisell says, every time he plays with Cantuaria he knows where to jump in: "I just follow along, it's like jumping into a river and you just get swept along. I don't really have to think so much it just feels so natural to me, in the melody and rhythm, just the whole world of what he does."

The album opens with a song in Spanish titled "Mi declaración" (My declaration). It's a sort of bolero, a romantic ballad Cantuaria heard on the radio when he was growing up in Brazil. The lyrics say:

Estoy perdido, caído (I'm lost, fallen)

Aunque intento, no te olvido, es mi amor
(Though I try, I cannot forget you, it's my love)

Tengo prisa, necesito de tus besos, tus cariños
(I'm in a hurry, I need your kisses, your caresses)

Tú lo sabes, yo no vivo, sin tu amor
(You know I cannot live without your love)

Lejos estás pero en mí
(You're far, but inside of me)

Tu presencia infinita
(Your infinite presence)

Siempre te puedo sentir, mi vida
(I can always feel you, my life)

Te escribo una carta de amor
(I'm writing a love letter)

Que es para ti (It's for you)

Mi declaración (My declaration)

Cantuaria says the inspiration behind many of the songs in this new album came to him on the streets of Brooklyn. The song "Calle 7" conjures up images of people speaking Spanish with a variety of different accents; Cantuaria explains: "Walking for five minutes, you just hear Spanish with different accents, Mexican, Colombian: 'cómo vas, está bien, vamos a comer, qué bonito...' Then this street with many many Latino situation happens there in different levels, musicians, restaurants, or just a simple café."

Frisell says the album reflects their own backgrounds as artists from two different worlds, each with his own baggage: "I come from America and Vinicius comes from Brazil but we both been all around the world. Also, we're the same age. We both grew up with rock-and-roll music and '50s, '60s, '70s. And just traveling, there's so much that comes into our lives." Vinicius Cantuaria and Bill Frisell say when they play, there are no rules or boundaries. It doesn't matter whether it sounds Brazilian or Latin, or if they're playing jazz or rock. They're simply making music.

Vinicius Cantuaria and Bill Frisell — Normal Life Pictures | Photo courtesy of Songline / Tone Field Productions

CUBA AND THE DIASPORA

ROCK IN CUBA

Change is slowly underway in Cuba — and the music is also changing. Now, in addition to Afro-Caribbean sounds and the state-sanctioned Nueva Trova, there is a burgeoning of Cuban rock-and-roll, from heavy metal to acoustic to pop rock. This music seems to be reflecting the angst and dreams of Cuban youth in the 1990s.

On a hot summer afternoon in Havana, members of the thrash band Zeus rehearse at an underground space called "El Patio de María." Zeus is an example of how rock bands in Cuba have managed to survive despite the official hostility and the economic hardships the island is facing. Drummer Aramís Hernández shows off a scratchy 15-year-old guitar he's converted into an American-style Gibson:

> "They're very old instruments, we repaired them a few times, they came from the former German Democratic Republic, from the Socialist block. They're not of very good quality but we try to make some sound. I think that if a foreign band would come and play our instruments, they would be unable to do it."

The music of Zeus is now reaching a wider audience, after being featured in David Byrne's compilation "Cuba Classics 3." Still, they have trouble finding places to play and ways to promote and distribute their music on the island.

These problems aren't hard to understand, says guitarist Dagoberto Pedraja, when you consider the history of rock-and-roll in Cuba. Pedraja, a founder of the well-respected rock band Gens, says rock-and-roll was considered synonymous with deviation and was not encouraged nor accepted by society: "It was as dogmatic as this: if you made rock-and-roll, you were an enemy. It was not written in the Cuban constitution nor did Fidel Castro ever say anything about it. No, it was the kind of cultural or social machismo on the part of those who handled the cultural policy of this country." Though there are only three officially recognized rock bands on the government payroll, it's estimated that there could as many as 300 throughout the island.

A song by the folk-rock band Extraño Corazón, "Viajeros del Tiempo," tells of the hardships experienced by those who left the island on a raft, but it also tells the story of the band itself and their struggles, trying to make music. "What we're demonstrating is that in Cuba rock has a wide acceptance, and it's a business. People are afraid to speak in those terms, that it's a business, because it sounds like capitalism. But music is a big business where the state is losing out because of their political and ideological stands," says guitarist Javier Rodríguez, leader of Extraño Corazón. Rodríguez would like to see the same access given to rock bands as there is to musicians interpreting traditional Afro-Cuban music and other officially sanctioned music styles.

One Cuban musician that has sidestepped the need for official sanction by signing with a label in Spain is pop rocker Carlos Varela whose music is now receiving international attention. In his latest album, released in the U.S., Varela captures the angst expressed by Cuban youth. The lyrics to the song "La política no cabe en la azucarera" tell this story: *Felipe left for the U.S. / there he is cold, here he was bored / there are two empty chairs / 90 miles away from mine / Politics does not fit in a sugar bowl.* Varela, who enjoys some airplay on Cuban radio stations, depending on the content of the song, believes the social climate will change as long as musicians continue to write lyrics that speak to the reality faced by Cuban society: "It would be a lot easier for me to write about flowers and butterflies, or say that everything here is fine. But the truth is that as long we keep coming back to Cuba, inevitably all those things are going to change."

Today, as more young Cubans find their own voice through homegrown rock-and-roll, musicians like Carlos Varela believe this musical culture can also be a bridge — back to the U.S. where rock originally comes from, and especially back to the Cubans who have left the island.

Extraño Corazón | Photo by María Torrellas, courtesy of the band

CARLOS VARELA

Cuban musician Carlos Varela has been in the United States for the past couple of weeks. Varela was barred from coming to the U.S. in 2004. Like other Cuban musicians he was denied a visa by the Bush administration. Now Varela has used his time lobbying for a lifting of restrictions on Cuba. He's also mixing a new album at Jackson Browne's studio in Los Angeles.

Carlos Varela is on a mission. He wants to help break the wall between the U.S. and Cuba so he's been visiting with Congress members in Washington, bringing along his guitar:

> "Everything I have to say to a congressperson is already in my songs. I sing to them and they look at me asking, 'well, what do you want?' And I tell them that I would like them to consider the possibility that it's a privilege for me to be here, and I tell them to open up, to find a way to open the door — at least in culture so we can learn about each other, to get closer and bring down the aggressive dialogue we've seen on both sides."

What Varela is talking about is a change of U.S. policy, to allow Cuban and American artists to travel freely to each other's countries. And change is also a theme in his new album.

Varela got some help securing his visa from the Center for Democracy in the Americas, a Washington-based group, working to end the travel ban to Cuba. Sarah Stevens is the group's executive director. At a reception held to honor Varela, she says they hope that with the change from the Bush to the Obama administration Varela and others would have a better chance of getting visas: "He got the visa in the context of other Cuban artists getting visas. Los Van Van have a visa to come and do a tour here, and some others did as well. We take it as a sign that at least in terms of culture, there is a policy change and that they're encouraging Cubans to come to the country."

Varela is one of the most popular singers in Cuba. Many of his songs have become anthems to thousands of young Cubans. In his latest album, "No es el Fin" (It's Not the End), Varela touches on the Cuban experience of loss and hope. He says the title song was inspired by a true story of a loved one lost out at sea: "Es una canción de esperanza, de fe. It's a love song dedicated to this young woman saying, 'it's not the end, girl, it's not the end, at this point, it's not the end.' I think that in the world we're living in today, having songs that give you hope is a blessing."

In between his Capitol Hill visits, Varela has been coming to Los Angeles at the invitation of singer Jackson Browne. They met a few years ago in Havana. Browne offered Varela his recording studio so he could finish mixing and mastering his new album. Browne also invited Varela to tour with him in Europe: "It's a relationship that is not too badly encumbered by the fact that I don't really speak Spanish. I don't really know anything he's saying when he speaks, but I find that in translation his songs are completely, utterly compelling."

Varela's album will be released next spring. He's hoping that by then, he will be able to tour the U.S. with his band and perform songs from it, like "Todo será distinto" (Everything Will be Different): *Perhaps tomorrow the sun will rise and everything will be different / the sad thing is that by then, we will not be the same.*

Carlos Varela at Jackson Browne's recording studio in Santa Monica, CA | Photo by Betto Arcos

THE ENDLESS TOUR
OF SILVIO RODRÍGUEZ

Singer-songwriter Silvio Rodríguez is one of the best-known performers in Cuba. But for the past six years he's been doing a special tour of the island, performing for people in the poorest neighborhoods. I was recently in Havana and got a chance to see him.

The concert took place in a barrio called "Jaimanitas," not far from the Marina Hemingway. There was a small stage, in the middle of the street, with the Cuban flag draped over the back. Silvio's idea is to bring music to people who can't afford a concert in a theater. When he walked on stage he spoke to the hundreds of people who came to see him. Silvio said, "We've been doing these concerts in different neighborhoods in Havana for a while. We took our music out of the theaters and we've done well, because what we get back is so much more than what we've given." Oroa Reyes, a young woman from this neighborhood, tells me Silvio says things she would like to say, but he says them easily and beautifully. There was also a large contingent of Chilean fans in the audience. Roxana Castillo is getting a degree in community-based mental health in Havana. She saw Silvio back in Santiago, in 1992, at the National Stadium, where hundreds of people were imprisoned and tortured during the Pinochet dictatorship. Castillo says, during the dictatorship Silvio Rodríguez gave voice to the cause of people who were against Pinochet. And during the rallies and gatherings against the dictatorship the most popular singer in Chile was Silvio.

The audience sang along to this 1991 song, "El Necio" (The Stubborn). It's a song addressing Silvio's concerns in the context of the new U.S.-Cuba relations. The song suggests that Cuba is not willing to give up the gains of the revolution, nor replace socialism with rampant capitalism. The chorus doesn't pull any punches: *I will die the way I lived.* He dedicated the song to Gerardo Hernández, one of the Cuban Five — the Cuban nationals arrested in Miami in 1998, and convicted of spying. They're all back in Cuba now and considered national heroes. Singer Kelvis Ochoa was also at the concert. A few years ago, Ochoa was invited to open the concert in the neighborhood where he grew up, one of the poorest in Havana. The area is called "Canal de Cerro," an open sewer runs through it. Kelvis says that concert was like a homecoming for him. He says, "I grew up there, I played there as a kid. I ate my first sweet plantains there, I remember it vividly — it's where I ate my first almonds on the sidewalk, and I relived all of that during the concert with Silvio, when I played in that barrio with him. It was incredible!"

This was Silvio's 75th concert in his "Gira Interminable" (Endless Tour). Silvio is now 70 years old. He says he'll continue to do these concerts until there is no more poverty in Cuba, or until he dies, whichever comes first.

Silvio Rodríguez during a concert in Havana's Jaimanitas neighborhood | Photo by Betto Arcos

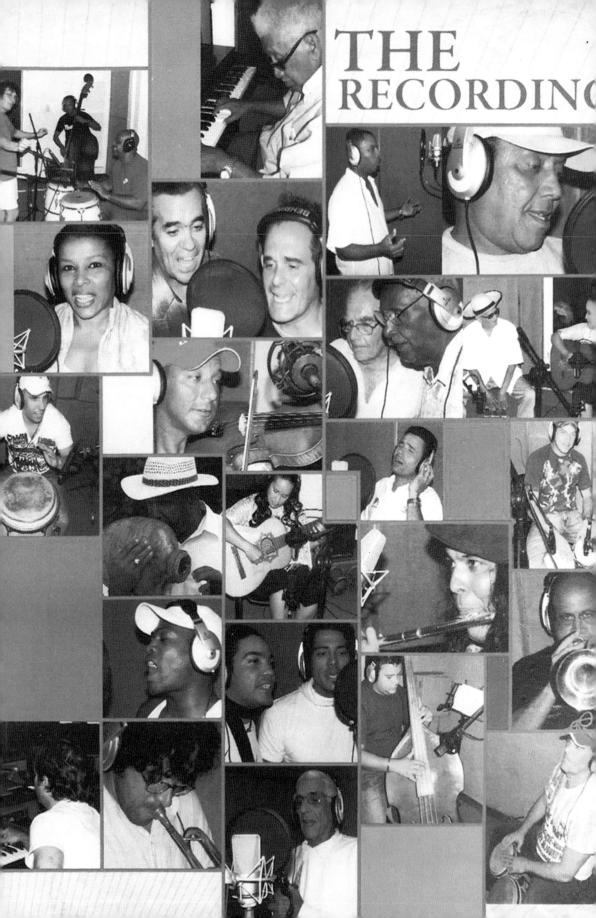

CIEN SONES CUBANOS

How do you decide what are the top 100 songs for a country like Cuba, with such a rich musical culture? For Cuban musician and producer Edesio Alejandro, the best way is to ask a question: "El día que te vayas del parque, ¿qué son te llevas?" (The day you leave the park, what song would you take with you?) That means, the day you die, what song do you want to hear them play? That's what Edesio Alejandro asked hundreds of people across Cuba. The result is "100 Sones Cubanos," a five-CD anthology and documentary DVD featuring the island's most popular sones. Son is the foundation of Cuban dance music, including salsa. The collection is rich and varied, from duets and quartets, to small groups and big bands. It includes classics as well as older and lesser known gems like "Retorna."

While the collection features some well-known names in Cuban music, Edesio Alejandro says the real star is Cuban son: "Porque no queríamos hacer un disco donde el cantante, donde la voz fuera lo más importante, como generalmente sucede en este tipo de proyectos." He says

he didn't want to make a record where the singer, the voice was at the center, just like every other project. The emphasis was on Cuban son and nothing else. Edesio Alejandro says one of the most exciting aspects of this project was finding music that built the foundation of Cuban son: "Encontramos al llamado padre del son, que es el "nengón." He says that in his search for the most popular songs he found a precursor to son. This tune called "nengón" is a very primitive style, still played the same way it was played more than a hundred years ago: "Hay tantos sones en Cuba, hay tanta música buena," says Edesio Alejandro — there's so much good music in Cuba that 100 is a small number to do it justice. That's why he decided to do the project based on people's favorites. He doesn't believe anyone is capable of saying one son is better than the other.

So which was the top choice among those surveyed? If you guessed the classic "Son de la loma" by Miguel Matamoros, you guessed right.

Cien sones cubanos | Photo courtesy of the producer

LEO BROUWER

Leo Brouwer is considered one of the most important living figures of classical music in Latin America. His works are played regularly in concert halls around the world, and he's scored more than 50 films. But at the age of 78, Brouwer finds it hard to reflect on his legacy. He's just grateful that people are moved by his music. "To be useful is something incredible, because you're at the service of the world," Brouwer says in Spanish. "Humans, when they communicate, when they teach, when they show, when they give ... they're doing one of the most beautiful things in life... Perhaps my roots in solitude, of being an orphan — it forces me to these reflections."

His parents divorced when he was very young, and his mother died when he was 11. So he decided to go look for his father. "I found him playing a guitar, and it was the instrument that fascinated me," he says. Brouwer taught himself everything he knows about music. Even though his grandmother was the sister of renowned composer Ernesto Lecuona, the wealthy family refused to pay for any kind of music education and wanted nothing do to with him: "I'd say that being in an orphanage made me reflect on the 'what' and the 'why' — especially the 'why' — of the essential things in life. What is a man? What am I doing here? What is culture? Why am I fascinated with this?"

Brouwer says he listened to Cuba's classical radio station all the time and learned how to read sheet music by haunting music stores in Havana when he was 15 years old:

> "I arrived and showed my clean hands, so I could touch the sheet music. 'Sure, come on in, boy,' they'd say. I spent four hours a day standing, studying Stravinsky, including one of Mozart's string quartets, who was one of my first teachers of the traditional forms... That's the world in which I began to compose. I didn't have a piano — I don't need it. I trained the ear and I wrote on the table. And I still write music that way. The guitar was a reference, for fingerings and things like that."

Brouwer's models were Bartok, Schumann, Rachmaninov and Stravinsky. He wanted to do for the guitar what they had done for instruments like piano and violin.

Brazilian guitarist Carlos Barbosa-Lima first heard Brouwer's music when he was touring in Europe, in the early 1970s. "For me it was a new experience, because I saw a composer-guitarist with incredible view of the music and different styles too, including the popular roots, and also his knowledge," Barbosa recalls. "I think probably he had his style, when he was in his teens, already defined." Part of that style is incorporating traditional music and Cuban instruments in classical music forms. But Brouwer is also a big fan of popular music and says it's just as important as anything written for the concert hall. "That's the case of The Beatles, among others, or a Leonard Cohen. So many. Including those that could be labeled commercial," Brouwer says. "The composers of boleros from Cuba and Mexico are absolute geniuses. Those boleros they wrote will transcend history because they're incredible." Brouwer has a special place in his heart for The Beatles. He decided to arrange their music for classical instruments because of a particular Cuban minister of culture and his views on music:

> "He even felt North American music deformed people. That view was widespread during the old Soviet era, that some music was degenerate, that it was a Nazi heritage. That minister banned my music, too, and that of composer Silvio Rodríguez, who was a hardcore revolutionary. We were forbidden, we became close friends, and here we are. The minister is long gone."

In addition to his prolific career as a composer, Brouwer also founded important cultural institutions in Cuba. In 1960, he created the Cuban Institute of Art and Film Industry and helped organize the conservatories on the island. He stopped playing the guitar in the late '70s, after an accident permanently damaged the middle finger of his right hand. Today, he focuses all of his energy on composing, noting that he still has a lot of work to do. "And now I have many more ideas. The problem is much more serious," he says. "It's a lot harder to compose — not because I don't have ideas, but because I have too many ideas ... and I have to be selective."

Leo Brouwer at home in Havana | Photo by Danay Nápoles

HAROLD LÓPEZ-NUSSA

You can hear Harold López-Nussa's training when he plays. The 33-year-old pianist is reluctant to admit the classical influence on his jazz playing, but he's quick to acknowledge that he, like many other great Cuban pianists, was classically trained. "This is the school that we have to learn music in Cuba; it's classical," he says. "I did all my stuff there from 8 years old to 25." Ned Sublette, author of the book "Cuba and Its Music, From the First Drums to the Mambo," says the education López-Nussa received in Cuban conservatories was unique. "He had a level of training that it's really hard to get anywhere else," he says. Sublette explains that the Cuban Revolution in 1959 led to more investment in music education. "The new revolutionary government made culture a priority," he says. He also points out that this robust system of conservatories is still operating. "You will meet Cuban musicians who have been trained from childhood to be competitive professional musicians — and most of them have a conservatory background," he says. But music school isn't the only part of a musician's education. Sublette, quoting British musicologist Geoff Baker, says Cuban musicians have four main streams of influence: "family, conservatory, street and religion."

Harold López-Nussa certainly draws on the first two. His grandparents were musicians, his father is a respected drummer and music educator, and his mother was a piano teacher. "I have the music in my body and my blood," López-Nussa says. "Eighty percent of what I'm doing today and why I'm a musician is because of my family." As for as the last two streams of influence, López-Nussa is not particularly religious, but he's certainly aware of the sounds of the street — and Cuba's long tradition of popular music. López-Nussa started listening to jazz as a teenager with his friends at the conservatory, and he says he's following in the footsteps of great Cuban pianists like Ernesto Lecuona, Frank Emilio Flynn and Chucho Valdés. He remembers seeing Valdés up close at the age of 10, when he came to play for the students at López-Nussa's school. "I was so impressed by his playing the piano, this kind of freedom that he has with the keyboard," he says. "I'm always thinking of this experience." It's no surprise, then, that a tune Valdés made popular with his band Irakere, "Bacalao con Pan," turns up on López-Nussa's new album, "El Viaje."

López-Nussa recently signed with an American label, Mack Avenue. He says improved relations between Cuba and the U.S. — ushered in by the Obama administration — have opened new opportunities that he hopes will continue under the new administration in Washington. He wants more Cuban musicians to play in the U.S., and he'd also like more American musicians to start performing in Cuba. "I have a lot of hope about this approach," he says. "It will be better for all of us."

Harold López-Nussa | Photo courtesy of the artist

OMARA PORTUONDO

Cuban singer Omara Portuondo came to international attention in the 1950s, when that country was less isolated than it has been since the Revolution. Her voice reached ears around the world again in the '90s, when she was featured as the only female singer on the hit Buena Vista Social Club album. Today, Portuondo is 85 — and she's still performing.

Sitting in the restaurant of the classy Capri Hotel in Havana, Portuondo remembers a Cuban composer, María Teresa Vera, who was part of the traditional troubadour scene from the 1920s to the 1950s. Portuondo has admired Vera's work for a long time. "I've been listening to her songs since I was a little girl," she says — which is why she chose Vera's song, "Veinte Años," for her showcase on Buena Vista Social Club. Danilo Lozano, a music professor at Whittier College who specializes in Cuban music, says that the 1997 album was Portuondo's reintroduction to international and American audiences. "And that was great," Lozano says, "because what she brought to it was, what can I say … It was magic."

Portuondo's career began in Havana, in places like the cabaret Salón Rojo and another club across the street from the hotel where we sit. "There at the Club 21, that's where I first started performing with Cuarteto D'Aida," she says. "All of these places are very important to me. They're part of my beginning." Cuarteto D'Aida was an all-female vocal group directed by pianist Aida Diestro. Portuondo says their gender was not all that made them different from the rest of the Cuban groups of the 1950s. "It was well distinguished because director Aida Diestro harmonized us perfectly," she says. "All the great musicians of Cuba admired and respected her for her approach, using notes in such an extraordinary way." Cuarteto D'Aida became a hit. The group toured the U.S. in the mid-1950s, performed with Nat King Cole and recorded an album for RCA Victor. According to Lozano, the group sang in a style called "Filin." "I would say that the equivalent to what 'Filin' would be like, would be listening to a jazz ballad," Lozano says. "Except that, instead of listening to it instrumentally, you're listening to it vocally, delivered with an instrumental passion — which is unique for Cuban music." Portuondo became known as "La Novia del Filin" (The Bride of Filin). It was a style of music that embraced both men and women.

Lozano says Portuondo's life spans the history of Cuban music from the 1940s to the present, and that she has championed many Cuban music styles during her time. But her greatest impact came with "Filin" music, where, he says, "she really, really makes a big 'marca-pauta' — she makes a mark in the music. And she becomes known for that, even though she's tremendously versatile."

Portuondo turns 86 at the end of this month during her U.S. tour, and she has no plans to stop working. "Ahora no soy tan niña, pero me siento como una niña," she says, laughing. She's not a little girl, but she feels like one.

Omara Portuondo at the Capri Hotel in Havana | Photo by Betto Arcos

DAYMÉ AROCENA (PART I)

In May of last year, 22-year-old singer Daymé Arocena was invited to take part in an open mic audition in Havana. She was one of a couple dozen Cuban artists getting a shot at a chance to record on a new album for Gilles Peterson's label. He's a world-renowned DJ and producer based in Britain. Daymé says she was tense: "Each person sang one song, I was so scared 'cause that open mic was huge — a lot of beautiful talent and so famous Cuban singers, and I was so scared 'cause nobody knows me there." Peterson had invited 10 emerging producers from around the world to go to Havana to record with Cuban artists. Daymé's friends told her, you should sing a song that everyone knows. But she decided to sing one of her own. When Daymé found out she was selected for Peterson's project, she was in shock. "I was like... What!!? 'Cause everyone there was like huge famous Cuban singers and they picked me!!?? I was like, 'maybe they drink a lot!!!'"

Next thing she knew she was in London for the launch party of the album "Havana Cultura Mix - The SoundClash" and Peterson invited her to perform that night: "He said, 'we bring Daymé from Havana 'cause all the DJs, the ten DJs picked her to work with her.' So I was at the stage like, What?! 'cause nobody told me about it before." After the show in London, as she was getting ready to fly home, she was asked to record her own album with Peterson's London-based label: "I was like, What?! My first CD in London? With Gilles Peterson's label? Am I dreaming? I was like what?! Are you joking with me?! Are you kidding me?! I was like c'mon man! They asked me, do you want it? I said, change the ticket right now!"

Daymé laughed all the way back to Havana. Her debut album comes out this week in the U.K. and later this month in the U.S. And with the way things are changing in Cuba, it couldn't have a more appropriate title. It's called "Nueva Era" (New Era).

Daymé Arocena | Photo by Betto Arcos

DAYMÉ AROCENA (PART 2)

Cuban music has long had a strong connection to the United States, and that includes the days when jazz trumpeter Dizzy Gillespie favored the sounds from the Caribbean island nation. And then the "Buena Vista Social Club" movie and soundtrack provided a huge boost to the Cuban music scene in the late 1990s.

Today's generation of Cuban artists is carving a new path. Singer Daymé Arocena is one of those artists. Her new album is called "Cubafonía." Arocena says the title carries a special meaning: "'Cubafonía' is the journey of the paradise that is Cuban music." Arocena lives a few blocks from Plaza de la Revolución. As she talks, the sound of the neighborhood comes in through the open windows of her fifth-floor apartment: "I'm just trying to bring alive again those rhythms, that music that made me dance, made me sing, when I was a kid, that gave me the pushing to make music, to write music."

This is Arocena's second album for renowned DJ/producer Gilles Peterson's London-based label. In 2014, Peterson invited Arocena to take part in his Havana Cultura Mix Project. Then came a record deal and her first album, "Nueva Era," released in 2015. Arocena, who is 25 years old, says that album was her opening to the world. But now that people know her name:

> "The next step is to take them into your heart, into your spirits. You have to show them who you are, more than just a name, more than just this person that Gilles Peterson met one day and decided to help. You have to show them where are you coming from. What is the music that is into your roots, is in your blood."

"Cubafonía" is a travelogue of Afro-Cuban music. The album opens with a song dedicated to the Santería spirit "Eleggua," who represents the beginning and the end. Arocena is a practitioner of the Santería religion. Another song on the album is called "La Rumba Me Llamo Yo" (My

Name is Rumba). It's inspired by a dream where Santería priests read shells and stones to tell Arocena about her life and her future.

While Arocena's album is steeped in Cuba, there's also an LA connection. Los Angeles-based Dexter Story was the album's producer. He has collaborated with saxophonist Kamasi Washington and Marie Daulne of Zap Mama among many others. Peterson recommended him to Arocena. Story says he was impressed by Arocena after listening to the album demos:

> "I was blown away by the progressiveness of the music. I've heard a lot of Cuban music. I thought she was actually taking it in a fresh direction. I was just amazed by her well-roundedness. She's a great singer. In fact she was raised as a choir director. In Cuba, they actually train you on different instruments. She's an accomplished pianist. On top of that she can arrange horns and strings. I was blown away by her talent."

Arocena has been to Los Angeles three times. The last time was to record her voice tracks for the new album. She's found Los Angeles has a certain affinity with Cuba: "I have to say that LA is my favorite city in the U.S. LA is more chill and you can see the mountains in the background, so I feel it closer to Cuba — and they have the beach. It's different. It's deeper, I think."

Arocena says this album has another purpose: to help people understand what Cuban music is and is not: "When people think Cuban music is just Buena Vista Social Club, when people don't know that rumba is the beginning of all the rhythms of Cuba, all of that makes me really angry, makes me sad." Daymé Arocena's "Cubafonía" adds up to a musical statement from a young singer living in the 21st century, supported by deep roots that have helped her find her own voice.

Daymé Arocena and her Santería altar at home in Havana | Photo by Betto Arcos

CIMAFUNK

U.S.-Cuba relations appear to be going back to the Cold War era. Last week, the Trump administration announced a new policy, reversing the changes president Obama had put in place five years ago. But that doesn't stop the island's wealth of musicians to continue making some innovative sounds. Billboard named Cimafunk — an artist called "the James Brown of Cuba" — one of the top 10 Latin artists to watch in 2019.

It's a Friday night at the No Name restaurant and bar on Fairfax Avenue in Los Angeles. The place is packed with a couple hundred people as Cimafunk and his seven-piece band deliver a blistering set of dance music. Cimafunk is the brainchild of 30-year-old Erik Iglesias, a self-taught singer who moved to Havana eight years ago from the province of Pinar del Río. After dropping-out of medical school, and landing a job at a car paint shop in Havana, he began to make friends in the music scene.

Iglesias did not attend Cuba's renowned music schools and he doesn't come from a musical family. But he grew up absorbing a wide range of music, especially Cuban and American pop, which he heard on cassettes in the family car: "Every time that I could, I'd get into the car and I put a cassette, I just literally killed the battery of the car, just listening music, like Lionel Richie, Michael Jackson with the album 'Invisible.' That is one of my favorites, it's my favorite actually. Stevie Wonder also."

After two years working in a car shop, Iglesias got his first break. He auditioned for pop singer Raúl Paz and got a gig singing background vocals at the Karl Marx Theater, Cuba's biggest indoor venue. That was the only concert he did with Paz, but he met many musicians, and a few doors started to open. He began collaborating with different bands and projects. Iglesias joined "Interactivo," a collective project with some of Cuba's renowned alternative music figures, led by pianist Roberto Carcassés. During the time he was with Interactivo, Iglesias and a couple friends created a cover band called Los Boys. He started to develop his own musical ideas:

"I was crazy with the rhythms and I said, man I need to start to experiment how I can know this way to sing, this way to perform the groove. So I said let's make a band and we're only going to do covers from Stevie and from Michael Jackson. Once we understand what is about this product that they have, then we pass to other stuff."

That was the plan, but instead Los Boys started making all kinds of other pop music. Then, they got a contract to work eight months in a cruise ship in the Mediterranean. When the cruise ship tour ended, Iglesias had saved enough money to buy the electronic equipment he needed to start recording his first album. But he didn't have a name. He found out that he was a descendant of people from Nigeria and learned about the Cimarrón culture — runaway slaves who created their own communities and lived in freedom in the forest:

"Black people from many places, from many tribes, from other countries, all they was living together, with different sounds, with different grooves, with different rituals, with maybe different gods even — and they all live together and they have to live together because was the only way to be, to live without being a slave."

Cimafunk | Photo by Daniel Arévalos

He called on some friends and together they came up with the name Cimafunk, combining Cimarrón and funk.

Cimafunk's manager is Argelio Rodríguez. He says renowned pianist Roberto Carcassés, Interactivo's musical director, was the first person who told him his opinion of the project. "We were in a car, leaving a concert and when he heard the record, he said, 'this is going to be a big thing.' That's the first time I heard that." Cimafunk has been touring the U.S. for the past six weeks, making stops in 16 cities, including SXSW, New York, Chicago and New Orleans. But this is not your normal U.S. tour. One afternoon, I caught the band having lunch and jamming at San Julian Park in Skid Row, an area filled with hundreds of homeless people.

Collin Laverty is the man behind Cimafunk's tour. Laverty is a leading expert on U.S.-Cuba relations — he runs Cuba Educational Travel, an organization taking Americans to Cuba: "We always try and make everything two ways, as much as we can bring Cubans and Cuban culture and thought leaders to the U.S., we do. So we bring a lot of entrepreneurs and cultural acts here. And that's how I got linked up with Cimafunk originally, by hiring them to do performances in Cuba for my clients and then also we came up with the idea to bring them to the U.S. and get them some visibility and opportunity to network."

During the tour, Laverty organized showcases for Google, Youtube and Netflix. I asked him why he took Cimafunk to skid row. He replied with the band's comments: "Two nights ago we performed for Leonardo DiCaprio and Sylvester Stallone, and a star-studded lineup on a 40-million-dollar mansion in Beverly Hills overlooking all of the city, and two days later we're here in skid row. And so I think in terms of getting a taste of America and understanding and also appreciating what they have."

The next day, Cimafunk took part in a Q&A and performance at the Grammy Museum's Clive Davis auditorium. Moderator Scott Goldman asked Iglesias if he considered himself a renegade, changing the perception of Cuban music. Iglesias was candid: "No, no, no, it's not like this. I'm just recycling what is done already. I'm not changing anything, I'm putting [a] music style, this stuff I'm putting together in a personal way. Everybody do the same, there's no new music now, man. We have been many, many years without new stuff."

After the Q & A, Cimafunk played a set of hits to an adoring audience that could not stop dancing. Collin Laverty says Cimafunk has the talent and the vision to become the biggest modern-day Cuban artist: "He is going to be the face of Cuba. He's going to be the cultural ambassador of Cuba, and I think that serves a very important role in terms of allowing Americans to understand the talent, the kindness and the warmth of the Cuban people, which he clearly represents." Laverty says for 60 years we've been relying on governments to figure it out and they haven't done a very good job. Maybe it's time to try something new and exciting, like Cimafunk.

Cimafunk | Photo by Marie Aureille

JAZZ PLAZA FESTIVAL IN HAVANA

Every year, the International Jazz Plaza Festival brings musicians and fans from all over the world to Havana for an intense week of performances across the Caribbean city. The festival includes a wide range of artists, some of whom are here this year for the first time.

On a cool winter evening at the Casa de la Cultura de Plaza, the group NG La Banda is playing Dizzy Gillespie's "A Night in Tunisia." NG La Banda created one of Cuba's most popular dance styles, known as timba. The band leader, flutist Jose Luis Cortés, used to play with Cuba's super jazz group, Irakere, and the iconic salsa band, Los Van Van. At the annual festival, jazz and Cuban music converge to create a potent mix unlike anywhere else. It was at this venue in 1980, where Cuban jazz singer Bobby Carcassés founded the festival, encouraging collaborations between jazz and Cuban artists. At the Festival's home, the historic Hotel Nacional, New York-based saxophonist Irwin Hall says he's playing here with singer Dee Dee Bridgewater for the first time. "The people here are very giving and very friendly," Hall says. "We've had a great time. We got to see some local musicians play and be able to play with them — and man, cats here are really [good]."

It wasn't always easy for American musicians to come to Cuba. But things began to loosen up at the end of 2014 when President Obama announced that the U.S. would resume diplomatic relations with Cuba. The Trump administration reversed some of the Obama policies, but it's still possible for individuals to come to Cuba. "This is smoke-and-mirrors from the Trump administration," says writer Ned Sublette, author of "Cuba and Its Music": "They got rid of one thing, which was individual [travel], which was the way the Obama administration put Cuba travel on the honor system. Well, you can't do that, you're not supposed to come for sun-and-beach tourism, but you can come to Cuba. For any musician coming to Cuba, its 'professional research.'"

Tenor saxophonist Joe Lovano was another of the Americans who came here this year. He played a set of ballads with the renowned Amadeo Roldán Conservatory Symphony Orchestra. Lovano first played at the festival in 1986, with Charlie Haden's Liberation Music Orchestra. In 2003, Lovano returned with his own band. He says Cuban music and jazz have been together for decades:

"That's because of the influences of the amazing masters that came to the States in the '30s and '40s from Cuba, and did collaborations with Dizzy Gillespie and Charlie Parker. There was some amazing music that was put together with the spirit of the life of the people."

The Cuban government is even welcoming expatriate musicians. Cuban bassist Yunior Terry is playing at the festival for the first time, performing with his older brother's group, Yosvany Terry Quintet. The brothers left Cuba for New York 20 years ago. Yunior says in addition to playing at a couple of the festival's major venues, this return to Havana is all the more meaningful because he and Yosvany performed at their alma mater, the National School of the Arts:

"We've been having a blast, sharing our experiences and bringing a little bit of the knowledge we have acquired through all these years. And it's always so great to give back and see so many young people so hungry for information. They heard us on record for many many years, but they've never seen us play before live, so this is a great opportunity and we're so happy to be here doing this."

The festival is organized by the National Center of Popular Music. Cuban dance music has been a key component of the festival since the beginning. One of this year's revelations was the 40-year-old singer Alain Pérez and His Orchestra. Pérez, who's played bass with major music figures, including pianist Chucho Valdés, singer Celia Cruz and flamenco giant Paco de Lucía, returned to Cuba a couple years ago from Spain and launched his solo career. Pérez says all the years he spent abroad have enriched his approach to music-making: "It's a different way of feeling, a much more open way to express — more sincere, more natural, closer to the public. But very Cuban, with all the jazz and folk music influences." Ned Sublette first came here in 1990 and organizes trips for his Cuban music seminars on the island. He says it was quite an intense festival back then: "It was overwhelming! And I had kind of forgotten what this kind of musical orgy feels like, even though I go to a lot of festivals. This is like my Spotify playlist has come to life! Coming to Cuba and immersing yourself in the music is an experience that transforms you."

Yunior and Yosvany Terry at Fábrica de Arte Cubano during Jazz Plaza Fest | Photo by Betto Arcos

CUBAN MUSICIANS in LOS ANGELES

Over the past decade, Los Angeles has seen a steady arrival of Cuban musicians who've integrated into the salsa and Cuban music scene. Many of these musicians play in multiple bands across the LA area. Their presence has enriched the music community, and helped turned LA into a powerhouse of Latin music.

Calixto Oviedo and Lily Hernández are a husband-and-wife Cuban music team. He's a percussionist, she's a singer, and together they play in no less than 10 Cuban and salsa bands, including three of their own. I caught them on a Saturday night, playing with their group Son Sabroso Quartet at the Madre Restaurant in Torrance. Oviedo and Hernández moved to LA from Denver, five years ago. Hernández says they're very happy they moved here: "At the beginning, when we were in Europe, we were thinking about Miami and everybody was, 'no, you're crazy, Miami no, you're going to be one more, one more Cuban. But you know, the destiny says, no, no, no. No Miami. Denver and then LA." In addition to the bands, Oviedo teaches drums and percussion at Cal State LA's Music Department. Oviedo says, LA has given them and other Cuban musicians many opportunities to find work: "Our work in Los Angeles is well respected and, modestly speaking, we are in great demand and that's comforting and feels good."

The nine-piece band La Charanga Cubana plays every Saturday at The Palms Restaurant in Downey. That's where I talked to Denis Medina who plays "tres" guitar — an essential instrument in traditional Cuban music. He moved to LA in 2015 and says now he plays with five different Cuban and salsa bands: "I learned about the music scene through Facebook, and started to look for bands, and found out there was also Cuban music in LA. That's how I found La Charanga Cubana," whose director is Edgar Hernández. He founded the group in 1997 and was nominated for a Latin Grammy in 2007. Hernández says when he first arrived in LA from Mexico in the mid-1990s, Cuban bands were almost non-existent. He says a lot has changed since then: "Now I can see a lot of movement of Cuban music in the area and appreciate it, because that's what I've been fighting for, from the beginning, and I'm finally seeing the fruits today. The doors opened and now I see that something beautiful is happening."

Guido Herrera is one of the hosts of the weekend program "Alma del Barrio" on KXLU, and a salsa and Cuban music promoter. He says it's clear why musicians come to LA:

"Why do immigrants move to another place? They will never have the opportunities that they will see in countries like these in their own places. That's the basics of the immigration wave. And I think that one musician came to Los Angeles, whoever that was and then his friend — I assume that one came and the other came behind him, and we have a great group of young musicians from Cuba in Los Angeles."

A couple weeks ago, I went to see five Cuban musicians who were jamming at the home of trumpet player Leider Chappotín. Bass player Azaris Manuel moved to LA five years ago, after living 15 years in Milan, Italy. He currently plays in five Cuban and salsa bands. He says, over the past 60 years, Cuban music has suffered from isolation dueto the U.S. embargo: "For a long time, Cuban music has been marginalized. Cuban music is vast, with many genres and types of music and now it's time to bring all that music back."

I went to see Calixto Oviedo and Lily Hernández & Orquesta at "El Floridita" in Hollywood. They played a set of all kinds of Cuban dance music — son, cha-cha-cha and timba, which is a more complex style of Cuban dance music combining rumba and son with funk. Oviedo, who is one of the creators of the timba sound, says that even with a bigger presence of Cuban musicians in LA, the music has yet to be fully embraced by club owners and promoters who still prefer the more traditional salsa — music made famous by singers like Celia Cruz. "It's difficult to play Cuban music because there are still a lot of taboos. They say, 'Don't play timba, play salsa.' And what is salsa? What are we talking about? What did Celia Cruz sing, 'La Sopita en Botella,' 'Cúcala' — Cuban tunes written by Cubans and performed by a Cuban."

But he says he's been able to prove that there is an appetite for something different: "When our band plays at El Floridita or The Granada — which is a tough venue, where people go dance to Celia Cruz, Cheo Feliciano and Marc Anthony — and we play timba, people go wild, and they shout at Lily, another one!" Salsa and Cuban music promoter Guido Herrera says dancers will ultimately have the final word: "They have to do what the public wants and the public wants to dance here in Los Angeles. But when they start creating their own music and their own sound, yes definitely will enrich what we already have, that's for sure."

The word is out that Cuban music is alive and thriving in LA. Percussionist Calixto Oviedo says his music friends in New York have commented on the vibrant Latin music scene here: "Los Angeles has turned into a very big place for Latin music. The city of music was always New York, and it will always be. But LA is now the competition. Truly, LA is now in competition with any city in the U.S."

Today in the LA area, there are up to 20 Cuban bands and more than 30 salsa bands. It's fair to say Los Angeles can give New York a run for its money.

Cuban musicians in Los Angeles. From left to right: Denis Medina, Chalo Chomat, Leider Chappotín, Santiago Santiuste, and Azaris Pijuán | Photo by Betto Arcos

ALFREDO RODRÍGUEZ

Alfredo Rodríguez was a relatively unknown jazz pianist when legendary producer Quincy Jones spotted him at a gig. A month later Rodríguez got a call and was told Quincy Jones would like to produce his first album.

When Alfredo Rodríguez enrolled in music school in Havana at the age of seven, he wanted to learn how to play the drums. But they told him he had to choose piano or violin: "I chose piano, thinking that I was going to change to percussion at 10 years old, but at 10 years old I was completely falling in love with the sound of the piano and I didn't change." When he was 14, his uncle gave him a CD of Keith Jarrett's legendary Koln Concert. Rodríguez says that was it for him: "I used to play just classical music at that time, and after that CD, I think that CD kind of changed my life because I found the improvisation. I said to myself, that was what I wanted to do with my life, since that moment."

Rodríguez is the son of a popular Cuban TV entertainer and singer of the same name. He started playing in his father's band when he was 14. He went on to graduate from the renowned Amadeo Roldán Music Conservatory. In 2006, Rodríguez was offered a spot at the Montreux Jazz Festival in Switzerland. One night, the Festival's director invited him to play at his house. That's where Rodríguez met Quincy Jones: "And I remember I played a Cole Porter song which is called 'I Love You.' That was how I met Quincy and Quincy was very happy to listen to my music at the time. So I just took that experience as something positive in my life. I had the opportunity to play one song for Quincy Jones."

And Quincy Jones remembers when he heard Rodríguez: "He blew me away. When we heard him that day, Herbie Hancock says I'm not going anywhere near that." After Montreux, Rodríguez went back to Cuba. A month later he got a call from Quincy Jones Productions offering to produce an album. But to do that he would have to move to the U.S. A few years later, Rodríguez made the difficult decision to go. He traveled first to Mexico where his father was living, but when he tried to cross the border into the U.S. he was arrested by Mexican border patrol officers:

"I had to speak with them three or four hours, about my situation about why I was coming to the United States, literally told them the truth, to meet Mr. Quincy Jones and to play my music, that it was something very positive in my life. And after four hours of speaking they understood whatever I was trying to tell them and they let me go to the border. So I took a cab, and took me like 15 minutes and I crossed the border."

So, on his first week in the U.S. he wrote the piece "Crossing the Border," which reflects all the stress of that experience. With his debut recording called "Sounds of Space," produced by Quincy Jones, Alfredo Rodríguez is now on a constant worldwide tour, waiting for the next surprise.

Alfredo Rodríguez | Photo by Anna Webber

RUMBANKETE

In the early 1990s, "Timba," a new style of dance music from Cuba, began to make its way around the world. Unlike salsa, timba has not taken root in LA. But that might change soon thanks to Rumbankete, an LA band specializing in original timba. To understand the difference between salsa and timba, you have to listen to both styles. Rumbankete percussionist Alberto López says Timba is a more complex dance music. "Timba is kind of like an updated version of salsa but with more folkloric elements and a richer base to draw upon." Trombonist Jim Miller says timba breaks down the barriers between the dancer and the band. "I feel it's more like a connection between the audience and the musicians, rather than dancers and a jukebox."

Rumbankete was founded in 2004. In the beginning, the band was kind of like a jukebox, a salsa cover band. They played music by Eddie Palmieri's band La Perfecta, Manny Oquendo's Libre and other groups from the 1970s and 1980s. Then in 2009, when Cuban singers Gonzalo Chomat and Iris Cepeda joined the band, they decided to record and play only their own original timba compositions. In the past few years, Rumbankete has been playing for large crowds at the Music Center's Dance Downtown series and more recently at Union Station, drawing hundreds of dancers. But playing original timba in Los Angeles has its challenges. It's hard for the band to get gigs at the local salsa clubs. Why? Singer Gonzalo Chomat says it's all about economics.

"The club owners don't understand what this music is about. What they understand is that they want to see their 500, 200, 60 people dancing salsa. It doesn't matter if it's from 1932. It doesn't matter." Percussionist Alberto Lopez has a simple theory to explain why Timba has not taken root in LA — because people don't know how to dance to it. "Timba is something that came out specifically out of Cuban dancers. Cuban audiences that danced a certain way, that asked for music to be played a certain way, so that they could move in a certain way and they invented a whole language of movement that doesn't exist here."

But maybe things are beginning to change. Singer Iris Cepeda says, in the past couple of years, she's been noticing a difference in the way people are dancing to their music. "I've been seeing a lot of groups of salsa dancers that have become timba dancers. Yeah, actually, they were like just salsa, one, two, three, four, five, six, seven, eight." Lopez says it's been happening naturally. "They're already hooked and they don't even know it. They're already moving their hips in a different way — they're doing all this stuff and they're like "oh my God." But then, that's our aim. Musically, we aim to create that transition for the dancers, from a regular salsa thing, to where they can feel good while their dancing timba." That's Rumbankete's mission: to create a more nuanced musical language for salsa dancers, so they'll be inspired to try out a little timba.

Rumbankete | Photo courtesy of the band

DAYRAMIR GONZÁLEZ

Pianist Dayramir González is the first Cuban national to receive the prestigious presidential scholarship from the Berklee School of Music in Boston. He's a rising star with humble beginnings and a solid music education.

On a recent weeknight, in a small club tucked inside a shopping mall in the Los Angeles neighborhood of Woodland Hills, Dayramir González and his trio opened their first set with an intense Afro-Cuban tune. The room of about 50 people responded with excitement. Most of the audience didn't know much about González, after all this was the first time he'd played this club. But they learned one thing: he's an extremely talented musician.

Dayramir González grew up in one of Havana's poorest neighborhoods, El Cerro. His father played trumpet in the legendary dance band Conjunto Rumbavana. González remembers vividly when the group would rehearse at his home. He was 10 years old: "Like sitting, watching the chart of the piano, and seeing the mapping: ok, you come introduction, repeat it four times, go to A, B, from B go to Coda, Coda repeat here, and then Montuno. On cue, this! Check out how to be aware of the cue of the leader. All of that, see, no one can teach you that, unless you experience it yourself, first hand!" When González was in eighth grade he wrote his first composition: *Mi salsa blue, mi salsa blue, tiene su swing y su onda cubana, mi salsa blue.* "Very simple but I already had that inclination."

That talent did not go unnoticed. In 2001, at age 16, González got his first big break. Oscar Valdés, a member of the renowned band Irakere, invited him to join his group, Diákara. After playing with Diákara for three years, González joined a band led by another major figure, Giraldo Piloto. González says he learned from both Valdés and Piloto how to be a leader and how to work with musicians: "How to handle when you're on the stage and having 16 members and you have to be very strong to give cue, very clear direction with enough time, this stuff that you have to learn, since I was very inclining to be a leader myself, I was learning from the maestros quietly." Then in 2008, González got a call to play in one of Cuba's top dance bands, Habana D'Primera. The concept behind this band was to assemble all the top in-demand musicians: "The top of the top. So everybody was fighting to have a spot, hahahaha! And I got it!"

While he was on tour in Europe with Habana D'Primera, González got an email from a music publishing company:

they were awarding one million dollars to support seven presidential scholarships at Berklee College of Music in Boston: "But, 'un negrito del Cerro' (a Black guy from Cerro). This is not going to happen." In February 2010, González and seven other Cuban musicians were selected to audition in Mexico City. He was among hundreds of applicants, vying for one of the seven scholarships. To prepare for the audition, González practiced something he learned from Tony Pérez, a Cuban pianist he once saw in concert in Havana. He noticed that during the concert, Perez took out a pen from his pocket and started tapping the Cuban Clave on top of the piano, with his left hand:

> "And then with the right hand, improvising … pah, pah, pah, poom, poom … super virtuoso with a lot of counterpoint, with a lot of rumba, quinto thing! I said, Wow, people went like Woooow! Watch that, watch that, watch that!!! I practiced that for two weeks, no stopping, because I wanted to bring that special thing to the Berklee audition."

González says that hard work paid off. He got the scholarship. "I became the first Cuban national in the entire country, Cuban national living in Havana to ever attend to Berklee."

The three years he spent studying at Berklee, plus all those years playing with some of the top Cuban bands are reflected in his U.S. debut recording, "The Grand Concourse." The album was released last June on a small label, Machat Records. González says he didn't want to present himself as only a piano player. He wants to show the world what Cuban music is today: "Cuba is a palate of classical with strong Yoruba traditions, with Conga Santiaguera, with cha-cha-cha, with danzón, with timba, with funk, with R&B, with jazz harmonies, with blues."

But González says, being a Cuban musician and composing Cuban music also encompasses many other things: "With politics, with Fidel Castro, with being hungry, with being resilient, with being 'I want to get out of Cuba, I cannot leave Cuba, I wish I could leave Cuba to see something.'" After attending the Berklee program, González has remained in the U.S. But he insists that he didn't defect — he says he's here for the sake of his career. He currently lives in New York, but he has family in Los Angeles and says he plans to move here within a year. Dayramir González is living the title of this song from his album "Moving Forward."

Dayramir González | Photo courtesy of the artist

SAN MIGUEL

A few years ago, a musician named San Miguel Pérez came to the U.S. from Cuba, hoping to advance his career as a guitarist. He was a sideman in Havana, but he had dreams of recording a solo album of his own songs. He always thought about making his first record with a traditional Cuban trio. Five years ago, that's as far as his vision could go. But now, he says he surpassed those expectations, and he believes it's all part of living in Los Angeles.

San Miguel hails from Río Cauto, a small town in the eastern Cuban province of Granma. He began playing music at age 9 — first, classical guitar. Then at 14, he started playing another instrument called the tres — a guitar of three double-steel strings. At 18, San Miguel moved to Havana to attend Cuba's top conservatory, Instituto Superior de Arte, to specialize in classical tres. He learned to play all the classical styles, from baroque to romantic music. In addition to his 13 years of classical music training, San Miguel also carries the roots of his hometown, a style called nengón, grandfather of the style known as son. "That's the music of my land," he says, "nengón, son and guaracha."

After graduating from the conservatory, San Miguel began working in Havana as a sideman. He received a couple of music awards and played with several bands, including the renowned orchestra Adalberto Alvarez y Su Son. In 2010, San Miguel got a call from a friend who was coordinating the production of an album for a singer who needed someone who could play the tres. Los Angeles-based singer Cecilia Noël was recording "Havana Rocks," an album of '80s pop hits arranged as Cuban dance tunes. She recalls: "They said, 'We have the perfect guy for you, and he's a young tresero.' They called him and I met him at the session. And I remember the first time, it was like, Wow! — that sound carried me, this is exactly how I wanted my album to sound."

Noël finished mixing the album in LA. When she returned to Havana she found out that San Miguel had moved to Florida. She called and asked him to join her band. "And he said, 'Absolutely!' I sent him the music and he learned every single note — everything, no papers, nothing.He came back and he played the show and everyone was, Ahhhhh, woooooow! And then, of course, Colin met him."

Noël introduced San Miguel to Colin Hay, founder of the band, Men At Work. Hay says when San Miguel first came to his recording studio in Topanga, he brought a song called "Lluvia." "He played the song perfectly. Very few people play the song and you don't have to go back and do it again or you don't have to fix anything, it's just a rarity." Hay says it's also unusual to find a musician who has all the skills, a novice songwriter whose songs have a structure: "Very rarely do you have somebody who's just embarking in what I would call that 'period of ascension,' where you're taking off, where mostly you do your best work, when you're almost ready. 'Cause when you're ready, you're a bit too sure of yourself. It's like if you're on a plane, the most exciting part is when you're taking off. Once you're there, you're like, Oh well, here we are."

San Miguel says, 10 years ago, when he was back in Cuba, he never imagined he'd record a song like "Un poquito de amor everyday" — mixing Spanish and English, and going for a pop sound in his music. San Miguel says he's a tres player first and a singer-songwriter second. As a tres player, he wants to make sure not to lose his Cuban roots and the instrument's identity. He says: "If you don't strengthen your roots and stay tight, you can easily get diluted." San Miguel wants to keep the natural quality of the instrument at a high level and respect the identity of Cuban music. If his debut album is any indication, that should not be difficult to accomplish.

San Miguel and his Tres | Photo by Vecc Schiafino

SILVIO RODRÍGUEZ

The poetry and politics of his lyrics have inspired generations across Latin America. His unwavering support of the Cuban Revolution has also drawn intense criticism from the Cuban exile community. Now Silvio Rodríguez has released an album that's both personal and political. It's called "Para la espera."

Silvio Rodríguez was 12 when the Cuban Revolution overthrew the country's dictatorship. Social activism has always been part of his songs. For the past 10 years, Rodríguez has been performing free concerts in some of the poorest neighborhoods of Cuba, in what he calls his Endless Tour:

> "That spirit of sharing culture comes from my generation of troubadours. We used to go sing everywhere: factories, schools, barrios and prisons. The Endless Tour started when a policeman knocked on my door inviting me to the barrio he cared for, 'La corbata' (The Necktie). We continued doing it and we've done 108 concerts."

His generation came together in 1967 to form a movement called "La Nueva Trova Cubana," The New Cuban Troubadours. Like the song "Ojalá," their lyrics dealt with all of the aspects of being in a relationship: love and pain, joy and sadness. Rodríguez says his songs should explain themselves. "Many times they're sudden feelings that create songs, words just come to me in a moment, and that's why it's hard to explain them." The song "La Maza" is a declaration of principles for being an artist. Fifty-year-old Kelvis Ochoa is part of the generation that came after Silvio Rodríguez. He says, the older singer is a hard act to follow. "He's one of the great Latin American poets. He's written so many songs, many of them are sooo good. It's overwhelming — it's way beyond our reach."

Singer and composer David Byrne and his partner licensed Cuban music in the early 1990s and released it on their label Luaka Bop — including a collection of 12 songs Byrne selected from Rodríguez's albums:

"Silvio's lyrics are sometimes very impressionist, sometimes abstract, and of course, no surprise, sometimes political. What really shocked me was that Silvio, despite being as popular as he is in Latin America, had never had a greatest hits record. Maybe he thought this was a kind of crass thing, and he thought the kind of commercial thing that only North Americans would do, but he'd never done it. But he agreed to do it with us. I think he might have been thinking that, and rightly, that we were going to introduce him to an audience that otherwise may not have heard his music, and there's some truth to that."

The album became their biggest seller.

Over the last 50 years, Rodríguez has recorded 24 albums. Before the pandemic, he was working on a new one with a large group of musicians. But he had to shut down the production. He decided to bring back the troubadour, after seeing what others were doing online: "I started seeing messages, songs, even concerts on the internet, so I thought about taking some of the songs I've already composed — which were not in the other record I was working on — and I began to organize the material and offer it to people, as a way to help them cope during the pandemic." Rodríguez says the title of his new album, "Para la Espera," alludes to the uncertainty of the pandemic and to the nearly two-decade wait for the release of the Cuban Five, intelligence officers arrested in the U.S. who become national heroes.

Rodríguez has always been an outspoken defender of the Cuban Revolution and a critic of the U.S. embargo. But he says he tries to look to the future. "I'm a man of hope. I'm a man who believes in the future, above all because I'm from this country and because we have this people. We're not perfect, but we're combative and hopeful. I'm part of all of this." And his music has been part of the soundtrack of life in Cuba and throughout Latin America for more than 50 years.

Silvio Rodríguez at a concert in Havana | Photo by Gabriel Guerra Bianchini, courtesy of Ojalá

ADVERSITY

NELLA

The 2019 Latin Grammys are set to take place on November 14. As a nominee in the category of Best New Artist, Venezuelan artist Nella knows she not only carries her own story, but also that of her homeland to the ceremony when she attends.

Nella was born Marianella Rojas in the beach town of Porlamar, on the Island of Margarita, the largest Venezuelan island in the Caribbean, and grew up singing American pop music: "I grew up listening to all the divas — Christina Aguilera, Celine Dion, Mariah Carey, you name it, all of them," Nella says. "I would lock myself in the room from like 3 p.m. until 9 p.m. and just sing." After graduating from high school in 2007, Nella moved to Caracas to study communications and music. Then, she applied to the Berklee College of Music in Boston, a pressure-cooker environment for singers.

"In Berklee there are 4,000 students. One thousand of them are singers," Berklee faculty member Javier Limón says. As a Spanish guitarist, composer and producer who has worked with some of the biggest names in flamenco, Limón saw something special in Nella when he first heard her at the college:

"In my opinion, the most valuable thing is the uniqueness, to be unique. Everybody sings amazing — perfect tune, perfect rhythm, perfect technique, whatever you want, any style. But to be original, to be different, to be someone special, that's what Nella had, and that's what she is now."

Two years ago, Limón was hired to compose music for Iranian director Asghar Farhadi's film "Everybody Knows" starring Javier Bardem and Penélope Cruz. Limón emailed Farhadi a link to a video of him and Nella singing the song "Fin de Fiesta." Farhadi loved the song and asked to hear Nella sing it over the phone. "So I did this song, and next thing I received a message saying that I had to go to Madrid, to not only record the songs of the movie but to also be part of this movie," Nella says.

This opportunity led to Nella's debut album "Voy," which was produced by Limón. One of the album's highlights is "Volveré a Mi Tierra," in which Nella touches on the humanitarian crisis affecting her homeland of Venezuela. Limón emailed Nella some lyric ideas for the song after reading a newspaper article about it. "I just started crying," Nella says. "And in the middle of all of this I told him, you know what, we should put music to this."

The song's lyrics translate to "I will return to my homeland. Venezuela is great, beloved and eternal. I will return to my homeland, to sing to the sea and its full moon, I will return to my homeland where my people are brave and awakened."

To capture the widespread impact of the crisis, Nella and Limón shot a video for "Volveré a Mi Tierra" full of the faces of Venezuelans around the world. As she heads to the Latin Grammys next month, Nella wants her music to be the voice of Venezuelans who hope for a better future for their country. "Sometimes people complain that, 'You don't care about Venezuela, you're not posting things about Venezuela,'" Nella says. "I don't need to post these things to make people know that I love my country and that I would love to go back one day."

Nella | Photo by Samantha López

MALAWI MOUSE BOYS

Malawi is a small, landlocked country in southeast Africa, one of the continent's least developed, the population mostly rural and agricultural. But over the past two years, some of its music has begun to reach the wider world, thanks in part to the efforts of Ian Brennan. Three years ago, the San Francisco-based producer set up a portable studio to record a group of gospel singers called the Malawi Mouse Boys. This year, he brought the musicians to the U.S.

The group took its name from the job the members had when Brennan found them, while driving the backroads of southeastern Malawi. "In that little stretch of freeway where they live, there's a tradition where they sell mice on a stick, as snacks, meals to the passing travelers," Brennan says. "And it's quite a labor-intensive task. It requires that they get up before dawn and hunt the mice. And their primary competitor for the mice are wild boars and black mamba snakes, so it can be quite dangerous." Brennan set up his gear near the road where they were working and asked one of them, Alfred Gavana, to play and sing. Brennan remembers:

> "And he played it so quietly it was almost inaudible. But when he came to the chorus, this group of 20 kids that was pressing in, from age 2, to age 18 or so, all kicked in on the chorus in multi-part harmony. And the sun was literally going down, with surround sound and one of the most musical moments I'd ever had in my life." After they recorded that first song, Brennan asked Gavana to invite other musicians to a session in his village a few days later. Brennan spent all day there, eventually zeroing in on a core group.

The Malawi Mouse Boys grew up singing in the village church, where Sunday services stretch for hours. When Brennan recorded them in May of 2011, the four members were in their mid to late 20s. Lead singer Zondiwe says from the get-go, the group had no real expectations. Foreigners had come through before expressing interest but never followed through. "But Ian, it's not like that," Zondiwe says, singer and percussionist Joseph Nekwankwe providing translation. "He came back and said 'OK, I recorded your songs. Here's your profit.'"

The Malawi Mouse Boys make their own instruments. Their four-string guitar was built with sheet metal and tree limbs. They use plastic water coolers and bicycle spokes for percussion. But Brennan says the instruments are secondary:

> "Their voices are really the core. They have such a unity that I think it's very similar to the Carter Family or The Jackson 5, where it's familial. They've been singing together their whole lives, people that have developed their voices literally together, that have learned to listen together, have opened their ears to each other and with each other."

Getting their voices heard became a mission for Brennan. First he got the album released on a British label. "That no record had ever been released in any substantial way, given a real fair chance in the world, is so absurd when you think about the tens of thousands, hundreds of thousands, maybe even millions, of records that come out of Los Angeles and New York and London — predominantly, mostly, in English," Brennan says.

Last year, he took the Malawi Mouse Boys to England to perform at the WOMAD Festival. It was their first trip outside their country, and they sang in their native Chichewa language to an audience of more than 10,000. They also recorded a second album. Nekwankwe says it's a miracle they've come this far. "Maybe we can say it's a plan of God," he says. "Because to us, to reach where we are now, using these local instruments, it's not a joke. In our country in Malawi, we have got many people who are using electric guitars and instruments, but they didn't reach America." Next year, they'll travel to Australia for the 2015 WOMAD Festival. And they hope to come back to the U.S.

Malawi Mouse Boys performing at McCabe's Guitar Shop in Santa Monica, California | Photo by Betto Arcos

COLOMBIAN MUSIC AND PEACE

This Sunday, Colombians will be voting on the peace agreement that was just signed by the government and the FARC guerrillas to end 50 years of war. I was in Colombia attending the annual music industry festival known as Bogotá Music Market or BOMM. I talked to young musicians about the prospect of peace and what it means to those who never knew a time when Colombia wasn't at war.

The Bogotá Music Market opened with a roar of sound from the electropical hip-hop band Systema Solar. This annual gathering was held during an emotional period for Colombia. The peace agreement and the vote coming up on October 2 were on everyone's mind. This is a very tense time. People going towards the Yes, people going towards the No.

Daniel Restrepo is in the Yes camp. He leads a jazz band called "FATSO":

"I'm more towards the 'if there's any possibility of no one getting killed anymore,' then I go towards the Yes. I'm not sure if it's going to work — I have my doubts, sometimes. It's been a long war, so there's a whole bunch of people who have been in it since they were kids, so it's very difficult. But I think if there's any chance of starting that peace process, it's very important. This time is awesome, I hope everything goes well."

Singer Maria Mulata is on the Yes side too. She's from the province of Santander, one of the regions that suffered so much during the war. When she was 6 years old, she wrote her first song, "Quiero Paz" (I Want Peace). "And it was a children's song, that said 'I want for peace to be in the world, you and I, let's play, but let's not play evil.' It was one of the songs on my first album that I recorded with my brother. And it's because we've never known peace."

At a concert called "Viche Por La Paz" (Hooch for Peace), hundreds of young people dance to the music of Canalón de Timbiquí, a traditional Afro-Colombian ensemble from the Pacific coast. Singer Nidia Góngora is the band's director. She says the Pacific coast of Colombia has also suffered a lot from the war, but she believes there's a lot of work to be done beyond the peace agreement. "Colombia is a country with a vast inequality, and as long as there's hunger, lack of education, and a [poor] health system for those least favored, and as long as the sons and daughters of the poor continue to be the bait of the war, the conflict will not end."

The issue of what happens after a peace deal is signed is something Stuart Bailie knows about. He's a co-founder of the "Oh Yeah" Music Centre in Belfast and was in Bogotá giving a talk about "Music, Conflict and Post-Conflict in Northern Ireland." Bailie says music played an important part during the '70s and '80s when the conflict in Northern Ireland was at its worst:

"We had a very lively punk scene which was very rebellious, which more or less told people to ignore the two traditions and 'find your own alternative Ulster,' to use a phrase from the band Stiff Little Fingers. So music kind of liberated my generation, it liberated our minds. And also a very famous moment in May 1998, which was three days before the referendum vote. And the vote was a little bit shaky. There was a very hastily put together gig, featuring U2 and a local Irish act from Northern Ireland, an act called Asch. And on that night, Bono got the two political leaders of the time, Trimble and Hume, to shake hands and that message went right around the world and that swung the vote in favor of Yes by 2%. So music saved the day, I believe, in Northern Ireland."

In Colombia, Bailie says he can feel a qualified optimism. No one is throwing a hat in the air just yet, he says, but people sense that things can and will change for the better:

"I met probably 20-30 individuals who are all working in their own way for the future of Colombia through music and that was very exciting and that was very good for my heart. I can't pretend to understand the absolute context of everything that goes on in here. But I just know, my expression is 'music never lets you down, music is always there and it is this incredible catalytic force.'"

Singer and activist Nidia Góngora, leader of the group Canalón de Timbiquí | Photo courtesy of the artist

LEÓN GIECO
AND MUNDO ALAS

León Gieco is one of Argentina's best-known singer-songwriters; he was among the first to fuse rock and folk music. Gieco has a new project called "Mundo Alas." I talked to him during his visit to Los Angeles.

One of León Gieco's biggest hits was the song "Sólo le pido a Dios," it was an anthem for millions of people in Latin America during the late 1970s and 1980s. This song and many others were censored by Argentina's military dictatorship and Gieco was forced into exile in 1978. He returned in 1981. Over the years, León Gieco has shared the stage with artists he's admired and he's recorded with everyone from Pete Seeger to Mercedes Sosa.

But Mundo Alas is a different kind of collaboration. Gieco led a tour of disabled musicians, dancers and painters throughout Argentina's provinces. Gieco organized the sold-out tour and co-directed a documentary about it. He also produced the soundtrack.

One of the artists is Pancho Chévez, a singer-songwriter who was born without arms and legs. He inspired Gieco to organize the tour when they played together at the presidential mansion in 2006. "Yo creo que tanto Sebastián (film co-director) como yo, actuamos solamente de puente." Gieco says his role in the project was to act as a bridge. He was the bridge so the artists could go on stage, then he and his co-directors were the bridge so the artists could be on the film.

One of the key moments during the tour happened when León Gieco wrote the lyrics to a tune by Alejandro Davio, a singer-songwriter born with a neural defect. Gieco recorded the song and they decided to include it at the end of the film: "Cuando yo la grabé, él habló con el técnico de grabación y se llevó la pieza." Gieco says after the recording Davio asked the engineer to give him the tracks so he could do his own version at home. The next day, Davio played the song for them and Gieco said it was much better than the one he recorded, so they ended the film with Davio's version.

"Estar con ellos me produce una especie de tranquilidad." Gieco says, spending time with these artists offers him tranquility and has made him a better person, one with more of an appreciation of life.

León Giego with Alejandro Davio and Pancho Chévez during their tour of Argentina | Photo by Karina Suárez, Magoya Films, Mundo Alas

1. NO ME IMPORTA - 3:05 Trio Zamora (A Zamora Rico)

2. VACILON - 5:22 Trio Zamora (Rosendo Ruiz Quevedo)

3. CHINITA - 3:02 Trio Zamora (D.R.)

4. UN LAMENTO EN LAS TINIEBLAS - 2:18 Trio Zamora (Marcelino Guerro

5. LA ULTIMA NOCHE - 3:00 Trio Melodicos (Bobby Collazo)

6. GAVIOTAS QUE PASAN - 3:59 Trio Melodicos (D.R.)

7. PIENSALO BIEN - 2:18 Trio Melodicos (Raul Diaz)

8. EL NEGRITO DEL BATEY - 5:03 Trio Melodicos (Alberto Beltran)

9. ROSA DORMIDA - 3:00 Trio Melodicos (Alexis Brau)

10. COSITA LINDA - 3:08 Trio Melodicos (D.R.)

11. YA ESTAMOS IGUALES - 2:27 Trio Melodicos (Francisco Canaro)

12. EL NEGRO SIMON - 2:41 Trio Melodicos (D.R.)

13. Studio Chatter - 0:25

14. BESAME MUCHO 2:57 Trio Melodicos (Consuelo Velasquez)

15. TRAICION - 2:59 Trio Melodicos (D.R.)

16. PERFIDA - 3:09 Trio Melodicos (Alberto Dominguez)

17. EGOISTA - 2:55 Trio Zamora (D.R.)

18. EL BURRO SACARRON - 2:36 Trio Zamora (Chucho Navarro)

19. ANOCHE SONE CONTIGO - 2:12 Trio Zamora (D.R.)

20. INTERROGACION - 2:39 Trio Zamora (D.R.)

21. EL TELEPHONO - 2:53 Trio Zamora (D.R.)

22. AMOR MIO - 2:32 Trio Zamora (Pepe Jara)

23. GAVILON COLORADO - 3:19 Trio Zamora (D.R.)

24. MI CAFETAL 3:38 - Trio Zamora (Farid Ortiz)

25. MONA LISA - 2:36 Trio Zamora (Livingston, Jay, Evans, Ray)

26. EL BODEGUERO - 2:52 Trio Zamora (Richard Egues)

DEDICATED TO THE MEMORY OF HARRY SCHRAGE

PRODUCED BY HARR
EXECUTIVE PRODUCERS MORRIE SCHRAGE & JIMM
ART/DESIGN BY WENDELL R. WIGGINS - L

Harry Schrage   Morrie Schrage

Recorded in
Mantanzas, Cuba 1958

THE LOST CUBAN TRIOS
OF CASA MARINA

The story of the Lost Cuban Trios of Casa Marina begins in 1939, when the Schrage family left Poland to escape the Nazis. "We got as far as England. And when the bombs started dropping in England, my father thought it was time to get out," says 80-year-old Morrie Schrage a successful car dealer in Los Angeles. "The only place you could get a visa for was Santo Domingo, but the boat stopped in Havana. And we got off the boat and that's how we got to Cuba."

Morrie Schrage and his older brother Harry were teenagers when they arrived in Cuba with their family in 1941. They lived in Matanzas, a couple hours' drive from Havana. Morrie Schrage says his brother was a budding audiophile and loved Cuban music: "He loved good sounds, good music, and when we visited Casa Marina, the trios were strolling among the clients in the nightclub."

Casa Marina was one of the many nightclubs the brothers frequented in the 1950s Havana. Morrie says his brother Harry came up with the plan to record some of the trios they heard on their rounds: "He built a studio in his bedroom in Matanzas, put cork on the walls and that was his studio. He went to Miami to buy the state-of-the-art equipment, the Ampex reel-to-reel and the microphones and all that stuff." Harry persuaded two groups to come to his home studio to record. You can hear Harry in the background on the recording of the bolero called "La última noche": "Ya pueden empezar, OK, ya." You can go ahead and start.

The recordings are a mix of classic boleros, "sones" and Latin American folk songs. They were done in 1958, a year before the Cuban Revolution. In 1959, the Schrage family left Cuba and moved to the U.S. and the tapes went with them. In 1973, Harry Schrage died at the age of 46. The tapes lay in a closet at his widow's house in Seattle. Then a few years ago, she gave the tapes to Morrie: "I knew about them but I didn't think that they would be good enough to do anything with them. So one day I asked Jimmy to listen to them and he liked them, so Jimmy took over."

Jimmy Maslon of the label Ahí Namá Music says the recording is unusual:

> "He recorded these groups directly (to tape), there was no multi-tracks or anything like that — he did directly to the stereo recordings. It's one reason the quality is so nice, it wasn't pointing to one tape and then mixed down to another. These were the exact tapes he recorded to and it's what we mastered on."

Morrie Schrage says the Lost Cuban Trios of Casa Marina is dedicated to his brother Harry. After all, it was his idea to record the music he loved so much.

The songs recorded by Harry Schrage in Matanzas, Cuba, in 1958 | Photo courtesy of Ahí Namá Music

MATEO KINGMAN

Mateo Kingman is a hip-hop artist who grew up in the Ecuadorean Amazon. But he didn't know the depth of his connection to the jungle until he moved to the city. When he was 5 years old, his parents moved the family to a small town deep in the Amazon. They were former leftist guerrillas who went to work with the Shuar Indigenous tribe "to help them fight what's happening there" and create a protected zone, the Condor Mountain Range.

Kingman was home-schooled, and he grew up immersed in the Shuar culture. His daily life was connected to this environment: "Get up, go gather fruits with my brother. In the afternoon, go play in the river with friends, walking and hiking on the Amazon trails." Living surrounded by nature led him to athletics, which later led him to music. Kingman was a runner. He became an accomplished athlete and joined Ecuador's national track-and-field team, competing in the Pan-American Games' 110-meter hurdles.

His athletic training came in handy one day when he found himself in an isolated Shuar village in the middle of the jungle. And had to make his way home. Alone. On a trail he didn't know. Kingman says he got really lost. He took some turns he should not have taken. "For a moment I thought, 'I'll never get out of here,

I don't know how I'm going to get out,'" he says. "I was really scared." He recounts the experience in the song "Sendero del Monte" (Jungle Trail). It's about how the trails can be beautiful but at the same time scary, magical yet unpredictable. At that point, running still meant more to him than music.

But four years ago, Kingman was competing in the track finals to represent Ecuador in the 2012 Olympics when he encountered a challenger he'd never seen before. "This guy had an incredible body, he was a giant. I couldn't believe it — I'd never seen him before. Nobody had beat me in four years in Ecuador." Kingman lost the race. He says his music helped him deal with the disappointment. He says music is one way to let go. It's the mechanism to release all the bad stuff that happens in life.

Kingman was dealing with other changes. He and his family left the Amazon for the capital Quito, and he was in culture shock. He says it took him a while to get used to the rhythm of the city, the people and the climate. But again, music helped him find the way. "I think music can take you through any river," he says. "Like a canoe. It doesn't matter which river, it just takes you along."

Mateo Kingman | Photo by Salvador Hernández & Francisco Rondón

CHÉJERE

Chéjere is an emerging band of musicians based in Mexico City who are taking Mexican roots music to a new global level. After more than a decade of touring and releasing a couple albums of traditional music, the Mexican roots ensemble Chéjere has found their own sound. Their new record is "Ojos de Luna." The opening track "Sobre la marea" builds from a soft ballad to an upbeat, dance-oriented composition. This song is a perfect example the band's rich palette of musical colors. Founder and musical director Alonso Borja says the record took a year to complete, though most of the songs were written and arranged a while back: "Este disco es cien por ciento original, que era una de las metas, los objetivos del proyecto de Chéjere." A completely original album — one of the goals of Chéjere's project:

> "One of our early goals was to record a completely original album. But this meant that we had to open up to a wide array of sounds. That's what makes it difficult to define what kind of music we play. It's a mosaic that reflects the group's identity, not just as Mexicans, but as Latinos in general."

This rich and colorful mosaic is evident in the song "Cocuyo" (Firefly). Borja says one night, he went out walking in the countryside in southern Veracruz and he saw fireflies. He says he was so touched by their beauty, that it inspired him to come up with these verses: *Cocuyo de madrugada / dame un poco de tu luz / para encontrar el camino / que va para Veracruz* (Firefly of dawn / give me a little light / so I can find the roads / that can take me to Veracruz).

Borja says the band also wanted to demonstrate the rich improvisational side of traditional music:

> "When musicians talk about improvisation, the immediate reference is always jazz. But if you don't have that language, traditional music also has a lot of improvisation. They're different languages, but still, it's a very explosive and spontaneous art form. That's what improvisation is all about."

With the current situation of violence in Mexico, Alonso Borja wrote a song specifically addressing it. The song is called "Pa' que se acabe la pena" (So That the Pain Ends). Borja says the band is committed to making music that helps people cope with the climate of despair, at all levels: "And not just physical violence of killing, but poverty and inequality are so widespread. And that is what's most needed right now, are expressions of love toward people, to cherish life."

Chéjere, from left to right: Mariel Henry, Jorge Cortés, Osvaldo Peñaloza, Natalia Cobos, Alonso Borja | Photo by Betto Arcos

CANZONIERE GRECANICO SALENTINO

The band Canzoniere Grecanico Salentino hails from Salento, in the southernmost part of Italy, on the heel of the Italian boot. Canzoniere Grecanico Salentino is modeled after a traditional ensemble from the 1950s called "Orquestrina Terapeutica." This sort of "healing orchestra" — violin, guitar, diatonic accordion and tambourine — traveled around playing music to exorcise the demons of the tarantate, those who had been bitten by a spider. The band would play and the patient would dance until he or she was healed. One traditional song in particular "Pizzica Indiavolata," which gives the title to their new album, was considered the most powerful cure for tarantate. "Today, we play it in a different way, in our own way, with new melodies, with new ideas, but still we want to save the function, the healing, the strong function that 'Pizzica Indiavolata' used to have," bandleader Mauro Durante says.

Durante acknowledges that the phenomenon of tarantismo has died. There are no more victims of the taranta. But there are still demons to exorcise. "There is the economical crisis. It is hard to find a job, it is hard to find your way in the world whenever you feel that you should be really able to express yourself," Durante explains. "And still this music can be a cure, can be a way to dance, sing and play out your own illnesses, your own demons."

In the same way the "orchestrina therapeutica" composed music to heal the tarantate, Mauro Durante composed a song with a similar purpose. It's called "Nu Te Fermare" (Don't Stop). The lyrics say:

> You've graduated, but there's no work, you have a master's, but there's no work and you're left with only your imagination wanting to buy a house, it's agony, wanting a family, it's crazy but if you stop, there's melancholy, get up, find a way, keep on going, don't stop find a way, take a chance, your voice is strong, make it heard.

Durante is well aware that music isn't a terribly practical response to all the ongoing economic problems facing Europe. But still, he says, when people dance they often forget their troubles, if only for a while. And so in that sense, he says the members of Canzoniere Grecanico Salentino consider themselves musical healers for the 21st century.

Canzoniere Grecanico Salentino | Photo by Vincenzo De Pinto

LOS ANGELES MASTER CHORALE

The Los Angeles Master Chorale is one of the country's most acclaimed choirs. For the past month, the ensemble has been touring the world, performing a deeply emotional a cappella masterpiece from the renaissance.

It's a Thursday evening in the city of Guanajuato, Mexico, and day two of the 46th Festival Internacional Cervantino, the biggest and longest-running performing arts festival in the Americas. On stage at the Teatro Juárez — built in the 19th century — the Los Angeles Master Chorale is performing a piece from the high point of the renaissance composed by Orlando Di Lasso, "Lagrime di San Pietro." Michael Lichtenauer, an alto singer with the Los Angeles Master Chorale says this masterpiece is focused on elemental humanity: "I think it's about the beauty and joy and anguish of just being human. And the thing I like about this piece is, instantly it's not people performing and people in the audience. It's just us, trying and living and giving and doing our best on this wild and anguish-filled ride."

The story is centered around one moment from the Bible: the night of the arrest of Jesus, Peter his disciple denies him three times. Associate conductor Jenny Wong says that moment of failure and regret keeps coming back to Saint Peter, even in his old age. She says that's why this piece is universal and speaks to many audiences: "Everyone, every individual, whether in Mexico, or in Los Angeles or in Hong Kong, where I'm from, everyone has had these moments of 'we've made bad decisions,'" whether it's as an individual or as a community. And there are things that we are not proud of, and things that we want to go back and fix. Although this piece is centered on failure, Wong says the resolution is uplifting: "Which means that for all of us, whatever anguish and shame and regret we go through, there is always salvation and there is hope. And that is what this piece I think is about."

"Lagrime di San Pietro" is not your typical choral piece, it's a hybrid of music and theatre. There are 21 singers on stage, acting out their parts. Alto singer Claire Fedoruk says,

"the wonderful aspect of the Master Chorale doing it, is that there is so much musicality we can bring and so many people also have tons of stage experience, but it's really quite much about that idea of bringing all of these different things into one endeavor that really can't be defined because, again, it's so special."

Associate conductor Jenny Wong says for a singing ensemble, renaissance polyphony is one of the highest art forms in vocal music. But she says this music gets often overlooked in programs and people think this music is one-dimensional: "Our job as artists is to bring that and highlight the beauty of that, so that more people can actually find access and relate to this music." To that end, the Master Chorale invited the renowned director Peter Sellars. Jenny Wong says Sellars invites every artist that works with him to dig into their personal life:

"And so when you experience this concert, there is a lot of movement but none of the movement is there so that we look good. Every movement stems from a word, a sentence, that goes back to an emotion. So that means that every singer, all 21 members, and the conductor, has to really dig and be vulnerable and find your own experiences with whatever the music calls for."

This is the first time the Los Angeles Master Chorale performs at the Festival Cervantino. During the performance, there were moments of pause and silence and the sound of the city of Guanajuato could be heard clearly inside the theater. That didn't bother conductor Jenny Wong. She says no music from any time period exists in a vacuum:

"The reason we perform music is that it can continue through history to speak to people, to communicate to people, to help people heal and cope with their shame and anguish. And the fact that we were able to actually perform tonight with our singing while participating with all of these other sounds from the outside world, to me was a very beautiful thing."

Lagrime di San Pietro | Photo by Tao Ruspoli and Marie Noorbergen

SOCIAL UNREST
AND VIOLENCE

EMEL MATHLOUTHI

Singer Emel Mathlouthi has been called "The Voice of the Tunisian Revolution." A video of one of her songs went viral and became an anthem for protesters in her homeland during the December 2010 uprising. She released her debut album in the U.S. last year.

Mathlouthi grew up listening to an eclectic mix of music — from traditional Tunisian songs to her father's record collection. "He was listening to vinyl of European classical music and some jazz and blues, old jazz and old blues from America, like Mahalia Jackson and Jack Dupree," Mathlouthi says. Mathlouthi started performing when she was 15 and joined a band in college. But she says there was no way for a young independent musician, let alone a woman, to get heard in Tunisia. "Because there were no structures, there was no help from the government for music like I was doing," Mathlouthi says. "I couldn't go on TV, I couldn't go to the radio, so I couldn't reach a larger audience."

Mathlouthi didn't help her chances of getting on government-controlled media when she started writing songs against the regime of then president Zine El Abidine Ben Ali. In 2008, she moved to France and began working on the songs for her first album. Mathlouthi says she was writing a lot of political songs like "Dhalem" (Tyrant), but nothing was happening in Tunisia:

> "I was posting my songs on the social media, and I was trying to reach a larger audience, especially in Tunisia, so I can talk to them, and I can give them all my strength. But I felt, from time to time — like everyone and every artist — I was desperate, and I was saying, so the dictatorship is growing and I am here, like, writing songs, and so what?"

Then, she remembered a poem by the Palestinian writer Mahmoud Darwish called "There Is on This Land What Is Worth Living." "I realize that that was the power," Mathlouthi says. "The power is to write songs, because the songs are eternal; the melodies will be here like witnesses. But the dictatorship and the persons will go, and this is why I wrote this song."

In the summer of 2007, at the iconic Place de la Bastille in Paris, where the French Revolution began, Mathlouthi sang "Kelmti Horra" (My Word Is Free) to an audience of tens of thousands. A video of the performance reached Tunisia and resonated with protesters in the streets. "She has so much courage to sing that around that time," says MC Rai, a 35-year-old Tunisian singer and composer based in San Francisco. "When the dictators in Tunisia, the old regime, were in the top of their power — and for her to even have the courage to sing that, when she was living still between France and Tunisia — I thought she really was a true artist, because that's what the art is about." Four years later, Mathlouthi returned to the streets of Tunis to sing "Kelmti Horra" just hours before President Ben Ali fled the country.

The last song on Mathlouthi's album is called "Yezzi" (Enough). It begins with a simple folk melody and unfolds into three cinematic images. In the first part, Mathlouthi sampled sounds of the Arab Spring street protests. The second part includes the last speech by the deposed Tunisian president. And the third part begins with an announcement of the resignation of Egypt's President Hosni Mubarak. The chorus says, "Freedom is in the street / Freedom is in the countryside / Not inside your house." "And I think it still can talk to Arab governments because we are not seeing so much changes, not really," says Mathlouthi. "We made revolutions, but maybe we are welcoming a new dictator, so we don't know."

Still, Mathlouthi has hope for the region. In her song "The Road Is Long," she sings: *My country stands above all tyrants and oppression / and despite the long road ahead / My heart will forever shelter / a love of freedom.*

Emel Mathlouthi | Photo by Ebru Yildiz

ARTURO MÁRQUEZ

Salón Los Ángeles is the oldest dance hall in Mexico City. The classic 1930s ballroom is located in a working-class neighborhood near downtown. nd every week, it sees dozens of well-dressed couples of all ages moving to an orchestra of saxophones, trumpets, trombones, clarinets and percussion instruments. The music is called danzón, and it was born in Cuba in the late 1800s. By early in the next century, it had couples gliding in set patterns in a kind of formal square dance. It was huge. But, like popular music in every era, danzón was eventually replaced by more modern styles. In Mexico, however, danzón is still a popular ballroom dance in cities across the country.

Composer Arturo Márquez caught the danzón bug when he started going to a Mexico City dance hall in the early 1990s. He says:

> "And that's where I really learned the way they play, the danzón sounds, the rhythms, the melodies, more or less the harmonies. And especially the connection between the dance and the music, which is very strong. I think it's one of the dances that the dance, the music, really goes together, all the time. It's like a marriage."

This kind of music and dance atmosphere inspired Márquez to compose not one, but a series of eight danzones for orchestra. "It allowed me to go into the symphonic world, into the classical world — I wouldn't say easily, but with a very natural sense," Márquez says.

Arturo Márquez was born in the northern state of Sonora. The family eventually moved to Los Angeles, where Márquez took up violin and later piano in high school. He eventually received a Fulbright scholarship to study composition with Morton Subotnick and James

Newton at the California Institute of the Arts. But Márquez did not follow their musical path, says Aurelio Tello, a Peruvian composer and researcher based in Mexico City. "Marquez signed the new epoch in music in Mexico because he refused the avant-garde style," Tello says. "When he presented Danzón No. 2, the avant-garde style was finished." Tello has written extensively about classical music in Latin America, as well as about Márquez's work. He says when Danzón No. 2 premiered in 1994 in Mexico City, the audience reaction was intense. "The audience was shouting, and for five or six minutes, the audience was clapping," Tello says. "It was amazing. I don't remember, never, in 30 years, 32 years that I'm living in Mexico, a similar occasion, a similar perception, a similar situation. The public was impressed with danzón."

Danzón No. 2 has been performed by orchestras around the world. Superstar Venezuelan conductor Gustavo Dudamel, who leads the Los Angeles Philharmonic, makes Márquez's music a regular part of his concerts. Márquez wrote Danzón No. 2 in early 1994. But he wasn't trying to conjure a bygone era so much as respond to the social and political upheaval around him, particularly the Zapatista Chiapas uprising against the Mexican government. "The social life around you really influences you, no? So that's what happened in Danzón No. 2," Márquez says. "Yes, there was this background, this knowledge background in 1993, of the salons, the dance saloons. But there was also this — what's happening in Mexico in January and February, and I think this piece, it shows — it has hope. I think it's a piece for hope, para esperanza."

It's music with echoes in an old dance hall and the streets of Mexico today — musical paths Arturo Márquez will continue to follow into the future.

An afternoon of danzón at Salón Los Angeles in Mexico City | Photo by Betto Arcos

ABJEEZ

The word "abjeez" is Persian slang for sisters, a fitting name for a band led by two Iranian sisters. Melody and Safura Safavi have a long-distance act: Safura lives in Stockholm, Melody in Los Angeles. Melody writes songs in Farsi, and Safura composes the music for the band they formed in Sweden six years ago.

Safura says when they started looking for musicians to join Abjeez, they already knew what sound they wanted. Their intention was to make Persian pop music and something else: "We wanted to give inspiration to young people in Iran. Because Iran has been very closed for popular music so we wanted our first CD to be a mixture of different styles so that they could listen and see that, 'wow you can sing Farsi on Bossa Nova, or you can do Persian reggae.'" Melody says she likes to write lyrics that are direct but delivered with a little humor: "Most of the songs are social, critical, but we express ourselves in a humorous way. So when people listen to it, usually they laugh and they can identify themselves with the situation that we are painting in the song. And also, most of the songs are written like small stories."

In their new CD titled "Perfectly Displaced" they sing in four languages, Swedish, Spanish, Farsi and English. The song "Bia" became popular in Iran last year. Abjeez recorded it right after the disputed presidential election and within a few days it went viral on the Internet. In the lyrics, the sisters ask the Iranian military to drop their weapons and join the peace movement. Melody says:

"Even though we're upset, even though we're angry, what's very beautiful about the green movement is that is a peaceful movement, it keeps asking everybody to be peaceful and calm and be resistant but in a peaceful way. That's what we emphasize in the song. Maybe that's why it touches people."

On their first self-produced tour of the U.S., Abjezz played a sold-out concert at the legendary Roxy Theater in Los Angeles. After the show, their fans, largely Iranian expats, had nothing but praise for the band. One of them said, "they're amazing, they're so much fun. I had one of the best times I've had in a concert in a long time." Another fan said, "I loved it, I love the way they sing, their political views, they send out messages for freedom, that's so moving, I love it."

Abjeez | Photo courtesy of the artist

ANOUAR BRAHEM

Anouar Brahem is one of Tunisia's best-known composers and musicians. He's released numerous solo albums, collaborated with a renowned French choreographer and an esteemed Greek filmmaker. Yet Brahem couldn't figure out a way to respond to the upheaval in his country that began at the end of 2010 — the one that launched the Arab Spring. So he waited four years. That response is captured on Brahem's new album "Souvenance," which is French for "remembrance."

Brahem wrote this short text for the album's liner notes: "Extraordinary events had suddenly shaken the daily lives of millions of people. We were propelled towards the unknown, with immense fears, joys and hopes. What was happening was beyond our imagining. It took a long time before I was able to write this music." Brahem says he's always been skeptical when artists suggest that they're influenced by political events, so he didn't want to be too specific in his notes. "I really wanted to leave the imagination of the people free and to try to listen to the music without this kind of indication. This was important for me," he says. "That's why I wrote this small text."

Brahem says he was at an artistic crossroads at the end of 2010, trying to find a new direction for his music. He'd written a few draft pieces, but a series of events then began to unfold in Tunisia. "It was really amazing, because in a few days, the regime fell down, the president left and we were in a kind of revolutionary situation, with a lot of hope and a lot of fear," Brahem says. "There were a lot of demonstrations on the street, and sometimes with a very chaotic situation." Brahem says he didn't want to leave, but it was difficult for him to write music. He says everything he tried to compose sounded banal and trivial in the wake of the Arab Spring. "I had a kind of fear that maybe I lost my inspiration," he says. Brahem was stuck.

But A.J. Racy — a professor of ethnomusicology at UCLA with a specialty in Arab music — says he understands why the composer stayed in Tunisia. "You can stay in your hometown, where you were born, and the advantage of that is you're in the consciousness of the society that you're living in," Racy says. "He senses the tensions of his being there."

Brahem says it was important for him to wait for things to settle down in Tunisia, to give himself some distance from the events. When he started composing the music for this album, he says, the creative process felt all too familiar. "To be honest, when I start to compose, I feel always that I am moving more or less in the fog," Brahem says. "I would say that I just try to follow my inspiration with a maximum of freedom." But amid the political and social uncertainty, Brahem says he wasn't hearing the instruments of his working quartet: the oud, piano, clarinet and bass for which he often composes. Instead, he heard a string orchestra.

It took Brahem months to figure out how to use that new set of tools. But when it finally came together, the music on "Souvenance" became the composer's personal tribute to what he'd experienced during and after the Arab Spring. "All these four last years were a little bit difficult, sometimes chaotic," he says. "But now I think we are in the good way. We just had a democratic election of the parliament and of the president, and the situation is more stable. We have much more hope than before." Although Brahem says the country is still fragile, he remains hopeful for its future.

Anouar Brahem | Photo by Arthur Perset / ECM Records

LOS AGUAS AGUAS

The Mexican state of Veracruz, in the Gulf of Mexico, has seen violence increase in the past few years. The state capital, Xalapa, known for its vibrant music and arts scene is also getting a share of criminal activity. The music of the band called Los Aguas Aguas was transformed by recent events in their hometown.

Los Aguas Aguas first album, called "Easy and Tropical Machine" carried an upbeat "party on" message, says bass player Danny Cruz. "Take it easy, just chill out, everything is going to be fine. Just dance and your problems will take care of themselves." But in the past couple years, violence has increased around them and the band admits they became numb to all the bad news. Guitarist and singer Demiss Arenal says when he heard about a neighbor or someone's friend being killed, all he'd say was "poor thing" and move on. "We kind of turned cold," he says. "We don't think about what happens to others. We just think it's best to keep to yourself and your family. Suddenly, there's an epidemic of fear."

Arenal says one day he noticed the state police had set up a compound next door to his home. "For the next two or three months," Arenal says, "they wouldn't let me walk through my street or wouldn't allow me to leave my house because they were doing some operation. They were harassing my wife and they almost killed my dogs because they barked at them, things like that. So I'd be inside the house, saying "how can I be a prisoner in my own home?" That's when he wrote the song, "El Sol" (The Sun): *At night the gunshots wake me up, in the streets they fight, rocks against bazookas. The army arrived grenades in hand... 'everybody get out or you'll end up in hell...' Five, ten, fifteen, twenty dead for no reason, people are tired of seeing so much destruction.*

Having the violence come to their door changed the band's attitude. And their new album, "Two, Three Karate Moves," reflects that, says Dany Cruz. "Now, we take a stand and say 'hey, we know how to fight, we're a brave barrio.' If you mess with our people we know how to respond, but not necessarily with violence. On the contrary, we created music to speak out, to show what's happening to many people." They noticed things were quiet in Xalapa because people were scared to come out. So rather than try to hide behind closed doors, the band played in the streets. Demiss Arenal says "come on, nothing is going to happen. And if it happens, we have to keep on living."

Los Aguas Aguas | Photo courtesy of the band

ARTISTS' REACTION TO VIOLENCE IN MEXICO

January 20, 2012

Mexico's federal attorney general announced a chilling number this month — in the past five years, drug-related violence in that country has claimed the lives of almost 48,000 people. The brutality has touched the people across society, and artists on both sides of the border, are responding.

Javier Sicilia is a novelist and a poet. In 2009, he was awarded Mexico's prestigious Aguascalientes National Poetry Prize. Last September, he read a poem dedicated to his son, Juan Francisco, at a rally:

> "There is nothing else to say, the world is not worthy of the word, they drowned it, deep inside of us, as they asphyxiated you, as they ripped your lungs apart, and the pain does not leave me. All we have is a world for the silence of the just. Only for your silence and my silence, Juanelo."

This was the last poem Sicilia wrote. His son was murdered in the central state of Morelos in March, along with six other people, by members of a drug cartel. Javier Sicilia renounced poetry and became the leader of a national protest against the drug war. Yet he says poetry has been an integral part of the "Peace with Justice and Dignity" movement. Sicilia says:

"Poetry has been present — the poets have been part of it. The problem is that the mass media don't like to cover it and don't understand that this movement was born out of poetry, and the reason why it's important is because it's filled with a poetic content that has transformed the language. And behind all of this is a profound ethics, as with all poetry."

Sicilia says the poet has a moral responsibility to tell these stories.

Other artists are also reacting to the violent realities in Mexico today. Singer Lila Downs addresses the violence in a song that deals directly with the consequences, called "La Reina del Inframundo" (Queen of the Underworld). The lyrics read: "Six feet underground, it's for a certain kind of weed, for which the bosses up north are making us kill each other off, and now I'm the queen of the underworld, and my crown is a tombstone."

"Well, this is a song that's more explicitly about what we're going through," Downs says. "It's something that I'm very afraid of. I've seen a lot of papers, a lot of women involved in the business, and a lot of women die." Downs'

whole album was inspired by her feelings about what's happening in Mexico today. "We're going through a very violent period where it's inevitable. You're always seeing these things on the news that are very sad and depressing," she says, "and you wish that you could do something about it. And I think, as an artist and as a human being, you're sensitive to what is happening."

Writer and performer Rubén Martínez is a professor of literature and writing at Loyola Marymount University, as well as the producer of a performance in Los Angeles about the drug war. He says that, in terms of artistic resistance to the drug war, the importance of Javier Sicilia cannot be understated. "As a writer, the only tools I have are language and representation to render a portrait of what is happening today. And Javier Sicilia was the first voice, artistically I think, to approach this," Martínez says. "[His final poem] moved a whole nation, and now it's moved us on this side of the border too, because ultimately, the war is on both sides." Martínez says that we may not see mutilated bodies hanging from bridges in this country, but that, according to the Centers for Disease Control, more than 22,000 people die every year in the U.S. as a result of drug overdoses. "That number of deaths should be added to the number of deaths every year in Mexico," Martínez says. "It's all part of the same conflict."

Singer and performance artist Astrid Hadad has addressed the current situation in Mexico from a different perspective. Hadad sees the roots of the current violence in a number of problems facing Mexico. She names a few of them in the song "Tierra Misteriosa" (Mysterious Land):

> "Poor motherland, vultures fly over you: army men, transnational corporations, presidents, hit men, businessmen. Yesterday they were called viceroys, today they're dignitaries. Five hundred years have passed, only the names have changed. Now the pillagers are called politicians. ... And if that's not saying something against what's happening today, I don't know what is. ... All of us who are fighting say that only a good education and the redistribution of wealth, called justice, will solve this. Otherwise, the current violence will never end."

But Downs offers some hope. In her song "Palomo del Comalito," she cites a popular Mexican expression: "No hay mal que dure cien años" (No evil can last a hundred years). Her hope is that it won't take that long.

Poet and activist Javier Sicilia with writer Rubén Martínez at the Los Angeles Public Library in 2012 | Photo by Betto Arcos

EDGAR QUINTERO

Edgar Quintero was born in Los Angeles, the son of Mexican immigrants. At 28, he's now one of the most successful writers of "narco corridos" — Mexican folk ballads about the drug war.

"I sing about it, I talk about it, but to a certain point where I don't get involved," Quintero says. "They are my clients. I get all sorts of people that come up to me and say 'Can you write a song for me?' Who am I to sit there and be like 'Oh, what do you do for a living, or can I do a background check?'"

Quintero is the focus of a new documentary film called "Narco Cultura," which opened last weekend across the U.S. It shows, in a very personal way, how the violence in Mexico feeds into popular culture. In the film, Quintero meets up with a client who hired him to write a corrido, and he sings an a capella version to the man inside an SUV. "I don't like the cheap stuff," Quintero sings, "only pure quality in the jar. The clients ask and pay, and I bring them what they requested." When Quintero finishes the song, the client pulls out a bundle of cash to pay him, and Quintero promises he'll record a version of it later. Quintero says when a client commissions a corrido, he asks questions and does research. But there are certain things you can say, and certain things you can't. "I'm not going to start pointing fingers," Quintero says. "That's when the problems come. That's when singers get killed."

Quintero says he grew up listening to corridos at home in Los Angeles, but they weren't as graphic as they are today. After he started writing his own songs, he was approached by a record label in Culiacán, Mexico, that helped him put together his band, BuKanas de Culiacán.

The documentary shows the band performing at a show in El Paso, Texas. Quintero gets the audience to sing along to one of their hits, which includes the lines, "With an AK47 and a bazooka on my shoulder, cross my path and I'll chop your head off. We're bloodthirsty, crazy and we like to kill."

But Quintero says he doesn't want people to think he's glorifying violence. He says he thinks of himself more as a reporter of what's happening in Mexico — though some might argue that he's doing PR for the drug cartels. "I don't condone violence, but I have to be real," Quintero says. "The music that I do is hardcore Mexican gansta rap. That's what it is." Quintero says that in the past year, as he's toured across Mexico, he's noticed a respect for drug traffickers. "They're the Mexican Robin Hoods. They're the ones that these kids in Mexico are looking up to, because they're the ones that are helping out their community when the government is not doing nothing about it."

Narco Cultura's director Shaul Schwarz, an Israeli American photojournalist, says he gets why Quintero would sing narco corridos — they're popular in Mexico and the U.S.: "Obviously, I don't share every view that Edgar shares. I'm more angered by it. It's not my cup of tea. But with that said, at the end of the day, I understand that the reality created him in the genre, not vice versa." Schwarz says if we don't want the narco culture to thrive, we have to talk about how to start changing it, on both sides of the border: "This has a direct effect on our next generation, on people who are not traffickers, who are not gangsters, and this is what I was really after in this film and in this coverage."

He'd also like Americans to understand that it's not just Mexico's war. "Without the money and without the guns coming from the American side, none of this could exist."

Edgar Quintero (with bazooka) and his band in Shaul Schwarz's "Narco Cultura" | Photo courtesy of Shaul Schwarz

"ÚNICAMENTE LA VERDAD"

Camelia La Texana is a mythical character from the U.S.-Mexico border and is the subject of an opera called "Únicamente la verdad," the first to be nominated for a Latin Grammy. Camelia La Texana, a female drug smuggler who killed her partner after he betrayed her with another woman, isn't a real person. But just try and tell that to many Mexicans.

The story of Camelia was first told in the song "Contrabando y Traición" (Contraband and Treason). It was made famous by the norteño band Los Tigres del Norte, and it was a big hit in the early 1970s — a totally fictional one, as confirmed by the song's writer, Ángel González.

Yet many Mexicans think Camelia is a real person.

"It's a very important myth in Mexico," says Mexican composer Gabriela Ortíz. "All the people know who is Camelia La Texana. Many people think that she's real, that she exists. There are many women who claim to be Camelia La Texana." Ortíz wrote an opera about the myth of Camelia named "Únicamente la Verdad," or "Only the Truth." The title comes from the slogan of a Mexican tabloid called Alarma! which hyped up reports of the "real" Camelia's existence.

When Ortíz and her brother, Rubén Ortíz Torres, researched the story, they were fascinated by the role of newspapers like Alarma! in sustaining the myth of a real-life Camelia. "The interesting thing is how the media contributes to form this myth," she says. "So basically, the inspiration of my opera, in terms of the music, comes from that."

When the opera was first performed in Mexico City in 2010, Ortíz Torres says some foreign news outlets saw it as a reflection of the drug violence going on in Mexico:

> "And for me it was kind of surreal. It's about a song from 1972, an incident from 1986. I wrote this somewhere in the '90s ... I mean, the song is the first 'narcocorrido,' it is true. But drug smuggling, as the composer of the songs says — as long as there's borders, there's gonna be smuggling."

The opera, he says, is more about how the media creates a character and makes it look real, and how that character becomes a myth in the popular imagination. And Ortíz knows just how firmly that myth has stuck. "I remember asking a taxi driver, 'Do you think that Camelia is a real character?'" she says, "He said to me, 'Yes, I really believe that, because if the corrido talks about her, it's because it's true. All the corridos tell the truth.'"

Mezzosoprano Nieves Navarro, surrounded by members of the Teatro de Bellas Artes choir in a scene from the opera "Únicamente la Verdad" | Photo courtesy of Gabriela Ortíz

JORDI SAVALL AND HESPERION XXI

Jordi Savall is a major figure in the early music scene. The Catalan native is a master of the viola da gamba. Savall is probably best known for his work on the soundtrack of the 1991 film "All the mornings of the world." The CD sold more than one million copies worldwide. Now Savall has turned his focus to a chapter in medieval history, one that involves the Catholic Church. The project is called "The Forgotten Kingdom — The Cathar Tragedy."

Jordi Savall says he first became interested in the Cathars when he recorded an album of medieval troubadour songs in the mid-1970s. The Cathars were a Christian sect that emerged in the 10th century. They were fierce critics of the Roman Catholic Church. The Church branded them heretics and launched a Crusade against them in Occitanie, what's now Southern France. Thousands were massacred, including women and children.

The Forgotten Kingdom — The Cathar Tragedy is the work of Savall and his ensemble, Hesperion XXI. It's one of their most ambitious projects. It includes three CDs of music as well as a book of historical essays. "For us, it's important to realize a project which makes work together from music, history, literature, philosophy and especially a dialogue between our time and these ancient times and also a dialogue between different musicians coming from different cultures."

The Forgotten Kingdom draws on the songs of 13th-century troubadours who recounted the violence unleashed on Occitanie. Savall says he used the troubadour composition called "Song of the Cathar Wars" as the main thread of the narrative. Savall says The Forgotten Kingdom has received a lot of positive response in France, though he notes, the French public doesn't know that much about France's role in the Crusade:

> "And this is not a very nice fact. I think Occitanie is still today very sad about all of this because at no time, the official government of France has [paid] attention to this. And also, I know from friends in Occitanie, they have sent several requests to the Popes in Rome to do a gesture of sorry about this history and nobody from the church is able to say sorry, it was not correct."

Even though the story and the songs date back hundreds of years, Savall says they remain relevant today, because history is a repetition of human tragedies and music helps to make sense of that: "Because music is essentially a moment of emotion, and it's a shared emotion. Only if we learn about that happened 800 years ago, we can be more sensitive about what happens today."

Jordi Savall and Hesperion XXI in concert | Photo by Alain Machelidon

IMMIGRATION

SB 1070 and MUSIC

For the 3600 people who got tickets, it was a night to remember. The rock band Rage Against the Machine, reuniting for a benefit concert, 10 years after their last show in Los Angeles. The reason for their reunion, Arizona's anti-immigrant law SB 1070. For Lydia Romero that's why it was such a special night: "We're standing in solidarity with our compañeros and our compañeras in Arizona, against SB 1070. I asked her if she'd be at the concert if it weren't for the Arizona law: "What do you mean? Would I be here to see Rage Against the Machine? I would be here to see them, but it wouldn't have the same feeling." During the concert, singer Zack de la Rocha mentioned some special guests: "What up, what up, raza! We have some brothers and sisters from Arizona that are here this evening, brothers and sisters who we love very much, because they wake up every day and they fight this shit on the ground, day in and day out."

Tonight's concert sold out in 30 seconds: 3,600 tickets, more than 300,000 dollars raised to help organizations fighting the law in Arizona. Marco Amador is a community activist in Los Angeles and one of the founders of The SoundStrike, along with Rage Against the Machine's Zack de la Rocha. The SoundStrike, says Amador, was created to reach out to artists who wanted to be part of the boycott against Arizona and also join an organized effort to raise awareness. Amador says De la Rocha led the way:

> "He knows a lot of these people throughout his years of being a musician, of being an activist, and so he reached out to them in a very personal way, with a very personal letter. And we just had all these artists hit us back about how they wanted to join in, how they wanted to participate. We had people in the very beginning like Michael Moore, like Conor Oberst, just jumping right on it and saying like, we have to do something about it. So right then and there we knew that it was something that was gonna be strong and survive."

The efforts of the SoundStrike are echoed by other LA artists such as Zul, Casillas and Malverde. They co-wrote a song called "Arizona Gonna Git Knocked Out." Casillas says the idea for the song came to him while he was stuck in traffic and listening to the radio. That's when he heard the LL Cool J classic "Mama Said Knock You Out":

> "The song came out, LL Cool J song came out and I thought, 'Man, we need to take that energy, that song and do a thing, an anthem about the Arizona controversy that's happening.' So just out of thin blue sky, the first couple of lyrics came up, 'Don't call me a wetback, we've been here for years,' and it was on its way — the rest is history. I called up Esteban Zul here and he took the lyrics to another level, and he suggested we call Malverde for some Spanish lyrics and we wanted to put something out in Spanglish. And we got a hold of Malverde and the rest just kind of happened by itself."

Community activist Marco Amador says The SoundStrike has received a massive response from people and artists all over the world including Mexico, where pop singers like Amandititita have been compelled to write songs protesting against SB 1070. Her song is called "Sheriff Arizona," and the lyrics address the issue head on: *We are against the law in Arizona / that's not the way you treat people / they mistreat you / they denigrate you / just for being brown they send you to the border patrol.* Amador says that's the reason why somebody like Amandititita felt compelled to write a song: "Especially her understanding — she's toured here, she's Mexicana, she understands the reality that happens to a lot of the communities here, the immigrants in this country. But I think in general, just the reaction from people across the globe has been huge."

Amador says since they started the SoundStrike they've had over 700,000 hits on their website from people around the world who are signing on in support of their cause. And given the overwhelming response to the concert by Rage Against the Machine last Friday, they will be organizing a series of concerts and festivals across the country to continue to raise money, and especially to help create a more positive awareness to the plight of undocumented immigrants in the U.S.

Rage Against the Machine performing at the Palladium in Los Angeles, in a benefit concert to help organizations fighting SB 1070, Arizona's anti-immigrant law | Photo by Betto Arcos

ARTURO O'FARRILL
AND FANDANGO AT THE WALL

Pianist Arturo O'Farrill is a composer, arranger and founder of the renowned New York-based Afro-Latin Jazz Orchestra. Last year, O'Farrill embarked on a monumental project: He took his 18-piece orchestra to the U.S.-Mexico border to record an album called "Fandango at the Wall."

It's a late Saturday afternoon, at The Soraya, the performing arts center at Cal State Northridge. Arturo O'Farrill and the Afro-Latin Jazz Orchestra are doing sound check, while rehearsing one of his signature compositions, "The Afro-Latin Jazz Suite." O'Farrill says it incorporates instruments and rhythms of the Americas: "It's a piece of music that we call 'All of the Americas,' because to me, I really believe strongly that all the elements for jazz are incomplete without all the elements of the Americas."

The idea to create an Afro-Latin Jazz Orchestra came to O'Farrill back in 2001, after Wynton Marsalis offered him a home at Lincoln Center. Marsalis's original request, says O'Farrill, was to start a resident Afro-Cuban jazz orchestra. During a press conference, to announce the Orchestra's new home, somebody said to O'Farrill:

"'Why not Afro-Peruvian, and Afro-Colombian, why not Afro-Mexican?' And I said, 'that's right, that's correct. I can't just do this repertoire orchestra. It has to explore all of the Americas because the truth of

the matter is that jazz is an inheritance, a legacy of a cataclysm called 'the slave trade' in which the people that were oppressed, returned love and divine love in music that enriches our souls. But it was not invented in the U.S. — it's part of a fabric that we inherited, that comes up through the Americas."

O'Farrill was born in 1960 in Mexico City, the son of renowned Cuban composer, arranger and bandleader Chico O'Farrill and Mexican singer Lupe Valero. He was five when his parents moved to New York City. He remembers growing up in the shadow of his father: "He was doing a musician's life — he was playing, rehearsing, recording. I got to see a recording of the Count Basie Orchestra — how crazy is that! Dizzy Gillespie would come to my house, or Machito, Graciela." At age 6, O'Farrill's parents enrolled him in the Manhattan School of Music where he studied the classical repertoire — Bach, Mozart, Beethoven. Late at night, he'd sneak into his father's writing studio and improvise:

"I would sit at the piano and I would make up music, but I thought I was just conducting an orchestra and I even provided myself with audience noise and cheer and roar. I think that's when the seeds for my life as a musician were really planted, when I just was back there creating my own sounds. That's kind of where the seeds for being a composer were planted as well."

Musician, activist Jorge Francisco Castillo — wearing a black hat — is the founder of Fandango Fronterizo, a celebration of music and dance, held every year on both sides of the Tijuana-San Diego border wall | Photo by Reynaldo Escoto

On a late afternoon, during last year's Memorial Day weekend, O'Farrill and his Afro-Latin Jazz Orchestra took part in the "Fandango Fronterizo," a celebration of son jarocho music and dance in a most unusual venue: the dividing wall at the Tijuana-San Diego border. "I thought this was the most elegant activism: to actually take a physical barrier and use it as a symbol of unification." O'Farrill first read about the annual event and its founder, Jorge Castillo, in the New York Times:

> "I thought, this man is a genius, and I thought this thing was so brutally touching to me — it just meant so much to me, the pueblo, conciencia, community and music-making, and the celebration of culture and dancing was so much more important than anything, any border wall that man could erect."

Jorge Castillo is a former librarian, a son jarocho musician and the founder of the Fandango Fronterizo, held every year since 2008, at the Tijuana-San Diego border:

> "It's kind of ironic that the wall is there to divide us and at the end it ends up bringing us together. Now it's bringing people from other places together, even it's getting bigger. The fandango is very inclusive, it's a feast that is very inclusive to the community and to the world. So now this concept is going beyond Tijuana — it's going even further, it's expanding to the world, through this 'Fandango at the Wall' project."

In addition to the Afro-Latin Jazz Orchestra, the "Fandango at the Wall" concert included two major son jarocho musicians, Patricio Hidalgo and Ramón Hernández. O'Farrill also invited jazz violinist Regina Carter, drummer Antonio Sánchez, Iraqi oud player Rahim Alhaj and many other international musicians. Twenty-five-year-old saxophonist and woodwind player Alexa Tarantino says joining the son jarocho musicians was exhilarating: "I found it to be just so much more raw and pure and much more direct to the listener. It just seemed like pure joy to me and I loved it."

Abdulrahman Amer plays trombone with the Afro-Latin Jazz Orchestra. He says he looked up during the performance at the Wall:

> "And there was a bird that crossed from Tijuana super easily to the U.S. side, and then I looked at myself — I can't do that. Nobody can really do that anymore. That made me think about how important this was to our current time because, you know, everyone wants to build these tall fences, but no one really wants to build longer tables anymore."

Jacob Hernandez is a son jarocho musician based in Los Angeles and Tijuana and a coordinator between the Afro-Latin Jazz Orchestra and the son jarocho musicians. He says "Fandango at the Wall" is about everything that the annual event represents: "It's about the larger relationship between our two countries and that border, that problem that we have, that we have to deal with and face. And this one story of how we came to face that problem."

From left, pianist Arturo O'Farrill, son jarocho musicians (standing) Ramón Gutiérrez, Wendy Cao Romero, Jorge Castillo, Patricio Hidalgo and Tacho Utrera | Photo courtesy of Varda Bar-Kar

IBRAHIM MAALOUF AND OXMO PUCCINO

Ibrahim Maalouf is a trumpet player born in Lebanon and raised in Paris. He has recorded five albums of original music. His latest project is called "Au Pays d'Alice," a collaboration with the Malian-French hip-hop artist Oxmo Puccino.

In the past couple years, Maalouf has been thinking a lot about the climate of intolerance in Europe, and the growing anti-immigrant mood. He wanted to do a project where he could express his opinion about it:

"I think we live in a society where more and more things are forbidden and that scares me. Especially in Europe now, and I'd say in France more than anywhere else, because this is where I live, it feels to me these last 10 years, less and less things are allowed to do, you cannot wear this, you cannot wear that, you cannot think like this, you don't have the right to say this. They try to find solution to the problems and to the crisis through things that divide people, instead of finding solutions with things that unite people, you know, and this really scares me."

A few years ago, Maalouf was asked to compose a musical inspired by Lewis Carroll's "Alice in Wonderland." He thought Carroll's book was the perfect vehicle to address what's happening in Europe today. Maalouf says Carroll's book may be considered a metaphor for his time, but:

"Almost 200 years later when Oxmo Puccino tries to see if this metaphor still exists, through this album, you notice that the metaphor is even more real and realistic now than it used to be two hundred years ago. 'Alice in Wonderland' for me is a very avant-garde book and this is what I wanted to show."

"Au pays d'Alice" follows the same storyline of "Alice in Wonderland" and the same characters of the story in a present-day context. The recording includes Maalouf's band, a classical orchestra, a children's choir, and the leading voice of rapper Oxmo Puccino, who reimagines the English author's most well-known work. Maalouf says he couldn't think of anyone else for this project:

"In all the people I've been working with, I think he's the one that writes the best in French. The way he writes is very autodidactic. He doesn't belong to any school, he doesn't follow any rule, he just writes the way I compose, which is without forbidding himself anything. And he's completely transparent in the way he writes and I love his writing. And also, he's very musical in the way he writes, he's very rhythmical — everything is about music when he writes."

The song "La Course au Caucus" is a sort of anthem, bringing people from diverse backgrounds together to face the hardships they experience across Europe. Maalouf says he'd like to see a society where different people coexist and respect each other's beliefs and culture:

"When I bring my child to the school, I want her to see all kinds of people — people who pray differently than she does, who think differently than she does, who don't see the world the same way. Because there's not one way to see the world, there are different ways, and you have to find the best, that is actually the addition of yours and mine and his and hers altogether — and that will make our world better."

Ibrahim Maalouf | Photo by Betto Arcos

LILA DOWNS

Mexican American singer Lila Downs became well known after she appeared in Julie Taymor's "Frida" in 2002, and her performance of a song from that film, which was nominated for an Academy Award. Over the course of her career, she has always engaged in political issues.

Last September, during the U.S. presidential campaign, Downs wrote a song called "The Demagogue." It was her critique of the Republican candidate: "Sometimes being explicit isn't very useful. That's what I felt when we wrote 'The Demagogue.'" After the song was released as a single and "nothing came of it," Downs says she was both depressed and angry:

> "After getting angry because people hate us, because we're racially inferior to them, well, you know what I think of you? I think you're envious of me. That's what you are. You may be white, but you know what? You don't know how to dance! Hahahaha! And I'm being very confrontational about that in this song and I really do think it's about envy."

Downs then wrote a song called "Envidia." On her new album called "Salón, Lágrimas y Deseo" she sings this tune in a duet with Argentine rocker Andrés Calamaro. It's in the aftermath of the U.S. election that Downs decided to make an album focused on romantic songs called boleros. These are ballads that are considered standards and are very popular in every Spanish-speaking country, including the U.S. But these boleros are not love songs. She says her selection is related to the way people are feeling today in Mexico, where she lives. She says the messages in the songs are political and universal in a profound way. The bolero called "La Mentira" (The Lie) speaks about the relationship between a politician and a person who helped elect him:

> "At the end, it says: 'Well, no problem, you can just leave and pretend like we have no relationship here, because this promise that we have between you and I is really a lie, it's based on a lie, right? That's what the song says. And it says, 'you can just go, because God is not involved in this decision.'"

Downs says at the center of the violence in Mexico is the loss of basic moral values:

> "People don't have a conscience and have no sense of what's right or wrong. Of course, not everyone. What I mean is that the violence has gotten stronger and stronger, the presence of the violence in this country. And it starts to make you wonder whether we're going to be able to live our lives the way we have been living them. It's really scary."

In the bolero called "Seguiré mi viaje," Downs says it's the voice of an immigrant who travels back and forth between Mexico and the United States:

> "The lyrics say, Oh, so now you think you're superior, you're above me and I'm beneath you? But you know what? I don't care, I'm going to continue on my trip, which I love, because 'seguiré mi viaje' is a very hippie kind of word — 'your trip, you're going to continue your trip.' And what I feel is that it's the paisanos you know, coming back and being strong and saying, I'm going to continue my trip, no matter what."

Despite the backlash against immigrants in the U.S., Downs is hopeful. Her new album opens with a song called "Urge." The voice of the immigrant makes a plea: *With my heartbreak, I'm just kind of rolling around like a rolling stone, I really just need somebody to listen to my failures and my successes.* Downs says now is a great opportunity to show who the immigrants from Latin America are. After all, they're just like others who came here before, in search of a better life.

Lila Downs | Photo courtesy of the artist

JOHN DAVERSA
AND AMERICAN DREAMERS

Trumpeter John Daversa's Big Band album, "American Dreamers: Voices of Hope, Music of Freedom," won three Jazz Grammys in February. A former UCLA student and CSUN professor, Daversa's album features 53 Dreamers born in 17 countries. When trumpet player John Daversa went on stage at Staples Center to accept the first of three Grammys he won for his album, he didn't have to make a political statement: "Thank you to the Recording Academy for recognizing our work together that features 53 Dreamers that came to this country as children. I'm a great-grandson of Italian immigrants, so this is a very personal project for me." Formerly based in Los Angeles, Daversa is now the chair of Studio Music and Jazz at the University of Miami. When we spoke before his recent show at a jazz club in LA, he said one of the most rewarding aspects of the project was getting to know everyone's unique story. It reminded him of his own family: "My great-grandparents immigrated from Sicily. They came through Ellis Island. I remember my grandparents talking about what being an American meant to them, coming here for a better life."

"My name is Salvador, I'm a Dreamer. I was brought from Mexico to the States at age 3 and I'm a clarinetist. The parts I remember from that journey are the airport. I knew at the time I finally get to go see my mom and dad again. They were already in the States before me."

Salvador Pérez is one of the nine Dreamers whose stories are interspersed between the album's 18 tracks. The three Grammys it won included Best Large Ensemble Album. Daversa says he's been wanting to do a project like this for a while: "I've been thinking a lot about intention, purpose and meaning behind music. Music is such a potent vehicle to relay expression and messages. So I want to be responsible with what it is, with the music that we're making." The idea for the album was born from a meeting between Daversa and three producers from his LA-based label, BFM Jazz. They were brainstorming about a recording project and they all had the same idea. Daversa says this is how it came up: "What if we made a record that was to heighten awareness about the DACA act and the human beings involved with this and we could have them involved and perhaps create some new arrangements, some new reimagining of themes of America."

The producers searched the internet for Dreamers who were musicians or singers. They reached out to immigrant rights organizations and through word of mouth: "And also, they had to be willing to be part of this too, 'cause they were giving up their anonymity to be part of this project." Tiffany del Río came to Los Angeles when she was 14 as an unaccompanied minor to reunite with her mother, after her father passed away in Mexico:

John Daversa and Dreamers during the recording sessions | Photo courtesy of the artist

"Our stories are powerful, the fact that people are getting to know who we are. People are getting to see our talents. People are getting to actually have this meaningful and powerful conversations that have to be. I was listening to some of the people giving their speeches when they were receiving their awards, and they were telling how they worked their entire lives for that award. And for us to be so young and to be able to have an achievement like that is amazing. For me, personally, just feeling so welcome, feeling so comfortable with being who I am. And being celebrated for it, being celebrated for being an immigrant."

I spoke with Tiffany del Río at BFM's office, along with another Dreamer, a hip-hop artist who goes by the single name of Caliph. He was born in Senegal and his parents brought him to the U.S. at age 7. He's been in the country for 22 years. For the album, he was asked to participate in a remake of Led Zeppelin's "Immigrant Song." Caliph says when he got to the studio in Miami, he felt a strong sense of community:

"I was instantly inspired. I walked out for 20 minutes, came up with the lyrics, came back inside, did the first verses. While they worked on other parts of the album, and then I walked out for about a half hour, came back and did the second verse. And then we did the same process for the intro. So it was all in that moment, it hit me in that moment."

Daisy Cardozo is a Dreamer who tells her story and performs a song on the album: "My name is Daisy and I am a Dreamer. I was brought to the United States when I was 9 years old from Venezuela and I love to sing. My sister had a tumor and my sister's medical treatment was in Houston. My mom and I came here in 1991." Cardozo was introduced to John Daversa by a colleague at the University of Miami. Daversa asked Steven Weber from his label to call Daisy. She told Weber that she lived almost her entire life in the shadows and always wanted to pursue a career as a singer but could not do it because of her status. Weber sent her the music, the background tracks and even a scratch vocal of Daversa singing the Woody Guthrie song "Deportee." She worked on it for two weeks, then Weber called her:

"Daisy, why don't you just sing into your iPhone with the background music going and let's just listen to what that sounds like. So she did, I have it still on my iPhone. It just was incredibly authentic. It was as real as anyone could sing a song. It was so moving that I knew immediately Daisy was going to get the gig. She was going to do this."

As he traveled across the country, recording the voices of the Dreamers who took part in the project, Daversa was struck by the lack of awareness about their plight. "But if we don't all know about it, we're not all supporting each other, we're not going to get anywhere. The main goal — and it still is, it continues, the journey continues — is about awareness, and for people to think for themselves." Daversa says jazz has been an agent of social change from the very beginning. "In New Orleans, it was a way for people to say: 'yes all of this stuff is going on around me, all this oppression and racism and all of it, but here I am, this is what I'm doing' — and the integrity in that is a lot of the core of what jazz is about. My freedom is within the music."

John Daversa says what he's doing with this album is no different. He's honored to be following in the footsteps of his heroes.

John Daversa and Dreamers during the recording sessions | Photo courtesy of the artist

GABY MORENO

On a chilly Saturday evening in Xela, a colonial city in the highlands of Guatemala, singer-songwriter Gaby Moreno performs her encore to hundreds of adoring fans who sing along. Moreno says this is one of the country's most beloved songs. "'Luna de Xelajú' is our second anthem," she says. "It's such a popular song in Guatemala — there's a sense of pride for that song, and it's a beautiful song. I love singing it." Her fans couldn't be happier. Outside the theatre, 20-year-old Adriana Guzmán says Moreno is a role model for Guatemalans: "She embodies the idea that we can do better, that Guatemala does have a future and it's because of her that all Guatemalans know that we have a voice, and that we can rise up and be better every day."

Moreno may not be a household name in the U.S., but she's a rock star in Guatemala, the country of her birth. She moved to Los Angeles 16 years ago. Since then, her career has gone in different directions. She's toured with a wide array of artists, from Tracy Chapman to Hugh Laurie, and she's shared the stage with Andrea Bocelli and Van Dyke Parks. She has released six albums since 2008. By the time she got a Latin Grammy for Best New Artist in 2013, Moreno had already spent almost 20 years singing and writing songs. Moreno says "Fronteras" is one of the songs she wrote for her new album, "Illusion": "Initially, I wrote it for Latin American people, in general, living in the United States, and how we are straddling the fence between two cultures. We keep our traditions and yet we have adopted new ones from the American culture."

Moreno has embraced a wide range of musical traditions. For her new album she worked with producer Gabe Roth, known for his work with Sharon Jones and the Dap-Kings. Moreno pours her heart out with lyrics and melodies steeped in the classic R&B sound of the 1960s. Moreno says she started listening to Blues and R&B when she was 12 years old. Over time, her love for this music and other genres has grown: "If you hear like my first and my second record, you'll hear a variety of styles because that's just who I am," she says. "I feel like the common denominator is always going to be my voice."

Jebin Bruni has been playing keyboards with Moreno for the past 10 years. Bruni says Moreno may not be well known in the U.S. right now, but in Guatemala she holds court: "She's like a rock star and it's amazing," he says. "She should be this big everywhere, but it's sort of Guatemala's little secret right now, but pretty soon it's going to explode." Moreno says she couldn't be happier, making a living as a singer, especially as an immigrant in the U.S. "That's what I came to this country for," she says, "to follow my dream of making music — and I'm doing it."

Gaby Moreno | Photo by Andrew MacPherson

LA SANTA CECILIA

La Santa Cecilia take their name from Mexico's patron saint of music. But you wouldn't call them a Mexican band. La Santa Cecilia's sound is a hybrid mix of music reflecting the city where they live and play — Los Angeles. Their Latin-flavored songs can combine a funky ska beat with a Gypsy-flavored guitar riff. Guitarist Gloria Estrada says when the band started playing four years ago, she noticed their music brought together their diverse backgrounds: "I think all six members have such different influences and we're all, I think, really open to everything, so I think it was a nice blend and it was refreshing for everybody to kind of be able to experiment freely with our music."

The musicians that make up La Santa Cecilia are children of immigrants. Three were born in Los Angeles, two in Mexico and one in Venezuela. La Marisoul is the lead singer and the band's main songwriter. She says she grew up singing boleros and Mexican rancheras with musicians who play at LA's historic Olvera Street: "So my base and what I know for music is from there, from what I learned with the musicians there. That's where I grew up, that's where I'm from. And La Santa Cecilia is the vehicle for me to express and explore and grow and I'm happy for that, I'm happy that I found them."

La Santa Cecilia began at a drunken party as a fun experiment. Today, they're one of LA's most successful Latin bands. And they're redefining a hip, Latin sound of Los Angeles. For the past year, they've been on a non-stop tour, playing gigs up and down California and recently in Texas, where they showcased at Austin's South by Southwest. They've put out two EPs, and a few months ago, they were signed to a label founded by a multiple Grammy-winning producer. Guitarist Gloria Estrada says it's a new opportunity: "We got to work with a producer this time, and got to have a nice-sounding album as opposed to our first EP. But I mean, you know, it's a work in progress I think for everybody."

Lead singer La Marisoul says they're working on a single due out this month: "I'm really excited 'cause we're really working on the artwork and the concept of how we're gonna release this." She says they've been keeping this secret from their fans. It's a new version of one of their most popular songs — "Chicle" or (Gum). Their plan is to release it as a single, in a specially designed little package that will include a code to download it and a treat to chew on.

La Santa Cecilia | Photo by Humberto Howard

EL CONJUNTO NUEVA OLA

When the band El Conjunto Nueva Ola first got together in Mexico City in 2000, lead singer Urbano Lopez says things didn't quite gel at first: "We tried to do rock music, but we couldn't have the rhythm right. So we gave up and decided to play cumbia," he says. And that, Lopez says, was one of the smartest decisions they made — along with moving to the Los Angeles area a few years ago. "We know that cumbia is a rhythm that is played from La Patagonia to Los Angeles now, so in every latitude it morphs; it kind of adapts to the culture there," Lopez says.

El Conjunto Nueva Ola, which translates as the New Wave Band, doesn't play traditional, acoustic cumbia, and they don't look like a cumbia band. The six members wear Mexican wrestler masks during their shows. During my interview with them, they kept their masks on. I never got to see their faces. These guys play covers, though they're not what you'd call a cover band. One of their covers is a popular tune called "La Cumbia de Los Luchadores" (The Wrestlers' Cumbia). Lopez says

they almost didn't want to do it. "It was kind of obvious and we don't like to do obvious. We pretty much think about something and we make a U-turn and we crash. That's the approach to how we get to a song. We really think, 'Oh how is this song good?' We're gonna do the exact opposite."

They recorded a singular rendition of the Sex Pistols' song, "Anarchy in the U.K." The band re-arranged it and named it "El Albañil de la Pensíl" (The Mason from the Pensíl Neighbourhood). Their version focuses on a mason who is a street-smart, hard-working citizen. Lopez says theirs is a much more positive take on the punk classic. "We are modernizing the cumbia and 'Cumbializing' the modern, adding a new flavor to it, so we use a lot of the keyboard-oriented sounds from the '80s — you know, the New Wave — and adapt them into the rhythm," Lopez says. The members of El Conjunto Nueva Ola think of themselves as 21st-century wrestlers, battling musical styles on stage. One thing's for sure — they don't take themselves too seriously.

El Conjunto Nueva Ola | Photo courtesy of the band

JON BALKE AND SIWAN

Al-Andalus was a region of Spain which, after the expansion of the Islamic Empire, was governed by Muslim rulers for nearly eight centuries — from 711 to 1492. During the first part of that time, followers of Judaism and Christianity were tolerated by most of the Muslim rulers, which encouraged a relative climate of cooperation between scholars of all three faiths. That climate of cooperation produced advances in math, science, art and music that influenced the rest of Europe.

The region's spirit has inspired contemporary Norwegian pianist and composer Jon Balke — who, with his group Siwan, recently released his second album drawn from those influences, titled "Nahou Houm." Balke first learned of Al-Andalus when he was commissioned to write music by a Moroccan promoter to celebrate a venue's 15th anniversary. "This was how I stumbled upon Gharnati music, which is the Andalusian music that existed in 1400 in Spain and was driven out," Balke says. The intellectual and social exchange fostered by its rulers helped make Al-Andalus one of the most culturally rich areas of Europe. But the Christian kingdoms to the north attacked repeatedly, and in 1492, the Spanish crown reclaimed the last vestiges of the region. Muslims and Jews were forced to convert, killed or expelled. Many sought refuge across the Mediterranean Sea.

"They left Andalucía and went to North Africa, and Tunisia, Morocco and Algeria," says Mona Boutchebak. An Algerian classical singer, Boutchebak is the lead vocalist on the new album by Jon Balke and Siwan. She says the culture of what came to be called Andalucía was carried and preserved by the exiles. "It is a mixture between Arabic music and Spanish," Boutchebak says. "Flamenco comes from this music, from this tradition. I'm from this tradition, from the Arabo-Andalusian one." It's a tradition that's still taught in schools: "what we call in Algeria the Arabo-Andalusian schools, where you can learn to sing the Arabo-Andalusian tradition. So I went and I said, 'This is what I want to do.' I started to sing when I was 11, to learn this tradition."

Jon Balke has taken this tradition's poetry and composed his own music around it. "It's a framing of the musical project," Balke says.

> "It puts the project in a framework that speaks about history and that speaks about a kind of a mentality that, from what you can read, existed in the best parts of this period — a kind of open, liberal practice of tolerance and coexistence. These poems, they speak about this kind of attitude, even if they speak about love or rain on the river or mystical experiences. You get the kind of a feeling of a period which was a really booming period in European history."

At first, Boutchebak resisted the idea of combining her ancient tradition with jazz improvisation and music from the north. "At the beginning, even for me, it was a little bit hard to imagine baroque music, improvisations, Andalusian music, and me in the middle," she says. "I was asking myself, 'What am I going to do?' At times I felt it like it was so far from me, but it isn't. We are all the same.

The title of the album is "We Are Them — Nahnou Houm." Balke hopes that by trying to recapture a long-gone period of cultural and religious coexistence, his Siwan project can offer an alternative to intolerance in the modern world. "It is possible to coexist," Balke says. "It is possible to respect even a person who believes something different from you or comes from a totally different background. And even if there are conflicts, it's possible to solve them in another way than shooting the person.

Jon Balke | Photo by Antonio Baiano / ECM Records

COMMUNITY
BUILDING

QUETZAL IN VERACRUZ

For more than 20 years, the Grammy-winning LA band Quetzal has incorporated the music and instruments of Mexico's son jarocho style into its sound. For its next album, the band wanted to revisit the source of this music, so the members recently traveled to Veracruz to immerse themselves in that world.

The first stop was on a hot and humid Sunday afternoon at the home of musicians Tacho Utrera and Wendy Cao-Romero. They live in a coffee region 10 minutes south of Xalapa, the capital of the Gulf state of Veracruz. Following tradition, the musicians opened with the song that marks the beginning of the jam session, "El Siquisirí." Cao-Romero welcomed the guests with verses that name-checked Sandino, the 10-year-old son of musician Quetzal Flores and singer Martha González, leaders of the band. Cao-Romero said the two families have kept a deep friendship and musical connection for many years and have collaborated on various projects: "For us, it's very important that they continue to be interested in our music, because they're so well known and they're a window into the world, as Chicanos and as American musicians." On Monday afternoon, the band visited Ramón Gutiérrez at his studio-workshop. He leads the renowned group Son de Madera and plays the five-string lead guitar called "guitarra de son" or "requinto."

Flores said the trip to Veracruz had a specific purpose: to immerse the band in the son jarocho environment and chronicle their time with the music community. Flores said they will bring back the field recordings and create soundscapes that will serve as the foundation for the band's compositions: "We're going to compose to these sounds, to these interactions, the voices that you hear of people having conversations, the playing together, the children interacting — all these things are part of the social fabric of who we are and this relationship that we have with the jarocho community." Gutiérrez says in the more than 35 years he's been playing son jarocho, he's never seen a rock band with the ability to absorb and distill this music like Quetzal:

> "I think it's the only group I've seen on stage playing jaranas and having a very exciting mix of today's music. It sounds like rock, but you see Martha playing jarana and Quetzal [playing] requinto with pedals."

On Tuesday afternoon, Quetzal visited a cultural center dedicated to the teaching of son jarocho in the port city of Veracruz. The center was founded in 2001 by Gilberto Gutiérrez, leader of Grupo Mono Blanco, the group that led the son jarocho music and dance renaissance in the early 1980s. Gutiérrez says Quetzal follows in the footsteps of the great Chicano artists Lalo Guerrero and Los Lobos:

> "It's admirable how they've become interested in Mexican culture. It would have been just as easy to disregard it, like many others have done. On the contrary, they have reaffirmed themselves as part of this culture and it's clearly reflected in the music they make."

On Wednesday, the band headed three hours south of Veracruz and arrived at El Hato, where in the early 1980s Grupo Mono Blanco jump-started the fandango tradition. Fandango is a celebration of music and dance and is the most significant aspect of son jarocho. Quetzal singer Martha González said this visit was enriched by the presence of her son, Sandino:

> "It's really special to see my son here, playing in the same space, to know that there's more than one generation and that he likes [the music]. Mainly, it's the fact that he really enjoys it. We don't make him play. He takes pride in his instrument and, any chance he can, he learns from the big dogs."

Quetzal Flores said their connection to son jarocho goes well beyond a visit to the source of this musical culture. It's also about reestablishing relationships with the community, like the musician and instrument maker Ramón Gutiérrez:

> "Sandino has a requinto from Ramón. So we have all these instruments that also have these voices of these people, extensions of their voices. It's important for us to not just to have an instrument, but know who made it, and the stories behind them and these incredible histories that we connect to in so many ways, and that have created a sense of home in multiple places — for them and for us."

Flores said this exchange, built on friendship and a strong musical connection, has created a spirit of reciprocity for both communities — in Veracruz and Los Angeles.

Quetzal at the shop of Ramón Gutiérrez in Xalapa, Veracruz | Photo by Betto Arcos

YO-YO MA in MEXICO CITY

World-renowned cellist Yo-Yo Ma has taken on one of the most ambitious endeavors in years — The Bach Project. The multi-layered initiative includes performing Bach's Six Cello Suites in one sitting, in 36 cities and six continents, and participating in cultural activities with local communities in each of those cities.

It's a cool and breezy Tuesday evening at the Plaza de la República, a large public square near downtown Mexico City. More than 20,000 people came here tonight to listen to Yo-Yo Ma's performance of Bach's Six Cello Suites. Right after he finished playing the Suite No. 4, Ma stood up from his chair and addressed the massive, captivated audience, in Spanish: "Me gustaría dedicar la siguiente canción a todas las personas valientes, desaparecidos y a quienes han sufrido de violencia" (I would like to dedicate the next piece to all the brave people, the disappeared, and those who have suffered from violence). Within a few seconds after speaking those brief, yet powerful words, hundreds of people spontaneously started counting from 1 to 43, in reference to the 43 college students who were abducted in the state of Guerrero, in September of 2014 — allegedly by police officers collaborating with criminal gangs. Their bodies have never been found. Then, Yo-Yo Ma began playing Bach's Cello Suite No. 5.

The next day, Yo-Yo Ma was at an event called "Community Culture of Peace Interaction," part of The Bach Project's "Days of Action." The event was held at "La Nana" cultural center in a working-class neighborhood near the city's historic district. At this event, attended by more than 100, the participants included teachers, dancers, visual artists, musicians and many people from the local community. The first activity was a free-form dance exercise — performed to "Danzón No. 2," by Mexico's renowned classical composer Arturo Márquez. Next, the group was led by musician Enrique Jiménez in a series of percussive exercises with their hands and feet. Jiménez attended Yo-Yo Ma's concert and was touched by the musician's gesture when he dedicated Bach's Suite No. 5 to the disappeared. He said it was a big lesson to musicians in Mexico:

> "Sometimes we're on our ivory tower thinking we're not affected by what happens around us, and just making music is enough. And it's good to make music. But when you give meaning to the music you play, that's when it reaches other dimensions. What Yo-Yo Ma did last night was very symbolic and meaningful."

Jiménez divided the group into four sections of about 25 people each, and got them to improvise a song, with their voices layered. The last exercise was a percussion routine, clapping hands and drumming on various parts of the body.

The group was then asked to keep silent for three minutes, to reflect on the theme of Peace, as they listened to music composed by Maricarmen Graue. Graue is a local cellist and teacher who was invited to write the music. She says it was especially meaningful to see an artist of such stature participate in a community event: "Yo-Yo Ma's humility and simplicity, integrating himself to the community and showing his human quality, has been very special for me to see up close." After a short video presentation focused on two artists working at the cultural center, Yo-Yo Ma sat down, tuned his cello and began to play Bach's Cello Suite No. 1. As the audience formed a circle around them, a man in a wheelchair and a woman in a beige dress, danced freely as Yo-Yo Ma played on. The event closed with a performance by the cultural center's 13-piece house band called "Ehya Disonante." Yo-Yo Ma grabbed his cello and joined the band as they performed a 15-minute medley that included The Beatles "With a little help from my friends."

After he was thanked and applauded for visiting the cultural center, Yo-Yo Ma offered his thoughts. He said this center is an example of culture in practice, a community where people do things together and everyone feels safe to create and share, in a common effort:

> "To bring timeless human expressions into the present and to be able to bring the sacred and the secular together under one roof. So we are doing things together, we are all equal in this house, and we get to a moment of common spirituality that gives us the energy and the hope and the determination, when we get out of this house, to practice the very values that we have found under this roof."

Maricarmen Legaspi, director of Conarte, the nonprofit that oversees La Nana cultural center, says Yo-Yo Ma has a similar vision of culture and community to that of her organization. Legaspi says the cultural center, located in a rough neighborhood of Mexico City, has a special function: to care for the people who live in this barrio:

"I think that's why Yo-Yo Ma was interested in it, because the theme of peace and community is a top priority for him. So his visit to a space like this, in a complicated barrio, where people are vulnerable, in violent situations, drug addiction and poverty, for him, it's important that this is the heart of this barrio, where there are opportunities to make art for everyone."

That's the essence of The Bach Project's Days of Action: to help people have a better quality of life, to help them be creative and contribute positively to society.

Yo-Yo Ma at the Centro Cultural La Nana in Mexico City | Photo by Betto Arcos

LAS POSADAS

Mexicans celebrate the holiday season every year with the reenactment of Mary and Joseph's journey as they looked for shelter on the eve of Jesus' birth. The tradition of Las Posadas dates back nearly 500 years to when Spanish missionaries wanted to tell the story of the birth of Jesus to the Indigenous people of Mexico. So they created this nine-day celebration. But the ritual has been modified, slightly, for today's Mexican Americans.

For the past 10 years, my own family and I organized Las Posadas at our home in Los Angeles. We invited close friends and neighbors and, at about 7 p.m., we walked around our neighborhood toward nearby homes asking for posada — or shelter. Tonight, there are more than 30 adults and about 10 kids walking around with us. As we approach the first house, about five of us go inside, while the rest of our group stays outside — each holding a songbook in one hand and a candle in the other. The group begins the posada song, singing in a call-and-response manner. One group starts singing:

In heaven's name, I ask for shelter, since my beloved wife, cannot be walking in the night.

Then, inside, the smaller group responds:

This is not a hostel. Go on ahead, I will not open the door, I'm afraid it might be a thief.

As we walk from one house to the next, we sing other traditional villancicos, or Christmas carols. At our second stop, the lyrics continue the story:

We're so tired of walking, all the way from Nazareth. I'm a carpenter, my name is Joseph.

Inside the house, the owners respond:

I don't care about the name, let me sleep. I insist on telling you, I will not open the door.

Continuing our journey, we sing another villancico — this time we sing "Campana Sobre Campana" (Bell Over Bell).

And finally, at our last stop, we get a different lyrical response:

Are you Joseph? Is your wife Mary? Please come in pilgrims, I did not recognize you.

As we walk in, everyone sings the welcoming verses:

Come in Holy pilgrims. Though our home is poor, we offer it to you, from the heart.

The end of our journey is our own home, and inside, we host a party for everyone. In Mexico, the family hosting the Posada is responsible for feeding everyone, but since we're in the U.S., guests bring tamales or bottles of wine. As the hosts of the Posada, it's our responsibility to make the ponche, a warm punch that's essential to this Mexican celebration. Ponche is made with apples, guavas and sugar cane, as well as raisins, prunes, hibiscus, cinnamon and brown sugar. But the most important ingredient in the ponche is a special seasonal Mexican fruit called tecojote.

Finally, we get to the exciting part — it's time to break piñatas. The piñata-breaking tradition dates back to the earliest Posadas in Mexico. Piñatas were made with seven points, to represent the seven cardinal sins: wrath, greed, sloth, pride, lust, envy and gluttony. The idea is to hit each of the seven points, blindfolded, to get rid of the bad stuff in your life and usher in a new life — and a new year.

Celebrating Las Posadas with family and friends at home in Los Angeles | Photo by Aaron Paley

JORGE DREXLER (PART 1)

Uruguayan singer Jorge Drexler has a new album called "Amar la Trama." Unlike his previous records, Drexler decided to record the entire album live, in front of a small studio audience, as a way to make a statement about the process of creating music.

If there's one thing that defines the work of Jorge Drexler it's his ability to keep finding new ways of making popular music. For "Amar la Trama," Drexler says he wanted to challenge himself by recording the album live in a studio:

"I wanted to have both, the definition and the control of sound that you have in a studio and at the same time avoid that stiffness, that lack of spontaneity when you record by tracks, and give to the recording a 'live' feeling. Like the way they used to do the records, for example in Frank Sinatra's records, a long time ago, where the singer is in the same room with the players and everybody plays together at the same time."

So to create the right environment, Drexler not only put his nine band members in the same room, he also added about 30 people, invited at random via his website, to be part of the recording process. He says, that

audience changed the whole approach to the recording experience: "You never play in the same way when you're alone or when you have another human being in front of you. There's a spontaneous intention of communication when you have another person in front of you and that was the idea in the record."

The recording took place over the course of four nights in a studio in Madrid. Drexler says he also invited some jazz musicians to participate, to give the songs a warm, acoustic texture. You can hear that texture in every song in the album. Drexler says he's gone through some changes in his career. The first was his move from Uruguay to Spain in the mid-1990s, where he says his music got more refined by incorporating acoustic instruments. The second was starting to work with electronic music and sampling. But he says he got too comfortable in that environment: "And I decided to do the last change, that is actually in this record, [to] go back even before than when I started recording, go back 50 years in the methodology and try to record the way that the old records were made. People playing in a room, like Ani di Franco says."

Jorge Drexler | Photo by Jesús Cornejo, courtesy of the artist

JORGE DREXLER (PART 2)

Jorge Drexler's songs have been called introspective and literary. He's been compared to Paul Simon. But a couple years ago, the Uruguayan musician began to wonder what it would take to write dance-oriented music. That's the assignment he gave himself on his latest album, "Bailar en la Cueva" (Dancing in the Cave). "I decided to start this record from the feet and from the movement centers in the body," Drexler says. The idea, he explains, was to shift focus "away from what was easy for me, writing from and about emotions, and from and about ideas — and move to the feet."

Drexler broke into the U.S. market in 2004, after a song he wrote for the film "The Motorcycle Diaries" became the first Spanish-language work to win an Oscar for Best Original Song. He says that adding a dance beat doesn't have to mean abandoning the scholarly qualities of his music: "If I'm going to talk about dancing, I'm going to try to look at a very deep and emotional and anthropological, even biological side, of it. What it means, music and dancing, for us, as a species."

Drexler is not your ordinary songwriter: He's an ear, nose and throat doctor who didn't launch a music career until he was 30. The awe he felt learning about the laws of science and the natural world still finds its way into tracks like "Todo Cae" (Everything Falls), which speaks of a love so powerful it can defeat gravity and entropy:

> "That awe [is what] I try to bring into songs, the awe at the perception and the contemplation of life and existence I feel through basic science. The only thing that I studied carefully in my life was music and medicine, especially the basic sciences like biology, chemistry and physics. And so I can't help but looking at the world from that point of view."

Drexler's parents were both doctors. His grandparents were German Jews who escaped the Nazis in 1939, taking political asylum at the Bolivian Embassy in Berlin. "And Bolivia was incredibly brave and generous," Drexler says. "They kept on giving visas to German Jews and they saved a lot of people. So my grandparents, very young, with a 4-year-old boy that was my father, had to leave Berlin and went to live in Oruro." He recounts that story in the song "Bolivia." Josh Kun, a professor at the University of Southern California Annenberg School for Communication and Journalism, says Drexler represents something rare — a contemporary singer-songwriter in touch with the cultural politics of memory:

> "He is somebody who [has] lived and felt and experienced the violences of movement and migration in his own family, and also the power of memory to make sense of the past. And then he has a gift of connecting those personal relationships to memory, to larger, social and cultural memories. And he somehow manages to do that, usually, in a space of a love song, where he can take something very minute and turn it into a much larger commentary about memory that is personal and historical."

For Drexler, history is very much a part of the present, and so is movement. He says people dancing around the fire in a cave, 45,000 years ago, are not that different from people dancing in a 21st-century club:

> "There must be something in common in the two situations, the deep reasons why we keep on doing that. We keep on getting together and dancing in closed places. Every generation thinks that they invented 'party,' and it's actually been with us since we came down from the trees."

As the title track of "Bailar en la Cueva" says, "We used to make music long before we knew about agriculture. The idea is eternally new: as night falls, we continue to dance in the cave."

Jorge Drexler | Photo courtesy of the artist

THE WORLD STAGE

For decades, Leimert Park has been a cultural hub for LA's African American arts community and The World Stage, one of its centers. Founded by the late jazz drummer Billy Higgins and poet Kamau Daaood, the performance space continues to nurture local artists with weekly educational workshops.

It's Saturday noon at The World Stage, and a group of 20 musicians are playing in a big band jazz workshop, led by pianist Billy McCoy: "One of the things we have in this workshop, we have people who are retired, we have younger musicians who are in college come here for this particular workshop, because they can't find it. And for the money, we hardly charge anything."

Rich Walker is 66, lives in Duarte and plays baritone saxophone. He's been attending the jazz workshop at The World Stage for the past two years:

> "This is like probably the only place in Southern California where you can come and hang out with people that are striving to understand the language of bebop, they want to get together and play, study it. It's in the African American community and it's like this focus of art and jazz and it's just like, I mean it's just heavy-duty."

For 30 years, Marion Newton was an officer for the Los Angeles Police Department, based in Leimert Park. He plays upright bass, and says the jazz workshop motivated him to start writing music: I don't know all the technical stuff about writing, I write what I feel and what sounds good to me... The players here are the springboard. They'll play it and they give me some input on what I did wrong or whatever, what they like or they don't like about it. And that's what I do. But I think this is fantastic. For alto saxophonist Beverly Milner, the World Stage helps fill a cultural void for people in the community: "They have taken the arts out of the public school systems, particularly music, and The World Stage is that bridge. Anyone can come here, they have all kinds of workshops, not just music, they have vocal, poetry, drumming."

"When it comes to this arts community, called Leimert Park, I think that The World Stage is undisputedly the cornerstone of this area," says Dwight Trible, executive director of The World Stage since 2013. He says two years

before it opened its doors there was another space that offered workshops, jazz performance and spoken word and when it closed down the community was in need of a new space to develop their skills: "There was the need for the young children to be able to come and learn how to play instruments or how to be involved in this music or to be exposed to the music." Instructor and pianist Billy McCoy says to learn to play the blues takes a lifetime: "And we have to pass that on in a 'Griot' tradition, where it's almost orally. There has to be this 'one candle, lights another candle, lights another candle. And that's my role here, to do that, to light another candle.'"

That candle is also being lit every Thursday at the women's drumming workshop. A group of 20 mostly African American women of all ages gather in a circle, singing and playing African songs. Tonight, they're rehearsing a South African Zulu song inspired by the spiritual healers called "Sangoma." The group is called "SHINE," which stands for Sisters Healing Inspiring Nurturing and Empowering. They're led by instructor René Fisher-Mims who started the workshop more than 15 years ago:

> "We go over the diaspora, African rhythms, songs, movement. It's a good healing tool, and a good communication tool that we use, and we get a chance to explore the culture, because I do a lot of folklore, and the medicine aspect of the drumming, not so much as a group, but as therapeutic coming in. And then from that we get together and we form a group."

Florence Penson, 77 years old, is the oldest member of the SHINE group. She's been coming to The World Stage for more than 15 years:

> "I call it my stress-buster. It's like the feeling and the drumming, it gets to your soul. It's very spiritual and you could actually just get lost with the drumming. It's like a magnet, if you will. It draws people because of the energy that it exudes when a person comes here. It's just the greatest, the greatest, OK."

The World Stage recently celebrated its 30th anniversary. Executive director Dwight Trible hopes the next generation that takes over the space will build on the solid foundation that's been established over the last 30 years.

Jazz musicians during a rehearsal at Leimert Park's The World Stage in Los Angeles | Photo by Betto Arcos

BOLEROS DE NOCHE

The romantic Latin ballad style known as bolero arrived in Mexico from Cuba in the 1920s and took off during the Golden Age of Mexican cinema in the 1940s. American singers such as Nat King Cole and Eydie Gormé helped to popularize it in the U.S., in the late 1950s and 1960s. In Los Angeles, a guitarist and his trio are bringing it back.

Thirty-year-old guitarist Roberto Carlos is the force behind the revival of Boleros in LA with his band, Tres Souls. His father introduced him to the romantic ballads when he was a teenager and encouraged him to learn the guitar. "Our teacher, our music instructor, he taught us bolero music," Carlos says. "My dad was pushing us to learn bolero music. At the age of 15 we started playing at small restaurants with my brother Pepe." A few years ago, Carlos started getting serious about bolero — gathering with friends, listening to boleros on vinyl records, and talking about the music and its composers. "And then from there we moved to, 'hey, how about if we take it from a small gathering dining room to an art gallery?'" he says. "From an art gallery we came to La Plaza de Cultura y Artes."

Since 2016, Carlos has been organizing "Boleros de Noche" concerts at multiple venues around LA. At a recent concert at La Plaza de Cultura y Artes, more than 500 people were in attendance, which speaks to the popularity of this music style among Latinos in Southern California. Martha González, lead singer of the Grammy-winning band Quetzal, also performs Boleros. González grew up listening and singing Boleros and said this music is part of the soundtrack of every other Latino home in LA:

"Bolero is yet another incredible music genre that we as Mexicanos have innovated on and made it our own. It's not exactly dance music, there are some that you can probably sway to, but mostly you listen; it's sit-down-and-listen culture that gets you to reflect on life, on love, lost love, new love, even hate and the capacity to go from love and hate. It's just an exploration of the human emotion and I think it's just a beautiful art form."

American audiences first heard boleros sung in Spanish in the late 1950s when Nat King Cole released the album titled "Cole Español." The album's orchestra was recorded in Cuba, though Cole recorded his vocals at Capitol Studios in Hollywood. One of the big hits from that album is the classic "Quizás, Quizás, Quizás." In the mid-1960s, boleros were introduced to a new audience by singer Eydie Gormé, who recorded a couple albums in Spanish with the Mexican trio that popularized the style around the world: Los Panchos.

In their own way, Tres Souls is following in the footsteps of Los Panchos and other trios. All three members sing, but the singular voice is lead guitarist Jesús Martínez. He says the requinto guitar plays in between the lead singer, and its role is to embellish the song: "It's those little licks that you hear in between the vocal breaks," said Martínez. "It's very much another voice and I think that's definitely what I try to get to — a singing voice with the requinto. And depending on the singer, depending on the song, how much you want to put in, how little you want to put in, how loud, how soft, all of that."

Tres Souls just released their first album, "Boleros Made in L.A." Lead guitarist Martínez says their Bolero style follows the classic sound of the trio, but they added the electric guitar to give the songs a richer quality. The album also includes samples of movies from the Golden Age of Mexican cinema, which Martínez said was inspired by hip-hop: "Wu-Tang Clan was probably the first or one of the first — they sampled movies from Japan, these Kung Fu movies, and then that's their whole style," he says. "And so I was like, 'hey we should just do Cinema de Oro, put it into our music, have it be a way to tell the story.'" Roberto Carlos says he wants people to enjoy timeless music that helps to bring families together: "I want people to appreciate what came before us — the trio románticos, the composers ... and share it now and celebrate it, something that's really iconic to our culture," he said.

The next "Boleros de Noche" concert is at the Downey Theatre in June, then a big show at the Ford Theatre in September — featuring the heirs of the legendary Trio Los Panchos.

Tres Souls | Photo by Jasmin Ramos

INSTRUMENTS

CRISTINA PATO

From an early age, Cristina Pato has been playing two instruments — classical piano and gaita, the Galician bagpipe. She always figured the path of these instruments would never cross, and she'd have to choose one or the other: "So to me, trying to find a space or a language that would represent me and my instincts and my traditions and all the things that I really love to listen to or to play — that was the challenge, in the last, probably like 10 years of my career."

In 2005, Cristina Pato moved to New York. She says she'd planned to leave the bagpipes in Spain and focus on classical piano: "And then I meet Osvaldo Golijov, who is an amazing composer from Argentina who fell in love with the bagpipe. I met him at the University while I was playing piano, and he opened the door to me to include the bagpipes in the classical world." Through Golijov, she met Yo-Yo Ma and started working with his Silk Road Ensemble. And that's when she started to discover the world of jazz improvisation and applied it to the bagpipe:

"Jazz is this amazing palette of colors, and of languages, and of cultures that are all represented in New York City. And being in this place, in which everybody comes from another place, and we all bring our roots and we all bring our traditions. But those roots and those traditions re-root again and they are born again with a different shape and with a different color and with a different motivation."

Cristina Pato invited the Argentinian pianist Emilio Solla to co-produce her record. One day, he called to tell her he'd composed a piece for her called "Gaitango" — a tango played on the bagpipes:

"And I started laughing like crazy because I thought he was joking. I mean, who am I to laugh also, because I play bagpipes. So, no matter what I do it's going to be out of context. But he heard this piece, which is very difficult because he knew already the instrument, because we were already working together. But I don't have all the notes in the instrument. I don't even have more than an octave and he was writing all these chromaticisms and he was challenging me like, 'oh yea you can get them, you can get them.'"

As a pianist, Cristina Pato can play anything from Mozart to John Cage to The Beatles. Now, immersed in the jazz and world music scene in New York, she says she's found the freedom to play any kind of music on the bagpipes:

"Probably, for me right now, after almost eight years living in New York and working with musicians from all around the world, I feel more confident about taking my instrument out of its comfort zone. I think I have an amazing instrument — I think we Galicians have an amazing instrument that is the Galician bagpipe, the gaita."

Cristina Pato and her gaita | Photo by Xan Padrón

IBRAHIM MAALOUF

Ibrahim Maalouf plays a four-valve trumpet — most just have three. The extra valve, attached to the button a trumpeter pushes down, allows the Lebanese musician to play quartertones — the notes between notes that characterize Arabic makams. "The makams are scales and modes with quarter-tones and three quarter-tones intervals," Maalouf says. "This is something that you cannot find in Occidental music." Maalouf credits his father, the renowned Lebanese classical trumpeter Nassim Maalouf, with the innovation:

"This trumpet that he invented is really pure genius. He invented the only Arabic instrument in which you blow, that allows you to play all modes, all scales, in all the tonalities. This does not exist in Arabic music. It's not only a trumpet that makes you play quarter-tones. He invented a way to blow in the instrument. He invented a new way to play the trumpet."

Maalouf says there are many links between Arabic and Western music. He says when he's playing jazz, he can incorporate Arabic scales thanks to one specific similarity:

"There's this note that we actually call 'the blue note' and I believe it's a heritage from African music. Those notes that are right in the middle, between a note and another note, those are 'blue notes' that you bend with the lips. Those are quarter-tones. From these kinds of scales, I can switch to music that is very close to Arabic feelings."

Ibrahim Maalouf's latest project is his first devoted exclusively to jazz: a score he was commissioned to write for the 1926 silent film by French master René Clair, "The Prey of the Wind." Maalouf's inspiration was another trumpeter's score for another French film: Miles Davis' music for Louis Malle's "Elevator to the Gallows." "This music really, really has been probably one of my favorite musics for years," Maalouf says. "So I used this opportunity to compose the music of a very, very old French movie of the '20s, and I decided to compose something that would sound a little bit like the music of Miles on his movie."

John Schneider, founding director of MicroFest, the country's largest microtonal music festival, says Maalouf crosses the boundaries between jazz and Middle Eastern music elegantly:

"He's using those seven notes in the scale, but when it comes time for him to improvise, he strays off the path just a little bit — he's breathing. It's like spicing food in a particular way. So sure, we've all had chicken, but tandoori chicken is different from Mexican chicken or Chinese chicken, right? It's still the same meat, but what you do with those spices makes all the difference. It's almost like an accent, too: an English accent, an American accent, a Southern accent. The words we recognize, but how they're presented, slightly different. The man obviously has Lebanese music, traditional music, in his ear. So when it comes time for him to ornament, he uses those strange, wonderful spices to get them an odd quarter-tone tinge and that gives you that flavor of the Middle East."

Maalouf moved with his family to Paris when he was a small child. His father still lives there and, according to Maalouf, is not too keen on his son's current career path. "In some way, I think that he believes that I should have taken some other way," Maalouf says. "Some other direction that would have been what he wanted me to do when I was young." He says his dad is not the only one. When he visits older musicians in Morocco or Cairo, he's always confronted with the same reaction to his music:

"So I usually take my trumpet off my bag and I play him this very, very old kind [of] traditional improvisation. And they start usually saying, 'Oh, this is what I prefer and this is what you need to do.' And I say, 'You know, I know how to do that and I love to do it. Today, I want to mix my music to the new world, to the new scene. I want to meet people who are discovering new colors — to participate, to create new music. I don't want to remain in an old white and black postcard.' Then, after this discussion, they usually understand what I mean and they say, 'You know what, you're right. Don't listen to your father. Do what you want.'"

Ibrahim Maalouf says he may not be playing or recording classical or traditional Arabic music, but he's still holding on to the heritage he received from his father.

Ibrahim Maalouf and his four-valve trumpet | Photo courtesy of the artist

GUILLERMO CONTRERAS

There's a place in Mexico City that's filled with thousands of musical instruments from all over Latin America — some of them more than 100 years old. It's not a museum or music school. It's an apartment. Actually, the collection's grown so much, it now fills two apartments. It's the result of a lifelong passion for the instruments and their history, as well as a determination to share them.

Guillermo Contreras is a brawny 63-year-old with gray hair and a beard, but when he opens the door — wearing blue jeans and a black dress shirt — you barely notice him. There are instruments everywhere. It's more than any museum collection I've ever seen. "No, I've filled one museum with 300 pieces," Contreras says. "I can tell you, there are more than 4,000 instruments here." He's got jaranas, vihuelas, guitarrones, bajo quintos — all Mexican offspring of the Spanish baroque guitar, which was brought here during the colonial period. There are also violins and harps of every size, marimbas, dozens of percussion instruments, and wind instruments of every shape, length and sound. He pulls out a reed flute and says it was played by the Aztecs. The instrument is still played in a region of northeastern Mexico.

Contreras was an architect by profession when he traveled to a small town south of Mexico City in the late 1960s. He met a group of old musicians, some born in the late 1800s, who were playing instruments from that period: "They thought it was amusing that a guy from the city would visit them and have so much interest in their music, which was sort of dying," Contreras says. "Many of them wanted to give me their 10-string guitars, and I couldn't take that away from the family." A few months later, he went back and found that some of the musicians had died. He asked their families about the centuries-old instruments — and says he was stunned by what he heard: "An instrument from the 19th century, already destroyed, had been turned into a chicken feeder; another one became a little kid's wooden horse." Contreras decided then and there that he would dedicate his life to documenting and preserving his country's musical heritage.

Contreras is not just an instrument collector. He also knows each instrument's individual history and how to play it. He pulls out a guitarra séptima, a 14-string guitar that was widely played across Mexico in the 19th century.

Next, he demonstrates how to play a five-string guitarra de golpe, a strumming guitar still played in the state of Guerrero. Contreras walks the walk, says Graco Posadas, director of programming at the CENART, the National Center of the Arts in Mexico City. Posadas says:

> "Every time you ask him about the music, he'll tell you he's already been to the mountains, he's already walked the kilometers, and he's the only one that's dedicated time to preserve those instruments, some of which have disappeared, unless he has them, and from every region in Mexico."

In addition to the instruments, Guillermo Contreras has also amassed a large collection of field recordings, old photos and music publications dating back hundreds of years. He spends 16 hours a week sharing what he knows.

In a small classroom at the National School of Music, three students tap small turtle-shell drums with deer horns as Contreras plays a small bamboo flute. It's the same melody that's been played by Zapotec people of Oaxaca for hundreds of years. One of the students is Dalila Franco. She's been studying music with Contreras for about a year:

"These rhythms, these melodic patterns, are calling us Mexicans; they're telling us who we are, even if we don't understand what they're trying to tell us. So the School of Music offers two tracks: the Western approach we inherited from Europe, where we learn the music of Beethoven, Mozart and Bach. But there's also this other one that has a lot to do with our identity."

For more than four decades, Guillermo Contreras has been a mentor and teacher to dozens of young musicians. He's tried to get funding to build a museum and a music school, without success. But he keeps collecting and teaching because, he says, these instruments and their history are precious reminders of our humanity: "I feel that this helps me understand a little bit more about life, as seen through the art of music and the musical instrument, which I believe are the most precious creations of humanity." With or without a museum, Contreras says that's reason enough to continue collecting them, though he says he's a little worried about finding space for more.

Guillermo Contreras and a "guitarra de golpe" | Photo by Betto Arcos

PARTCH ENSEMBLE

On a recent Tuesday morning, musician Erin Barnes arrives at the home of John Schneider in Venice and carefully removes an odd-shaped instrument from the back of her car. As we step into the house, other instruments are spread all over the living room. This is not your typical marimba, says Barnes:

"The keys are arranged in the shape of a diamond, and if you could imagine that there's a horizontal row, of six bars and on either side of that, close to your body and far from your body. There's a row of five, and then four, and then three, two, one. It forms these diagonal rows of six bars, and so that's actually how the notes are arranged."

Barnes studied percussion at Cal Arts and has been playing the diamond marimba since 2002. She says she won't let go of this special instrument: "And I feel really, really lucky to be playing it because I feel like this music utilizes what my own personal strengths are as a musician and the things I'm interested in as a musician, so I feel like it's a happy match."

The diamond marimba, and more than 30 other instruments, were invented by composer Harry Partch. He was born in Oakland in 1901. Guitarist John Schneider is the founding artistic director of the Partch Ensemble:

"He was a very good keyboard player, he played in silent movie theaters for a living, while he was in high school, and he got so good at it he thought that he would like to become a piano virtuoso, and he came to Southern California, and went to USC. He lasted three months. He also had some very interesting ideas about the human voice, and the relationship of musical instruments with that. And he found out that there's a lot more we can hear than he was being offered by the instruments he already knew how to play."

Partch learned that there were hundreds of notes that people hadn't heard before. And there's a whole new way of tuning where notes can interact in a different way. Partch caught the bug and he started making musical instruments and composing for them, says Schneider:

"Basically, he invented 24 or 25 classes of instruments. But sometimes he built three or four different versions of the same one, because the first one didn't go so well. So eventually he made 36 or 37 absolutely custom musical instruments, some of them adapted from normal instruments, but after about 1945, he just created his own."

The first instrument he created was the "adapted viola." And he replaced the neck on it with a cello neck and a cello fingerboard — and then tuned it an octave below the violin. Next, Partch made an adapted guitar:

"And they're beautiful chords, but he said, 'it sort of plays like a mandolin, it doesn't sound like a guitar and a mandolin either, it's sort of in between the two.' And he wrote a famous piece of music called 'Barstow,' that was probably his biggest hit. He was stuck in Barstow, California, hitchhiking in the early 1940s, and wrote down a bunch of graffiti and set it to music, and he did it on this musical instrument."

John Schneider has been on a personal mission: he wants more people to know that Harry Partch is as important as any other composer. Over the past 20 years, he's been building many of Partch's instruments and performing the composer's music with the Partch Ensemble. Many of the instruments are here in the living room of his Venice home:

"He's been one of the best kept secrets in American music. He made a lot of recordings — he actually made a living selling his recordings in the 1950s. We talk about indie music now, people get together their own bands, and sell stuff on Bandcamp. He was doing this; he was pressing his own records in the 1950s. Because nobody else would."

Partch was a well-kept secret until the late 1960s, when Columbia records discovered him. He made three records for the label, including "The World of Harry Partch." Despite his achievements, Schneider says Partch is considered an oddity, and those who know about him describe him as the weird guy who made all the strange musical instruments:

"That's the tip of the iceberg. It turns out that when you get to know this music, play it, study it, which I've been doing for the last 30 years, you realize this is great music, this is well-written, highly-crafted, integrated music, just as important and satisfying and structurally relevant as Bach or Beethoven or anybody else. He's one of the biggies. And yet nobody knows about him. So that's my job."

The Partch Ensemble just released a new record called "Sonata Dementia." It's fitting that the release of the album was an intimate concert at the MorYork Gallery in Highland Park. This is not just any gallery — it's a private collection of artifacts and unusual art made with recycled materials. Partch's 10 odd-sounding instruments made for a perfect evening of strangely beautiful music in a strangely beautiful space.

Partch Ensemble performing at Jacaranda | Photo courtesy of John Schneider

RODRIGO y GABRIELA

The guitar duo Rodrigo y Gabriela released a new album last month called "Mettavolution." The Mexico City-born guitarists came through Los Angeles recently to tape a performance for the Jimmy Kimmel Show. I talked to them at the Old Style Guitar Shop located in a residential area of Silver Lake. There are two rooms filled with all kinds of acoustic and electric guitars, and other string instruments.

Rodrigo Sanchez and Gabriela Quintero, better known as Rodrigo y Gabriela, arrived and began looking around. The owner told them they could try anything they liked. I asked Gabriela about the instruments they play:

"We play Yamaha custom-made guitars and they have a special kind of little 'piezo' so they can absorb all the acoustic sounds and the percussion on the acoustics. But then without the feedback so then we'll be able to play it in a big PA, almost like a rock ambiance and so it will sound big as a rock band, but without the feedback."

Rodrigo y Gabriela's sound is a combination of different elements. They were previously in a metal rock group; the sound of a full band was already part of their DNA. Rodrigo plays most of the melodies while Gabriela builds the rhythms and the bass lines — both powered by loud amplifiers. Rodrigo y Gabriela are constantly on tour. When they're on the road they each take about five guitars. Gabriela says unlike some of their rock friends who may take a Gibson and a Fender, their situation is different:

"We have like clone guitars, just in case one of them breaks. Because, even though they're very good guitars, every day we kind of evolve in our sounds, the way we play and all of that, and sometimes the things break — and sometimes things are not captivating the new way, the new riff or the new whatever — so we need to be safe, having all of those guitars."

I asked Rodrigo and Gabriela if they play or practice when they're not touring. At first, they hesitated how to respond, then Rodrigo said: "Yes, I mean, when we're not on the road, we spend, I mean have a studio, and it's at least my favorite place. I mean, I do other stuff, I play soccer and all that. But we have like an office job, even though we're not on tour, but we always have something to do. I mean we have a next tour coming in a month, so we want to work on something, or we want to just write new music, so we spend every morning in the studio from 11 to 3 to 4 — that's our office job."

As we were talking in the guitar shop, someone was playing an electric guitar in the background. It got me thinking again about the sound Rodrigo y Gabriela create with their two acoustic guitars. Gabriela says it was their precarious financial condition that helped them create a rock band sound: "It needed to be done because it was survival, it was a way we were surviving. We wanted to travel and play, without knowing anybody, without any security." In the late 1990s, Rodrigo y Gabriela split from the metal band, left Mexico and moved to Dublin. Their only goal was to make a living from playing music. They couldn't find a gig at a restaurant or pub so they became buskers on Dublin's famous Grafton Street. Their music took off and they started to build their career playing in pubs. In 2002, they started touring all over Ireland, then the rest of Europe, says Rodrigo: "We didn't want to become like a Guitar Hero, like the fastest, or the fastest scales, or the fastest rhythm or something like that. It just came out naturally, we wanted to find a sound that emerged. And it was mostly subconscious, it wasn't like intentional."

Carlo Polli has worked as Rodrigo y Gabriela's road manager from the beginning. Over the past 15 years, Polli has seen them play everywhere — from the smallest comedy club in Cardiff, with 50 people, to 10,000 at Red Rocks Amphitheater in Colorado. He says he never gets tired of seeing the crew's reaction:

"What's this? That we're supposed to be selling 10,000 people and they turn out with a van, and then of course out come two guitars, click! click! plug them in, and some lights get set up. The local crew just literally cannot believe. 'We get like four trucks full of gear turning up and it's nowhere near as close to what you've just done with regards to the performance.'"

Rodrigo says much has changed in the music industry since their early days as buskers, more than 15 years ago. But he says one thing remains clear to both: "If you want to create your own sound you really need to know how to play — that's real. Because otherwise, everyone can make music with a computer and all that. But to transcend, you need to really practice, and that's something that we did and we still do."

Before they left the guitar shop, I showed Rodrigo y Gabriela a tiple I bought in Colombia last year. It's a 12-string precursor of the guitar, and they'd never seen one before. Gabriela strummed a few bars, smiled and said she liked it. Who knows, maybe they'll record something with a tiple in the future.

Rodrigo y Gabriela at the Old Style Guitar Shop in Los Angeles | Photo by Betto Arcos

LOS ANGELES BALALAIKA ORCHESTRA

Iryna Orlova runs a tight ship as director of the Los Angeles Balalaika Orchestra. At their weekly rehearsal, held at Saint Vladimir Ukranian Orthodox Church, she directs an ensemble of more than 30 musicians. Peter Rothe, a founding member of the orchestra plays the balalaika, a triangular string instrument ubiquitous in Russian folk music: "One thing that is very special about the balalaika is the fact that two of the strings are tuned to the same pitch and it's plucked." Rothe says the orchestra has different sizes of balalaikas:

"If you include every triangular-shaped instrument, there are over 10: three are small balalaikas, and then several medium size, which play sort of viola, or a middle voice; and there's one that plays the cello range, and one that plays down in the double bass range. It's really a challenge to fit that one in most cars. If you play that instrument, you have to take it with you when you go to buy your car."

The balalaika is clearly the star in this orchestra, but there's another solo instrument, the "domra." That's what Yrina Orlova plays: "It's a round-board instrument like a mandolin, it's tuned like mandolin and like violin, and in our orchestra it carries the function of violin in a symphony."

The orchestra's main focus is classical, Russian and Ukranian music and the members range in experience and in age. Fiona Fetter is 14, she and her 11-year-old brother Tommy have been playing domra in the orchestra for more than five years: "I started out playing violin and my dad wanted me to learn mandolin. [Orlova] said it was the same thing, so we started domra. We've been playing ever since."

The Balalaika Orchestra recently played a 15th-anniversary concert at Schoenberg Hall on the campus at UCLA. The concert opened with a classic piece by the creator of the modern balalaika orchestra, Vasily Andreyev. But the concert also included Irving Berlin's "Puttin' on the Ritz." Director Iryna Orlova looks back to when she first took over the orchestra in 1995: "When I landed in Los Angeles, 16 years ago, I did not have an expectation of an orchestra which we have today. And these children whom I'm teaching, they are showing how much we can do all together. And I think it exceeded the expectation I had 16 years ago."

Los Angeles Balalaika Orchestra | Photo by Oleg Kbarchenko

RUBÉN LUENGAS

Almost 20 years ago, a young student at the Universidad Nacional Autónoma de Mexico went in search of a very old instrument in the mountains of the southern state of Oaxaca. Today, he has become a leading force in the revival of the instrument called the bajo quinto and the music played on it. Rubén Luengas was working on a research project at the National School of Music in Mexico City in 1995. He wanted to focus on the music of his hometown, in the Mixtec region of Oaxaca, so he asked his 97-year-old grandmother to tell him about the music played at her wedding. "She tells me it was played on violin and 'bajo.' That's what they played at the parties," he says. "I imagined an upright bass, then I thought an electric bass, so I asked her if she could describe the bajo to me. I had no idea what she was talking about."

The bajo quinto looks like an oversized acoustic guitar, with five courses of doubled steel strings. It's played with a pick, with an emphasis on the bass strings. But Luengas did not know any of this. He went to his professor, Guillermo Contreras, who invited him to his studio and showed him a collection of more than 15 bajo quintos from the states of Puebla, Morelos and Guerrero — but none from Oaxaca. Luengas says: "He said to me, 'this is the bajo quinto.' I was speechless. I became captivated by the instrument. So I asked my teacher, 'Where can I get one?' And my teacher says, 'You have to go find it and learn how to play it. It's part of your tradition.' And he gave me a whole lecture on it."

Contreras, who's still a professor and researcher at Mexico's National School of Music, says the bajo quinto likely evolved from the Italian baroque guitar, called "chitarra battente," brought to Mexico during the colonial period. "Chitarra battente is very similar to the bajo quinto because it has five courses of strings — 10 strings in total — and metal strings," says Contreras. "And the body is very similar — big body, large neck." He says in the mid- to late-1800s, a German music store had branches all over Mexico, including one in Oaxaca. He has also found evidence of instrument builders there: "In Oaxaca, there were two important centers for building musical instruments: Coicoyán, in the heart of the Mixteca, and Oaxaca City."

It was that first town, Coicoyán de las Flores, that ethnomusicologist Luengas' grandmother had told him about. She — and just about everybody else — said it was a dangerous place, and advised him not to go. But one day he mustered the courage and took off to the tiny hard-to-reach town deep in the Mixtec mountains. Luengas says that when he arrived, he had the odd feeling he was going back in time. A colleague at the university had given him her grandfather's contact. By now, he felt that everything seemed prearranged:

> "My friend's grandfather told one of his workers to take me to the luthier's house. We went down a very deep ravine, then up a hill. I knocked on a little wooden house, and out comes a man, about 80 years old. He speaks very little Spanish. I told him I was there to get a bajo quinto. He didn't say anything. He turned around and got a brand-new instrument he just finished, for whoever needed it, and he said he was waiting for me. That day completely changed my life."

Luengas is now one of the leading bajo quinto players in Oaxaca. He has formed several groups to showcase the instrument, including an eight-piece band, Pasatono Orquesta, modeled after the traditional Mixtec orchestras of the 1920s. Luengas says Don Telesforo, the luthier he met in Coicoyán, has died. Nobody there learned his secrets: his respect for the trees, the music and all the mysticism that goes with the craft of making the bajo quinto. "But the truth is, it's not dead," says Luengas. "I had the opportunity to learn from him. Now I'm reproducing his bajo quinto models, his singular style. And as long as I'm here, I'm not going to let it die." Luengas says he now has the responsibility to pass on the tradition, but first he needs to find apprentices interested in learning it.

Rubén Luengas and his bajo quinto | Photo by Johnny Moreno

CANDELAS GUITAR SHOP

Candelas Guitars, a neighborhood fixture in East Los Angeles, has been hit hard by the coronavirus shutdown. The shop has been serving customers since 1947, and Tomás Delgado says his family has been making guitars in Los Angeles for three generations. But the business, named after Delgado's great-uncle Candelario, dates back even further, when his family lived in Mexico. "My grandfather, Porfirio Delgado, and my great-uncle, Candelario Delgado, started the business in 1928 in Torreón, moved to Juárez in 1932, then opened the shop in Tijuana in the early '40s and then ultimately opened the shop here in Los Angeles in 1947," Delgado says. "They were two orphan brothers, basically just trying to eat and survive, and started a really solid business."

That business, however, has been seriously threatened. Delgado says their regular clientele included musicians who came to the store for strings, accessories and repairs, but that side of his business has dried up. "All of that is gone," he says. "The things that are keeping me busy right now are the custom orders that I've had on backlog." Since the pandemic shut Candelas' doors more than two months ago, Delgado says, he has been building more classical and flamenco guitars, and he's doing more restoration work.

Musician Stephanie Amaro was one of Candelas Guitars' steady customers and plays a mariachi guitar she bought from the store. As a solo artist, she plays at concerts and festivals, and as a gig musician, she plays at private events such as weddings and quinceañeras. Much like the store she gets her supplies from, Amaro says her business has been severely affected by the pandemic. "Any kind of gathering is completely forbidden right now, which means no live performances and all of the concerts scheduled for the summer, and for the spring, and wedding season, actually, is canceled," she says.

Delgado says the daily income he has been losing over the past two months will never be recovered. "My grandpa, my dad, made me promise that I would keep the hours and keep the business going, but this revenue, we're never going to get it back," he says. "So it's going to have long-term effects on my small business and I'm sure everybody else's."

While the store is closed, Delgado put all but two of his employees on paid leave. To generate much-needed income, he hired guitar instructor Kenneth Del Río to do online classical guitar lessons. "That's helping a little bit. We're hoping that will pick up and help sustain us through the next couple months," he says. "But other than that, on the retail side of it, phone calls and walk-ins and anything else — there's not much more we can do."

Master Luthier, Tomás Delgado "Candelas Guitars" | Photo by Morelucas, courtesy of the artist

PRODUCERS

GABE ROTH

If you've listened to the music of Sharon Jones and the Dap-Kings, Charles Bradley or Antibalas, you probably know about Daptone Records. The indie record label was co-founded by a musician, producer and engineer from Riverside. I went to visit the recording studio to learn about the man behind the Daptone sound.

It's a Wednesday afternoon at the Penrose Studios, located on the second floor of a building in downtown Riverside. Producer Gabriel Roth is at the helm, playing organ, as the San Diego-based group Thee Sacred Souls rehearses a song they're about to record today. Most of the Daptone Records operation is in Brooklyn. But about a decade ago, Roth moved here to set up shop. And in the past year, he noticed a re-emerging music scene in Southern California:

> "I started to meet more and more musicians out here and kind of discovered this kind of local scene, this kind of resurgence. It's hard to say resurgence, 'cause the scene has always been here in California, this kind of soul scene, which is mostly a Chicano scene, but just a lot of people out here that have always been into oldies and old soul records."

Roth was born in the San Bernardino area and grew up in Riverside: "And when I was 17, I moved to New York and I was there for most of my adult life." In 2001, Roth and saxophonist Neal Sugarman launched Daptone Records and ushered-in a revival of Soul music. Since then, the label has released more than 50 albums — and more than 130 45s — of soul, R&B, funk, gospel, rock, Afrobeat and Latin music.

One of Daptone's biggest artists is soul singer Sharon Jones. Roth produced and wrote most of the songs for her group, the Dap-Kings. He recorded hundreds of songs with Jones, including "Fish in the Dish" from the album "Naturally":

> "'Fish in the Dish' is a song I wrote for Sharon and she sang it and it was about fishing, 'cause she loved to fish. I think we had a different song that was supposed to be on a record that we were working on and the song didn't work out in the studio, so I kind of quickly wrote that for her — just thinking like, 'oh, she loves to fish,' and she just dug her teeth into it. It's beautiful just hearing the joy when she sings that song."

Jones died more than three years ago from pancreatic cancer.

> "Playing behind Sharon was probably the thrill of my life and it was probably, in a lot of ways, always be the high point of my musical career, when I was playing the music at the highest level for myself, I just felt the strongest musically, and touching the most people. With her passing, it's definitely a little bit disorienting trying to find my footing. It's not as much as 'oh, I gotta figure out how to make money, or hustle, or find another singer' or some shit like that — it has nothing

to do with that. It's more about just kind of, taking a real step back and 'what do I really have to contribute at this point?' I'm not trying to do what I did again. We did that and we crushed it. The Dap-Kings is still to me the greatest band in the land. But we're not trying to replace Sharon and find another singer."

Another artist whose career was launched by Daptone Records was soul singer Charles Bradley. Sadly, he died about a year after Sharon Jones: "Charles Bradley has a lot of great songs," says Roth. "'In you, I found a love' — that's a great one. 'The World' was obviously a big one. 'The Telephone Song' is one of my favorites." Bradley and Jones put the Brooklyn-based label on the map, but somewhere along the way, Roth started to feel a tug: "In 2010, I believe, my wife and I, we had our daughter Penelope, we wanted to live a mellower life so we moved back out here, moved back to Riverside." Roth found an old building downtown and rented part of the second floor. There are no computers in the studio. All the music is recorded on analog tape. Simón Guzmán, 29 years old, has been working as an engineer with Daptone Records for the past seven years:

> "It's a process, that takes a little bit longer, it's a little bit more time-consuming, working with tape, working with all the musicians at the same time. At the end of the day, when the record comes out it sounds like it was recorded by a bunch of people in the same room and they were all throwing ideas. If Daptone has a sound, that's the sound."

Looking back at the success of his work with all these artists, Roth — now 45 — says he's in a different phase of his life and career. He has the resources to contribute to the R&B scene in Southern California:

> "I'm in a great position to help these younger artists who actually have their own scene, that isn't my scene, it's not something I created, it's not something I take credit for, it's not something I lay claim to or put my flag-in necessarily. But it's something that I feel like, I kind of was were they were twenty-something years ago, me and my friends and the scene — you sing backgrounds on my record and I'll play bass on your record — these kind of bands that are working together and starting to appreciate similar music."

Adriana Flores is a singer in two East LA groups, Thee Altons and Thee Sinseers. Both groups have been recording at the Daptone Studios in Riverside: "First of all, it's a dream — like if anyone ever asked me, what label or anything I would want to do it, it would be Daptone, anything associated, 'cause I'm a huge fan of all their acts." And next Spring, the music of both R&B groups will be released on a new Daptone imprint called Penrose.

Gabe Roth directing a concert rehearsal at the Apollo Theater in New York | Photo courtesy of Matt Rogers

SEBASTIAN KRYS

On a recent afternoon at a music publisher's office on Sunset Boulevard, 50 people from across the Latin music industry gather for an exclusive artist showcase. The host is producer Sebastian Krys: "Today, we're going to present a duo, which is rare these days, called Mitre." After showing a video clip, the duo of Andrea Sandoval and Luis Mitre play a few songs, including their first single "Los Santos del Amor." Singer Luis Mitre says working with Krys has helped him and Sandoval become better musicians:

> "We arrived in the studio with 20 songs and he was like, 'It's not enough.' But I think this is a really good song, people say it when we sing it. He's tough. But it comes from a place where if he's tough with you is because he sees the potential. That's his magic. He's like an alchemist of music."

That magic began 20 years ago, when Krys was an assistant engineer at Gloria and Emilio Estefan's Crescent Moon Studios in Miami. One night, he was given a chance to mix a song by Colombian pop singer Carlos Vives: "It was one of the mixes for a song called 'La Piragua.'" It was a tight deadline. Krys knew that whatever he did to the song would be final. As we spoke at his recording studio in Woodland Hills, he said working on that album gave him the confidence he needed to find his voice as a producer.

> "So at that point, you have a choice to make: you can either be really conservative about what you're going to do or you can be really bold about it. And I chose the latter, just to go for it and really rearrange the intro of the song. And we spent all night, from six o'clock at night till they came back in at 10 AM and we had created this entire movie scene in the jungle."

Krys was born in Buenos Aires, Argentina. In the late 1970s, when the political climate took a turn for the worse, his parents moved the family to Miami. At age 15, he decided he was going to pursue a career as a musician. But shortly after he was diagnosed with a rare disease, he changed his mind:

> "And the day I told my mom I was giving up music I went to Blockbuster video and got a copy of Sting's 'Bring on the Night' and 'The Police Around the World,' 'cause I was just really into that band at the time. And when I saw 'Bring on the Night' and I saw all those guys in the background I was like 'I'm not good enough to be Sting but I don't know what those guys do, I can probably be one of those guys in board shorts turning knobs.'"

Krys got an audio engineering degree. For two months, he called recording studios around Miami, including the Estefans' Studio, to no avail:

> "Until one day the receptionist was late and the studio manager picked up and I told her 'I studied audio engineering, I'm looking for an internship.' So I had an internship there for three months, just grunt work. And that's how I got in. I didn't know anybody in the business or anything like that. It was just persistence."

Over 20 years, that persistence has paid off. Krys has produced albums by Alejandro Sanz, Carlos Vives, Lori Meyers, and mixed albums by Shakira, Jennifer Lopez and Marc Anthony, to name but a few from a very long list. When Krys moved to Los Angeles in 2008, he came upon a yet unsigned band, La Santa Cecilia: "I started courting them to try to sign them and it took about eight months to get a deal done." The day La Santa Cecilia was to sign with Universal Music Latino, Krys says they were a little glum. "I finally said: 'guys, sign or don't sign. But sign with somebody. More people need to find out about what you guys are doing musically. You can't be LA's greatest kept secret forever." Krys also worked as the A&R director for the mega hit "Despacito," putting together the production team. When "Despacito" got to a billion views on Youtube, he wrote a note to the song's co-writer and performer, Luis Fonsi: "And he knows me pretty well, he knows that I'm fairly serious about everything. I said, 'wow, one billion views, now the real work begins.' And he wrote me back and he said 'I thought you were going to say congratulations!'"

Recently, Krys produced the 30th album by Eugenia León — one of Mexico's most renowned singers. León says they didn't meet until the day they started recording her vocals for the album:

"He told me, 'I'm very serious, but don't think I'm in a bad mood, that's how I am.' So you learn to adapt to it and be respectful, just the way he was with me. He said, 'what do you think, did you like the sound of your voice?.' He would comment or give me a suggestion."

Krys says as a producer he can make an artist sound the best they can possibly sound, but in the end, the artist has to deliver: "Anybody who does this for a living knows that you're only as good as the artists you work with. Period." And currently, Sebastian Krys is working with a pretty good artist — a guy named Elvis Costello.

Sebastian Krys | Photo courtesy of the artist

GUSTAVO SANTAOLALLA

If you listen to Mexico's most famous rock band, Café Tacvba, you likely recognize Gustavo Santaolalla's name as the group's producer. That's just one of the dozens of Latin American bands he's worked with. And if you saw the films "Babel" or "Brokeback Mountain," you've heard the Oscar-winning soundtracks he composed. But you may not know his history as a musician and performer.

Santaolalla's recording studio is in the hills of Echo Park. From the street, it looks like a normal 1950s ranch-style house. But just inside the entrance, there's a wall with more than 50 covers of the albums he's produced over the last few decades. He walks in, singing a melody, and starts talking about the new album from his group, Bajofondo. The band plays contemporary dance music, reinventing tango and other styles from Rio de la Plata, in Argentina. At first, he hesitates to tell me the name, but then: "I'm going to say it. The album is called 'Aura.' Aura, for us, means the same thing [as] here, the energy field that surrounds living things. But also in Argentinian, aura it's like slang to say ahora — now." Santaolalla's studio is called La Casa (The Home). This is where he has recorded the bulk of his work as producer, composer, bandleader and solo artist: "It's impossible to count the amount of amazing music that has come out of this place and that has been created here," he says. "All major alternative Latin acts have done something here. All the music of the movies, at a certain point, most of it gets done here. So it's very charged, the place."

Before he came to Los Angeles, in the late 1970s, Santaolalla was in a couple of successful bands in Argentina. In the late '70s, when the military dictatorship ruled with an iron fist and things turned ugly, he moved here and formed a band called Wet Picnic. Eventually, Santaolalla felt a different calling: "I wanted to put my talent at the service of other people, instead of being so obsessed just with my project." Next, he went to Mexico City and saw the emergence of a rock scene that recalled what he lived in Argentina, in the late '60s and early '70s: "It reminded me of that vibe, of that energy, that quality, that freshness, that innocence, that danger." Santaolalla recalls the first time he saw Café Tacvba. It was 1989, before he had his own record label:

"They were playing with cheap instruments, the sound was terrible, but they had something unbelievable. I thought, these guys are so unique! At the time I didn't

have [my own label], so when I saw a band that I liked I had, to go and convince a record label to sign them so I could produce the record. In this case, it took me almost two years to get Tacvba signed. [The labels] didn't want to sign them."

In the late '90s, Santaolalla was approached to work on the soundtrack of the first feature-length film by a Mexican director. Santaolalla was so busy producing bands he told his assistant to decline on his behalf. He had not read the script or seen any of the film. Then, something happened: "That night, I woke up in the middle of the night and I started thinking, 'What if? What if he's a genius?'" Santaolalla gave his assistant an urgent task: "'Call and tell them that if they come to Los Angeles and they show me the film, I will consider it.' Sure enough, they came. We saw the first five minutes [and] I was like, I'm in, I'm doing this. Yes, it was amazing." And that was how Santaolalla came to work on "Amores Perros" by Alejandro González Iñárritu.

Santaolalla followed that with the music for "The Motorcycle Diaries." Then, "Brokeback Mountain," which garnered his first Academy Award for original score. Then came a reunion with Iñárritu for "Babel," and a second Oscar, followed by more than a dozen film and TV projects — and, of course, producing albums by many Latin alternative bands and his own, Bajofondo. More recently, he's been collaborating with songwriter Paul Williams on a musical version of Guillermo del Toro's "Pan's Labyrinth." And if that's not enough, Santaolalla has also jumped into the world of video games, composing the music for the wildly popular "The Last of Us." But one thing he's been wanting to do for a while is to play his solo albums live: "At this point in my life — I'm now 66 years old — I felt the need to look back at my life through my songs and through my music. This is basically a look at my songwriting since I was 15 to now."

Before I leave Santaolalla's studio I ask him to tell me about his work in the forthcoming season of the Netflix series, "Narcos." Once again, he hesitates: "… which is very exciting because … ahhhh — I don't think I can tell." But this much we know: the next season of "Narcos" is set in Mexico in the 1980s. Santaolalla says he can relate to the period. It's the same time when he was in Mexico looking for the next rock band to produce.

Gustavo Santaolalla in his recording studio with ronroco | Photo courtesy of Alejandra Palacios

EDUARDO LLERENAS

More than 40 years ago, four friends — three scientists and one musician — went to the Huasteca region in Northeastern Mexico in search of music they wanted to record for their own enjoyment. Now, some of their work has been released on a two-CD compilation titled "El Gusto." The four friends found a wealth of music in Ciudad Valles, in the state of San Luis Potosí. One member of the group, Eduardo Llerenas, even chose to dedicate his life to recording the music of the area, giving up a career in biochemistry:

> "It was because I just couldn't afford the time to do both things. Being a scientist and a researcher, you need 24 hours a day, and to do this work with the music, I think you need the same sort of time. So it was impossible to continue in that way. So, back in 1986, I stopped and I moved into the music field."

Llerenas used the observational skills he honed as a scientist to try to understand the community. "We have developed an ear, like the local people, in order to be good judges of this, because we don't normally record whatever we listen to," he says. "You have to adapt your ear to the local ear, and in that way you could actually make judgments and do recordings of what we think are the very best musicians." Son huasteco, as the musical style came to be called, is also commonly known in Mexico as huapango. It's played by a trio of musicians: one playing a small, five-string rhythm guitar called a jarana huasteca, one on an eight-string bass guitar called a quinta huapanguera, and another playing a violin. The two guitarists sing coplas, or short poetry stanzas, alternating verses between them. When Llerenas and his colleagues were collecting the music for "El Gusto," they found themselves at a bus stop in Ciudad Valles where they met a trio called Los Camperos Huastecos. Their violinist, the late Heliodoro Copado, is considered one of the top musicians of the son huasteco style. The recording they made of the trio — at a motel restaurant — produced the classic song "El Sacamandú."

Son huasteco has two unique trademarks: improvised violin ornamentations based on a melody and the high falsetto voice. The style has spread beyond Veracruz and San Luis Potosí, where Llerenas and his friends recorded much of this music, to other states including Hidalgo, which is now the wellspring of son huasteco. Llerenas says the reason for the music's popularity is the demand for it at family parties, weddings, baptisms and birthdays. "So it is the desire of the community, they love this music they have been born to, they dance to it [and] they drink to it," he says. "So it's the meaning of the fiesta for them, where the huasteco music is associated."

Writer Mary Farquharson co-produced the "El Gusto" compilation. She says contemporary groups are not reinventing the sound, but building on the roots that make the music remarkable. "The emotional range that can go from joy to great tragedy within one song, but there's always emotional relief," Farquharson says. "It sort of pushes you up and drags you down and whirls you around, all in one song. It's such a complete music and it's played by three musicians."

Roy Germano was filming his documentary "The Other Side of Immigration" in 2008, when he and a friend picked up a CD in a market one day. He says he was blown away by the sound. Last summer, Germano began shooting a new documentary about son huasteco music called "A Mexican Sound." For him, the recordings are great, but to really get the feel of the music, he says, you have to see it live. "When you throw into the mix a live performance — where people are dancing on the tarima and creating their own rhythm — I think it's just a magical sound," Germano says. One of the musicians Germano interviewed for his documentary is Marcos Hernandez. More than 40 years ago, Llerenas and his friends discovered Hernandez, who at the time was a 17-year-old singer and guitar player with a group named Los Cantores de la Sierra. Hernandez says he's thrilled to see children learning son huasteco. He says his grandkids are starting to like it, and even kids as young as 6 are playing almost like professionals because parents are exposing them to the music at an early age.

When Llerenas and his three friends went to the Huasteca region to record this music, they thought it was on the verge of extinction. Today, it's thriving, perhaps more than ever. Thanks to their efforts, even more people will have the pleasure — El Gusto — of hearing it.

Enrique Ramírez de Arellano & Eduardo Llerenas en Huejutla, Hidalgo, 1985 | Photo courtesy of Discos Corason

JOE CASTRO

Just before he died in 2009, Joe Castro sat down with his son James to listen to some tapes. The reel-to-reels were full of Castro's own decades-old recordings, in which the jazz pianist jammed with his contemporaries. "It was kind of like a shock," James says, "because right when we put the first tape on, it sounded like it was recorded yesterday." Father and son went through more than 40 hours of tape. James says he was used to hearing his dad back up other musicians. "He was being reserved for others," he says. "He always played down for others because, you know, he was just that way. But when he wanted to go off, he could go off."

Joe Castro was part of the jazz scenes on two coasts in the 1950s and 1960s. He led his own small groups and played with some of the top names in jazz. Dave Brubeck was a fan. And yet, most of the music Castro made for his label was never released — until now. This winter, Sunnyside Records unveiled "Lush Life: A Musical Chronology of Joseph Armand Castro," a career-spanning box set of the musician's work.

Joseph Armand Castro was born into a Mexican American family in 1927, in a small mining town near Phoenix, Arizona. The family moved to northern California and Joe started playing piano. By the time he was 15, he was in the musicians' union. In 1951, Castro was leading his own group when he met the millionaire heiress Doris Duke, and began a relationship with her. James Castro says that while his father enjoyed the perks of their union, his career stalled. "With Doris caging him, wanting him to be with her at all the times — 'Let's go here, let's go to Switzerland, let's go to Morocco,'" James says, laughing. "He was caught in between, 'I'd love to travel and see these places and spend time with the woman I love,' or play jazz. I mean, there were so many conflicts."

In 1953, Duke purchased Falcon Lair, a Beverly Hills mansion formerly owned by Rudolph Valentino. She financed a state-of-the-art recording studio; Castro invited many of his musician friends to jam there, and recorded them. These recordings became the stuff of legend among musicians and jazz aficionados, says Kirk Silsbee, who writes about jazz for DownBeat magazine:

"People would look at the data. They would look at the names: Zoot Sims, Lucky Thompson, Oscar Pettiford — all the great people who played at Falcon Lair when Joe presided over the music there and, as we now know, recorded it. They could only imagine what was recorded for history. But now we have this box set, and it's nothing less than a treasure trove."

Castro made his New York debut in 1956, and before long landed a deal with Atlantic Records. And while Castro wasn't necessarily an innovator, he made up for it in other ways, says Daniel Richard, a former executive at Universal Jazz France and co-producer of the box set: "He has a great technique, and he swings all the time. That's very, very important. For him, it was the purpose of playing music, swinging." By the early '60s, the relationship between Joe Castro and Doris Duke had soured. Duke threw him out of Falcon Lair. He sued, and she counter-sued. Richard says when the dust finally settled, the two tried to salvage their relationship by creating a record label. "At the end of this fight, they wanted to have something in common," he says. "And they start the label Clover — in that purpose, just to have something to do. But it was not enough to keep the couple together."

After Castro and Duke separated, she kept the recordings until 1992. A year before Duke died, she called her old flame. "She said, 'I'm going to start giving you what you deserve,'" James Castro says. "My dad said, 'No, no, you don't need that. But the Clover stuff would be great.' And the next day, all the Clover stuff was on the doorstep." It was more than 200 reels of tape. But by then, Joe Castro's career as a jazz soloist was pretty much over. He married singer Loretta Haddad and they moved to Las Vegas. Castro got a secure job as music director of the Tropicana Hotel so they could raise their children, including James. "He was a very underrated musician," James says. "I think this first box set shows who he is. But there's so much more music still to be heard."

James Castro says he wants his father to be remembered as a man with the highest integrity — caught up in a world of money but also accomplished in the art form he loved most: jazz.

Joe Castro with Philly Joe Jones and Cannonball Adderley | Photo by Jerome Lee

PLACE AND NATION

JORDI SAVALL AND *EL NUEVO MUNDO*

Two hundred years ago, in 1810, Mexico declared independence from Spain. But for three centuries before then, Mexican culture was woven from Spanish and Indigenous traditions. Now, Spanish musician Jordi Savall is exploring that hybrid with the help of a group of Mexican musicians.

It's fitting that Jordi Savall met the Mexican group Tembembe Ensamble Continuo in Guanajuato, one of Mexico's oldest colonial cities. The new album, "El Nuevo Mundo," is a reflection on the music born when two cultures collided in the New World. Jordi Savall says it's important to remember several things about this encounter. First, when the Spaniards landed they brought with them Africans. "The Africans was the slaves in this — they had to do the most difficult works. And then come the Indians, the native people, and the music that we still today are singing in the baroque music at the end of the renaissance is a mix of this confluence of old Spain, African rhythmical and songs, and Indian influences — all this mixed together."

One of the music styles the Spaniards brought with them is son, created in the 16th century. Guitarist Eloy Cruz, one of the founding members of Tembembe Ensamble Continuo says it flourished and changed in Mexico:

> "We take old sones — we call them sones, pieces for baroque guitar from 17th- and 18th-century manuscripts — and we put this music together with sones that are from today, that are alive today. And they just work perfectly together. It's just like one single piece, but it's always a pair of pieces, one from 17th-century Spain, another from 21st-century Mexico."

Cruz says this collaboration with Jordi Savall not only creates a bridge across cultures but across time. "It's not a confluence, not a meeting of different forms, of kinds of music. It's one and the same."

The piece called "El Cielito Lindo," starts with a Cumbes, a dance by Santiago de Murcia, one of many composers who came to the New World. De Murcia was a Spanish guitarist who lived in Mexico in the early 1700s. He absorbed the Indigenous musical traditions and began to compose informed by his experience, says Jordi Savall. "We use the music from Santiago de Murcia, like many other music from this period, to make the bridge to the ancient to the New World. Savall points out that Spanish music before 1492 was very different. He says many people don't realize that as soon as 50 years after the encounter, the musical language of Spain — and, by extension, Europe — was forever changed:

> "Fifty years after this, in Spain, we invented chaconas, folías, jácaras, seguidillas — all lot of the dances, who they had never exist before and dances that were so exciting and so beautiful and so different from everything. And this was in Spain. And I think this has a very strong relation with this meeting between the old Spain and the New World."

Jordi Savall says this music shows the diverse influences of all the cultures coming together in the Americas. And he says that's one of the most positive aspects of the tragic encounter between Spain and the New World. Eloy Cruz of the Ensamble Continuo says this musical collaboration is an opportunity for Spanish people to see themselves through Latin American music. "It's like they spread their seed out in the world, and now they are finding pieces of themselves that they thought to be lost to be very much alive and healthy in the other side of the ocean." The same might be true for Latin Americans.

Jordi Savall, Hesperion XXI and Tembembe Ensamble Continuo in concert at Cité de la Musique in Paris | Photo by David Ignaszewski

SAMBA AND BRAZIL

It's a Saturday night at the Mangueira Samba School in Rio de Janeiro, where students are getting ready for Carnival. Millions of people will be dancing to the rhythms of Brazil's most popular music: samba. Osvaldo Martins, one of the school's organizers, has put together a competition for the best samba-enredo, or samba story. Standing at the edge of the throbbing crowd, he explains that each group vying for a spot in the Carnival parade has to tell a story, kind of like a moving opera. "And just like an opera, the parade has a plot for the story being told," he says. "With that story in mind, a visual artist will take that plot and will 'carnivalize' it: create the fantasies, the costumes and the floats."

The Mangueira Samba School isn't really a school, but a community organization that spends most of each year preparing for Carnival. There are more than 40 samba schools across Rio, each of which has 3,000 to 5,000 members. Here at Mangueira, dancers crowd the floor of this warehouse-like building. Four singers are perched on a balcony, and on stage, what looks like about a hundred drummers pound out a parade rhythm. A samba can be fast or slow; it can propel a parade or insinuate sensuality behind a song. It's the child of African rhythms brought to Brazil by slaves, born in Rio in the late 1800s. The first recorded song to be called a samba was "Pelo Telefone," from 1917.

Today, the type of samba played in Rio's clubs and recorded by most singers is classic or traditional samba, and composers are still writing in that style. One of them is Leandro Fregonesi, who says samba is a complete music genre in terms of rhythm, melody and harmony — it offers a musician limitless possibilities. "If you have a boy that plays power chords on the guitar to play rock 'n' roll, he'll never play samba," Fregonesi says. "If you get a boy who plays samba and choro, he can play

everything. That's the difference, the richness." It's that richness and its infectious, feel-good quality that's made samba a popular sound in the clubs of Rio's historic Lapa neighborhood. At the club Carioca da Gema, you can hear today's emerging samba voices perform every night. Julio Estrela, 27 years old, lives near downtown Rio. He's been singing in a samba group for the last three years. "For me, samba came to me like a surprise," Estrela says. "I don't have musicians in my family, I began to listen to music and one day I began to listen to samba. I was playing cavaquinho. Cavaquinho is a little guitar with four strings, and I began to play and listen, listen and play."

Samba is not just for the musicians who work the scene in Rio. Singer Maria Rita is from São Paulo in southern Brazil; she recorded a samba album a few years ago and is about to release a second one this spring. Rita says sambistas expect you to get their music right: "For the first album that I recorded, I was really scared that I could offend people more than I could add to it. But that didn't happen, thank God. I'd be somewhere and meet a sambista and they're like, 'That was so good you did that, thank you! Do it again!'"

Much has changed since samba came of age in Rio. For decades, the music was a vehicle for Black people to integrate into Brazilian society. But over time, samba helped to transform Brazilian culture. Francis Hime, a renowned composer and arranger of Brazilian music, explains that samba is an integrated genre: "It belongs to everybody. It not belongs only to Black people, as it was before. Before it was a kind of way of opening the door, for being accepted." As the great composer of sambas in the 1930s Noel Rosa wrote in "Feitio de Oração," one of his classic songs: *Samba doesn't come from the hills, nor the city / anyone who bears a passion can feel that a samba comes from the heart.*

Saturday night at Escola de Samba Mangueira in Rio de Janeiro | Photo by Betto Arcos

VALLENATO AND COLOMBIA

Colombian writer Gabriel García Márquez once said that "One Hundred Years of Solitude" was a 400-page vallenato: a traditional music of Colombia's Caribbean coast. The songs are mini-epics, filled with local characters and poetry. It's a style that stretches back 200 years and is still thriving today. You don't have to look far for signs of Gabriel García Márquez's love of vallenato. It's right there in his 2002 memoir, "Living to Tell the Tale": "I had dreamed about the good life — he wrote — going from fair to fair and singing with an accordion and a good voice, which always seemed to me to be the oldest and happiest way to tell a story."

At high noon in Valledupar, the capital of vallenato, a traditional trio takes the stage. The occasion is the Festival de la Leyenda Vallenata, which has been held in the city that has given the music its name for almost half a century. Its goal is to promote the traditional elements of the style, which is played on three instruments: caja, or drum, guacharaca (scraper), and the diatonic accordion. In addition to a competition, the festival includes daily concerts held in a 25,000-seat amphitheater. Among the headliners this year was superstar singer Carlos Vives, who helped popularize vallenato around the world in the early 1990s. "For me, vallenato is connected to the countryside, to the cattle rancher, to the farmer," Vives says. "That's vallenato. And then there's us, the new generation who have reinvented it. But when I talk about vallenato, we have to remember the 'minstrels.'" The minstrels go back to the early 1800s, when troubadours traveled from town to town, singing songs about local and regional news.

García Márquez would often mention vallenato in his stories, even name-checking a beloved composer, Rafael Escalona. He made vallenato a central part of his most famous book, "One Hundred Years of Solitude," turning a real-life vallenato accordionist, "Francisco El Hombre," into a mythical balladeer. Vallenato composer and historian Tomas Darío Gutiérrez says:

> "The problem is when people confuse one thing with the other. And people think vallenato began with 'Francisco el Hombre' taking an accordion, a drum and a 'guacharaca' instrument, and traveling all over the region, teaching the music he had invented. That story was invented by García Marquez. Back in the day, the news was spread through songs. News that today could be transmitted in a matter of seconds — for instance, about an epidemic."

In "One Hundred Years of Solitude," one of the main characters learns of her mother's death through a famous vallenato accordionist named Francisco el Hombre, inspired by a real-life minstrel. Gutiérrez says people may think García Márquez wrote about a fantasy world in his novel:

> "No, no. He takes the history, the social and cultural reality of our people, and runs it through the sieve of fantasy and creates that monumental work. García Márquez took the real character and processed him thru his 'magical realism.' Many times, the same phenomenon happens in vallenato songs. For instance, the song 'The House in the Air': *I'm going to make you a house in the air.* It's the same thing!"

Artists at a parranda vallenata in Valledupar. From left to right, singer Carlos Mario Zabaleta, composers Deimer Marín and Robi Oñate and guitarist Calixto Mendiola | Photo by Betto Arcos

The song tells the story of a man who wants to build a home for his daughter up in the air to protect her from unwanted suitors, so that only the one who can "reach that high" can win her hand.

It's all part of the oral tradition the novelist was steeped in, says Raymond Williams, a professor at UC-Riverside who has written extensively about García Márquez. Williams says he kept the tradition alive through the book, and also through the annual vallenato festival where he was a regular: "It's a happy marriage for him literarily, and eventually it became a real cultural marriage because he was famous for going to the Festival de Vallenato every year. I guess until he became so, so famous that he just couldn't do it comfortably anymore."

The minstrel tradition of vallenato is still very much alive at the festival. I saw some of it when I dropped-in on a "parranda" in the city of Valledupar. These are small gatherings of friends and musicians who sing, tell stories, eat, and drink Old Parr whisky. The one I went to was hosted by the composer Deimer Marín. He sang and played guitar — no accordion. After a while, Carlos Mario Zabaleta, a well-known vallenato singer, arrived and told me a story: in October of 2006, while on tour in Mexico with the group "Reyes Vallenatos de Colombia," he was invited to sing at a Parranda hosted by the Colombian ambassador in Mexico City. The guest of honor was García Márquez:

> "He started asking me about Armando Zabaleta, a great-uncle of mine, a vallenato composer. You cannot imagine the nostalgia I saw in his face — I had no idea how long it had been since he last heard a drum, a 'guacharaca,' an accordion. I will never forget when he said he would love for me to sing 'La Diosa Coronada.' So when he died two years ago, I dusted off his books and re-read them, and I found the epigraph he

included in 'Love in the Time of Cholera,' two verses from 'La Diosa Coronada': *The words I am about to express, they now have their own crowned goddess.*"

Up until the late 1800s, vallenato was played on Indigenous Colombian flutes called gaitas. When the accordion came to Colombia from Germany in the mid-1800s, it became the primary voice playing four distinct "airs" or rhythms: paseo, merengue, son and puya. Last December, UNESCO declared vallenato "intangible heritage, in need of safeguarding." Efraín Quintero, vice-president of Fundación de la Leyenda Vallenata, says the acknowledgment brings with it a big responsibility:

> To promote and support music that does not stray from the melodic and literary structures of traditional vallenato. That said, I'm a firm believer that we have to evolve — we can't restrict or stigmatize new musicians. We just have to make sure that they have all the necessary elements of traditional music and, based on that, create new work.

The Vallenato Festival recognized accordionist Emiliano Zuleta and his brother, singer Poncho Zuleta, for their efforts to preserve the music. "We must follow the rules and parameters of traditional vallenato, to conserve its essence," Zuleta says. "That's the work we do and the recommendation we make to new generations, so they don't distort the truth about Vallenato."

Carlos Vives agrees. It's important to continue recording vallenato and to encourage younger musicians. "It's also important that minstrels continue to thrive, like Emiliano Zuleta, the elder, or Luis Enrique Martinez or Carlos Huertas. Composers that were born free of the recording industry — who were not born to make records, but to carry messages from town to town."

Gabino Andrés Molina and his proud father at the Festival de la Leyenda Vallenata in Valledupar, Colombia, April 2016 | Photo by Betto Arcos

CARLOS DO CARMO AND PORTUGAL

Carlos do Carmo is known as the Sinatra of fado, Portugal's national music. In 2014, do Carmo became the first Portuguese artist to receive a Latin Grammy Lifetime Achievement Award. This past weekend, the 78-year-old singer made his New York debut at Town Hall NYC as part of the Fado Festival of New York.

Often called the Portuguese blues, fado (literally, "fate") is emotional music. "People think that fado is connected with sadness only. It's not true," do Carmo says. There is fado menor — sad fado in minor — joyful fado and really joyful fado, sung in a major key. A corrido is an example of really joyful fado. "The 'corrido' is something you even can dance and there's got to be a smile when you sing it," do Carmo says.

Carlos do Carmo grew up in Lisbon, Portugal and is the son of Lucília do Carmo, one of the great singers of the golden age of fado, which began in the late 1920s. His mother's club in Lisbon became a gathering place for all of the older fado singers, says musicologist and author Rui Vieira Nery. "He absorbed that tradition, but then he went on to re-process that heritage and he was always very curious about the interaction between fado and other genres," explains Vieira Nery, the author of "A History of Portuguese Fado." Vieira Nery cites the singer's keenness on Frank Sinatra and "the crooners." "Sinatra was the best fado singer I ever heard," do Carmo says. "I mean it. You heard Sinatra. The same song in different records — never the same song. That's fado." Do Carmo took Sinatra's approach and applied it to his own records.

Until do Carmo came along in the early 1960s, fado was usually performed by a singer and two guitarists. He brought in the orchestra. Vieira Nery says do Carmo also invited musicians who were outside the scene to compose music for fados. "He managed to attract people from pop rock, from jazz, from art music and convinced them to actually try to get into the language of fado and write melodies for fado, just as much as he attracted some of the very best contemporary poets to write for him," Vieira Nery says. Ary dos Santos was one of those poets. In 1977, three years after the collapse of Portugal's Estado Novo dictatorship, the two men collaborated on an album called "Um Homem na Cidade" (A Man in the City). "We lived in a dictatorship for almost 50 years. There was censorship. So if you sing under censorship, you can't express yourself. And I lived that, I know what I'm talking about. It's terrible, it humiliates you," do Carmo says. "My good friend Ary dos Santos, that was a very, very good popular poet. We had an idea together: Let's make an album about Lisbon in freedom."

Before that album came out, fado had become old-fashioned, aligned with the regime even as do Carmo was pushing its boundaries. "Um Homem na Cidade" was a watershed. It was a call to artists, poets and musicians according to director of the Museu do Fado, Sara Pereira. "Carlos was fundamental, so that [the people] could understand that fado, it can also be a song of intervention, can also be a song of protest," she says.

Vieira Nery believes that do Carmo has helped ensure that the fado tradition will live on. And whether a fado is sad or happy, do Carmo says the music has to be deep; the lyrics have to be strong and go straight to the heart: "For me, it's life, love, it's my entire life, fulfilling my dreams, the love of my hometown, the love of my country."

Carlos do Carmo | Photo by Fernando Bento, cartel de la película de Ivan Dias "Carlos do Carmo, un hombre en el mundo"

ASTRID HADAD AND MEXICO

For Astrid Hadad, everything is fair game, whether it's the Mexican government, the Catholic Church, or Mexico's Independence festivities. The title song of her latest album is called "Tierra Misteriosa" (Mysterious Land). It was inspired by Mexico's Bicentennial celebrations last year. Hadad wanted to offer her own take. The lyrics say:

> Oh poor Motherland, vultures fly over you, priests, military men, multinational companies, presidents, hitmen, and businessmen. Five hundred years have passed and the only thing that's changed is that those who pillage and plunder are referred to as politicians.

"My intention is to say what I feel. We all know that in this country, corruption is at full steam, that governors have become little kings, and nobody keeps an eye on them. The best business right now is to become governor or a politician."

Astrid Hadad has released seven albums and produced more than 20 different stage shows, since the early 1990s. In that time, she's become one of the country's most engaging critics, combining music, performance and political satire. In the song "La Cucaracha," Hadad refers to Mexico's revered president, Benito Juarez. He signed a law in the mid-1800s, limiting the catholic church's power in Mexico. She says, leaders in Mexico aren't as willing to confront the church: "People told me 'are you crazy?' In this song, I sing 'if Juarez lived today, the things he would do, he would hang the pedophile priests by the cojones.'"

When it comes to one of the most high-profile issues in Mexico today, drug-related violence, Hadad says people are so afraid they've become paralyzed. But they shouldn't be: "I think that it's better to be out in the streets. Protesting the violence is the best thing we can do. We can't just stay indoors, because that's what they want." For the classic Mexican song "La Llorona" (The Crying Woman), Hadad wrote these new lyrics: Leave your sorrow, crying woman, because crying paralyzes, and if you stay still, they will beat you up.

> "I never lose my humor. I think it's necessary to keep the spark of humor, the depth of humor. And love too, otherwise life is not worth living. Despite the pains and despite the horrors we're living in Mexico, life is still very beautiful. We have to tell people, 'remember if you step on poop, it will bring you good luck.'"

She closes her new album with the song, "Toca Madera-Knock on Wood." These are hard times, she says, but it's always good to remind people not to lose hope.

Astrid Hadad performing at the Teatro Diana in Guadalajara, Mexico | Photo by Betto Arcos

KIOSK AND IRAN

When Iranian rock musicians can't get government approval to play in public, they jam and perform in friends' basements. They call them "kiosks." And it's a name adopted by an Iranian band in the U.S.

Imagine this: you live in Iran and you want to make music. More precisely, you want to play the blues and sing the things blues singers take on in their music. Arash Sobhani, the lead singer and songwriter of the Persian band Kiosk says it's a musician's nightmare:

"Your lyrics had to be approved, your music had to be approved by the government so you won't say anything politically wrong. You couldn't talk about sex, you couldn't talk about love in a more human way. You cannot talk about political stuff, definitely. You couldn't talk about the economy, you couldn't talk about anything. So you're left with nothing."

With those kinds of restraints, you don't rock, you can't make music. So you leave. That's what Sobhani did.

In early 2000, Sobhani arrived in the U.S. and met up with an old friend, Babak Kiavchi. Kiavchi started a recording label to promote music made by Iranians in exile. So with their credit cards in hand, Sobhani and Kiavchi released Kiosk's first album, "Ordinary Man." The song "Bent Rules Blues" says: *I'm a second-class citizen, with a third class life and full of debt. How did this happen in the first place? Was it by choice or by accident?*

Arash Sobhani says the band's initial rock-blues sound was inspired by the music of Bob Dylan, Eric Clapton and Leonard Cohen. But he says, after he moved to the U.S. he wanted to create a new sound:

"And moving to the U.S., I kind of started feeling like, 'relocating, leaving your country, leaving your home and now you live somewhere else,' I started relating to Gypsy music, because I thought, these people have that in their blood, they're constantly being relocated, and I kind of related to that whole culture a lot. Now I think we're at a stage where we're exploring tango, waltz and Gypsy music, to come up with a sound that relates to our situation as immigrants outside of Iran. So it's tricky to create these songs. I think we're still trying to come up with a signature sound for Kiosk but I think the last album was a big step for us."

At a concert in Los Angeles, Kiosk played for an audience filled with hundreds of Iranians expats. Yatrika Shah-Rais, a world music programmer says the band's music appeals to Iranians here because their songs bring together elements of social and political satire and commentary:

"And I think that because the tunes are very catchy, and the music has a reminiscence of a little Dire Straits, a little Leonard Cohen occasionally, and it rings the bell to those people who are acquainted with Western culture, pop music or rock music, it has a tremendous amount of appeal among the Persian community. Across the board, younger people, as well as people in their 40s and 50s, and especially also those people, the older generation that have come out of the experience of the (Iranian) revolution and who decided to live in exile, as a result."

Kiosk now has fans across the globe. The band has played in Sydney, Berlin and in several cities in Canada and the USA, but they've never played in public in Iran. After the LA concert, I asked Arash Sobhani if he hopes to do that someday: "every time I go on stage, I'm thinking, oh my god, is it going to happen, am I going to be playing in Tehran, can I ever do this? Yeah, that's my dream."

Kiosk band members Arash Sobhani, Ali Kamal and Shahrouz Molaei | Photo courtesy of the artist

DANIEL "TATITA" MÁRQUEZ AND URUGUAY

This week at the South by SouthWest music Festival in Austin, the South American country of Uruguay will be have a strong presence. Seven groups will be performing everything from rock to tango, and a percussionist who wants "candombe" to be better known outside Uruguay.

Daniel "Tatita" Márquez started playing candombe drums when he was 8 years old. He grew up in the Palermo neighborhood, one of three barrios in Montevideo known as the cradle of candombe: "El hecho de que me guste es el candombe es porque nací justamente ahí y lo traigo de nacimiento este ritmo y es de acá. Entonces me gusta impulsar esta tradición que tiene mucho para dar y que en el mundo no es conocida." Tatita says because he was born in that neighborhood, he carries the candombe rhythms since he was born. He says, candombe may not be well-known around the world, but it certainly has a lot to offer. Candombe rhythms are played on three barrel-shaped drums called chico, repique and piano. The chico and piano drums carry the base rhythm, and the middle drum or repique improvises over it. candombe music was brought by African slaves to Uruguay more than 200 years ago. It was initially played only in the Afro-Uruguayan community, but with time, it became everybody's music. Today it's one of Uruguay's essential musical styles, especially during the Carnival season.

Tatita says you can hear candombe in Montevideo every day — it's music that's played in the streets: "El candombe se escucha en Montevideo todos los días porque es una tradición que se practica en la calle. Es un ritmo que se toca caminando, son agrupaciones que se llaman comparsas. Y que se practica en un toque que recorre las calles de Montevideo y eso está hoy en día en todo el Uruguay." It's a rhythm played while walking, by groups called comparsas. And today this tradition is practiced all over Uruguay. In the last few years, Tatita has been on a mission to make candombe better known outside Uruguay. His new project is called "Mukunda" — a fusion of candombe rhythms and jazz. Unlike his previous recordings, the music in this album is anchored in the candombe rhythms, using drums as the basis for composition: "Pienso y compongo los temas a partir de la percusión, porque es lo que estudié, y a partir del candombe que es la música que más me gusta del Uruguay. A partir de eso se suceden las otras cosas. Aunque tiene una melodía, una armonía, como cualquier música instrumental."

As a percussionist, Tatita says he conceived all the music with the candombe drums as the foundation, and because candombe is the music he likes the most from Uruguay. But he says all the compositions in this album have melody and harmony, just like any instrumental music. Tatita says his main goal is to take this music project to New York this Summer. He says candombe needs to be played and heard in the jazz capital:

"Es un proyecto para Nueva York, el proyecto 'Mukunda.' Así como pasó con el bossa nova, de que en algún momento se instaure esa música en otro lugar del mundo y que ahí empieza a ser reconocida como una tradición de determinado país, pero nació ese querer, esa forma musical partir de otro lugar." (Just as it happened with bossa nova and other musical styles, he says, candombe needs to take root in another part of the world, and from there, it can begin to get the recognition as a musical tradition that came from Uruguay.)

Tatita says he and his band are really excited to be playing this week at the South by SouthWest Music Festival in Austin. This will be a big step on the road to make candombe more well-known outside Uruguay.

Daniel "Tatita" Márquez | Photo courtesy of the artist

3MA AND AFRICA

The story of one of Mali's most prominent musicians and how his instrument was destroyed in transit made news all over the world. Ballaké Sissoko accused the Transportation Security Administration of taking his kora apart sometime during a flight from New York to Paris. The TSA says it never opened the instrument's case. But Sissoko and 3MA, the band he was touring with, are much more than a few weeks of international headlines.

3MA stands for Madagascar, Mali and Maroc — Morocco in French — and the band is comprised of three musicians from three different African nations playing three different stringed instruments. Rajery is from Madagascar and plays an instrument called the valiha; the second "m" is for Malian kora player Ballaké Sissoko and oud player Driss El Maloumi is the Moroccan. "It's not music from Morocco, not from Madagascar or from Mali," El Maloumi says. "It's, at the same time, [using] our culture to make something completely different." The trio first came together 12 years ago and each of the musicians also has a successful solo career.

Ballaké Sissoko is probably the best-known internationally: He's the son of Djelimady Sissoko, a renowned kora player. The instrument traditionally has 21 strings and that number has a specific meaning. "Seven strings represent the past, seven the present and seven the future," Ballaké Sissoko explains. He says he adapted the instrument slightly to play with 3MA, plus he added an extra string to honor the luthier who made the instrument." I created the chromatic kora with two and half octaves for this project, to dialogue better with other instruments," he says. "I think music and instruments should evolve and not remain static." Sissoko's bandmate Rajery plays the 18-stringed valiha, considered Madagascar's national instrument. "It's made of bamboo. In the middle there is a fissure that separates the two parts," Rajery explains. "A series of movable bridges tune the instrument: You slide the bridge upward to get the bass sound or downward to get the treble sound. It has two octaves."

Last but not least, there's Driss El Maloumi's oud, an instrument that's played all over North Africa and the Middle East. It has 11 strings (in case you're keeping track, that's 51 strings under the fingers of 3 musicians). El Maloumi picks his oud with a plectrum, which is sort of like an elongated guitar pick. For even longer than El Maloumi has been performing with 3MA, he's been touring and recording with ancient music scholar Jordi Savall. In 2014, Rajery and Ballaké Sissoko joined El Maloumi for "The Routes of Slavery," Savall's large ensemble project exploring the cultural impact of the slave trade.

Ballaké Sissoko says the project wasn't just about music. "Jordi's personality helped me understand that music is not about virtuosity," he says. "It's about wisdom." Driss El Maloumi says working with Savall also helped 3MA as a whole. "Jordi Savall played a very important role in this group. He is all about wisdom and history and he's a great teacher," he says. "As three cultures coming together in our trio, we came to understand how our countries have been deeply affected by the pain that humanity has gone through." El Maloumi says 3MA's music is all about spirit. "For me the question is in l'esprit," he says. "Because if you are open in your spirit, you can make anything, and you can go and you can make evolution." And that's exactly what the trio wants to do says Rajery: present a new image of an ancient continent. "Mali, Madagascar and Morocco are together to show that before anything else, we are human beings," he says. "We are united through the universal language of music. We want to show Africa from a different point of view: three cultures, three musicians and three emblematic instruments."

The members of 3MA, from left to right: Ballaké Sissoko, Rajery and Driss El Maloumi | Photo by Fred Pluviaud

WORLD FESTIVAL of SACRED MUSIC

The World Sacred Music Festival in Fes was created 16 years ago to celebrate spiritual music from around the globe. And from the start, the festival has invited American musicians to bring blues, jazz and, especially, gospel music to Moroccan audiences. One of this year's headliners was supposed to be the rock singer Ben Harper, but he canceled at the last minute. Still, that didn't discourage young Moroccans from coming to see one of their favorite groups, The Blind Boys of Alabama.

"My name is Iman. I'm 18 and I'm here to listen to gospel music because it's something that I enjoy." I asked Iman Remel why Moroccans are so crazy about gospel music: "It's very popular among Moroccan youth, because with the globalization and the communication means and everything, we tend to listen to every kind of music from all the nations. And I think that there's something that makes Moroccans feel it and like it, so we're here for the gospels of the Blind Boys of Alabama."

The organizers have picked up on that, says Festival president Mohamed Kabbaj: "Often, we finish the Festival with gospel because the young people love gospel and we love people to dance. We love people to enjoy the last day and the gospel is the music. At the same time it's sacred music, but at the same time it's music which the young people enjoy." Kabbaj adds that gospel brings in a younger crowd, one that's been hard to attract to the Festival.

The popularity of gospel music in Morocco may also have something to do with the popularity of Sufi sacred music here, says Alain Weber the Festival's artistic director: "Sufi music is the mystical and emotional part of religious expression and most of the gospel music is coming from the holy spirit, the idea of the trance, the idea to have a direct relation with god through the holy spirit, so it's a common thing between Sufism and gospel in that sense, I think."

Whether it's American gospel or Sufi music, one thing was evident at this year's sacred music festival in Fes: Moroccan youth are eager to listen to music that goes deeper than the pop hits they hear on the radio.

Lalla Rahoum El Bakkali Group performing at the Festival of Sacred Music in Fes, Morocco | Photo by Betto Arcos

SON JAROCHO IN LOS ANGELES

Son jarocho is a music genre from the Gulf Coast region of Mexico, in the state of Veracruz. "La Bamba" is the most well-known tune, made popular in the early 1950s by Ritchie Valens, an early rock-and-roll musician from Los Angeles. But the music and dance emerged more than three hundred years ago and its popularity is on the rise again, not only in Mexico but also in the USA.

It's a warm evening at Tia Chucha's Bookstore in Sylmar, in California's San Fernando Valley, not far from the neighborhood where Ritchie Valens created a rock-and-roll version of the most famous son jarocho tune "La Bamba." Tonight, Aaron Castellanos is one of eight students in a music class held at the store. He's learning to play the eight-string jarana, the main instrument in the musical style of son jarocho: "I like the way that the jarana sounds," he says. "I like how son jarocho invokes so much energy into the playing and into the singing." Son jarocho comes from Veracruz, a state in the Gulf Coast region of Mexico, where three different cultures — Spanish, Indigenous and African — came together more than 500 years ago. Castellanos is actually learning the "mosquito," one of the smallest jaranas, which has a noticeably high pitch. "This is the first instrument that I've ever learned, so I want to keep playing," Castellanos says. "I want to buy my own jarana and just continue practicing." Castellanos' teacher is César Castro, a key figure at the center of the son jarocho explosion in Los Angeles. Castro says that, since he moved to LA from Veracruz eight years ago, the number of son jarocho musicians has been growing, and the quality of the music has been improving. "When we had the first fandangos here in Los Angeles, the music was not that good. But the energy, the will to do these fandangos, it was very strong," Castro says. "The music is getting better, still in a very respectful traditional format."

Fandangos are at the heart of son jarocho. They're kind of jam sessions, where musicians gather to play, sing and dance for hours around a wooden platform called "tarima." At the Zona Rosa Café in Pasadena, the fandango is hosted by Castro's band Cambalache, one of a dozen son jarocho groups in the LA area. Within an hour, more "fandangueros" arrive and join in, playing, singing and dancing. About 10 years ago, Castro says, young Mexican Americans got into son jarocho as a way to connect to their Mexican heritage. "They felt more comfortable, more invited to participate," he says. "It doesn't matter if you don't dance, if you don't play, if you don't sing — you could be around it. It's a whole experience that people, little by little, got the chance to be part of and

feel something good." One of the groups that grew out of this evolving scene is the primarily female Son del Centro, an ensemble created at the Mexican Cultural Center in Santa Ana, the heart of the Mexican American community in Orange County. All of the members sing, dance and play instruments. Son del Centro member Ana Urzúa says the music's ability to get everybody — musicians and audiences — to do everything is part of its appeal." It's a beautiful music," she says. "It's a music that is welcoming. But I think it's also that it is a part of something bigger. It's a part of a people, their traditions and their culture."

Los Angeles has been hosting a son jarocho festival for the last 10 years. This year, Mono Blanco, the group that helped revive this music in the late '70s in Veracruz, came to play in South LA. Gilberto Gutierrez, the group's leader, says the traditional way of playing son jarocho has not changed. What's new and exciting is how young Latinos in the U.S. have taken up the music. Gutierrez explains:

> "The fandango celebration has the ability to bring together families, generations, different social classes and that's really positive. Especially because these days, different generations tend to separate, but now suddenly there's an activity that unites the family: youth, old, kids, rich or poor and so on. I think that's what's been attractive to people here in the U.S."

Rafael Figueroa, a writer and radio host from Veracruz, agrees. He's been recording and documenting son jarocho, both in Mexico and the U.S. "If you become interested in son jarocho, you belong to a community almost right at the start," Figueroa says. "Of course, for us from Veracruz, it's important, but [also] for people from Mexico City, from California, like Chicanos, Anglos, whatever. They feel like they're participating, right from the start, in a community."

Libby Harding is the leader of a son jarocho group called Conjunto Jardín. When she was a child, she learned the music through her father, who learned it from the masters in Veracruz. "I've always wanted to do it and share it with other people — share at least what I've learned and help maybe turn other people on to son jarocho by hearing us," Harding says. "Maybe they'd go and look at some of the roots of the music." As long as son jarocho musicians learn and hold onto the roots of the music, the tradition will thrive wherever it's played.

Son Jarocho festival in Los Angeles | Photo by Betto Arcos

GUARANIA AND PARAGUAY

I'm standing at the edge of lake Ypacaraí, about an hour East of Asunción, the capital of Paraguay. This lake was made famous by one of the most romantic love songs ever written anywhere, "Recuerdos de Ypacaraí" by Demetrio Ortíz. This song has been performed and recorded by countless musicians and singers around the world. "Recuerdos de Ypacaraí" is a "guarania," Paraguay's national music genre, created in 1925 in the capital Asunción by composer José Asunción Flores. Flores, in collaboration with poet and lyricist Manuel Ortiz Guerrero, established the guarania as the emblematic music genre of Paraguay. In the words of Flores: "The guarania is from my people, written for and by my people."

Paraguay is a country with two official national languages, Spanish and Guaraní. In the 1930s, the guarania had a crucial role in reclaiming the Guaraní language by the people of Paraguay. Today, there are as many guaranias written in Spanish as there are in Guaraní — and many guaranias are sung in Jopará, which is a mixture of Spanish and Guaraní. In 1935, singer Agustín Barboza recorded "Nde Ratypykua" in Buenos Aires accompanied by Orquesta Ortiz Guerrero. This song is a guarania composed by the creator of the genre, José Asunción Flores. At the beginning of the song, one can hear Flores speaking in Guaraní and singing the melody of his song.

The guarania reached its height of popularity in Paraguay in the 1950s. A few years later the style reached a larger international audience, when singers from all over the world began performing and recording it. In 1963, Los Panchos, the internationally renowned Mexican trio, released an album of Paraguayan music which included several guaranias. In the 1970s, the vocal trio Los Troveros de America performed and recorded guaranias composed by Flores and Ortíz.

A few years ago, Paraguayan musician Ricardo Flecha produced a series of four albums focused on the guarania. One of the albums, "La Guarania Crece Sin Fronteras" (The Guarania Grows Without Borders), was intended to show the style's popularity and influence outside Paraguay. The album featured musicians from Argentina and Brazil, including "Saudade," a guarania written in Portuguese in the 1960s by Mario Palmeiro, a Brazilian composer. The song's arrangement is by Mauricio Cardozo Ocampo who also plays the guitar, and singing in a duet is Ricardo Flecha with Brazil's Chico Buarque.

Singer and composer Ricardo Flecha says for Paraguayans the guarania is not only a musical genre:

> "It's a state of mind, a place, a way of recognizing and seeing who we are inside, in relationship with the original native cultures. They used to say that 'Guarania' was a place with fabulous trees, extraordinary flora and fauna, a place that exists. Our native cultures talk about a place called 'Yvymarané'y' — Land without Evil. Our ancestors marched toward the sunrise saying that this place existed. It's contrary to the Christian notion that says that when you die you go to Paradise. In that long march, they created the Land Without Evil inside each one of them. It's a beautiful story of this country. Paraguay is almost a secret, but it's important for people to know about its history and culture, through its music. Flores, the creator of the guarania was a chronicler of his time, a pacifist, and lover of nature, with firm convictions and utopias created through his songs."

It's early evening at the home of music promoter and producer Lucas Toriño in Asunción. He invited me to an "asado." We're joined by two world-renowned master musicians, harpist Sixto Corbalán and guitarist Pedro Martínez — and they brought their instruments. Right after the feast, they start playing a most touching, instrumental version of the guarania called "Mis noches sin ti" (My Nights Without You). Tomorrow, I return home to Los Angeles.

Guarania creator José Asunción Flores. Street art in Asunción's Chacarita neighborhood | Photo by Betto Arcos

CHAMAMÉ AND EL LITORAL

I'm in the city of Formosa, in Northeastern Argentina, in a region called "El Litoral." This cultural and historic region is surrounded and by three major rivers: the Paraná, the Paraguay, and the Uruguay rivers. The "chamamé" genre covers a large region over four South American countries: Argentina, Brazil, Paraguay and Uruguay. The tune "Kilómetro 11" was composed by bandoneón player and composer Mario del Tránsito Cocomarola leader of the legendary Trio Cocomarola, one of the pillars of chamamé music. This is considered the top anthem of the genre, which exploded in Argentina in the mid-1930s, when musicians such as Tránsito Cocomarola, began recording chamamé in Buenos Aires. My guide to the world of chamamé is musician and promoter Marcos Ramirez. We begin the chamamé route on a Sunday evening, at a music festival in his hometown of Formosa, capital of the Formosa Province. One of the singers is Gicela Méndez Ribeiro. Gicela Méndez is originally from the province of Corrientes but her grandparents are from Rio Grande do Sul, Brasil, another region where chamamé is very popular. She sings in Spanish and Portuguese.

The City of Corrientes, capital of the Province of Corrientes, is the birthplace of chamamé. It's Monday, and as luck would have it, a group of chamamé musicians get together every Monday night to play fútbol, enjoy an asado, and gather around the table to sing chamamé. But it's not just any group of friends. There are a few significant chamamé names here: Angel Montiel is a bandoneón player, but tonight he's playing guitar, he happens to be the grandson of a major chamamé figure, accordionist Ernesto Montiel; Juan Pablo Rivas is another important guitarist; and tonight, playing accordion is 27-year-old Alan Guillén. It's common that when a song reaches the heart and soul of a person, he or she releases a "sapukai," a holler in the middle of the song. Tonight's sapukai is courtesy of Fernando "Chingoli" Bofill, son of the great singer Mario Bofill.

Since we're in Corrientes and this is where chamamé originated in the countryside, more than 100 years ago, I wanted to find out more about the origins of this musical tradition. At its heart, this is mestizo music, the result of the confluence of several cultures and music traditions: it has Guaraní roots, African rhythms, and European music and dance influences. The main chamamé instruments are bandoneón, several types of piano and button accordions, the 6-string guitar and occasionally the violin. There are as many instrumental pieces as there are songs with lyrics. But the lyrics are filled with regional lore and profound poetry, describing life in the countryside, the natural landscape, and the rivers. From the mid-1930s to the 1950s, chamamé was one of the most popular music genres in Argentina; in fact, the most widely sold record in the history of Argentina's music industry was "El Rancho de la Cambicha" recorded by singer Antonio Tormo — in 1955, this record sold a whopping 5.5 million copies.

I'm now in Posadas, the capital of the Misiones Province, the red land, the land of yerba mate. Marcos Ramírez and I arrive in Posadas in the evening and we're invited to a traditional asado at the home of brothers Juan and Marcos Núñez, known in the chamamé world as Los Núñez. After a sumptuous dinner, we sit down in their living room and they start playing — Juan plays bandoneón and Marcos, his younger brother, plays acoustic guitar. Then, their father, Moncho Núñez, joins them for an encore, playing the diatonic accordion called "Verdulera."

After driving back 600 kilometers from the Tierra Colorada of Misiones, we return to Formosa, Marcos' hometown. It's a Sunday night at Pista La Colonia, one of two dance halls in Formosa where locals come to dance chamamé played by a live band every weekend. There are 200-300 people here tonight, some of the men are dressed in the traditional gaucho attire: bombachas or loose-fitting trousers, a large scarf around their neck, and a black hat. This scene is replicated across cities and towns in the Litoral, and also in the outskirts of Buenos Aires, where the music was first recorded and played on radio stations in the early 1930s. Every year, the City of Corrientes, hosts the annual Fiesta Nacional del chamamé — the National Chamamé Celebration. I hope to return to El Litoral in the future to attend this festival of music and dance.

Juan Núñez on bandoneón, Marcos Núñez on guitar. The duo called Los Núñez and their father Moncho Núñez on the accordion called "verdulera", playing at their home in Posadas, capital of Misiones province, Argentina | Photo by Betto Arcos

CHAMPETA in CARTAGENA, COLOMBIA

I'm in Cartagena, Colombia, at the Bazurto Social Club, a medium-size dance venue, very close to the historic part of the city. I just happened upon this club and found a fantastic local band called "La Soukursal" playing an infectious style of music called "champeta." Bazurto Social Club takes the name from Mercado Bazurto, the popular market where champeta was born, in the late 1970s.

Champeta is an Afro-Colombian music genre that is the confluence of music from various African styles, but specially Soukous, from the Democratic Republic of the Congo, and Afro-Colombian rhythms from the Cartagena region. The music began to flourish in the late 1970s, when Colombian sailors started bringing vinyl records of African groups to Cartagena and Barranquilla. The local DJs started spreading the music in their sound systems called "picós" (slang for pickup truck). A picó then implies a certain mobility of sound systems as they take them around in pickup trucks, all over the working-class areas of the city. The song "Quiero a mi gente" is one of the early hits by champeta guitarist Abelardo Carbonó and his Conjunto. It's important to note that Abelardo Carbonó is from Barranquilla, the biggest city on the Caribbean coast of Colombia, an hour away from Cartagena. While champeta is always associated with, and has become a major symbol of Cartagena, Barranquilla can also lay claim to its origin, especially through Abelardo Carbonó's contribution in the early 1980s.

I'm now at the Bazurto fish market, in one of the most populated areas of the city, a working-class neighborhood of Cartagena. I'm standing in front of a fish stand where a man is cleaning the fish with a knife called "champeta." And if you're wondering if that's why the music style is called champeta, you're absolutely right. Champeta got its name from the knife used to clean and slice fish in the Bazurto market. And the people who dance the music and practice the lifestyle and fashion emanating from champeta are called "champetúos."

During my visit to the Bazurto Market in Cartagena, I had the chance to meet one of the great figures of champeta, Louis Towers. He told me that champeta's significance in the Afro-Colombian community of Cartagena could not be underestimated: champeta and the lifestyle associated with it, was the main vehicle through which the Afro-Colombian community was integrated into mainstream society in Cartagena. One of Louis Towers' hits is called "El Liso en Olaya." Some champeta artists, such as Towers, are known for writing lyrics with social

commentary. This song is about a man who wants to take advantage of a married woman in the barrio of Olaya, in Cartagena. Towers doesn't sing in Spanish in this song but in "Palenquero," the language spoken in San Basilio de Palenque.

Champeta musician Charles King is from a small town called San Pablo, near San Basilio de Palenque, the first town to be free from slavery in the American continent, in the late 1600s. In San Pablo, Charles King met Anne Swing, a major important champeta figure, and became one of his vocalists. Within a few years, King launched his own solo career. Charles King's tune "El Chocho" is a song with a double and triple meaning — one refers to a popular market in Cartagena called El Chocho; it's also what people say when a woman's skirt has a hole. And the third, well, we have to leave that to your imagination...

You may have noticed that the names of the last two artists are in English. The major figures of champeta all have names in English. Most of them, simply translated their names literally into English. Luis Torres became Louis Towers; Carlos Reyes became Charles King, and so on. The only explanation behind the name change is that the artists felt it would be more "commercial" to use a name in English than their original name in Spanish. Then there's Anne Swing, whose real name is Viviano Torres. I suppose it was impossible to translate his name into English, so to stand out from the rest, he chose a more unusual name. Anne Swing's "Mini-Mini" song became the first major champeta hit on the radio in 1986.

In Cartagena, and by extension all over Colombia, the name Bazurto is synonymous with champeta. There's a band called "Bazurto All Stars," a group of young musicians who got together at the Bazurto market a few years ago, and decided to form a group, using champeta as its main music style but also incorporating other influences.

La Soukursal was playing a set when I walked into the Bazurto Social Club. La Soukursal is an example of the widespread popularity of champeta, outside the working-class neighborhoods of Cartagena. There are new groups who play this music across the country, but most of the musicians come from the Caribbean coast of Colombia, and DJs around the world are spinning classic or remixed versions of champeta tunes to hundreds of people who love dancing to it.

Champeta artist Louis Towers, outside Bazurto Market in Cartagena | Photo by Betto Arcos

FESTIVAL DE LA MEJORANA, PANAMA

"Mejorana" is one of the many traditional styles of music from Panama, it's a musical genre related to punto cubano from Cuba, son jarocho from Veracruz, Mexico, and joropo from Colombia and Venezuela, among others. These musical genres emerged in the Caribbean in the 16th century as a result of mestizaje or the confluence between three cultures — Spanish, Indigenous and African.

I'm at the Festival Nacional de la Mejorana (National Mejorana Festival), held annually in the town of Guararé, province of Los Santos, in Panama. If you look at a map of Panama, you'll see that right in the middle of the country, there's a Peninsula facing the Pacific Ocean called Peninsula de Azuero — the town of Guararé is right in the middle of the Peninsula, facing the Gulf of Panama.

One of the major figures of the mejorana is composer, singer and mejorana guitar player Juan Andrés Castillo. He was born in 1932 in the city of Chitré, he started playing the mejorana guitar at the age of 9. Castillo has accompanied some of Panama's great singers and has recorded and performed internationally. He's also written 2 books about the mejorana, the music and the tradition. In 2017, he was honored at the Mejorana Festival with the "Dora Pérez de Zarate" award for his 70-year career dedicated to composing and performing traditional music. I was lucky to spend time with him at his friend's home in Guararé and he played one of his best-known songs called "Hojitas de tamarindo" (Tamarind Leaves).

The National Mejorana Festival was founded in 1950 in the town of Guararé by the Zárate family. More than 70 years later, the Festival has become one the most important gatherings of Panamanian Folklore and an emblematic space of national identity. The mejorana tradition originates in the countryside, so this musical genre has peasant origins. There are different voices in the Mejorana Festival. Fernando Ramírez is one of the participants of the Concurso de Toque de Guitarra Mejoranera (Mejorana Guitar Competition). He's 13 years old and is the winner of the first place, receiving the prize of one thousand Balboas, equivalent to one thousand dollars. The mejorana guitar contest is dominated by male musicians, while the contest of "décimas," or improvised verses, is dominated by women. In addition to the mejorana guitar and singing of décimas, the Mejorana Festival also celebrates two fundamental instruments of Panama's traditional musical: the drum and the accordion. In both cases, the contest is dominated by men. This year, the Mejorana Festival included the first ever contest of "grito" (shouting). The tradition of the gritos comes from the countryside — it's a common language among peasants who use it to call each other across the hills, during their hours of work, tending cattle or working in the fields. Alfredo Sáez and Melvin Rodríguez are the winners of the first place in the grito contest. In the accordion contest, there were 16 participants, 15 men and one woman, Erica Chávez and her group.

Before and after the competitions, next to the Palacio de la Mejorana, I met different musicians, some participants in the Festival this year, and others who participated in previous festivals. Oscar Díaz is a 12-year-old participant; he won third place in the Mejorana contest. One of the most touching moments I enjoyed at the Mejorana Festival happened on the street in front of the Palacio de la Mejorana. Two older singers, Mara García and a man who did not give me his name, suddenly began to sing décimas, verses accompanied by Oscar Díaz.

There's great a song inspired by the Festival de la Mejorana — a composition by the Panamanian music giant, composer, singer and accordion master Dorindo Cárdenas, who was honored at the Festival for his long and rich career. The song is called "Festival de Guararé" and it's performed by none other than the fantastic Colombian super-group Los Corraleros de Majagual, with accordionist and lead singer Alfredo Gutiérrez.

Singer and Mejorana guitar player Juan Andrés Castillo | Photo by Betto Arcos

CARRANGA AND BOYACÁ

It's midday in the town of Ráquira, in the highland province of Boyacá, Colombia. At a local restaurant, a trio of musicians are playing "Caballito de acero" or Little Horse of Steel, a song by Jorge Velosa, the creator of the style of music called "carranga." This is Velosa's homage to Colombia's great cyclists who have competed internationally. The song fits the spirit of the moment: cyclist Egan Bernal just won the Tour de France and people are celebrating across Colombia.

Ráquira is the hometown of Jorge Velosa, the composer and singer who single-handedly created a new music style called carranga, in the late 1970s. Jorge Velosa and Los Carrangueros de Ráquira's first big hit is a song called "La cucharita," from their self-titled album released in 1980. As the story goes, in the mid-1970s, Jorge Velosa left his hometown of Ráquira to attend Veterinary School at the National University of Colombia, in Bogotá. There, Velosa found his calling. He began writing songs and founded a group with some of his musician friends. Soon, they began playing at a small club in Bogotá called "Arte y Cerveza" (Art and Beer). In 1977, they performed at a music festival called "Guitarra de Plata Campesina" in the town of Chiquinquirá. The festival was sponsored by a local radio station, Radio Furatena. The band was so successful that the owner of the radio station offered Velosa and his group, a radio show. Velosa called the program "Canta el pueblo" (The People Sing). The focus of this radio program was all about peasants and their livelihoods. It became the most popular radio show across the region, and it also nurtured the inspiration of Velosa, his gift of storytelling and his songwriting style. Some of his first hits were created during this period, including the song "Julia, Julia, Julia."

Carranga is country music, with an emphasis on the lives of peasants. The songs tell stories, and many of them are full of humor. The two main rhythms of carranga music are merengue carranguero and rumba carranguera. But carranga music is also a confluence of other music styles from the Andean region of Colombia, including bambuco, pasillo, guabina, torbellino, rajaleña, and it's also influenced by other neighboring genres such as joropo and vallenato. The traditional group has four members and the music is played with these instruments: tiple, a guitar-like instrument with 12 steel-strings; the high-pitched tiple requinto, also a 12-steel string instrument; a scraper called guacharaca; and the nylon-string guitar. The group Campo Sonoro is led by composer Eduardo Villarreal, founder of "Convite Cuna Carranguera," the annual carranga festival held in August in the town of Tinjacá.

Although carranga music is mostly dominated by male groups, there are also groups of women. The group called El Son del Frailejón is a collective who give voice to women peasants as guardians and caretakers of water, seeds and food in the mountain region of Guasca. In Tunja, the capital of Boyacá 15-year-old María Estefanía Mesa Dueñas leads her own carranga group. Estefanía started playing tiple four years ago, encouraged by her teacher in the music school of her hometown, Belén. Then she decided to take a chance and move to the Boyaca's capital. Today she's studying at Tunja's Music School and she recently formed her group called Estefanía y su Grupo Carranguero.

Carranga turns 40 this year, and it's still Colombia's youngest music genre. Thanks to the work and popularity of Jorge Velosa and Los Carrangueros de Ráquira, the music style took off like wildfire across the country and today, there are carranga groups all over Colombia, including the capital. Los Rolling Ruanas is a group from Bogotá with a completely new take on carranga, fusing it with a rock edge. A "ruana" is the traditional wool poncho worn by peasants in the highlands. The band honors that tradition with the song called "Ruanas on":

Una prenda mística, un hermoso telar,
una capa mágica que va sin cardar
Olor a tierra y color de ciudad,
que son las alas de mi libertad
Porque esta fiesta es con traje de lana,
Y que lo bailen de Tunja a Tijuana
Pa'que lo goces con Los Rolling Ruanas, onnnnn!
Put your ruanas on, yeah!
Put your ruanas on, c'mon!

Carranga creator, composer and singer Jorge Velosa | Photo by Yezid Campos

GALICIAN MUSIC AND EL CAMINO DE SANTIAGO

El Camino de Santiago is an ancient pilgrimage trail that begins at various points in Europe and goes to Santiago de Compostela in northwestern Spain. My wife Josephine Ramirez and I walked the Camino for a week, October 20-27, 2018. This story combines my report for NPR and a Road Trip piece I produced for the program Music Planet on BBC Radio 3.

Our journey begins in O Cebreiro, a Celtic mountain village from the 9th century 1,300 meters above sea level in the eastern region of Galicia. Tonight at the chapel of Santa Maria Real do Cebreiro, four people from different parts of the world read a farewell in French, Italian, Spanish and English to a group of 20 people walking the Camino de Santiago: "And when the moment comes for you to reach your goal, may love embrace you eternally." This church hosted pilgrims as far back as the 12th century. From here, it's a seven-day walk to Santiago de Compostela. Father Paco Castro says, if you ask a typical 21st-century pilgrim why they do the Camino, they'll tell you a series of evasive answers. Father Castro says there's always something deeper: "Human suffering, fears, the need to give sense to one's life, finding one's self, the encounter with others — which is to me one of the treasures of the community. It is a historic landmark because there are no borders. There's only one family called humanity. And you see it all on the Camino de Santiago."

When I think about the music of Galicia, I think of bagpipes. As the story goes, researchers from the British Museum found that the oldest bagpipe goes back to Galicia, more than 1,000 years ago. One of the most important ensembles of traditional Galician music, Os Montes de Lugo, was founded at the beginning of the twentieth century. Their song "Alborada Gallega" refers to a special moment in the early hours of the morning when the sun is coming up in Galicia.

On our second day of our walk on the Camino, we descend into the valley of Samos, we're on a stretch of the trail surrounded by walls made of shale rock. Birds are chirping all around and suddenly, as a sort of welcoming, we hear the sound of church bells at the medieval monastery of Samos. Later that afternoon, I meet Rosario Garcia, a 48-year-old woman from Rota in southwestern Spain who's hiking with her husband. She loves the atmosphere, the camaraderie and meeting new people. But she tells me today is a rough day: "There are days I just want to cry. I don't know. Maybe it's the quiet of the Camino. It makes you think more, and I'm thinking too much. I'm also thinking about all the things I'd like to do, but you can't fix everything."

The Camino de Santiago takes around four to five weeks to walk. We only walked seven days. Coincidentally, while we were on the trail, one of the most popular musicians from this part of Spain, Carlos Núñez was performing at the Catedral de Mondoñedo and invited us to the concert. Núñez plays all kinds of traditional Galician music, such as Muiñeiras, Alboradas, Jotas, Gaitas, some of the music he plays is based on the research he's done over the last couple decades. He recently published a book called "La Hermandad de los Celtas," where he brings together all the cultures of the Celtic world into one and talks about the connections between them. Carlos plays all kinds of medieval flutes but his main instrument is the gaita. Carlos played with his five-piece band but at one point during the concert, he was joined by a group of 15 gaiteiros (bagpipe players), it was truly a fantastic experience, one of the most exciting shows I've ever seen. His composition "Camino de Santiago" evokes our experience that night at the Catedral de Mondoñedo.

On day four, I meet Hillary Haye and Daniel Ong a young couple from Malaysia walking the Camino as their honeymoon. Daniel Ong says the Camino gives you an opportunity to discover a resilience that you never knew you had:

"What we wanted to achieve was we wanted to make sure that we walked every step of the way and we carry our backpacks. And we've done that so far. But, you know, there were lots of challenging moments. There were lots of people encouraging us to drop our packs

El Camino de Santiago | Photo by Betto Arcos

and send them ahead and all that. And it was really about listening to our own bodies and understanding ourselves better and knowing, you know, if that was something we wanted to do or if we wanted to push ourselves."

On day five, I catch up with Kathleen Riley. I've seen her a few times on the Camino and noticed her American accent. She's from New York, recently retired and has been on the Camino for a month: "I think you can't finish this without finding a little bit more about yourself, whether it's things you want to improve on, understanding your own strengths and weaknesses better.

Josephine and I had been wanting to walk the Camino for a while. Last year, when our son left for college, we decided we could finally do it. The Camino has been the perfect place to reconnect. We're here, our final destination — Santiago de Compostela. As we descend into the large Praza do Obradoiro in front of the cathedral, where all the pilgrims gather to celebrate their journey, I hear a gaitero. He seems to be welcoming everyone who came here. Our muscles are sore, our knees are aching. But beyond the pain is a deeper feeling of accomplishment. We did it. We know we will return and meet new friends on the Camino de Santiago.

Santiago de Compostela, the capital of Galicia, is where a lot of the exciting music scene is happening — it's the city with the richest cultural history — a very vibrant and exciting place. Uxía is one of the best-known vocalists from Galicia. She shared with us a very special moment when she sang a poem by Rosalia de Castro, right next to the tomb where she is buried in Santiago. There's a song by Uxia called "A Tribu Maxica" that conjures up the magical spirits of the Galician land, asking them for protection and the purifying rituals of the night of San Juan — water and fire. The song is also about the mythical tribe that links Galicia to all the other Celtic cultures. Uxia is joined by her Scottish friends from the band Capercaillie and the violin of Quim Farinha, one of the founding members of the legendary Galician band Berrogüetto, and who is now part of Uxía's band.

I met Uxía and Galician singer-songwriter Fran Pérez, known as Narf, in Los Angeles. Uxía and Narf together were touring the U.S. and performed at the Getty Center songs from their album called "Imaginary Galicia." When Uxía and Narf stepped on the stage, the audience sensed it would be a special concert. Besides their soulful, naked voices, Narf was strumming a red electric guitar and Uxía

had a tambourine at her feet. By the time they finished the first song, "Sempre en Galiza," an anthem summoning Galician immigrants from all latitudes, they had enchanted the audience. At the core of their performance is the warmth and richness of the Galician language, as rhythmic and melodic as its cousin and neighbor to the south, Portuguese. They sang original and traditional songs and a poem by the renowned 19th century Galician writer and poet Rosalía de Castro. Introducing the songs in English, with a full smile, Narf resembled a storyteller and a medieval troubadour. Sometimes taking turns singing verses, Uxía and Narf let the magic unfold when they sang in harmony. But there were also moments when they elevated their native language to universal heights, beyond their "Imaginary Galicia." In the song "Esta noite," Uxía and Narf sang of *having all the power to fight, all night to dream, and every minute to remember who I am and where I am.* Fran Pérez died on November 15, 2016 at the age of 48.

Galician music is rich and diverse. One of the musical discoveries during this trip took place one night in Santiago, when our friend Uxía invited us to magical concert at the Cidade da Cultura. Before the show, we were treated to a feast of chestnuts and wine. When Xoselois Romero and Aliboria came out on stage with their unusual instruments, we sensed it was going to be a special concert. The group has 10 musicians, seven women and three men, who sing and play everything from empty olive oil cans, frying pans, kitchen utensils, to large frame drums, and tambourins. In Galicia, traditional songs usually carry the name of the place where they come from and many of these towns are a wellspring of many good songs. Aliboria's songs come from the towns of Liñares, Gargamala, Toutón, and Arcos, just like my last name — a small hamlet in the county of Mazaricos on the Costa da More. The song "Mangüeiro," also known as "Olvídame," is from a small hamlet in the county of Avión in the province of Ourense — a region famous for the immigrants that went to Mexico from the middle of the 20th century. "Olvídame" is a "paso doble" popularized in Galicia in the '90s by the group Leilía, the first group of Cantareiras that released an album and toured in the folk music circuit. This song is well known in Galicia but no one sings it, but when Aliboria performs it outside of Galicia, it's received with a lot of passion and people in the audience start singing it. Aliboria's concert felt like the perfect ritual to celebrate our journey on the Camino de Santiago.

Uxía and Fran Pérez — Narf — performing at the Getty Center, March 12, 2016 | Photo by Betto Arcos

LA CHIVA RUMBERA IN CARTAGENA, COLOMBIA

I dreamed I was in vallenato heaven at Cartagena's Parque de los Zapatos Viejos, surrounded by a dozen accordionists and their percussionists, playing the deepest grooves I've ever heard. I woke up and realized I had arrived at the park on a "chiva rumbera" — a bus carrying passengers on a nocturnal tour of Cartagena, Colombia.

A "chiva" (goat) is what people in the small towns of Colombia call a bus. The name derived from the sound of the horn the old buses had — people thought the horn sounded like a wailing goat, so when the bus came to town people said "ya llegó la chiva" (the chiva is here). A rumba is a party — so the chiva rumbera is... a party bus! It may appear that the service only caters to tourists, but chivas rumberas are also popular with Colombians and you can find them all over the country. Here's the genius behind the chiva rumbera: fill a bus with people, charge them $10 each, bring a vallenato trio, serve them cheap rum, take them for a 3-hour ride around the city, and then have a big party in a park — with a bunch of chivas rumberas.

I was excited to ride the chiva rumbera for one main reason: the chance to listen to vallenato music on a bus seemed like a dream come true. So at 7:30 PM on a warm Saturday night in Cartagena, I climbed on with the fantastic vallenato accordionist Santander Monroy Fontalvo and his trio. The minute he started playing my favorite vallenato called "La hamaca grande," I was the happiest man on earth. Traditional vallenato played with the three essential instruments — accordion, caja (drum) and guacharaca (scraper) — is deeply soulful music. Within the first 30 minutes of the ride, the trio played a mix of different tunes. While there is an emphasis on the vallenato and cumbia repertoire, the trio also played the classic Mexican ranchera "El Rey" and the global hit "Lambada," both in a Colombian rhythm called "paseaito."

About an hour later, the chiva made a pit stop. Santander Monroy told me they were picking up the booze. Before too long, the staff of three started passing plastic cups, pitchers with ice, two-liter bottles of soda and a small bottle of cheap rum. After a couple of drinks and more upbeat music, the passengers seemed a bit happier. The bus stopped briefly — an MC got a microphone and said: "good evening, let's give a hand to the group, Los Elegantes del Vallenato!" The MC went around the bus asking passengers where they came from — there were people from Mexico, Argentina, Bolivia, USA, Chile, Australia, and from all over Colombia. After a few announcements, the MC finally said "iahora sí empezó la rumba!" (now the party really started!)

We rode for another 30 minutes and arrived at the Parque de los Zapatos Viejos. It was around 9 PM, there were vendors selling trinkets and food — arepas, sausages, sodas and beer. Santander Monroy and his trio started playing and more chivas started arriving. By 9:30, after a dozen chivas dropped off their passengers, the park was teeming with hundreds of people, and several Vallenato trios were playing in different areas, people were dancing, others were singing. This was like a dream. Then, at about 10:15, I walked to the area where the chivas were parked. A chiva rumbera is a mobile work of art — all the buses are painted in bright tropical colors of orange, green, blue, red, purple, yellow, with intricate designs. And the names are something else: El Cacique (The Chief), La India Catalina (Catalina The Indian), La Jefa (The Boss), La Latina, La Patrona (The Boss), La Quitasueño (The Dream Stealer). Right before we boarded the chiva to continue the journey, the staff lined up the passengers and treated them to a sampling of fried food delicacies. Then we boarded the chiva but the music changed. The MC started playing the latest reguetón hits. There were two more stops at discotheques. I decided to get off the Chiva near my hotel. The dream was over.

Chiva Rumbera | Photo by Betto Arcos

CANDOMBE AND MONTEVIDEO

I'm in Montevideo's Palermo neighborhood, one of the traditional and historic barrios of the Afro-Uruguayan community. It's early evening on Sunday, and a group of more than 30 drummers are rehearsing a "llamada," a traditional drum parade. This group along with many others, is participating in the annual Carnival, which starts in late January and concludes Tuesday, February 25th. I was invited to the Palermo neighborhood by two major figures of Afro-Uruguayan music, drummer and drum-maker Fernando "Lobo" Núñez, and legendary singer-songwriter, Rubén Rada. I spent a couple hours with them, talking about candombe and its history. Visiting Montevideo with them is akin to visiting London with members of the Rolling Stones. In the mid-1960s, Rubén Rada and another major figure of Uruguayan music, Eduardo Mateo, formed the group 'El Kinto.' Rada and Mateo created a style called "candombe beat," a fusion of candombe with the influence of The Beatles. In 1969, Rubén Rada recorded his first big 'candombe beat' hit, a song called "Las manzanas."

Candombe is played by everyone, black or white, rich or poor, young and old, male and female. But it wasn't always like this. In the beginning, candombe was mostly played by Afro-Uruguayans in their neighborhoods, at their events and gatherings. candombe was beginning to be integrated into popular music in the early 1960s. One of the first artists who introduced candombe into the mainstream was the popular folk singer Alfredo Zitarrosa. The first time I heard candombe was his song called "Doña Soledad," recorded by Zitarrosa in 1968. Candombe is traditionally played on 3 different drums each with a different size and distinct sound: chico, repique, and piano. I asked luthier Lobo Núñez to tell me about the type of drums played in candombe. Lobo says in the beginning, the drums were made from barrels that were used for all kinds of products:

"Later, they started using barrels from vineyards that had been used to store wine. They started making the drums with the three different sizes, creating a traditional Uruguayan instrument which is now played today by everyone in society. This is a folklore with African origins, but today everyone takes part in it, and you can see that the people who participate are from all kinds of ethnicities. It went from being only ours and now it's everyone's folklore."

By the mid-1970s, as musicians of various music styles mixed the candombe rhythm into their songs, the folkloric style became part of the national identity. Today, candombe is the national music of Uruguay. Rubén Rada says candombe is "the most powerful rhythm left by Africans in Latin America. But it so happens that we're in between Argentina and Brazil. If you see Argentina from Geneva, Argentina is in the world's behind, and Uruguay is right behind it. So it's very hard for people to listen to our music and it's difficult to tell them about the richness of our music." But one thing is for sure, today candombe has become one of the most sought-after rhythms for Uruguayan musicians in every other music genre — jazz, tango, rock and pop music.

When the Rolling Stones toured Latin America three years ago, they played a show in Montevideo. One of the background vocalists knew about Lobo Núñez and wanted to meet him and learn about candombe and the drums, so he went to visit Lobo on his birthday, February 16, 2016, a couple hours after their concert in Montevideo. Mick Jagger and a large entourage of people also came along. A moment from that visit is included in the Rolling Stones documentary called "Olé Olé." Here's Lobo's recollection of the special visit: "I showed Mick Jagger the way I make drums and he was quite impressed. But he's the one that surprised us and through the drums we tried to surprise him. It was an exchange of surprises. He was very thankful, he's a well-educated person, very respectful. I felt he was not that pop star, but a simple musician that came to visit other musicians, to learn about our folklore, with a lot respect and humility." Uruguay's biggest pop artist Jorge Drexler wrote a song called "Memoria del cuero," featuring Lobo Núñez on the piano drum, and his son Noé Núñez on the repique drum. The lyrics say: *In the hold of a slave ship, came the prisoner's candombe. In the prisoner's memory, the candombe sleeps waiting for the skin, curing fear and dizziness, healing the jailer's blows. They come playing, they come playing, they come playing...*

A traditional "llamada" or drum parade in the Palermo neighborhood of Montevideo | Photo by Betto Arcos

LA TROVA SURIANA

I'm in the city of Cuernavaca, the capital of the state of Morelos, in central Mexico. I'm at the home of musician Francisco Ocampo. He and his mentor and friend Jesús Castro are singing a song from one of the most enduring musical traditions in Mexico known as Trova Suriana or Southern Troubadours. Francisco is 25 years old, he started singing this music about 10 years ago. Jesús is 44 and he's been performing songs from the Trova Suriana for more than 25 years.

The Trova Suriana is a music and lyrical style based on the oral tradition. Historically, the Trova tradition is part of a large region in the central part of Mexico, in a radius covering five provinces surrounding the state of Morelos and Mexico City. The lyrical foundation of the Trova Suriana goes back to the theatre tradition that flourished during the "Siglo de Oro," the Golden Century of Spanish letters, whose towering figures are Miguel de Cervantes and Lope de Vega in Spain, and Sor Juana Inés de la Cruz in Mexico, among others. The teaching of this lyrical art form during Mexico's colonial period, was carried out by nuns and friars of the many diverse religious orders that worked in Mexico, from the conquest to the mid-1850s. All of this musical and literary education was conducted in verse, in Spanish, unlike the liturgy which was in Latin, so the population was trained in the rhythm, metrics and phonetics of the Spanish language. It's one of the reasons why there's still a vibrant art of improvising verses in by peasants in the countryside in different parts of Latin America, in countries like Cuba, Puerto Rico, Venezuela, Colombia, Mexico, Panamá, Chile and so on.

There's something to be said about this style of singing in two voices, first and second. The first voice is usually sung by the bajo quinto player, and the second voice follows behind the first voice — instead of singingin harmony. And there's a reason for that: many of the second voice singers don't always remember the lyrics of the repertoire, so they look closely as the first voice sings and follow them behind. The instrument that accompanies singers in every style of the Trova Suriana is called "bajo quinto." The bajo quinto is a precursor of the six-string guitar, its origin goes back to the early to mid-1800s. It has a bigger body than the guitar, five courses of doubled steel strings, and it's played with a pick, with an emphasis on the bass strings. There are two basic styles of playing bajo quinto. Jesús Castro says the bajo quinto is played in a simple way in the mountain region, and it's played in a double-way, in the southern and eastern region of the State of Morelos. Jesus demonstrates the simple way and says there are notes that remain in the air, like the pedal in a piano. But Jesus says, one of his teachers, Mauro Vargas, told him the bajo quinto must be played in a double-way. Jesus says the bajo quinto is such a versatile instrument, it easily adapts to either style. Then, Francisco Ocampo tells me that one of his mentors, Bajo Quinto player and composer Rubén Luengas once told him that the instrument is also part of a rich tradition of town orchestras and he tells him not to play the bajo quinto in the northern style, which is very different from the southern style.

Don Ignacio Vargas and Jesús Castro performing at the Museo Morelense de Arte Popular in Cuernavaca, Mexico | Photo by Betto Arcos

Francisco Ocampo and Daniel Hernández recorded an album called "Poesía y Canto del Siglo XIX." Most of the pieces in this record were arranged by them, since they couldn't find the music. The verses were found many decades ago, in an old big book in a church and were transcribed by hand by Victor Capistrán. In the town of Yautepec, I met 26-year-old Andrés Rubio, a bajo quinto luthier. In addition to making the Trova Suriana's main instrument, he's also a bajo quinto player and singer. He's been performing songs from the Trova for the past 10 years and with his mother María del Rocío Zavala, they formed a duet called Alazán y Rocillo.

For more than 200 years, the Trova Suriana — mainly through the corrido style — has been a sort of daily gazette, and one of the main ways of documenting the memory of events in cities and towns. Luz María Robles has been researching the history of the Trova Suriana for a few decades and says the Trova Suriana has specific metric and rhythmic qualities which go well-beyond the popular corrido of northern Mexico:

> "The Trova's verse style is written in a high art form, in 10, 12 and 14 verses, more complex than the octosyllable verse, the form most commonly used in the Spanish language. The Trova's command of the Spanish language is highly sophisticated, especially since it comes from troubadours who are peasants. Rhythmically, it covers a wide range of music genres, including polkas, tangos, schottische, danzón, habaneras and many more. The content of the lyrics could be about love, humor, satire, history."

In 1984, the National Institute of Anthropology and History, or INAH, released two albums called called "Corridos de la Revolución," part of a collection of field recordings. In one of these albums, they include perhaps the most emblematic Trova musical styles called "bola suriana," a playful and often times social and political song form. "La Bola de los Presidentes" is an exceptionally critical, fierce political satire against the political system during the Mexican Revolution. The author, Elías Domínguez, metaphorically places the listener in hell, through what he calls a "revelation dream." In this corrido, the luminous presence of revolutionary leader Emiliano Zapata, contrasts with that of dictator Porfirio Díaz and presidents Venustiano Carranza and Francisco I. Madero who are presented as ambitious, weak and resentful. The recording features a legendary figure of the Trova Suriana, Mauro Vargas on Bajo Quinto and first voice, and his son Ignacio Vargas on second voice.

In Cuernavaca, I was invited to emcee a performance by one of the last great singers of the second generation of the Trova Suriana, 83-year-old Ignacio Vargas, who sang with his father in that historic recording. But the best part was listening to Jesús Castro play Bajo Quinto and sing first voice while Ignacio Vargas sang the second voice on "La Historia de la muerte del general Emiliano Zapata." This is one of the longest corridos, 26-27 minutes long. The verses never repeat and as the singers move from one stanza to the next, the story unfolds in photographic detail.

One of the most sublime, and still unreleased, recordings of Jesús Castro singing and playing bajo quinto is called "La Muerte de Bárcenas." This is a "corrido esdrújulo," a very complicated verse form where the accent is on the third to last syllable. Castro's composition is an homage to one of his mentors and singers of corridos, Aniceto Araiza, also known as Tío Bárcenas. A few years ago, Oaxacan composer, arranger and director Rubén Luengas invited Jesús Castro and his brother Santiago to take part in a concert featuring some of the most popular corridos of the Trova Suriana, with the fantastic Pasatono Orquesta Mexicana from Oaxaca. These collaborations are a good sign that the Trova Suriana is in good hands. The new generation of troubadours will continue to play and promote this old musical style and renew it with their own compositions.

Andrés Rubio and his mother, María del Rocío Zavala, a duet called Alazán y Rocillo | Photo by Betto Arcos

INDEX

3MA. 335

A

A. J. Racy. 235

Abelardo Carbonó and his Conjunto. 345

Abjeez. 233

Accordion. 19, 49, 51, 55, 75, 89, 145, 150, 163, 165, 225, 323, 325, 343, 347, 355

Aceves Mejía, Miguel. 71

Acoustic cumbia. 267

Acoustic guitar. 297, 301, 343

Adams, West (neighboorhod in Los Angeles). 147

Adapted viola (instrument). 295

Africa. 5, 7, 19, 43, 75, 77, 81, 89, 95, 101, 157, 165, 211, 269, 283, 291, 319, 321, 333, 335, 339, 343, 345, 347, 357

Afrobeat. 77, 307

Afro-Cuban music. 33, 121, 171, 187

Afro-Latin Jazz Orchestra. 251, 253,

Agbabian, Alidz. 119

Agbabian, Areni. 119

Agbabian, Lucina. 119

Aguas Aguas, Los. 237

Aguascalientes National Poetry Prize. 239

Aguilera, Christina. 209

Ahí Namá Music. 217

Air (French band). 129

Ajamian, Mher. 59

Aka DJ Sultán Balkanero. 149

Alain Pérez and His Orchestra. 193

Al-Andalus. 269

Albarrán, Rubén. 35

Aloradas (rhythm). 351

Alejandro, Edesio. 177

Alfaro, Mary. 97

Algeria. 269

Alhaj, Rahim. 253

Aliboria. 353

Alizadeh, Hossein. 7

Allende, Isabel. 109

Alma del Barrio (radio program in LA). 195

Almodóvar, Pedro. 63, 143

Alonso, Checo. 131

Álvarez, Adalberto. 203

Alves, Andrea. 159

Amadeo Roldán Conservatory Symphony Orchestra. 193

Amador, Marco. 249

Amanditita. 249

Amaro, Stephanie. 303

Amazon (jungle). 9

Amer, Abdulrahman. 253

America. 7, 9, 19, 25, 27, 37, 39, 41, 47, 49, 51, 59, 63, 65, 67, 71, 75, 77, 79, 81, 83, 85, 87, 89, 95, 97, 99, 101, 107, 109, 113, 115, 119, 127, 131, 153, 161, 165, 167, 171, 173, 179, 181, 183, 189, 191, 193, 205, 209, 211, 215, 217, 219, 225, 229, 231, 241, 251, 257, 259, 263, 273, 277, 283, 285, 291, 293, 295, 311, 315, 319, 333, 337, 339, 341, 343, 345, 353, 357, 359

Amigo Girol, Vicente. 7

Andalucía. 33, 79, 85, 127, 129, 269

Andean region (Colombia). 349

Anderson, Laurie. 85

Andrews, Reggie. 125

Andreyev, Vasily. 299

Angeles Balalaika Orchestra, Los. 299

Angeles Master Chorale, Los. 225

Ángeles Negros, Los. 9

Anthony, Marc. 195, 309

Antibalas. 307

Apelian, Teni. 59

Arabic makams (melodic system). 291

Araiza, Aniceto. 361

Aratani Theater. 137

Arcos, Esther. 9

Arcos, Luis. 9

Arcos, Quinto. 9

Arenal, Demiss. 237

Argentina. 57, 99, 105, 215, 289, 309, 311, 341, 343, 355, 357

Arias, Estrella. 135

Arizona. 249, 315

Armenia. 59, 119, 127

Armenian National Symphony. 129

Arocena, Daymé. 185, 187

Arroyo, Hugo. 41

Art&co Recording Studios. 21

Arte y Cerveza (club in Bogotá). 349

Asia. 7

ASUJAZZ. 125

Asunción. 125 341

Asunción Jazz Festival. 125

Atlantic Records. 315

Auditorio Nacional. 149

Auserón, Santiago. 7

Austin, Tony. 125

Australia. 211, 355

Avant-garde (style). 231

Azaris, Manuel. 195

B

Baba, Masato. 27

Baca, Susana. 7, 83

Bach Project, The. 275

Bach, Johann Sebastian. 251, 275, 293, 295

Bagpipes (instrument). 85, 289, 351

Baik, Jen. 27,

Bailey, Patrick. 77

Bailie, Stuart. 213

Bajo quinto (instrument). 25, 293, 301, 359 361

Bajofondo. 311

Baker, Chet. 67

Baker, Geoff. 181

Balalaika (instrument). 299

Balkan music. 145

Balke, Jon. 69

Bamboo flute (instrument). 293

Bambuco (genre). 349

Banda (genre). 75

Bandolim. 165

Bandoneón. 343

Barbosa-Lima, Carlos. 179

Barboza, Agustín. 341

Barcelona. 103

Bardem, Javier. 209

Barnes, Erin. 295

Baroque guitar. 293, 301, 319

Baroque music. 57, 79, 269, 319

Barranquilla. 345

Bartók, Béla. 95, 179

Bartra, Bruno. 145

Basie, Count. 39, 251

Bass. 77, 79, 89, 103, 113, 121, 125, 129, 135, 141, 149, 193, 195, 235, 237, 283, 297, 299, 301, 307, 313, 335, 359

Bastos, Waldemar. 7

Bazurto All Stars. 345

Bazurto Social Club. 345

BBC Radio 3. 7, 351

Beatles, The. 9, 143, 357

Bel canto. 161

Belfast. 213

Bello, Lara. 65

Beltrán, Lola. 71

Benson Latin American Collection. 7

Berklee College of Music. 201

Berklee School of Music. 201

Berlin. 281, 331

Berlin, Irving. 299

Berlin, Steven. 49

Bernal, Egan. 349

Bernstein, Leonard. 161

Berrogüetto. 353

Berry, Chuck. 45

Bethânia, Maria. 153

Beverly Hills. 191, 315

Big band (jazz ensemble). 39, 133, 177, 259, 283

Blades, Rubén. 47, 49,

Blanc, Enrique. 111

Blind Boys of Alabama, The. 337

Blues. 41, 59, 67, 105, 201, 229, 263, 283, 327, 331, 337

Bocelli, Andrea. 149, 263

Bofill, Fernando (Chingoli). 343

Bofill, Mario. 343

Bogotá Music Market (BOMM). 213

Bola Suriana (music style). 361

Bolero. 5, 9, 69, 115, 167, 179, 217, 257, 265, 285

Bolivia. 281, 355

Bollani, Stefano. 165

Bomba Estéreo. 23

Bombu Taiko. 27

Bono. 213

Border. 9, 41, 79, 111, 197, 239, 241, 243, 249, 251, 253, 341, 351

Borja, Alonso. 221

Bossa nova. 91, 145, 233, 333

Boston. 59, 201, 209

Boulder. 7, 9

Boutchebak, Mona. 269

Boyacá. 349

Boys, Los. 189

Bradley, Charles. 307

Brahem, Anouar. 31, 235

Brazil. 5, 7, 9, 67, 123, 153, 155, 157, 159, 161, 163, 165, 167, 179, 321, 341, 343, 357

Brazilian Carnival. 157

Brazilian Drumming Ensemble. 123

Brazilian Hour, The (radio program). 165

Brel, Jacques. 63

Brennan, Ian. 211

Brenner, Vytas. 87

Bretons, The. 85

Bridgewater, Dee Dee. 193

Brighton Park. 131

Broadway. 155

Brooklyn. 167, 307

Brouwer, Leo. 5, 179

Brown, James. 77, 189

Browne, Jackson. 173

Brownsville border. 197, 239, 241, 243, 249, 251

Brubeck, Dave. 315

Brunner, Ronald. 125

Brunner, Steven. 125

Buarque, Chico. 101, 153, 155, 157

Buena Vista Social Club. 341

Buenos Aires. 105, 309, 341, 343

Bugbee, Grace. 113

Buika, Concha. 61, 63, 127

Buitrago, Fabio. 83

Bukanas de Culiacán. 241

Button accordion. 343

Byrne, David. 159, 171, 205

C

Cabaret Salón Rojo. 183

Café con Pan. 57

Café Tacvba. 35, 37, 311, 343

Cafeteras, Las. 49

Cage, John. 163, 289

Cairo. 291

Caja (percussion instrument). 355, 323

Cal State LA's Music Department. 195

Calamaro, Andrés. 257

Calarts Salsa Band. 121, 123

Calaveras, Los. 71

California. 9, 27 41, 75, 77, 97, 111, 121, 139, 211, 231, 265, 281, 283, 285, 295, 307, 315, 339

California Institute of the Arts. 121, 231

Caliph. 261

Camarón de la Isla (José Monje Cruz). 43, 91

Cambalache. 137, 339

Camelia La Texana. 243

Camino de Santiago. 143, 351, 353

Camperos Huastecos, Los. 313

Camperos, Los (ensemble). 131

Campo Sonoro. 349

Canada. 27

Canalón de Timbiquí. 213

Candelas Guitar Shop. 7, 303

Cândido, Joyce. 155

Candombe (genre). 333, 357

Candombe beat (music style). 357

Cano, Nati. 131

Canta el Pueblo (radio program). 349

Cantores de la Sierra, Los. 313

Cantuaria, Vinicius. 167

Canzoniere Grecanico Salentino. 223

Cao-Romero, Wendy. 273

Capercaillie. 353

Capistrán, Victor. 361

Capitol Studio B. 135

Capitol Studios (Hollywood). 285

Caracas. 209

Caravan Palace. 7, 39

Carcassés, Roberto. 189, 191

Cárdenas, Dorindo. 347

Cardiff. 297

Cardozo Ocampo, Mauricio. 341

Cardozo, Daisy. 261

Carey, Felix. 7

Carey, Mariah. 209

Caribbean coast (Colombia).
  5, 89, 323, 345

Carneiro, Carlos. 153

Carpenters, The. 9

Carranga (genre). 349

Carrangueros de Ráquira, Los. 349

Carrillo, Álvaro. 43, 115

Carroll, Lewis. 255

Cartagena. 9, 345, 355

Carter, Regina. 253

Cartola. 155

Carvalho, Beth. 155, 157

Casa Grande (theatre). 153

Casa, La (studio). 311

Casillas. 249

Casillas, Martín. 9

Castellanos, Aaron. 339

Castillo, Jorge. 253

Castillo, Juan Andrés. 347

Castillo, Roxana. 175

Castro, César. 137, 339

Castro, Fidel. 171, 201

Castro, James. 315

Castro, Jesús. 359

Castro, Joe. 315

Castro, Joseph Armand. 315

Catalan folk. 103

Catalonia. 103, 143

Catalonia College of Music. 103

Cathars, The (religious movement). 245

Cavaquinho (instrument). 321

Cavaquinho, Nelson. 155

Cello fingerboard (instrument). 295

Cello neck (instrument). 295

CENART, the National Center of the
  Arts (CDMX). 293

Cenzontles, Los. 41

Cepeda, Iris. 199

Cereté. 45

Cha-cha-cha. 195, 201

Chacona (dance). 319

Chamamé (style). 343

Champeta (genre). 345

Chao, Manu. 7

Chapman, Tracy. 263

Chappotín, Leider. 195

Charanga Cubana, La. 195

Charchetta (instrument). 75

Charlie Haden's Liberation Music
  Orchestra. 193

Charro. 35, 97

Chaurand, Andrés. 47

Chaurand, Juan Carlos. 47

Chávez, Erica. 347

Chéjere. 221

Chévez, Pancho. 215

Chi, Diego. 47, 49

Chi, Enrique. 47, 49

Chicago. 125, 131, 191

Chico (candombe drum). 333, 357

Chieftains, The. 85

Child, Desmond. 63

Chile. 9, 95, 99, 101, 105, 109, 175,
  355, 359

Chiquinquirá. 349

Chitarra battente (instrument). 301

Chiva Rumbera, La. 355

Chocquibtown. 21, 23

Chomat, Gonzalo. 195, 199

Choro (style). 165 321

Cimafunk. 189, 191

Cimarrón. 7, 189, 191

Ciudad Valles. 313

Clair, René. 291

Clapton, Eric. 331

Clarinet. 133, 145, 231, 235, 259

Classical (genre). 125, 127, 147, 153, 179,
  197, 203, 229, 231

Classical guitar. 57, 129, 161, 203, 303

Classical saxophone. 103

Clave Festival, La. 115

Cline, Patsy. 111

Club 21. 183

Cohen, Leonard. 179, 331

Coicoyán de las Flores. 301

Coimbra. 67

Cole, Nat King. 183, 285

Cole, Tom. 5, 7

Colibrí, Las. 29, 97

Colina, Javier. 103

Colombia. 5, 7, 9, 19, 21, 23, 37, 45, 51
  77, 89, 123, 167, 213, 251, 297, 309,
  323, 325, 345, 347, 349, 355, 359

Colorado. 7, 9, 297

Commendation of Arts and Letters.
  (recognition). 153

Compa Negro, El. 75

Comparsas (carnival floats). 333

Compay Segundo (Máximo Francisco
  Repilado Muñoz). 7, 85

Concurso de Toque de Guitarra
  Mejoranera (mejorana guitar
  competition). 347

Congas (percussion instrument). 139

Congo. 101, 345

Conjunto Bernal. 41

Conjunto Jardín. 339

Conjunto Nueva Ola, El. 267

Conjunto Rumbavana. 201

Conservatorio Nacional de Música. 95

Contreras, Guillermo. 293, 301

Convite Cuna Carranguera (festival). 349

Cooder, Ry. 7, 85

Cooper, Alice. 85

Copado, Heliodoro. 313

Copenhagen. 55

Corbalán, Sixto. 341

Córdoba. 45, 129

Corea, Chick. 125, 163

Corraleros de Majagual, Los. 9, 347

Corridos. 49, 75, 241, 243, 327

Corrientes. 343

Cortés, Jose Luis. 193

Costa Chica (South of Mexico). 115

Costello, Elvis. 309

Count Basie Orchestra. 251

Couto, Bernardo. 67

Coyoacán. 145

Crescent Moon Studios. 309

Criteria Entertainment. 21

Crosby, Stills and Nash. 71

Cruz, Celia. 193, 195

Cruz, Danny. 237

Cruz, Eloy. 319

Cruz, Penélope. 209

Cruz, Ricardo. 67

Cuarteto D'Aida. 183

Cuba. 5, 7, 9, 33, 61, 63, 81, 103, 107, 115, 121, 165, 171, 173, 175, 177, 179, 181, 183, 185, 187, 189, 191, 193, 195, 197, 199, 201, 203, 205, 217, 231, 251, 347

Cuban Five. 175, 205

Cuban Institute of Art and Film Industry. 179

Cuernavaca. 359, 361

Culiacán. 241

Cumbes (genre and dance). 319

Cumbia. 51 75, 77, 83, 89, 113, 123, 267, 355

Cuneta Son Machín, La. 81, 83

D

Daaood, Kamau. 283

Daft Punk. 129

Daltrey, Roger. 85

Dance. 9, 27, 29, 39, 65, 75, 89, 95, 133, 137, 155, 177, 187, 189, 193, 195, 199, 201, 203, 213, 221, 223, 231, 237, 251, 253, 257, 273, 275, 281, 285, 311, 313, 319, 327, 337, 339, 343, 345

Dandys, Los. 9

Danzon. 201, 231, 275, 261

Dap-Kings. 263, 307

Daptone Records. 307

Daversa, John. 259, 261

Davio, Alejandro. 215,

Davis, Miles. 91, 141, 163, 291

Day, Doris. 115

De Castro, Rosalia. 353

De Cervantes, Miguel. 359

De Holanda, Hamilton. 165

De Ita, Marina. 145

De la Cruz, Sor Juana Inés. 135, 359

De la Rocha, Zack. 249

De León, Joey. 123

De Lucía, Paco. 91, 127, 129, 193

De Vega, Lope. 359

Deep funk. 77

Del Barco, Mandalit. 5

Del Morao, Diego. 33

Del Río, Kenneth. 303

Del Río, Tiffany. 259, 261

Del Toro, Guillermo. 311

Del Tránsito Cocomarola, Mario. 343

Delaporte, Charles. 39

Delgado, Candelario. 303

Delgado, Porfirio. 303

Delgado, Tomás. 303

Delmiro, Hélio. 161

Democratic Republic of the Congo. 345

Dempster, Alec. 7, 57

Denver. 195,

Desjardins, Richard. 53

Di Franco, Ani. 279

Di Lasso, Orlando. 225

Diákara. 201

Diamante Eléctrico. 21

Diamond marimba. 295

Diatonic accordion. 223, 323, 343

Díaz, Oscar. 347

Dibango, Manu. 77

DiCaprio, Leonardo. 191

Diego El Cigala. 33

Diestro, Aida. 183

Dion, Celine. 209

Dire Straits. 331

Do Bandolim, Jacob. 165

Do Carmo, Carlos. 7, 327

Do Carmo, Lucília. 327

Domínguez, Elías. 361

Domra (instrument). 299

Don Telésforo. 301

Dora Pérez de Zárate (award). 347

Dorothy Chandler Pavilion. 97

Dos Santos, Ary. 327

Downbeat magazine. 315

Downey Theatre. 285

Downs, Lila. 7, 239, 257

Drazan, Ivonne. 29

Drexler, Jorge. 279, 281, 357

Drum. 27, 123, 141, 323, 325, 333, 347, 355, 357

Dudamel, Gustavo. 95, 147, 149, 231

Dueto Heredia, El. 107

Duke, Doris. 315

Dupree, Jack. 229

Durán, Alejo. 19

Duran, Dolores. 153

Durante, Mauro. 223

Dúrcal, Rocío. 9

Dylan, Bob. 331

E

Echo Park. 311

ECM (record label). 119, 235, 269

Ecuador. 9, 219

Edición Semanaria (radio show). 7

EDM (electronic dance music). 129

Egypt. 79

El Din, Hamza. 7

El Maloumi, Driss. 335

El Rey Theater. 113

El Salvador. 123

Electric bass. 125, 301

Electric guitar. 45, 89, 125, 137, 285, 297, 353

Electronic music. 39, 87, 143, 279

Elegantes del Vallenato, Los. 355

Ellington, Duke. 39

Equatorial Guinea. 63

Escobar, Diego. 35

Escoleta (traditional music school). 133

Estefan, Emilio. 309

Estefan, Gloria. 309

Estefanía y su Grupo Carranguero. 349

Estrada, Gloria. 265

Estrada, Ramón. 115

Estrela, Julio. 321

Europe. 153, 173, 179, 195, 201, 223, 255, 269, 293, 297, 319, 351

Extraño Corazón. 171

F

Fado (rythm). 67, 165, 327

Fado Festival. 327

Falcon Lair (Beverly Hills manssion). 315

Fandango (dance). 57, 137, 253, 273, 339, 351

Fandango Fronterizo (festival). 253, 351

Fantasmas, Los. 9

Farhadí, Asghar. 209

Farinha, Quim. 353

Farquharson, Mary. 313

FATSO. 213

Faudel. 101

Fedoruk, Claire. 225

Feliciano, Cheo. 195

Fernández, Miró Raul. 103

Fernández, Pedro. 35

Ferreira, Bibí. 153

Ferreira, Procópio. 153

Ferrer, Ibrahim. 7

Fes (Morocco). 7

Festival de Guararé. 347

Festival de la Mejorana. 347

Festival Internacional Cervantino. 225

Fetter, Fiona. 299

Figueroa, Rafael. 69, 137, 339

Fiol, Shae. 107

Fisher-Mims, René. 283

Flamenco. 33, 63, 65, 85, 91, 103, 127, 129, 143, 193, 209, 269

Flecha, Ricardo. 341

Flor de Toloache. 107

Flores, Adriana. 307

Flores, José Asunción. 341

Flores, Quetzal. 273

Florida. 203

Floridita, El (club). 139, 195

Flynn, Frank Emilio. 181

Folía (composition). 319

Folkloristas, Los. 95

Fonda de Los Camperos, La. 131

Fonsi, Luis. 309

Ford Theatre. 27, 29, 285

Forgotten Kingdom, The (album title). 245

Formosa. 343

Fortaleza. 153

Four-valve trumpet. 5, 291

Frame, The (radio show). 7

Francisco el Hombre. 323

Franco, Dalila. 293

Fregonesi, Leandro. 157, 159, 321

Frisell, Bill. 7, 167

Fukawa, Halle. 27

Fulbright scholarship. 231

Funk. 77, 83, 191, 195, 201, 307

Funky ska beat. 265

G

Gaita (instrument). 19, 89, 289, 351

Gaita (rhythm). 85

Gaiteros de San Jacinto, Los. 89

Galicia. 85, 351, 353

Galindo, Gustavo. 37

Galliano, Richard. 165

Galstian, Samuel. 59

Gamboa, Hernán. 87

Garcés, Javier. 9

García Márquez, Gabriel. 19, 323, 325

García, Celia. 115

García, Chucky. 21, 23

García, Judith. 147

García, Laura. 115

García, Mara. 347

García, Mariano. 115

García, Patricia. 25

Garcia, Rosario. 351

García, Sergent. 51

García, Susie. 97

Garcia-Fons, Renaud. 79

Gardel (prize). 105

Gardel, Carlos. 91

Garza, Oscar. 7

Gavana, Alfred. 211

Gavilán, Francisca. 99

Gens. 171

German Democratic Republic. 171

Germano, Roy. 313

Gieco, León. 215

Gil, Gilberto. 159

Gilberto, João. 67, 161

Gilles Peterson (producer). 185, 187

Gillespie, Dizzy. 187, 193, 251

Gismonti Egberto. 165

Global Village (public radio show). 5, 7

Goldman, Scott. 191

Golijov, Osvaldo. 289

Gómez, José Manuel. 143

Góngora, Nidia. 213

Gonzaga, Luiz. 159

González Iñárritu, Alejandro. 311

González, Ángel. 243

González, Dayramir. 201

Gonzalez, Jerry. 83

Gonzalez, Martha. 273, 285

Goran Bregovic. 145

Goren, Jennifer. 7

Gormé, Eydie. 115, 285

Gospel. 211, 307, 337

Gotan Project. 39

Goya (prize). 103

Grafton Street (Dublin). 297

Grammy (award). 81, 83, 97, 105, 107, 131, 141, 195, 243, 263, 265, 273, 285, 327

Grammy Museum's Clive Davis (auditorium). 191

Granada. 65, 103

Granada, The (club). 131, 195

Granda, Chabuca. 105

Granma. 203

Graue, Maricarmen. 275

Graves, Cameron. 125

Greece. 79

Greenland. 55

G-Strings (radio show). 5

Guabina (genre). 349

Guacharaca or scraper (instrument). 323, 325, 349, 355

Guadalajara. 35, 111, 131, 149, 329

Guanajuato. 225, 319

Guaracha (rhytm). 203

Guarania (genre). 341

Guararé (Panama town). 347

Guelaguetza (traditional music and dance festival). 133
Guerrero. 275, 293, 301
Guerrero, Dan. 73
Guerrero, Lalo. 273
Guillén, Alan. 343
Guillén, Carlos. 81
Guinga (Carlos Althier de Souza Lemos Escobar). 161
Guitar. 5, 7, 9, 29, 37, 45, 55, 57, 67, 89, 91, 99, 109, 127, 129, 131, 137, 141, 143, 161, 165, 167, 171, 173, 179, 195, 203, 211, 223, 265, 273, 285, 293, 295, 297, 301, 303, 313, 319, 321, 325, 335, 341, 343, 347, 349, 359
Guitarra de golpe. 293
Guitarra de Plata Campesina (festival). 349
Guitarra de son. 137, 273
Guitarra séptima. 293
Guitarrón. 107
Gulf Coast (Veracruz, Mex). 43, 69, 237, 339
Gulf of Panama. 347
Guthrie, Woody. 261
Gutiérrez, Alfredo. 347
Gutierrez, Gilberto. 273, 339
Gutiérrez, Manuel. 129
Gutiérrez, Ramón. 253, 273
Gutiérrez, Tomás Darío. 323
Guzmán, Adriana. 263
Guzmán, Simón. 307
Gypsy jazz. 39, 331
Gypsy-flavored guitar riff. 265

H

Habana D'Primera. 201
Habanera (dance). 361
Hadad, Astrid. 7, 239, 329
Haddad, Loretta. 315
Haden, Charlie. 7, 193,
Hancock, Herbie. 125, 141, 197
Haney, Steve. 77
Harding, Libby. 339
Haro, Julio. 35

Harper, Ben. 337
Harrington, David. 7
Havana. 171, 173, 175, 179, 183, 185, 189, 193, 197, 201, 203, 205, 217
Havana Cultura Mix Project. 187
Hawaiian (dance). 29
Hay, Colin. 203
Hemingway, Marina. 175
Heredia, Miguel (Dueto Heredia). 107
Hermanas García, Las. 115
Hernández Portilla, Griselda. 9
Hernández, Aramís. 171
Hernández, Daniel. 361
Hernández, Edgar. 195
Hernández, Gerardo 175
Hernandez, Jacob. 253
Hernández, José. 97, 131
Hernández, Lily. 195
Hernandez, Marcos. 313
Hernández, Ramón. 253
Herrera, Guido. 195
Herrera, Magos. 43
Hesperion XXI. 245, 319
Hidalgo. 253
Hidalgo, David. 41, 49
Hidalgo, Patricio. 253
Higgins, Billy. 283
Highland Park. 295
Hime, Francis. 321
Hip-hop. 21, 75, 83, 101, 125, 213, 219, 255, 261, 285
Holiday, Billie. 63
Hong Kong. 225
Hora de Agustín Lara, La (radio show). 9
Horn (instrument). 121, 187, 293, 355
Hotel Nacional. 193
Huapango. 149, 313
Huertas, Carlos. 325

I

Iba, Rachel. 135
Iglesias, Erik. 189, 191
Iman Remel. 337
Indie (genre). 111, 113, 295, 307

Infante, Lupita. 29
Infante, Pedro. 29
Infante, Pedro Jr. 29
Instituto Superior de Arte. 203
Internacional Sonora Balkanera, La. 145
International Mariachi Festival. 131
Inti-illimani. 9
Inuktitut. 53
Irakere. 77
Iran. 7, 209, 233, 331
Ireland. 85, 213, 297
Isaac, Elisapie. 53
Island, Ellis. 259
Istanbul. 119
Italy. 79, 195, 223

J

J Balvin. 21, 23
Jácara (composition). 319
Jackson 5 (or Five), The. 9, 211
Jackson, Mahalia. 229
Jackson, Michael. 141, 189
Jara, Víctor. 95, 101
Jarana. 137, 273, 293
Jarana (eight-string). 339
Jarana huasteca. 313
Jarrett, Keith. 197
Jazz ballad. 183,
Jazz Plaza Festival. 193
Jeanette's Place (club). 131
Jerez de la Frontera. 33
Jiménez, Enrique. 275
Jiménez, Flaco. 7
Jiménez, José Alfredo. 61, 111
Jiménez Cruz, Miguel. 113
Jimmy Kimmel Show. 297
Jobim, Antonio Carlos. 91
John, Elton. 71
Jon Balke & Siwan. 269
Jones, Quincy. 141, 197
Jones, Sharon. 307, 263
Jopará (paraguayan colloquial language). 341
Jorgensen, Erik. 139

Joropo (genre). 347, 349
Josephine. 7
Jotas (rhythm). 351
Juan Gabriel. 9
Juanes. 21, 23
Juárez. 303
Juárez, Benito. 329
Juarez, Melanie. 131
Jungle Fire. 77

K

Kabbaj, Mohamed. 337
Kansas City. 47
Karl Marx Theater. 189
Kennedy, Will. 141
Kerpel, Anibal. 37
Keyboard. 47, 89, 113, 125, 181, 263, 267, 295
KGNU (radio station). 7
Khaled. 101
Kiavchi, Babak. 331
Kibler-Vermass, Elsje. 147, 149
King, Carole. 71
King, Charles (before Carlos Reyes). 345
Kingman, Mateo. 9, 219
Kinnara Taiko. 27
Kinto, El. 357
Kiosk. 7, 331
Kitsune Taiko. 27
Klaver, Ellen. 7
Koln. 197
Komitas. 59
Kora (instrument). 335
Koreatown. 147
KPCC (radio station). 7
Kronos Quartet. 7, 95
Krys, Sebastian. 309
Kun, Josh. 281
Kuti, Fela. 77

L

LA Philharmonic. 95, 147
Lafourcade, Natalia. 51, 111
Lamar, Kendrick. 125
Landau, Greg. 81, 83

Lantello, Tiffany. 123
Lara, Agustín. 43, 69
Larson, Megan. 7
Las Vegas. 315
Latin America. 47, 51, 65, 81, 83, 85, 95, 99, 109, 115, 179, 205, 215, 231, 257, 293, 357, 359
Latin Grammy Lifetime Achievement Award. 327
Latin Jam (radio show). 7
Latin jazz. 33, 251, 253
LATV Studios. 107
Laurie, Hugh. 263
Laverty, Collin. 191
Lebanese music. 291
Lebanon. 79, 255
Lecuona, Ernesto. 179, 181
Led Zeppelin. 261
Lee, Cameron. 141
Legaspi, Maricarmen. 275
Legend, John. 107
Legión Infantil de Madrugadores, La (radio show). 9
Legrand, Michel. 161
Leigh, Ann Hahn. 39
Leilía. 353
Leimert Park. 125
Leñero, Pablo. 123
Leon Chancler (Ndugu). 141
León, Eugenia. 309
Leona (instrument). 135
Leonardo Favio. 9
Libre. 199
Lichtenauer, Michael. 225
Lily Hernández & Orquesta. 195
Limón, Javier. 91, 209
Lincoln Center. 251
Lincoln, Abbey. 63
Lisbon. 67, 327
Litoral, El (Argentina region). 343
Little Tokyo. 27, 47
Liza Minnelli. 153
LL Cool J. 249
Llerenas, Eduardo. 313
LLILAS Benson Latin American

Studies. 7
Lobos, Los. 49, 85, 137, 273
London. 95, 115, 185, 187, 211, 357
Lopez, Alberto. 77, 199
López, Antonio. 75
Lopez, Jennifer. 309
Lopez, Urbano. 267
López-Nussa, Harold. 181
Lora, Alex. 51
Los Angeles. 1, 5, 7, 9, 21, 27 29 33 39 47 49 59 71, 73, 79, 95, 97, 115, 127, 129, 131, 133, 135, 137, 139, 143, 147, 149, 161 173 187 189 195 199 201 203 211 215 217 225 231 233 239 241, 249, 253, 259, 263, 265, 273, 277, 283, 285, 297, 299, 303, 309, 311, 331, 339, 341, 353
Lost Cuban Trios of Casa Marina. 217
Louvre (museum). 99
Lovano, Joe. 193
Lowery, Rhyan. 75
Loyola Marymount University. 239
Lozano, Danilo. 183
Luaka Bop (label). 205
Luengas, Rubén. 25, 301
Lund, Elsa 135
Lynge, Simon 55

M

Maal, Baaba. 7
Maalouf, Ibrahim. 5, 255, 291
Macarthur Park. 131
Machat Records. 201
Madagascar. 5, 335
Madrid. 143, 209, 279
Magnificent Seven, The. 141
Majumdar, Ronu. 7
Making Movies. 47, 49
Mala Rodríguez, La. 103
Malawi Mouse Boys. 211
Maldita Vecindad, La. 83
Maldonado, Cesar. 131
Mali. 255, 335
Malle, Louis. 291
Mallorca. 61, 63